Book Awards for *The Universe Builders*

*** GRAND PRIZE WINNER ***
Writer's Digest Self-Published e-Book Awards

*** BOOK OF THE YEAR (1st PLACE) ***
Independent Author Network Book Contest

*** GOLD ***
Readers' Favorite

*** GOLD ***
eLit Awards - Digital Publishing Excellence

*** GOLD ***
San Francisco Book Festival

*** OUTSTANDING YOUNG ADULT ***
Independent Author Network Book Contest

*** SECOND PLACE ***
New York Book Festival

*** FINALIST ***
Stargazer Literary Prizes

*** FINALIST ***
Beverly Hills Book Awards

*** FINALIST ***
Next Generation Indie Book Awards

*** FINALIST ***
International Book Awards

*** AWARD ***
Literary Classics Book Reviews

Praise for *The Universe Builders*

"Highly recommended. One of the most unique and well-written young adult books I've ever read."

Judge, Writer's Digest Self-Published e-Book Awards

"...smart, witty, creative, and captivating like nothing I have ever read before. Almost impossible to put down. Awesome!"

S. Fisher, Readers' Favorite

"...a rare literary treat with a genuinely likable cast of characters sure to win the hearts of readers. ...imaginative and unpredictable, whimsical and heartwarming. ...will appeal to readers of all ages and is highly recommended.

Literary Classics Book Review

"...a top pick for teens and adults interested in ... unique stories filled with unpredictable action!"

D. Donovan, Midwest Book Review

"...had me hooked from start to finish. I must say I have had a lack of sleep as I couldn't put it down, and when I did, I still thought about it."

Miriam Davison, author

"This book was fantastic! I was riveted, wanting to know what was going to happen to Bernie. The story has humor, a well thought out world of gods and their creations, and subplots interwoven in a way that makes this book difficult to put down. ... a fascinating tale of good vs. evil and of a young hero on a journey of self-discovery."

S. M. Lowry, blogger, The Fringes of Reality

"This book totally took me by surprise! The author does a great job of building empathy for his main character. It definitely kept me turning pages to find out what poor Bernie would have to go through next. There are some twists and turns that keep you guessing, and it ends wonderfully, leaving the door open for many possibilities. This story will undoubtedly capture your heart, as well as make you wonder if WE have our own Bernie."

Felicia Madura, author

"This book was just wonderful! The story was captivating, and the characters were interesting and fun. I absolutely loved the original storyline, and thought it was brilliant. It's a wonderful new twist on how worlds and such are created. The ending ... was just what I wanted it to be."

Hayley Guertin, blogger, *Hayley's Reviews*

"Everybody loves an underdog story, and I'm no different... but this is the first time I've read one where the underdog was a god. Mr. LeBel's creative genius shines throughout the entire book, and I can only hope that this is the first in a series of Universe Builder novels. I would love to see this made into a movie..."

Chris Snead, reviewer

"...a fascinating world populated by weird, crazy characters that will tickle your funny bone and, at times, tug at your heartstrings."

Linda Watkins, author

"I expected to enjoy it, after all, every review I read was very positive, but I did not expect to be drawn in so quickly. The story had me captivated until the end, and an overwhelming desire to see Bernie victorious kept me hooked."

Lynne Fellows, blogger, *Just 4 My Books*

"Hands-down the best indie novel I have ever read. Best book, period, that I have read in at least a year. The writing is so descriptive you forget where you are. I could picture every moment, every scene, every person, as vividly as if I were watching a movie. Comparable to some of C.S. Lewis' work."

Rachael Snead, author

"There are times when the technical jargon flows so smoothly that you would swear Mr. LeBel was an Astrophysicist. Then at times he wraps the story like a mixture of Pratchett (they wear the same kind of hats) and Hans Christian Andersen. A story that can be enjoyed by any age. The possibilities for future adventures are limitless."

H. William Ruback, author

THE UNIVERSE BUILDERS

BERNIE

AND THE

PUTTY

A young adult fantasy

Steve LeBel

Copyright

The Universe Builders: Bernie and the Putty

Published in the United States of America by Argon Press
Library of Congress Control Number [LCCN]: 2014900580
ISBN (ebook): 978-0-9910554-1-8
ISBN (CS-print): 978-0-9910554-0-1
ISBN (IS-print): 978-0-9910554-9-4

(v 2.91)

ARGON PRESS
www.ArgonPress.com

www.TheUniverseBuilders.com

The Universe Builders Series

Genre(s): young adult fantasy, fantasy, science fiction, young adult, epic fantasy, coming of age, time travel, humorous, visionary and metaphysical, first contact, teen and juvenile fiction, fantasy and magic, science and technology, space opera, myths and legends, witches and wizards, fantasy adventure, and adult fiction.

Dedication

To the Bernie in all of us.

Cast of Gods & Goddesses

Bernie, a young god
Suzie, a good friend of Bernie's
Lenny, a year older than Bernie
Billy, a bully
Shemal, Bernie's boss

Hannah, Bernie's mother
Simeon, Bernie's father

The School
Beatrice, Bernie's favorite teacher
Gabriel, creation ethics teacher
Other Teachers: Caleb, Phoebe, Ester, Griffin

Judges
Jazelda, Michael, Thomas

Other Characters

Lookies
Bowin, Catila, Renot, Gower, Sibot, Gingi

Zardok, high priest
Gondal, leader of the Senate
Ministers: Landor, Nottag, Tonst, Branton, Wadov
Alcandor, a scientist

Prologue

Have you ever wondered about the universe? How it came to be? The purpose of it all?

Well, the answers may surprise you.

Actually, there are a lot of universes out there. They come in every size and shape and flavor you can imagine. And the answers to your questions are very different, depending on which universe you're in.

Some universes are amazing. They're full of beautiful planets, intelligent races, technological marvels, and other wonders. But some of them are, well, not so amazing.

Each universe is created by a god, of course, as is required for such things. But one of the inconvenient truths is: not all gods are created equal. Oh, they have the best teachers and the best educations possible, and, over the ages, the gods have developed a good work ethic and a strong desire to do their best. But gods are pretty much like everyone else. They have their own share of overachievers and underachievers, motivated and unmotivated, and talented and not so talented, which explains why some of the universes out there are not really up to professional standards.

This is a story about those gods. They live in The Town, on a planet they call The World. Their primary occupation is building universes, which they call The Business. You needn't be much concerned about their lack of creativity in naming things. They all live in the same town on the same planet. And there isn't anyone else in the god business, so they don't need a lot of fancy names to differentiate these things.

No one remembers how The Business began. The gods have been building universes as far back as anyone can recall. They will always be doing it. It's what gods do. It isn't like they can just quit The Business and do something else. Their whole economy depends on the universes they create. And since it's the only thing they will ever do, they make it fun by seeing how well they can do it.

In fact, the only real competition on The World is the Annual Universe Awards. This is when a special committee looks over the new universes to see if anyone has come up with something worthy of an award. After so many millennia, there is an award for every category you can imagine. But they don't give out awards for every category each year. To win an award, your universe has to be the *best ever* in that category. So, if you're going for the *Most Beautiful Planet*, and there have been forty-seven winners before you—each one more beautiful than the last—you have to be exceptional if you want to be winner number forty-eight. The competition is everyone's favorite event, and the gods work hard to outdo each other. It's the best and fastest way to gain recognition for your work.

Not every god is cut out to be a builder, of course. Some gods are better at other things, which is good, because The Town needs cooks, librarians, plumbers and all manner of other professions as well. In school, everyone has a chance to become a builder, but as classes keep getting harder and more challenging, there are more reasons to change your major to something else.

To help you understand The World, we'll take a look at an ordinary boy. He isn't the smartest, although he isn't dumb. He certainly didn't distinguish himself in school, unless you count his reputation for being picked on more than most kids. He had few friends, perhaps because he came from a broken home. His mom worked hard to raise him the best she could, but after the divorce, it was a struggle just to make ends meet. Our boy's only claim to fame is his dad, who won three universe awards and became a major celebrity all over The World.

We take you to our young god at a special time in his life. He has just finished school and is about to start his first job.

An exciting time to be sure…

The Time of Waiting

Bernie was being watched.

Tiny eyes followed his movements as the young god closed the door to his home. Glancing from force of habit at the path to the bridge that led to The Town, Bernie turned away. He had not taken that path for several days, nor would he today. Instead, he circled around to the back of the small home he shared with his mother. There, he chose a less used path that would take him into the woods.

"Where shall we go today?" he asked, although he appeared to be alone. "I know. Let's go to Lookout Point. We haven't been there for a while." His invisible friend did not reply, although a small group of twigs quickly assembled on the path behind the boy and began merrily hopping along in single file after him.

Bernie would never have called his companion a friend, any more than he would have called his finger a friend. But he had developed a habit of talking to him as if he understood—and perhaps in some ways he did. He was usually better behaved when Bernie talked to him. If left to his own devices, well, then anything might happen…

During his younger years, he'd often thought of his companion as an evil force, something to be fought or battled into submission. For a long time, he felt shame, as if it were a dark curse or terrible flaw. He tried to hide it—still did, really—but that usually made things worse. Other gods had clouds, of course, but not nearly as strong. Nor as chaotic.

'It's not your fault,' they had told him. 'When each child is born, Order and Chaos fight for dominance. For most children, it's a close battle, and the child ends up with a slight inclination toward one side or the other. This imbalance is what we call the cloud, and, for most people, their cloud is rarely heard from. But for people like you, Bernie, your cloud is very strong. When

Order and Chaos were supposed to fight for you, Order never showed up, and Chaos won by default,' they said.

'You can't win by fighting it. You have to make friends with your cloud. Try to understand what it wants. Learn to live with it,' they counseled. 'After all, it's part of you.'

Bernie tried. Really, he did. But it was hard to be friends with something inherently chaotic. It was unpredictable, disorderly, unreliable, and often just plain stubborn.

As the young god entered the woods, the sky seemed to darken. In the woods, the gods took no responsibility for encouraging or discouraging the trees from doing whatever they wanted, although the Town Council had discussed it often enough. One tree in particular—the Old One—was the subject of perennial discussions. The tree's big offense was having attained a height so great it blocked the sun in much of the Northeast Quadrant of The Town. An exaggeration, perhaps, but that didn't explain why no one ever volunteered to take it down. It didn't explain their fear.

Bernie's path took him to the trunk of the great tree.

"Hello, Old One," he said as if greeting a friend.

Even from the far side of town, the great tree could be seen as it towered above their world. Bernie hands stroked the soft warm bark. The tree had been created by a god, of course, but so long ago no one remembered who had done it or why. Even its placement in the woods was a mystery. Had it been an accidental passenger, riding in the entrails of some exotic creation, excreted on fertile ground, and left to grow? No one knew. Bernie had been delighted the first time he'd touched its side and discovered it was warm-blooded.

Bernie put his ear against the great tree and listened to the slow quiet rumble of its great heart as it pushed the sap through its veins. "I think you will outlast us all," he said as he stroked the soft bark.

Bernie was startled by a small tap on his leg. Expecting a cloud-prank, he found instead a green vine rearing up like a snake in front of him. Although it looked like a plant, he knew it was not.

"Ah," he said as understanding dawned, "are you sure you want to go up there?" The vine creature tapped higher on

Bernie's leg. "Okay, okay," he said, "I'll help."

Gently grasping the slither, Bernie lifted it upward, its head snaking higher as it reached for a low branch. Bernie laughed as the slither wrapped itself around his arms and neck in its struggle to ascend. Finally, its head reached a low branch where it twisted around twice before pulling the rest of its long body up the great tree. Slithers were always looking for tall trees where they could reach the sunlight. Once there, tiny leaf-like scales that covered their bodies would fan outward, capturing the sun's precious energy. If they found the right tree, they would spend their entire lives there.

Bernie smiled. "You've found the ultimate home here, little buddy."

Slithers were a refugee species. When a god brought one of their creations to town, they were careful to sure the species was harmless. The most common offense of a new species was over-population. If enough people complained, the Town Council would take action and impose a ban. Usually the banned species was rounded up and thrown into an empty void. Occasionally, a handful escaped the roundup and found safety in the woods. Slithers were one such species.

In the woods, they were safe from the gods... and safe from other refugees that may have found their way to the woods. But the indigenous life forms that crawled up the side of the plateau from time to time, well, that was a different story. They could be dangerous. Perhaps it was a good thing slithers spent their lives in the treetops.

Bernie felt a guilty pleasure for his love of the woods. He didn't know anyone else who felt the same. Other gods shunned the woods and the danger, but this was Bernie's backyard, and his youth had been spent here. In school, he seldom talked about the woods, having learned it was best not to give reasons for people to see him as different. Most already thought him strange.

Too far away for the young god to hear, the watchers made soft rustling sounds as they scampered behind. Even if Bernie had heard the creatures, he would not have seen them. The woods were filled with brushes, tall ferns, and dark hidden places. The tiny eyes had little fear of discovery as they followed the boy deeper into the wood.

When the path separated, Bernie took the right fork, knowing it led to the stream. This was one of four streams that began at the artesian well in the center of town. Each stream spiraled through the town once, before finally reaching the rim of the great plateau and cascading over The Edge. Bernie discovered a crossing years ago where a tree had fallen across the stream; this had become his bridge.

As he climbed on top of the fallen tree, he said, "Okay now, let's be careful. We don't want to get wet."

Once, his invisible cloud had not understood the precarious nature of balancing high above rushing waters and decided to lighten the mood by tickling Bernie. That had resulted in wet clothes, angry words, and a long walk home. Since then, no chaotic episodes had intruded on Bernie's river crossing attempts. But, each time, he made a point of reminding his cloud to be careful.

He'd learned a lot about his cloud over the years. It was easily agitated. Strong emotions of any kind guaranteed chaotic consequences, so Bernie learned to keep his feelings hidden. That was the best way to avoid unpredictable incidents. Out of habit, Bernie sent gentle, calming thoughts as he balanced on the log. The cloud rewarded him by confining itself to creating ripple patterns in the water, which were quickly carried away by the current. Neither Bernie nor his cloud noticed the tiny watchers as they crossed the bridge after him just moments later.

Strolling down the path leading to Lookout Point, Bernie heard the sound of water colliding with the rocky slope as they approached the North Fall. Gentle breezes whispered in high branches. Near Bernie's feet, where no breeze blew, leaves and twigs twirled in a windless dance as the young god passed by.

Strange creatures called out from hidden places. Many, he'd never seen up close. Some, glimpsed out of the corner of his eye, vanished whenever he turned to look.

If I had my powers here, he thought, *I'd love to know what they look like.*

"We're almost there," he said as the shaded woods began yielding to the openness beyond The Edge.

The prominence Bernie called Lookout Point was a flat-topped boulder that rose above and extended beyond the rocky border that made up The Edge. There was little vegetation that chose to live on the bare rock, although a handful of refugees, and perhaps some indigenous creatures, scrambled from their warm sunny places when they detected the young god's approach. Bernie climbed the short distance to the top. From here, the trees blocked any view of The Town, but he had a magnificent view of the wilderness that extended on down the side of the plateau and all the way to the horizon. Other places along The Edge were less steep, and it was possible to walk down the slope to the Unknown Territory, although, of course, no one ever did.

The wilderness reached in every direction, thick and overgrown. Somehow, the colors of the indigenous life below seemed more drab than the life forms created by the gods. But, that was mere speculation, since no god had ever explored the Unknown Territory. In the distance, Bernie could see lakes and large ponds, and, always, there was the mysterious blue mountain barely visible in the distance. He had spent many hours on this very rock, wondering about that mountain.

"Someday, we're going exploring," he said. Bernie smiled as he felt invisible hands press on his chest, holding him back. "Don't worry. Not anytime soon." Here, in the woods, he was at ease with his cloud. It was a safe place, and the cloud could do little to embarrass him there.

Had there ever been a time before when Bernie felt so relaxed or so content? The young god smiled as he thought of everything he'd accomplished. Graduating as a builder was the highest achievement possible for any god. And he was a good builder, too. Not as good as his dad, of course, but then, who was?

"Did you think we would make it? There were lots of times when I wasn't so sure." He suppressed the temptation to point out that most of those times were directly attributable to the cloud. "They threw everything they could at us. But we mastered it all. We can build suns, planets, moons, and everything in between. And we're not half-bad with life forms, either. We graduated. We're builders!

"Mom is so proud of us," he said, savoring the feeling. Then, unbidden, his thoughts turned to his father. "I wonder if

Dad even knows I've graduated. Do you think he would be proud of me?"

There was no answer. But then, there never was.

Bernie sighed.

His gloomy thoughts turned into a chuckle when he felt something patting him on the head. "Yes, I know. We did great. All we can do now is wait for the interview. Suzie said it takes a few days because they look at your file and talk to your teachers before they call you in."

After working so hard for so long, it was a true pleasure just to relax. No classes, no homework, no extra-credit assignments, no part time jobs. It was the closest Bernie had ever had to a vacation. As the shadows lengthened and the day drew to a close, Bernie felt at peace.

~

As the young god made his way back through the woods, the tiny eyes watched him. Stealthy and careful, nothing betrayed their presence as they followed the boy all the way back to his home.

Personnel Department

It was a busy month for Ezrah. This was the time of year when they hired the young gods who graduated with degrees in universe building. He'd worked his way through the list of applicants, and still had five more students to interview.

Suzie stepped into his office, pot in hand. "More coffee?"

"Yes, thanks."

"I filed all the evaluation forms that came in." She poured fresh coffee into his cup. "I flagged the ones I thought you would want to review. I also made a list of the supervisors who are late with their evaluations so we can follow up."

"Thanks, Suzie. You're doing a great job."

Ezrah smiled when he saw how his compliment affected Suzie's godly shimmer. The outer edge of her aura broke out in tiny gold sparkles. This time of year, he was so busy he always fell behind. She was making him look good.

"Is there anything else I can do?"

"I'm all set for now. Thanks."

Ezrah picked up the remaining stack of applications. As the Director of Personnel for The Business, he decided whom to hire for the most coveted job in The World. The School forwarded all the records and transcripts for the builders from its most recent graduating class. So far, he'd hired everyone he'd interviewed, as he did almost every year.

Ezrah took his responsibility seriously. He knew there were times when an applicant might look good on paper, but he knew things wouldn't work out. Usually, the rejects were found among the students last to apply, which was the group he was looking at now.

He picked up the next file and paged through years of transcripts, teacher comments, incident reports, and parent-teacher conferences. Ezrah enjoyed looking at the files. Each file was a complete record of the candidate's school experience from elementary school all the way through graduation. This young god, Bernie, looked about average. As usual, Ezrah skipped the first half of the file—he wasn't concerned with the early years. Bernie had mostly B's with a few C's, which wasn't bad. He flunked Advanced Quantum Mechanics 307, but repeated it and got a solid B. His performance in creation lab classes had been poor; his teachers suggested a need for better planning and preparation. His performance improved as he got older. There was one class where he had a D+, and that was Creation Ethics 200. His teacher said Bernie understood the material well enough, but he refused to accept it.

Hmm, thought Ezrah, *problems with authority?*

The thick file showed only one extracurricular activity, the Off World Technology (OWT) group, which Ezrah recalled as a bunch of geeky kids who swapped technology from other worlds. The file included Bernie's placement in co-op jobs over the years, including summer jobs. His supervisors gave him good reports.

That's a plus, he thought. *It shows the kid's willing to work.*

Ezrah made a list of people to talk with and questions to ask. To make sure he understood Bernie's early weaknesses, he started with Caleb, one of the boy's elementary school creation lab instructors. He added Gabriel, the creation ethics instructor who had written the long note about Bernie's ethics problems. He paged through the file looking for the name of Bernie's last co-op supervisor. When he found it, he added Peter to the list. He smiled when he noticed Beatrice's name on several classes. He always enjoyed an excuse to talk to her, so he added her name as well. Something was missing.

Oh, I think this is the kid Suzie told me about. I should talk with her too.

Caleb's Story

With his list in hand, Ezrah walked across Central Plaza to The School. He'd start with Caleb, the elementary lab instructor, although he wondered if the man would remember Bernie.

"Of course I remember him." Caleb broke into laughter. "Bernie gave me the best laugh I've had in centuries. Not just me, either. He made quite a reputation for himself."

"What happened?" Ezrah found himself smiling at Caleb's infectious laughter.

"I gave the kids a basic sun-planet-moon project—nothing tricky at all," Caleb explained. "The lab manual called for a yellow sun, a rock planet with atmosphere and hydrosphere, and a moon. Just the basics, you know."

"No kits?"

"No, they had to make everything from scratch. But Bernie didn't read the manual before he came to class. That was his first mistake," Caleb said. "By the way, have you met Wanda?"

"Yes. I certainly have." Ezrah recalled the young goddess with a perfect straight-A record and glowing reports from all her teachers. "She was the first person I hired this year. A very impressive young lady."

"That's true, although her skills didn't make her popular with the other kids. They usually kept one eye on what she was doing while they worked on their own stuff. Bernie was no exception.

"Well, Bernie jumped right in and made a red sun. It was supposed to be yellow, but since he hadn't read the manual, he missed that. When he noticed everyone else making yellow suns, he started reading the manual. By the time he finished, half the class was over. That's when he went into overdrive.

"He decided to keep it red because he didn't have time to redo it. To make up for points he would lose on the sun color, he figured he would go for a really big planet—twice what the specs called for. He got the planet revolving around the sun, and he made an ocean that covered half the surface. His planet started out pretty well.

"But there was a problem. As soon as the oceans rotated to the dark side of the planet, they froze. And when they got back to the light side, it took most of the day before they thawed out." Caleb was grinning.

"I assume that was because of the cooler red sun."

"Exactly. Bernie tried to fix it by spinning the planet faster so the ocean wouldn't have time to freeze on the night side. Unfortunately, he hadn't considered the centrifugal forces involved. The faster spin caused the oceans to slide toward the equator with such force, it threw a stream of water vapor into the atmosphere, where it escaped from the planet's gravitational field."

Ezrah laughed. He visualized the planet zipping along through space, spinning like a drunken top and dragging a long vapor tail behind it.

"Bernie was worried. He feared the escaping water vapor would cause his planet to be reclassified as a comet since it now had a tail, so he slowed the rotation down until the water was no longer achieving escape velocity. Fortunately for Bernie, there was still water left on the planet.

"But he needed a way to keep the dark side of the planet warm so it wouldn't freeze. Do you know what he asked me?" Caleb's eyes twinkled.

"Not a clue."

"He wanted to know if it was okay to have two suns. He had the bright idea to put his planet between two suns and have the planet spin in place. That would keep both sides of the planet warm and solve his frozen ocean problem. I reminded him his planet had to revolve around the sun, so that wouldn't work. He was so disappointed.

"Finally, he moved his planet closer to the sun, which solved the problem. That was when he looked over to see what Wanda was doing. She had finished her project and decided to add two extra moons just to show off.

"Bernie decided to try the same thing. Maybe he wanted to make up for the points he would lose for the red sun or maybe he was trying to compete with Wanda. Or maybe he never finished reading the manual and really thought he was supposed to have three moons. Who knows?

"Bernie was running out of time, but he rushed ahead anyway. He decided two of his moons would circle the third moon instead of the planet. He made a large moon and got it into a good orbit. Then he put the two smaller moons in orbit around the big moon. And, in a clear play for extra credit, he made them circle the moon in a vertical orbit instead of the traditional horizontal orbit. Now, that would have given him a passing grade, except for one problem. He needed to verify orbital stability." Caleb struggled to keep a straight face.

"He pushed into the future to see how the orbits looked, but found the second moon had crashed into the first and pieces of both had smashed into the planet — definitely a failing grade. He came back to the present time and tried a do-over by adjusting the orbits. But every time he did a future check, he found the planet in ruins."

"How far in the future do they have to verify a stable orbit?"

Caleb's eyes twinkled again as he said, "We usually tell the kids their solar system has to be stable for long enough to give any advanced life forms a fighting chance to evolve, invent space travel, and escape to a safer planet."

Ezrah laughed, and Caleb laughed with him.

"It finally dawned on Bernie his fancy moons were a problem. That is when he decided any passing grade was more important than outdoing Wanda. So he grabbed all three moons, mashed them together into one large moon, and put it into orbit. He did a future check, and the orbit was stable.

"I could see the relief on his face until he noticed a two-thousand foot tidal wave racing around the equator." Caleb could barely tell the story because he was laughing so hard.

"I assume that was because the moon was so big and heavy."

"Yep. Now, most of us would know to make the moon smaller or lighter or move it farther away from the planet so the gravitational forces wouldn't be so strong. Bernie was so frazzled he didn't think it through.

"Instead, he panicked. He squished the planet, thinking that would force the oceans away from the equator and closer to the poles. All he accomplished, of course, was to subject his oceans to even greater centrifugal forces, which increased the depth of the oceans and the height of the tidal wave." Tears of laugher rolled down Caleb's cheeks.

"The saddest part was next. I saw Bernie's face the moment he figured out what to do. All he had to do was move his moon farther away, which would have solved the problem. But, that's when I had to tell everyone their time was up. Poor Bernie. So close and yet so far."

"That's funny. I wish I'd seen it."

"You can," exclaimed Caleb. "His universe is one of few I've saved over the years." He brought Ezrah to a viewing window hanging on the wall.

As Ezrah gazed into the window, he saw a large red sun; around that sun rotated a sad little planet. The planet, instead of being round, looked squished, just as Caleb had described. Its oceans were concentrated around the equator where two massive tidal waves, one on each side of the planet, were dragged around the world by its gigantic moon. It looked like a fat little world swinging a Hula-hoop ocean around its middle.

Ezrah saw every detail of Caleb's story written on the planet. Even the moon looked like a lump of clay with two smaller lumps squished into it. They both laughed some more.

"I must admit I feel badly about one thing, though," Caleb said as his laughter subsided.

"What's that?"

"I told the other teachers about Bernie's universe. We got such a kick out of it, we put it in the Alumni Newsletter. Unfortunately, it got back to the kids at school, and Bernie took a lot of abuse from his classmates. I heard kids making up expressions like 'Don't Bernie it.' or 'What a Bernard!' I didn't mean for that to happen."

"Just one more question for you, Caleb. Would you recommend Bernie for a builder job with The Business?"

"Sure, I'd probably hire him. I'd keep an eye on a couple of things, though."

"What?"

"First, make sure he reads the manual before he tries to do anything."

"Okay. What's the second thing?"

"Don't let him sit next to Wanda."

The Waiting Continues

The young god closed the door to his home and turned toward the woods. The tiny eyes noticed him right away. For years, they had watched him leave in the morning and not come back until late afternoon. Three or four times a week, he found time to walk with them in the woods. Well, not really… He didn't know they were there, but they walked with him nonetheless.

Bowin, whose job was to watch for the young god, alerted the others the boy had been seen heading into the woods. The watchers came together, careful to make no noise. They liked the boy. They'd seen many gods in town before they became refugees and fled to the woods. This one was gentle, and they knew he would not hurt them. Even so, they never let him know they were there.

Two weeks earlier, something had changed. The boy no longer left home in the mornings. And he was spending more time than ever in the woods. They liked seeing more of him, but they wondered what had happened. For the first few days, he walked along the path and even hummed tunes. His shimmer had been strong, with flecks of gold and blue. He seemed very happy. Bowin had to caution the other watchers not to be caught up in their joy at seeing so much of the boy. There was great danger in the woods, and they needed to be cautious.

Following the boy was always an adventure. Strange things happened near him, like branches breaking or things moving by themselves. Once, when Gingi was watching the boy, something pushed the branch she was lying on, and she had to hold tight or she would have fallen. It was as if an invisible force surrounded the young god. And that wasn't all. Often things from the boy's pockets often ended up on the ground. They were sure the boy didn't mean for this to happen. Bowin always assigned two members of their troupe to recover lost items and return them to the boy's home.

Bowin wished he understood the language of the gods. It

was very different. The gods communicated mostly with sounds, but the sounds were very complex. There was also a relationship between their sounds and the colors in the shimmers that surrounded them. The young ones, like their boy, often displayed constantly changing colors, while the older gods showed few color changes. Interestingly, the gods seldom talked with other parts of their bodies. Lamona speculated the gods had been forced to learn complicated verbal sounds because they had no tails or even ears they could move to make their meaning clear. Bowin was not convinced. He thought the gods were so powerful, they simply had no need for soundless ways to talk. But, in the final analysis, no one really knew what the gods were thinking. And that was reason enough to keep your distance.

Today, and for the last three days, they saw none of the gold and blue colors in the shimmering light that surrounded the boy. The young god's head was down, seeming to stare at the path in front of him. Several times, he changed direction without warning, as if wrestling an inner demon. Even the odd things that happened close to him were happening farther away. Once, the boy turned around so fast, he almost saw them, and they had to scramble for cover.

Still, they followed.

~

After a time, Bernie's thoughts slowly untangled and began to make sense. He'd come a long way, but it wasn't over. Everything depended on getting hired by The Business. He'd put in his application over a week ago.

"Why is it taking so long?" he asked as he walked along.

If his cloud heard him, it did not respond. But then, it never did. Clouds didn't talk. In fact, even listening was rare. The cloud seemed to know what was going on, but it was more of an emotional understanding than an intellectual one. Clouds had access to your senses, but they didn't process things through a full brain. They seemed limited to the primitive, instinctual part that housed your needs and your desires. And clouds never thought about consequences. If Bernie could have changed one thing about his cloud, he would have made it think about the consequences of its actions before acting. But there was no cloud anywhere that did that. So Bernie's strategy was simple: keep himself calm, which tended to keep his cloud calm. Usually. Sometimes. But not always…

Bernie had been to The Edge twice already today. He tried to relax in the moss-covered clearing near the stream, but his nervous energy wouldn't let him sit still. Doubts he didn't know he had emerged to trouble him. So he walked.

"My grades were good—I was in the top third of my class," he said, as if trying to convince someone else. How long did it take to speak with his teachers? Did they talk to all of them? There were some he hoped they wouldn't talk to at all.

"Beatrice would say good things. She was the best," he said, thinking immediately of his favorite teacher. "But what would the others say?" Most would only remember him as the kid who fought with Billy. No matter how many times he thought about the fight, the intense feelings never diminished. Going over the edge like that was the worst thing he'd ever done.

"Ouch!"

Bernie felt the pull on his hair and quickly slapped it down before it could tie itself into a knot. He calmed his mind and turned away from thoughts of the fight, lest his cloud become even more upset.

As if on cue, he found himself at The Edge. Had some part of his sub-consciousness sent him here again? *What is it that keeps calling me out here?* At this point on the rim, the land sloped gently downward. It would be a leisurely stroll down into the Unknown Territory. *That's crazy*, he thought. *I'm just nervous about my future.* Did such thoughts make him insane? No. He was as sane as anyone else. It was just the pressure.

A tug on the cuff of his pants brought him back to reality. He wasn't surprised to see a snarl of unraveled threads dragging behind him. The threads, once part of his pants, had been used to capture small twigs, leaves, and even an unwary stone that had failed to move out of range quickly enough. It was one of his cloud's favorite pranks.

"Stop that," he said automatically. "We can't afford to buy more clothes right now. We already bought new clothes for my interview," he said, hoping he would have a chance to use them.

The threads twitched once and stopped.

"And don't even think about doing this with my new clothes. They have to be perfect."

The threads and their stranglehold on the collection of sticks and stones loosened in response to Bernie's words. Suddenly the captured sticks raced off in different directions, free at last from the threads that had held them tight. The stone rolled drunkenly down the path.

"That's not funny," said Bernie. "And please don't do it again."

After a time, Bernie resumed his walk. He found no answers. Everything was already in motion. There was no test he could retake, no class he could study for, no extra-credit assignments to do.

There was nothing he could do except wait.

~

And so, the watchers with the tiny eyes, they waited with him.

Bad Ethics

Ezrah found Gabriel's office easily. After all these years, he knew his way around The School very well. He didn't often have reasons to interview the creation ethics teacher, but Gabriel's note in Bernie's file couldn't be ignored.

"Bernie was a big problem in my class." Gabriel thundered his complaint with the voice qualities of an elder god. Ezrah, no youngster himself, struggled not to succumb to its power.

"In what way?" Ezrah got out his notebook.

"He rejected the basic building principles we've taught for millennia. He just didn't get it."

"What do you think was going on?"

"I've seen it before. Some kids can't stay objective," said Gabriel. "They get attached to their creations, and then nothing you say makes any difference."

"Did Bernie violate the rule against communicating with higher life forms?"

"It makes you wonder, doesn't it?" Gabriel replied. "Well, I never heard about it if he did. I checked with some of his teachers, but they never saw him break the rule either. But, who knows? Maybe he did with a personal universe at home. Lots of kids have them."

"What kind of things did he challenge?"

"Where to begin? One day I was telling the class about the importance of instilling death directives into their life forms. I'm sure you know, Ezrah, finite life spans are essential for any kind of evolutionary process. No one gets complex life forms right on their first try. You have to weed out the bad ones so your superior specimens can make more contributions to the gene pool. If none of your creatures ever die, what are you going to do with the inferior specimens you don't want anymore?

"I couldn't believe Bernie's response. He said, 'It doesn't seem fair. The gods don't have a death directive, but we give one to everyone else. Why should we make everything else die if we don't?' I couldn't believe he was comparing us to something we created.

"I tried to be patient with him. I said, 'If you don't instill a death directive, your planet will end up overpopulated with misfits. You won't be able to accomplish your evolutionary goals, and everything will eventually starve.' 'But we don't have death directives, and we don't overpopulate,' he said. 'We're different, Bernie. We're gods. Besides, our retirement rate matches our birth rate, so it's not a problem for us,' I said."

"What did Bernie say?"

"Well, I'll give him credit for one thing. He always had an answer. 'You could always increase the food supply,' he says. So I asked, 'What about when the planet is full?' He says, 'Then make the planet bigger and, after that, make more planets.' The kid was just plain stubborn."

"Did he have any other hang-ups?"

"Don't get me started on his issues with blinking out a population. That one made him nuts. Sometimes you realize your creation isn't going to make it, and the best thing is to start over. So you blink them out and begin again. Everyone knows that."

"But not Bernie?"

"Nope. He thought once you created something, you take on some sort of parental responsibility for it," said Gabriel. "I thought I could force the right answer out of him by asking him what he would do it if his main life form was being destroyed by a second life form. Makes sense to get rid of the invasive species, right?"

Ezrah nodded.

"Not to Bernie. 'I would split the continent so they are not on the same land mass,' he says."

"He's creative," Ezrah acknowledged.

"One day he asked me to prove the things we create are any different from us. I naturally pointed out that created beings don't have thoughts or feelings like we do. 'How do you know?' he asked. 'Because they don't have souls,' I said. 'How do you know?' he asked again. 'Because we didn't give them any,' I said. 'If I wanted to give a soul to one of my creations, how would I do it?' he asks. 'You can't, because we're not sure exactly what it is,' I explained. 'If we don't know what a soul is, how do we know we have them and they don't?' he says."

Gabriel shook his head. Ezrah wasn't sure if he saw disgust or anger. "My days were spent in this kind of debate."

"Did this cause problems with the other students?"

"Oh, no. I don't think anyone took him seriously. Most kids come from good builder families, and they understood this stuff before they got in my class. I think Bernie got his ideas from one of those fringe groups around town always protesting one thing or another."

"What makes you say that?"

"He used to wear T-shirts from protest rallies. Things like: 'All life is sacred', 'Save the Lookies', 'Why destroy at all?' He always wore torn jeans and old tennis shoes. I've never seen him in anything else. I think it was his way of defying The School's unwritten dress code."

"I saw you gave him a D+ for the class."

"It was the lowest grade I could give him. He knew the right answers so he did well on the exams. But in class, he disagreed with everything. I changed the final exam to essay questions hoping I could flunk him, but I couldn't quite justify it."

"Is that why you wrote the special report and put it in his file?"

"Yes. I knew he would eventually get to The Business, and I didn't want you guys blind-sided."

"Well, thanks for the warning, Gabriel. I appreciate it."

Beatrice's Version

Ezrah stuffed the notes from his meeting with Gabriel into his briefcase and walked down the hall to see Beatrice. He couldn't help smiling as he approached her office. If she'd been one of his teachers, he might have ended up a builder instead of going into personnel.

"Hello, Ezrah." Beatrice beamed a bright smile at him. "Who are you sleuthing out today?"

"Today, it's Bernie."

"Sure. He's been in my classes for several years. One of my favorite students, actually. What do you want to know?"

"In looking over his file and talking to Caleb and Gabriel, I have some doubts about him."

"Why?" She looked puzzled.

"Gabriel said Bernie argued with him about numerous ethics issues. Bernie challenged the death directive, argued against blinking out his mistakes, insisted created life has feelings, and more. I assume you observed similar behavior."

"Well, you have to understand Gabriel is very 'old school'. He doesn't like it if anyone questions anything."

"No kidding. Listening to one of the elder gods is always intense. My ears are still ringing," said Ezrah. He knew they would say the same thing about him someday, but not for a while yet. "I'm concerned, though. He described some very stubborn behavior by Bernie."

"Bernie has, on occasion, resisted doing things. But I've always been able to get him to do what was needed." She flashed Ezrah a pretty smile, and to make sure he understood her meaning, she radiated her shimmer at him. Ezrah found himself watching a hypno-wheel of swirling colors pulling him into its center.

"I can see how that would be hard for any young god to resist," Ezrah said. And then they both laughed.

"Well, you have to understand. Bernie is a pacifist. He doesn't want to hurt anybody or anything, and this influences everything he does, including his building assignments. But he listens well and whenever I made suggestions, he did his best to carry them out."

"So he had no problem blinking things out when you asked him to?"

"I didn't say that. He still had problems with it, and if there was any way he could think of to accomplish the same thing without blinking, he did. He was quite creative, actually. I think he takes after his mother in that way."

"You know the family?"

"Sure. His mom attended all the parent-teacher conferences, and she's active in the PTA, too. I wish more parents were as involved."

"Where does she work?"

"She's a waitress in one of the restaurants in Central Plaza. Her name is Hannah. You've probably seen her around."

"What about his dad? What's he like?"

"Oh, gosh. You didn't know? His dad is Simeon."

"You're kidding! Simeon?" Ezrah exclaimed. "He's amazing. I went to one of his lectures after he won his second Universe Award. He has three now, you know. I can't remember the last time someone won that many."

"Neither can I."

"So you got to meet him. What's he like?" Ezrah leaned closer.

"No, I've never met him. He and Hannah are divorced. Let me think… It was right after he won the second award. Bernie would have been about eight or nine then, I think."

"Divorce is hard on kids. How did Bernie handle it?"

"Oh, that happened before I knew him. I remember his mom said it was rough on Bernie when they had to move out to Fifth Circle. He lost most of his friends."

"That would be hard on anyone. I don't think there's anything out there but a few project homes and the woods. And then the wilderness."

"That's about right, I think. I've never been out that far."

"I have. I went all the way to The Edge once. You have to walk a long way through the woods. At The Edge, you can see the wilderness below. It goes on forever."

"Did you go past The Edge?"

"Not me. Who knows what might be lurking there? I have too much to live for." Ezrah chuckled. "It was scary enough just being in the woods."

"Well, it doesn't seem to have done Bernie any harm. He told me he likes to walk in the woods."

"So you're telling me Bernie is a lonely guy with a death wish?" Ezrah asked with a twinkle in his eye.

Beatrice laughed. "Seriously, I like the boy. He might be a little different, but wouldn't you be if you grew up in the shadow of a famous father?"

"How does he get along with the other kids?"

"Quite well. Much better for the last couple years. There was a little cabal that used to pick on him. I think they were jealous of the attention he got because of his dad."

"It doesn't seem like it would be hard to rise above that."

"Well, remember, a lot of things happened when his parents separated. For one, they went from being comfortable financially to, well… Fifth Circle," she said.

"Tell me about this little cabal."

"The ringleader was a guy named Billy. Do you know him? He graduated a year ahead of Bernie."

"Oh, yes. I hired Billy. I still get the creeps when I think about his scar. It's really hard to… Oh, wait! Wasn't Bernie the one who fought with Billy? I remember now—it was Simeon's kid who did it."

"Yes, but remember, Bernie was only eight when it happened," she said a little defensively.

"But still." Ezrah recoiled as he recalled the incident. "What Bernie did was awful! Nobody deserves that."

"Wait a minute, Ezrah," said Beatrice. "It wasn't Bernie. It was his chaos cloud that did it."

"But still."

"Ezrah, let me explain. Billy was a bully. He'd been after Bernie for years. Bernie never responded to his provocations. But one day, one of the students, a girl named Suzie, stuck up for Bernie. When she did, Billy hit her. That's when Bernie hit Billy. He was defending Suzie."

"I know Suzie. She works for me." *Trying to protect a friend sounds like something she would do,* Ezrah thought. His mental picture of Suzie faded as he thought of the scar on Billy's face. "But he shouldn't have lost control of his cloud."

"Billy had him down on the ground and was hitting him over and over. Do you know anyone who could control their cloud with that going on?"

"No, I guess not."

"Zachariah, the headmaster, banished Bernie from school until he could be evaluated. He also commanded that Bernie get training to control his cloud. Finally, they decided it was an isolated incident, and they let him come back."

"But still…"

"Will you stop saying that? Bernie felt awful about it. I think that's why he's such a pacifist. He can't stand the idea of hurting anyone ever again."

"What happened after Bernie returned to school?"

"Billy never stopped picking on him. Billy's a mean-spirited kid, and he and his buddies made life hard for Bernie. I remember a story that went around the teachers' lounge about Bernie's clothes—"

"I heard about the way he dresses," Ezrah interrupted. "Gabriel told me he dresses in T-shirts and torn blue jeans. He said it's in defiance of the school's dress code."

"That's not true. Let me tell you what really happened. One day Bernie came to school dressed in new clothes. He was very proud of them. Billy told him in a voice loud enough for everyone to hear that he really liked Bernie's new clothes. Then, smirking, he said they used to be his before his mom donated them to the secondhand store. Poor Bernie was mortified."

"Ouch. That was mean. Something like that leaves emotional scars."

"That's when he started wearing the blue jeans and T-shirts."

"He couldn't compete, so he went the opposite way, huh?"

"I'd say that's a good guess. By the time I met Bernie, I found someone who doubted he was as good as the other kids. But he has a lot of talent. He did well in my classes because I demanded more from him."

"How did you do that?"

"Let me give you a mental picture of Bernie. He was picked on by other kids, which made him doubt his self-worth. And most of his early building experiences hadn't gone well. Add to that his chaos cloud, which he can't always control. Now you have a kid who doubts whether he can succeed. And because of that, he wasn't doing the preparation or planning he should for his building projects.

"To be really blunt, I wouldn't let him get away with that mind-set. I told him I knew he had the talent, and I insisted he do the proper planning. After that, his performance improved dramatically."

"It sounds like you left your mark on him," Ezrah said.

"No builder gets out of school without taking at least three of my classes. I leave my mark on all the kids." She laughed.

"So, it sounds like you're an advocate for Bernie to get a job as a builder."

"Absolutely. You won't be sorry."

"Thanks for filling me in on Bernie. It's always fun to talk with you, Beatrice."

Stock Boy

Ezrah found his way to the company where Bernie had his co-op job. It was located in Northeast, Second Circle, where most of the importers were located. Peter, the owner, stood in the doorway waiting to greet him as he arrived.

"Thanks for taking the time to talk with me, Peter. I appreciate it," said Ezrah.

"I'm glad to help. You wanted to talk about Bernie?"

"Yes. He's applied for a builder job with The Business, and I'm doing background checks to see what kind of young god he is. I talked with his teachers, and now I want to know how he performed as an employee."

"Okay. Before I try to answer that, can you tell me what you know about my business?" Peter asked.

"Not a lot, really. I know your business is called Good Shimmer Imports, and you're a supplier to some businesses around town. Maybe you should fill me in."

"Sure. We specialize in non-tech products like books, furniture, hand tools, clothes, and kitchenware. We also have a fine range of office supplies, so if you could put in a good word for us with your Supply Division, I sure would appreciate it."

Ezrah just smiled.

After a moment of awkward silence, Peter continued, "We have contracts to maintain the inventories of our retail customers. For example, we supply several bookstores with books. You know how the publishing business works, right?"

"Not really. It's a bit outside my normal work."

"Okay. If you're an author and you want to publish something, you go to the bookstore. They review your book. If they like it, they work out a payment arrangement with you. The bookstore contacts us, and we negotiate a price to publish and deliver the books. We're then responsible for getting them printed and keeping copies on their shelves until they tell us they don't want it anymore.

"It works the same for other products too. If you're a

hardware store, and someone comes in with a new idea, you buy it from them and give us the design specs. We manufacture it for you and maintain your inventory of the product."

"You do all that here?"

"Yep, back in the manufacturing section. Come on. I'll show you." *The man is proud of his company*, thought Ezrah.

Peter led the way into a large well-lit back room that boasted four skylights. The square room was divided by three long walls running the length of the room, leaving plenty of room for the push-carts to move up and down the aisles between the walls. Viewing windows had been mounted every twenty feet, and next to each window was a neatly printed label with planetary reference points for the manufacturer's location, the contact person, and contract terms. Dozens of windows were hung on the walls.

"I've never seen this done before."

"See the youngster over there?" Peter pointed to a boy who looked about sixteen. "That's Tony. He works in the hardware section. See the paper in his hand? That's his shopping list. Tony made it when he visited one of our customers an hour ago. It's a list of what's been sold and what needs to be replaced to bring the inventory level back up."

Tony pushed a large flatbed cart to one of the windows and positioned himself between the window and the cart. Ezrah watched the boy as he prepared to enter the universe on the other side. The boy reached through the window and appeared to bend down. Moments later, he returned to this side holding several small boxes, which he carefully placed on the pushcart. He repeated the process several times, each time adding to the pile of boxes on the cart. Finally finished, he looked at his cart, crossed several items off his list, and pushed the cart to another viewing window where he began the process again.

"When he's done with his list, he brings the new supplies back to our customer and places them on the shelves."

"That's very interesting," said Ezrah. "I assume you have contracts with higher life forms on those worlds to do the actual manufacturing for you."

"Yes. We keep track of what they've provided, and we pay them once a week."

"And this is what Bernie did?"

"Yes, he was a stock boy, just like Tony. Bernie worked mostly in the book section. He did a good job. We also used him as a paymaster when he wasn't too busy."

"What did that involve?"

"He would go to the manufacturer's contact person, make sure our paperwork agreed with their billing, and he would pay them in whatever form they wanted," said Peter. "And, by the way, I wouldn't trust just anyone to do that job."

"What was so special about it?"

"It can be a delicate business. You want to pay your manufacturer fairly, but you have to avoid misunderstandings. Bernie is someone I trusted to pay them and not show off."

"Show off?"

"You don't want your paymaster to create gold or diamonds right in front of your manufacturer. If they see that, they start thinking it's easy for us, and then they start wanting more. I've lost good manufacturers because they got greedy. I finally realized the problems were caused by my paymasters. So now I only send people I trust."

"Was there anything about Bernie's performance that makes you think he would not be a good builder?"

"No. He's a good boy. The only complaint I ever had was the way he dressed. His clothes were in bad shape. I talked to him about it once. I asked him what he spent all his money on. I was going to suggest he buy clothes instead of games or toys or whatever it is kids spend their money on nowadays, but he said, 'I give it to my mom, sir.' I didn't have the heart to say anything else, so I bought him a company uniform, and he wore that when he worked for me."

"Well, thank you for your time, Peter. This has been an enlightening experience."

"My pleasure. And don't forget to talk to your Supply Division about us," Peter said with his most ingratiating smile.

The Interview

Ezrah had expected to see a tall, thin boy with long hair and glasses. The young god walking in the door was pretty close. Bernie's hair was more unruly than Ezrah had expected, with multiple cowlicks sticking out in random directions. *I can't hold that against him*, he thought. *Neat hair would be impossible for anyone with a chaotic cloud like his.* He'd half-expected to see Bernie wearing a T-shirt and torn jeans; he was pleasantly surprised to see him wearing nice, although worn, shirt and pants. His belt did not match, and his old scuffed tennis shoes, with one lace dragging on the ground, seemed out of place. *Well, it's easy for a cloud to untie even the best knots*, thought Ezrah. He could see from Bernie's shimmer how nervous he was. It was probably all he could do to keep his cloud under control

Ezrah put on his professional manner and said, "You must be Bernie. My name is Ezrah. I've been looking forward to meeting you."

"Thank you, sir," said the young god.

"Let's go to my office and sit down. Would you like some coffee?" Ezrah asked.

"Ah, no... Thank you."

Ezrah led the way into a large office with a beautiful dark wood desk. Nearby bookshelves and the conference table were made of the same dark wood, leaving no doubt of Ezrah's importance in The Business hierarchy. The sun shining through a private skylight illuminated the far side of the room, furnished with a small sofa, a coffee table, and three chairs. Ezrah gestured to the sunlit corner.

"Let's sit over here. It's always nice to enjoy a little sunlight. Have a seat wherever you feel comfortable."

Bernie chose the sofa, but he remained standing until Ezrah, who selected one of the side chairs, said, "Please sit." *Bernie's mom certainly taught him manners*, Ezrah thought as he reached for his notebook and pencil.

Ezrah glanced again at Bernie's shimmer. *Hmm*, he thought,

we need to work on your anxiety level, Bernie, or we're not going to have a very productive interview. Let's start off easy.

"How was your graduation ceremony?"

"Ah… It was great, sir."

"You've been working on your building degree for a long time. It must feel good to have finished it."

"Yes, sir."

Ezrah smiled inwardly, and said to himself, *Okay, let's try some open-ended questions.*

"Can you tell me about the graduation ceremony?"

"Yes, sir. We had one hundred and seventy-six graduates this year. There were twenty-three of us in the Builder Program. Zachariah, our headmaster, made a speech about how proud he was of us. The weather was beautiful so the ceremony was outdoors. It was great."

"I imagine everyone is very proud of you. Getting your degree in Building Sciences is hard work."

"Thank you."

"Bernie, I'd like to get to know you better. Can you tell me something about yourself?"

"Sure. What would you like to know?"

"Well, let's see. What classes did you like best?"

"I always liked math and physics. And, ah… the creation classes were great too."

"What did you like about math and physics?"

"I like solving problems. That's why I like math. Physics is even better because there're lots of different ways to solve the same problem. It's fun to find a solution no one's thought of before." Bernie's enthusiasm began to show.

"I noticed you were active with the Off World Technology group. Is that related?"

"Oh, yes. Some of the technology they've invented on other worlds is amazing. A lot of it works in our world too, you know. I love that kind of stuff."

"Can you give me an example of something you've done with this technology?"

"Sure. I have a planet at home that was developing a problem with overcrowding. One of the OWT guys mentioned a portal device that lets life forms teleport across space. He gave me one of the portals. I made a duplicate planet on the opposite side of the sun for them. Then I made a hundred portals and put them all over both planets. It didn't take long before they figured out it was less crowded on the new planet, and thousands of them migrated. It was a great solution."

"Why didn't you just cull the population? You know, introduce a disease or a predator. That would have done the same thing."

"I didn't want to hurt them."

Oh, yes, thought Ezrah. *Now we're seeing Bernie's problem with not wanting to hurt anything.*

"Then why didn't you just talk to them about birth control or something?" Ezrah asked.

"We aren't allowed to talk to our life forms, sir. I could get in a lot of trouble for that." Bernie seemed surprised Ezrah would make such a suggestion.

"I see. Are there other classes you liked?"

"Well, I liked classes that combined different disciplines, like social engineering, anthropological design, social-psychology, physiological-psychology, genetic engineering, social-anthropology, astrophysics, and stuff like that. I like learning new things."

"How do you do with repetitive tasks?"

"Hmm... I'm not sure. I can't remember ever doing the same thing twice in school, sir. There's always so much to learn. They were talking about changing the five-week semesters into four-weeks so they can squeeze more classes in."

Ezrah thought back to his days in school. He'd stayed in the builder program for many years. When he finally changed majors, his world had changed. He went from constant studying to having a social life and friends. He still had plenty of classes, but the homework dropped to almost nothing. The kids in the building program, on the other hand, never had time for themselves.

"Can you tell me how well you get along with others?" Ezrah asked, thinking of his conversation with Beatrice.

"Ah... Pretty well lately, sir."

"Hmm... Beatrice told me you had problems with some of your classmates." Ezrah fumbled through his notes. "Yes. Billy and some of his friends."

"That's true, sir. I had problems with Billy until a couple of years ago, but I haven't had any problems since then."

"What happened a couple of years ago?"

"Billy and I were in a lot of the same classes, but his schedule changed during his last year, so we weren't in the same classes anymore. He graduated a year ago, so I haven't seen him for almost two years now."

"Did you have problems with anyone else?"

"No, sir. I've never had problems with anyone except Billy."

"Another question I have is about dressing properly for work."

The disappointment on Bernie's face was clear as he said, "Isn't this okay? We bought these clothes just for work."

"What you're wearing now is fine. I'm talking about what you wore at school. You need to know torn jeans and T-shirts are not appropriate here."

"I understand." Bernie looked visibly relieved.

"Bernie, I have to ask you about problems Gabriel said you had in your creation ethics class."

"Yes, sir."

"Can you tell me why he says you refused to accept even the most basic ethical standards?"

"Sir, it started when Gabriel said we have to install death directives in everything we create. He said it's the only way to evolve life forms and avoid overpopulation. I asked him about situations where that could be handled in other ways, and he got mad at me."

"He says you argued with him almost every day."

"Sir, I didn't try to. I... Every day when he was lecturing, he would say something like, '...but I'm sure Bernie has a different opinion on this. Tell us what you think, Bernie.' I didn't want to argue with him, but I couldn't just lie."

"He said you're opposed to blinking out life forms even if they're interfering with your creation goals. Is that true?"

"Sir, I don't think we should destroy the life we create. There are times we have to, but that should be the last resort. Gabriel was upset because my definition of 'last resort' and his are different. He's ready to blink them if they get in his way. I would do it if it was the only way."

"Okay, I think I understand your position." Ezrah glanced through his notes and jotted down a couple more.

"Can you tell me why I should hire you as a builder?"

"Yes, sir. Being a builder is the only thing I've ever wanted. I've been working for it my whole life. If you give me this job, I promise, you won't be sorry. I'll do my very best for you and for The Business."

Ezrah liked the conviction and sincerity he heard in Bernie's words. "Thank you, Bernie. Now, before we finish, is there anything you want to tell me or you think I should know about you or your qualifications?"

"I don't think so."

"Are there any questions you would like to ask me?"

"Yes, sir. How long will it be before I hear from you?"

"You should know something, one way or the other, within a week."

"Thank you for seeing me, sir. If there's anything else you would like to know, please ask."

"We will, Bernie." Ezrah stood, and they shook hands. "Thank you for coming in."

~

Ezrah watched as Bernie walked out of the Personnel Department and back toward the main entrance.

He shook his head. "You have some serious limitations, Bernie. I don't know how we can work around them."

Ezrah sighed as he reached his decision.

Shaking his head again, he said, "I'm sorry, Bernie. I know you've worked really hard, but I don't think you've got what it takes to work here."

Suzie Protests

Ezrah called Suzie into his office. He knew her interest in Bernie was more than casual. She'd been hovering over Bernie's application for two weeks now. She would be upset by his decision, but he was prepared to get it over with.

At the same time, Ezrah wrestled with a second issue. Suzie had been a co-op placement with him for two years. She was one of the most talented students he'd ever seen. She recognized what needed to be done and took the initiative to do it. When she graduated a month ago, Ezrah had been delighted to offer her a full-time job. Suzie had accepted on the spot and had jumped up and down in an uncharacteristic display of happiness. Ezrah planned to cross-train her in all aspects of personnel work. After all, he wasn't going to be there forever. In fact, he had his eye on a couple of nice retirement worlds that looked very comfortable. And who knew? In another few millennia, they might be too tempting to resist.

This Bernie situation is sticky, he thought. Suzie needed to learn she couldn't hire someone just because they were friends. She had to make the best decision for The Business, even though it might be painful for her or someone she cared about. The Business had to come first. What was the best way to teach her this lesson?

If she's going to be a full member of my department, then I need to respect and invite her input. But if I've already made up my mind, it doesn't seem fair to ask her opinion. In the end, Ezrah decided the direct and honest approach was best.

Suzie came in with two fresh cups of coffee and set them down. She sat in the chair opposite his desk with pen and notebook in hand.

"What can I do for you, boss?" she asked with a smile.

"Suzie, I need to have a serious talk with you. It's about Bernie."

Suzie did a quick intake of breath as she sat straighter in her chair. "Okay."

"I've been doing background checks on him. I talked with three teachers and his co-op supervisor. Yesterday, as you know, I interviewed Bernie. I promised to talk with you about him, and that's what I'm doing now."

"Great. I've known Bernie for—"

Ezrah interrupted her. "I need to tell you, based on what I've heard so far, I can't justify hiring him. I don't believe he's a good fit for us."

"Oh, no! Ezrah, you're wrong. Bernie's a great guy. Please don't do this," Suzie said as tears filled her eyes.

"Suzie, I'm willing to listen to everything you have to tell me, but I had to tell you what I see right now." Ezrah tried to ignore the first tear as it fell. "I'm sorry. I know this is upsetting, but I can't just pretend to listen when my mind is almost made up." Ezrah moved a box of tissues closer to her.

"Why are you doing this? What do you think is wrong with him?" Suzie took the tissues.

"First of all, there are a lot of good things I can say about Bernie. Just graduating with his building degree means he's a hard worker, he's smart, and he's dedicated. One of his teachers, Beatrice, said very positive things about him, and so did his co-op supervisor, Peter. Bernie's work ethic is not a problem. The real problem is his building ethics.

"Let me tell you a lesson I learned from Leviticus, the Personnel Director before me. He asked me a question once. 'If you hire someone and later have to fire them, whose fault is it?' I said, 'It's the employee's fault because he didn't do a good enough job.' He said, 'No, Ezrah. It's *your* fault.' When I asked him why, he said, 'You knew what the job required, and you had the chance to interview the employee and learn what they had to offer. It was your job to decide if it was a good fit. You're the only one who had all the information to make a good decision.'

"He taught me an important lesson, Suzie, and one I can't ignore. When I look at Bernie, I see a young god who, although talented, is not willing to perform the basic functions required for the job. If you're unwilling to erase your mistakes, regardless of whether they're alive or not, how can you ever be a successful builder?"

"But, Ezrah, there are positions in The Business where he

wouldn't have to do anything with life forms. Maybe he can work in the Sun Division and just build suns."

"But that would mean having an employee we can't transfer to another department if we need him somewhere else. Anything involving life forms will stop him cold. We can't have someone who takes two or three times longer to do something because he doesn't want to hurt the life forms. We have production requirements and deadlines."

"But what about the talent you want to cultivate here?" Suzie asked. "Some really talented builders have serious shortcomings. I've seen their personnel evaluations. They're amazing in one or two areas, but they have other areas where they're really bad."

"That may be true for some of the star builders, Suzie. But Bernie hasn't shown us anything that suggests he has that kind of skill."

"But how would you know? No one's given him a chance. If you saw what he could do, I know you'd be impressed. Please, Ezrah," begged Suzie. "Please just give him a chance."

"I don't know." As soon as the words were out of his mouth, Ezrah realized his position was weakening. *Hmm*, he thought, *the pilot program for new employees would give Bernie a chance to show what he can do.*

"Don't forget, Ezrah. Bernie's dad is Simeon. How do you know he doesn't have the same talent as his father?" Ezrah watched as Suzie sit up straighter in her chair, somehow sensing the growing strength of her argument. "You wouldn't want to find out you'd refused to hire the next Universe Award Winner, would you?" she asked in her most winsome tone.

Ezrah knew he'd lost. The only thing left was to save as much face as possible. "Okay, Suzie. I'll give him a try. Maybe we'll both learn something from this."

Suzie jumped up from her chair and ran around the desk and hugged a protesting Ezrah. "Oh, thank you, Ezrah! You won't be sorry. You'll see!" Then she hugged him more.

Finally, Ezrah said in his gruffest voice, "Okay, now get out of here and close the door behind you. I have important work to do."

As soon as Suzie closed the door behind her, Ezrah got up

and kicked the wastebasket into the wall. Then he turned to the credenza and the picture of his wife and daughter and growled, "It's bad enough there are two women who can do that to me. Now I have a third."

Tomorrow, It Begins...

As they followed the young god through the woods, the watchers with the tiny eyes knew something was different.

Four days ago, they'd been overjoyed to see the change in their boy. His shimmer was stronger than ever before, almost as bright as the sun that shined through the treetops. Something had happened to make him very happy. They saw it in the way he walked with them, sometimes even bursting into a run along the path, forcing them to race to keep up. What had happened to make him so joyful?

Each day since then had been similar. He still didn't go away in the mornings. He still spent most of the day walking with them. But each day he seemed to lose a little of the radiant joy he had shown four days earlier.

Other gods all went into the town for part of the day. Why didn't the boy? Was there something wrong? They couldn't think of anything to explain why he had stopped going into the town.

Today, the boy wore his usual torn jeans and an old T-shirt that said "Life is Sacred" in faded ink. The lace from one tennis shoe dragged on the ground, making occasional attempts to lasso twigs or small plants that came into range. The young god's shimmer was mostly greens and yellows, and red made an occasional appearance.

The watchers all agreed the boy was lost in his thoughts, more than usual. They worried for him. Gingi, not usually known for her courage, suggested revealing themselves to the boy. But no one, not even Bowin, the bravest of them all, had agreed. And so, once again, they just followed. Had they known how long it would be before Bernie returned to the woods, they might have decided differently.

But there was no way for them to know how much the boy's life was about to change.

~

Bernie liked to think he had a logical mind, but today he would not have made that claim. His head was bursting with thoughts. Each thought came with emotional baggage, and Bernie flitted from thought to thought and emotion to emotion, accomplishing little beyond giving a certain cloud an excuse to unleash even more chaotic forces upon the world.

Without conscious thought, Bernie's course through the woods led him to his favorite place. Trees gave way to a clearing where tall green grasses swayed in the gentle, ever-present breezes that caressed the plateau. Sunlight was unobstructed in the beautiful clearing where Bernie sat on a large rock. Bernie, like all gods, loved the sun. Here, in his forest sanctuary, no outsider ever disturbed him.

After a time, Bernie became aware of new thoughts.

"I really am at a transition point," he said, thinking of the headmaster's words at his graduation ceremony. His old life was over. For him, the world of school and homework and part time jobs was forever behind him. "Tomorrow, I begin a new life."

There was a lot to be excited about. He had worked hard and, finally, it was here. "I'm a *builder*, a member of the most respected profession in the world," he said with pride. Nor was he the only one who felt pride in his accomplishment. His mother was just as proud. Bernie felt as if he was about to fill an empty hole in his family. He was going to make big money, which they certainly needed.

Although his thoughts should have remained full of excitement and hope, they drifted instead to his father, Simeon. The questions never changed: Why had he left them? They needed him, but he'd closed the door and never looked back. *Was it me? Was it my fight with Billy?* In all these years, why hadn't he ever come to see them?

People have different ways of dealing with their hurt. Some people turn it into anger against the person who hurt them. This was not Bernie's way. If his dad rejected him, there was probably a reason. If he could only prove himself, things would be different. The best way to do that was to become a builder. And someday, he would win Universe Awards too, just like his dad. When that day came, his dad would know he had misjudged his son. He would come back and say how sorry he was for everything. *Then things will be the way they're supposed to be*, said the worn-out storyboard pictures in Bernie's head.

Bernie shrugged off thoughts of his father and the stupid daydreams that came with them. After all, he had worked hard to make it through the builder program. Plenty of times he'd been ready to give up. *Maybe there really is something wrong with me*, he thought. His efforts had often backfired and turned him into the school joke. He was always afraid of being kicked out of the builder program. Even the other day, when he interviewed with Ezrah, he'd been sure he wasn't going to get the job.

His gut tightened more, remembering his teachers talking about how much harder things are in the real world. Things were already hard in school. *No*, he thought. *These are just normal self-doubts. If the rest of my classmates can do it, then so can I.*

He forced himself to think uplifting thoughts, thoughts of his new life, his new job, and all the exciting things that waited for him in the future.

"The woods will always be here for us," he said in a weak attempt to calm his doubts. "Whenever we need to think things through, we can always come here."

Unfortunately, that was not to be.

Weekend at Billy's

The weekend had finally arrived, and Billy was alone in his suite. His parents never disturbed him on weekends, having learned their son put a high value on his private time.

Billy's weekend plans seldom changed, and this weekend would be no exception. He would spend it in a 'play world' he called Klash.

Billy had created Klash six years ago, when his building skills were still growing. Unable to create the kind of higher life forms he wanted, he solved the problem by purchasing a seed population from a hobby supply store. They transferred one thousand people to the planet, and, although he lost a third of them during their first few years, eventually they learned to survive on his world.

After six thousand years, the Klashians numbered one hundred thousand and had developed a rudimentary culture, which was perfect for Billy. They had reached that 'sweet spot' when they had the agrarian skills needed to support specialized professions such as soldiers, artisans, and, of course, priests and priestesses.

"Playing God," Billy said, "is always more fun if you don't have to worry about mundane things like keeping your people from starving. It's better if they've solved those problems already. People struggling to survive, worrying about food, water, shelter, and other boring stuff, aren't much fun." Billy grinned. "With more advanced civilizations, you get to manipulate more interesting things like power, wealth, social status, and recognition, which makes for much better game."

Of course, that could be carried too far. Billy had no interest in highly technical civilizations. Fighting with swords and spears was infinitely more entertaining than laser beams and rocket launchers. Palace intrigues with slow-acting poisons were preferred over a genetically engineered killing agents designed to wipe out specific families by targeting unique biometric profiles. Billy knew he could simply smash any technology they might develop, but once they had the idea, it was difficult to get them to forget it. It was better if they never learned.

Between his weekend games, he let time advance on Klash, giving the people time to rebuild their population and their cities; usually fifty or sixty years was sufficient. If he killed off more than thirty or forty percent of the population, he might give them an extra thirty years before the next game. That gave things a chance to change on the planet, which gave Billy a fresh new game every weekend.

And things were always changing. Sometimes, in the absence of his godly interference, the authority of the temples and priesthoods would decline. Sometimes, rival kingdoms went on to achieve peace, either through truce or conquest. Billy actually liked this. It made each new game like a chess match, requiring new strategies and new moves.

Billy was an excellent strategist. He could provoke conflict in any situation. In the end, it was about control and power. And, of course, the body count. The body count had to be high, or how could you ever tell a god had been involved?

Billy's first step was always to find out what had changed from the previous weekend. The old leaders were dead and gone, so discovering who the new players were was the best place to start. And there were always secrets to discover—although few secrets really mattered when weighed against the powers of a god.

As Billy surveyed his world, he discovered the Klashians had once again found peace. "They seem to be doing that a lot lately." Billy frowned. "I wonder if I'm killing off the violent ones and leaving the pacifists behind. Well, no matter. I've never had trouble getting them to draw blood." Billy chuckled as he thought of past games.

Studying the game map, Billy selected 'civil war' as the theme for this weekend's game.

"I think we'll have a little insurrection. It's always fun to see what the underdogs do when they get their own power," he said. "Hmm… I don't see a lot of oppression going on. Dungeons are empty. No bodies swinging from the gallows. The population appears well-fed. The king appears to be taking good care of his subjects."

Billy paused for a moment. "That shouldn't be much of a problem. It's easy enough to create a food shortage. That'll bring down the social order as fast as anything, especially when people see how the remaining food gets divided up, it's easy to get them to riot."

Billy shook his head. "No. That's too easy." Billy noticed a poorly maintained temple on the outskirts of town. "Oh, that's an idea. I'll use the remnants of the Temple of Zinnew. I'm surprised anyone still remembers him. It's been, let's see…" he counted the weekends back, quickly converting it into Universe Time, "about three hundred and forty years now."

Billy, also known as the Great Lord Zinnew, laughed. "I must have made quite an impression, since you're still burning incense at my altar. Well, your patience and your loyalty are about to be rewarded."

Billy jotted notes on a pad. When he finished, he said, "Okay. The temple will rise up, overcome the godless tyrant-king, and they will form a theocracy and rule the world, by divine right," he declared. "At least until next weekend." Billy laughed.

He took a box of many-sided dice from his desk drawer. "And how many godly interventions will we allow for this game?" Rolling the first die, he announced, "Only three." Rolling again, he added, "But I get four miracles. That's good."

With the game parameters decided, Billy settled into the game. It would take just a few manifestations by Lord Zinnew for people to know the god of vengeance was back. According to the *Book of Billy*, it didn't count as a godly intervention or even a miracle if he appeared to three people or less. He chose key opinion-makers for his visitations, beginning with the high priest of the Temple of Zinnew. Even though the high priest was an elderly man, it was inspiring to see how energized he became upon learning his god had returned. At this stage of the game, it was mostly a matter of glitz and glitter; Billy saved his miracles and interventions for later.

Breeding dissent was easy. The temple had lost a priest last year under mysterious circumstances. It was child's play to convince them the king had been involved. Punishing the king was the obvious solution. However, the king was well-regarded, and there was some reluctance to assassinate him. Nor was the

Great Zinnew interested in such simple solutions. This was just the opening move. Billy needed to build the strength of the all-but-forgotten temple before he was ready for open confrontation.

So how do you punish the king for his treachery? The answer was simple: you hurt him back. The king's daughter was eleven. She was chosen to pay the price for her father's evil deed. They chose poison and were careful to leave no evidence.

The king and queen, heartbroken over the loss of their daughter, had no suspicion of foul play—until Billy, appearing to the king as the ghost of his dead grandfather, planted the idea in his head. The ghost 'revealed' that his daughter had been murdered by the tradespeople because of a recent tax increase. Billy was not ready to put the priests in play yet; they were still far too weak.

To keep things moving, Billy used the first of his three godly interventions to kill a priest, leaving his body hanging from the castle wall where all could see. This outraged the temple, and they had no choice but to retaliate again.

And so it went. Planting seeds of distrust and disharmony, Billy watered them with whispers and doubts, making them grow. Billy used his godly power to move through time, often going days and even months into the Klashians' future, watching as his deadly seeds were harvested. For Billy, only moments passed, but the people experienced months of assassinations, kidnappings, tortures, and other outrages. And for every act, there were reprisals as each side sought justice. And the great god of vengeance, Lord Zinnew, cheered for them all.

Billy used another of his miracles to create gold for the temple so they could hire mercenaries. No one believed the official story—that the temple needed guards to protect their priests and priestesses. And, as chaos reigned in the world of Klash, the temple grew in strength. Followers of Zinnew, though often victims of the raging conflict, were known to suffer less than others. 'The Mighty Zinnew protects his chosen,' they said.

Finally, the tradesmen, furious over the capture and torture of so many of their own, began allying, one trade after another, with the temple. As the temple's power grew, so too did their boldness.

In fairness to the king, it should be acknowledged he did his best to maintain order and keep the peace. But even with the best intentions, the overwhelming provocations soon turned the king into a back-street fighter, little different from any of Billy's other pawns.

Manipulating the groups was easy, and Billy delighted every time he found someone who resisted Zinnew's suggestions. They became examples for the rest. The wrath of the Great Zinnew was terrible indeed, and there were never any second chances.

At last, the strength of the temple rivaled that of the king. But Billy wanted nothing left to chance. So the Great Zinnew demanded a declaration of loyalty from the people; they must pledge their allegiance to the Temple. They were given one day to comply. Those unwilling or unable to change sides paid a terrible price. They woke the next morning to discover their youngest child had died in their sleep. Soon, Zinnew had all the soldiers he needed.

By the end of the weekend, Billy had both sides lined up on the battlefield—ready to die for the greater glory of their cause.

And they did.

Oh, how they did…

Suzie's View

Suzie arrived early and was sitting behind her desk in the Personnel Department. She wore a special dress from her school days. It was the one she wore the day she and Bernie almost had a conversation about something other than school. Her long blonde hair was pulled into a ponytail, and the seahorse earrings she always wore dangled with every turn of her head. Only her shimmer revealed her anxiety, as it occasionally altered intensity.

Suzie's teachers described her as a serious student, self-conscious and quieter than most, but polite and eager to please, which went a long way. She had worked in the Personnel Department as a co-op student and learned a lot about The Business. Her boss, Ezrah, liked her, and when she graduated, Ezrah had offered her a full-time job. She had been thrilled to accept.

Her crush on Bernie had begun in the third grade. She liked the way he got excited about everything. She was pretty sure he liked her. Well, maybe he didn't. He never said so.

Although, she thought, *your cloud tells a different story, Bernie.* Suzie chuckled, remembering the time his cloud had tied their shoelaces together. Bernie had been terribly embarrassed, but she knew it was the cloud's way of trying to keep them close. Nor, of course, would she ever tell Bernie of the times she felt an invisible hand patting her on the shoulder. She learned not to react when it happened—Bernie would have been mortified. But, she didn't mind. In fact, she rather liked it.

Ever since she had known him, Bernie had been afraid to show his feelings. Whenever she tried changing the subject to something besides school, Bernie would get tongue-tied, mumble some excuse, and run away. It might have been different if he'd known she liked him, but she'd never told him. And she knew Bernie would never be able to figure it out for himself.

Guys like Bernie didn't understand girls. Well, no one did, really. The School Board tried many times to come up with a special Understanding Females program, but never found enough material to fill a semester, let alone an entire curriculum. Suzie, as a member of the girl world, took some pleasure in knowing she was unfathomable to half of the population. Some elder gods even called females one of the Great Mysteries. And perhaps they were.

Suzie hadn't seen Bernie since the graduation ceremony a month earlier. She had been seated with the graduates who had chosen non-builder professions, dressed proudly in multi-colored caps and gowns that contained every color of the rainbow. Bernie wore the special all-white cap and gown reserved for the builder grads. The white robes were special, chosen because they included all the rainbow colors and yet were a special color of its own. She had been so very proud of Bernie that day.

Today was another big day. Bernie would arrive soon, and she was excited. For days, she had been thinking about how to make Bernie's arrival a perfect experience. She decided Bernie would see her sitting at her desk, full of papers—a clear display of the important work she did. She would time it so their eyes met at exactly the same moment. As he looked at her, a familiar face in alien territory, she would smile, get up, and walk over to him. She would graciously welcome Bernie to the Personnel Department and his first day at work. She had practiced what to say and even planned to wink at him as she spoke, so he would know she was still the same Suzie, even though she had an important job now.

As she sat thinking, Bernie walked in, all wide-eyed and excited, as usual. But when he noticed Suzie, he jerked and quickly looked away. Suzie didn't even have time to smile. Bernie looked everywhere except at her. What was wrong? Had she done something?

Ezrah greeted Bernie, and the moment was ruined. She slumped at her desk. She couldn't bring herself to look up as Ezrah escorted Bernie into his office. She sat at her desk, pretending to be busy, while Ezrah and Bernie talked and filled out paperwork. When Ezrah's door opened again, she kept her eyes on her desk as they left to meet Bernie's new boss.

Why had he done that? She wanted to impress Bernie with

her job and how professional she had become. Maybe
something had changed with Bernie. Maybe he had a girlfriend.
The knot in Suzie's stomach growled out its hurt. Suzie turned
back to her desk and the stack of papers.

She re-stacked them again, as a tear trickled down her
cheek.

Orientation

Bernie showed up wearing pants with frayed cuffs and a shirt with two buttons undone. Looking at him, Ezrah wondered again why he'd given in to Suzie. He'd seen people like Bernie before—he was just a rube from the outer edge of town, who somehow got through school, but would never amount to anything. *Well, this is a necessary part of Suzie's education,* he thought. *Bernie will be an object lesson for her. It will teach her what happens when hiring decisions are made for the wrong reason.*

"Hello, Bernie," said Ezrah as they shook hands. "Are you ready for your first day?" Ezrah maintained his professional smile as he pointed to the buttons on his own shirt and then pointed to Bernie's unbuttoned shirt.

"Yes, sir, I think so," said Bernie, as he quickly re-buttoned his shirt.

"Good. Then let's get the paperwork out of the way." Ezrah led the way into his office where he handed Bernie a folder of forms and invited him to sit in the chair in front of his desk.

Ezrah watched Bernie extract a pair of wire-rim glasses and adjust them on his nose. One lens had a crack across the lower left corner, and the wire frames had bends in places that weren't supposed to bend, mostly because Bernie carried them in his pocket. As he slid the glasses in place, a newborn cowlick rose up in all its glory over one ear. "I mostly just need them for reading," Bernie said as he patted his empty shirt pocket. "May I borrow a pencil?"

"Sure."

As Ezrah waited for Bernie to finish, he thought of how different their world was from the universes they created. *The kids here don't know how easy they have it. Life is simple for them. They don't even have last names, for goodness' sake.* Ezrah had seen planets with so many people they used numbers to keep track of each other.

As Bernie filled out papers, Ezrah reminisced about the retirement party he attended the previous Friday. That was another part of their world that was simple. Some universes had to take care of people when they got old and couldn't work or support themselves. That wasn't a problem for the gods—and not just because they didn't get old.

Sure, gods retired from time to time, but it was usually because they got bored. Then they moved to some universe they bought or had built over the years. It wasn't as if they needed a pension check. If they needed anything, they could just create it. The biggest problem retirees complained about was the crowds. No matter how much they disguised themselves to blend into the world they had chosen, people knew they were different— probably the shimmers—which made it hard to find a life of quiet solitude. Unless they were careful, that darn shimmer would shine through. Females had more control over it, of course, since most of them took classes in shimmer management. But even they had problems.

Ezrah managed an inward smile recalling the toasts at Friday's retirement party. They were honoring a builder who was settling on a system he'd created eons earlier. It had three suns and eight or nine planets, typical of retirement worlds—at first. Many retirees became bored and ended up filling their universe full of star systems. The standard toast at builder retirement parties was, 'May you never build another world.'

"I'm done, sir," Bernie said, abruptly ending Ezrah's reverie.

"Oh, thanks, Bernie. I'll take that. We'll use this to get your personnel file started. We'll fill your file with performance reviews, transfer requests, and all that other stuff. Before we get started, do you know about our pilot program for new employees?"

"No, sir. We didn't study much about The Business," said Bernie as two buttons on his shirt quietly unbuttoned themselves.

Ezrah was about to say something, but before he could, the buttons re-buttoned themselves.

"Umm…" Ezrah collected his thoughts. "The pilot program started a few hundred years ago. It was designed to give new employees a chance to show us what they can do. You'll be given complete freedom to create a universe of your own.

Anything you want—anything at all. No one will tell you what to do or how to do it. And you'll have whatever supplies and materials you need.

"I can see from your expression this is all new to you. Let me tell you why we started this program. The Board of Directors feared we might be missing out on the creativity of new employees because they ended up in some specialized division before we had a chance to learn what they're really capable of doing. This is your chance to shine, Bernie. We want you to wow us. Knock our socks off. Show us what you can really do.

"You'll have six months to complete your project. Then we'll take a look at what you've done. When we see your work, we'll make decisions about your skills and decide what division to put you in.

"While you're working on your universe, you'll be assigned to one of the regular divisions. That division's head will be your supervisor, and he'll review your performance on whether you follow the work rules, get along with coworkers, and things like that.

"Even though you're in the pilot program, you're still a probationary employee. And if your boss decides you don't measure up, he can terminate your employment, regardless of how you're doing on your universe. Have you got all that?"

"Yes, sir. Follow the rules, and build a great universe."

"Yep. That's about right. Well, let's go meet your new boss." Ezrah glanced away, unable to look at Bernie.

The poor kid, he thought. *His enthusiasm is about to get dashed. Shemal is the toughest manager in The Business. He demands high performance, and if he doesn't get it, he has no problem terminating someone before their probationary period is up.*

Ezrah felt badly about assigning Bernie to Shemal, but he thought it would be more merciful for everyone if things ended quickly.

Meeting the Boss

Bernie followed Ezrah up three flights of stairs, down two long corridors, and up another flight of stairs as they moved through the strange 'inner space' the gods used to make their buildings. Buildings in town were invariably larger on the inside than the outside. Thinking of the building in three dimensions lead to getting lost, which is why Bernie paid attention instead to the twists and turns and ups and downs as he memorized the route.

All the major divisions had their own skylights; some said you could tell the power of a division by counting their skylights. This bore some truth. Divisions were always being reorganized, restructured, and renamed in an attempt to improve their efficiency, although some argued it was more about power struggles that raged among the corporate officers.

Today was no field trip where Bernie and fellow students had come for a tour. Today he started work as a builder. So far, everything was going perfectly. Ezrah seemed nice. He spoke to him like an adult instead of a student. Bernie wasn't sure anyone had ever done that before. It felt really good. In fact, the only bad thing today was the weird way Suzie had acted. When he first saw her, his cloud got excited and he was afraid it would do something to embarrass him. By the time he got it calmed down, he couldn't catch her attention. He was sure she'd seen him. Well, maybe she was having a bad day or something. He hoped that's all it was.

Finally, Ezrah stopped and opened a door for Bernie. The sign said Standard Model Final Assembly Division. As they walked inside, Bernie saw cubicles stretching from wall to wall. Bernie couldn't suppress a shiver of excitement as he surveyed the large room. These were all builders, hard at work creating new and wonderful things. And he was about to join them.

Ezrah steered Bernie to the long corridor in the center of the room. At the far end, in an office with glass walls on three sides, they found a big man wearing an angry frown as he stared at a paper in his hand.

As Ezrah knocked, the angry man looked up. "Ah, Ezrah. Come in," he said as the frown disappeared. "I see you brought me some fresh meat. Come on in, kid. I almost never bite on the first day."

"This is Bernie. He's our newest employee. He's only been on the payroll for an hour, Shemal, so treat him gently. They only graduate once a year, you know." They both laughed.

"Pleased to meet you, Bernie. You can call me Shemal. Thanks, Ezrah. I can take it from here."

"Okay, then. Good luck, Bernie."

"Thanks, Ezrah. I'll do my very best."

Ezrah closed the door behind him.

~

"Now, Bernie. I'm going to tell you the way things work around here," said Shemal with a voice that thundered and echoed in the small office. "It's very simple. I'm in charge. I'm the boss. You do whatever I tell you to do whenever I tell you to do it. Got that so far?"

"Yes, sir." He remained still even though he felt the grip of invisible fingers digging into his shoulders.

"I used to spend a lot of time trying to teach people to do exactly what I want. But I found out most of the new kids aren't very good at building, and they don't follow instructions very well either. So I developed my own little evaluation system for new employees. So here's how it's gonna work.

"You have your universe to build. I'm sure Ezrah told you about it. You're going to work on it. I'm not going to tell you a thing, although I'll come over once in a while to see how you're doing. You can build whatever you want.

"While you're in my division, you'll follow the rules and whatever else I tell you to do. I will be watching to make sure you do. And if I decide I'm wasting my time on you, then I'll show you the door. Got it?"

"Yes, sir." Bernie's heart was pounding so hard he could hear it in his ears. His invisible friend had hunkered down behind his back; he could feel it shaking.

"Now that we have the orientation complete, let's get you settled in. I'm giving you work station number seventeen. There are two manuals waiting on your desk, so read them. They will tell you most of the stuff you need to know. Any questions?"

"No, sir."

"Good. Then get out of here."

As Bernie walked out of Shemal's office he noticed a dozen or more heads raised above the cubicles watching him. He walked to the closest head, a young man who quickly turned back to his desk. Bernie said, "Hi, I'm Bernie. Can you tell me where station seventeen is?"

The young man, without looking up, pointed at the small numbers in brass on the outside of the cubicle. Bernie noticed the number forty-two. Everyone who had been watching him earlier was now too busy with their own work to respond to his attempts to say hello. He walked down the row of cubicles in the direction of descending numbers until he reached seventeen.

Inside the cubicle, he found two thick manuals and a beautiful set of builder equipment and supplies neatly stacked on the floor next to his desk. A rolling chair with an adjustable tilt sat waiting for him. Bernie walked into the cubicle and sat down. He tingled with excitement. His cloud, terrified just minutes earlier, was now patting him on the back. He closed his eyes and breathed in the satisfaction of having reached what had once looked like an impossible goal.

Life is good, he thought. *No, life is great!*

Billy Bully

Just a year ago, he'd been a new graduate from The School, standing in line and hoping for a job with The Business. Well, there had been little doubt he would be hired. He had good grades, and his family tree was full of builders.

In the last year, lots of things had changed. Billy hadn't changed, but he sure changed things around him. The division was a good example. When he first arrived, he was just the 'new kid'. Unfortunately for some of them, they hadn't treated him with the respect he deserved. But they had learned. They'd had no choice.

On the first day of each week, Billy made a point of arriving early and walking around the maze of cubicles that made up the Final Assembly Division. This morning, as he followed his weekly routine, he paused in front of empty cubicle number eighty-four. He had smiled. *Poor Stacey. You were the first to feel my wrath. Would it have been so hard for you to accept my invitation to lunch? Well, you gave me an opportunity to teach an important lesson to your co-workers, although I'm afraid it was too late for you.*

As if taking a regal stroll around his kingdom, Billy sauntered up one aisle and down another, pausing in front of several more empty cubicles. *And, you, Jason. I heard you now have a job stocking shelves in a grocery store. You should have shown me proper respect. You might still be working here.* Billy smiled, recalling how Jason had approached him on the street and begged for his job back. Billy had laughed in his face.

From a nearby cubicle, another god witnessed Billy's smile as he stood before the empty cubicle. The god shuddered and quickly looked away, lest Billy notice him.

The first few victims had been for the sake of example, really. It had been necessary to get everyone's attention and make them understand that things had changed. The strategy was similar to what he did on Klash: size up the battlefield and then, without mercy, destroy any who dared to oppose him. There was only one difference here: he couldn't kill his enemies.

He had to content himself with getting them fired. It was better in some ways—a god's pain lasted for an eternity. A Klashian's pain lasted for only an instant.

Naturally, there had been the predictable counterthrust when some had tried to resist what he was doing. They were the most fun really, because they knew what he was doing, had made a conscious decision to oppose him, and yet were powerless to stop him. Billy took more pride in their termination than in the others. In just six months, the battle had been won. No one who remained dared to oppose him. These were smart people. They saw his power. They knew what he could do.

They learned if they wanted to keep their jobs, they did whatever it took to stay on Billy's good side. A simple rule, really.

Anyone should be able to understand it.

~

The door to Final Assembly opened. The personnel director, Ezrah, entered, followed by a young god. Billy couldn't believe it. He hadn't seen him for two years. Could it be that Bernie was going to be working in this division? Billy smiled his first genuine smile in days. This was the perfect opportunity to settle old scores.

While Bernie met with Shemal, Billy thought back to all the times Bernie had wronged him. It was a long list. Billy and his posse had been the most-respected and envied guys at school. They'd been the cool kids with the best clothes and special tutors—all from good homes where both their moms and their dads were builders. All the girls liked to hang out with them.

Well, that wasn't quite true. Suzie didn't, and that was another thing to put on the list. Billy knew she would have been another of his groupies, but for some reason, she followed Bernie around like a love-struck puppy. Billy tried on numerous occasions to show her how unworthy Bernie was, but it just made her like him more. *Bernie is a nothing*, he thought. *He lived in one of the project homes the Town Council built for poor people out in the Fifth Circle. They weren't even like real homes. They were even smaller on the inside than on the outside. It would be like living in a shoebox. His mom didn't even have a real job; it wasn't like she was a builder or anything.*

Okay, Bernie's father was a hot-shot builder, but he'd had the good sense to dump them both years ago.

Billy's feud with Bernie had gone on for years. Bernie deserved it. Everybody treated him differently because his dad was the 'Great Simeon'. *So what? Somebody had to show them Bernie was nothing but a dumb geek in secondhand clothes. He always had his head in the clouds; if I hadn't poked him from time to time, he would have walked into walls.*

Usually Ber-Nerd would just take his lumps and go away. Things changed when Suzie came along. Old Bernie had this little audience of one so he felt the need to stick up for her. At least that was Bernie's excuse for the fight.

Billy seethed as he remembered what Bernie had done. Nothing could ever excuse it. *He turned me into a monster. Whenever someone looks at me, I see their shimmer flicker as if they're about to faint. Everyone gets the same sick feeling. And who wouldn't?* The horrible scar that ran half the length of Billy's face reminded everyone of their own mortality. The healers had said there was nothing they could do. It was the first thing people saw, and it was how they remembered him. *They think this is the greatest injury they can imagine, but it's not. The greatest injury is what I'm going to do to Bernie. And even then, it won't be enough.*

Over the years, he tormented Bernie at every opportunity. Just two years ago, everyone knew to avoid Bernie. If they didn't, one of his buddies, RedDog or Butcher, would have a little talk with them about the danger of hanging out with social misfits.

But Bernie couldn't leave well enough alone. The little nerd started fighting back. Without warning, Billy's class schedule was changed, and they weren't in the same classes anymore. A few more changes, and soon, they didn't have classes near each other; Billy was reassigned to the toughest teachers who gave the most homework. He was forced to run from one class to another to make it on time. He could never prove it, but he knew Bernie was behind it. Everyone knew Bernie was a geek. He probably hacked into the school's computers. Or maybe he used something from that Off World Technology group he was in.

One day, Billy caught up with him after school. When he confronted him, all Bernie would say was 'Really? You don't say.' or 'And you think I did this?' and other such nonsense.

Everyone knew he did it. And for proof, the next day Billy's classes were changed again. This time, his last class didn't end until thirty minutes after Bernie had left for the day. Billy was going to nail Bernie before school the next day, but he never did. He was afraid his schedule would get changed again, making him come in earlier so they would never see each other. Everyone was laughing behind his back. It was all Bernie's fault.

As Billy pondered the best course of action, a frown darkened his features. Billy's frown bore an uncanny similarity to the scowl on Shemal's face just minutes earlier.

Billy knew he could get everyone to shun Bernie, but the way his Uncle Shemal ruled this division, Bernie might not even notice people weren't talking to him. No, he needed a much better punishment. He needed full-strength Righteous Retribution. Bernie needed to go. Bernie needed to be fired. And to sweeten his revenge, Billy would tell his coworkers he was going to do it. They would watch it happen. It would be a great double lesson: punishment for Bernie for his crimes, and a not-so-subtle reminder of how important it was to respect Billy.

Out of the corner of his eye, Billy saw a tall figure walk by and go into the cubicle next to his. He heard someone sit in the chair. He waited thirty seconds for Bernie to settle back and relax. Timing was everything.

Billy stood up, looked over the cubicle wall, and waited for Bernie to notice him. As Bernie turned toward him, Billy smiled as Bernie's face registered the shock of seeing his longtime foe.

And, because quiet is more powerful than loud, Billy slowly whispered the words, "Hello, Ber-Nerd. I haven't forgotten that I still owe you." Then, before Bernie could do or say anything, Billy lowered himself back into his cubicle, smiling with satisfaction.

This is going to be fun, thought Billy.

Bernie's Journal

Journal Entry

I never thought I would make another journal entry after I finished school. But Mom's still working, and I just have to tell someone about my awesome day.

I spent time with the personnel director, Ezrah. He's a really cool guy. He took a lot of time with me and made sure I understood everything.

Ezrah gave me the most incredible assignment. I get to build *my own universe*. I can make anything I want. I even get whatever I need. No one will tell me what to do. I can do *anything*. This is so exciting! My biggest problem will be trying to figure out what to do.

When we were done, Ezrah took me to meet my new boss.

Shemal seems like a good guy. I mean, he seems kind of strict—he scared my cloud—but I'm sure he's fair, and everyone does a good job because of it.

I wonder what Dad's first day was like. I read in his book that he started in the Custom Planets Division. I wonder if he was nervous on his first day. Probably not.

I saw Suzie in the Personnel Department. I was so excited I forgot she would be there. When I saw her, my cloud grabbed my shirt and started pulling me toward her. Every time I'm near her, that stupid cloud goes crazy. It's always doing something to embarrass me, especially around her. When I finally got it under control, I tried to get her attention, but she wouldn't look at me. I hope I didn't hurt her feelings. It's frustrating.

One bad thing happened. After two years of not seeing him, I bumped into Billy again. He works in the cubicle right next to mine. He said he still owes me. I can't imagine he's still carrying a grudge after all this time.

I'm sure we can work it out.

The Manuals

Bernie's brain was reeling. He finally finished reading the thick manuals Shemal had given him. Although he was anxious to begin his universe, it had to wait. Learning the employment rules was the priority; he didn't want to make any mistakes.

It took three days to read them all. Fortunately, he found the bathroom rules early on the first day. He was relieved to find he could go whenever he needed to, although excessive time spent in the bathroom could be a rule violation. He didn't discover the section about lunch breaks until late the third day, so he missed three lunch breaks. Bernie couldn't find anything about whether people from Personnel and people from the other divisions ate at the same time, but he hoped he could see Suzie there. He found a section about a water cooler, but in spite of a full trip around the office, he couldn't find one, although he did see a place where it might have been once.

There were so many rules. Many of them contradicted each other. In school, they said there are only two kinds of rules: hard rules and soft rules. Hard rules are clear-cut and never contradict each other. Students learned to pay attention to hard rules because if they didn't, their universes wouldn't work right.

On the other hand, soft rules were different and confusing. The most confusing soft rules were in psychology and sociology where there weren't any hard rules at all. Well, there might be a few, but sooner or later someone would figure out a way to break them just to show they could. The School Board got tired of rewriting textbooks, so they added a paragraph saying any hard rule, under certain circumstances, could become a soft rule. And, just to cover all their bases, they added 'and vice versa'. That cut down on the rewrites.

The Business' manuals were full of soft rules disguised to sound like hard rules. For example, if you stole something from The Business, then you would be fired. But if you stole something and nobody caught you, then would you still get fired? If it didn't happen, then this was really a soft rule. And, making it more confusing, none of the rules were prioritized. If two rules conflict, which one do you obey? Bernie wanted to obey all the rules, but it made his movements jerky. Every time he started to do something, he stopped while he did a mental search for any rule he might be breaking.

For some rules, Bernie needed to ask someone. He tried asking people in the other cubicles, but they wouldn't talk with him. At best, they answered him with a head nod or a head shake, usually followed by a shooing-away motion with their hands. When he asked one young goddess if he should ask Shemal instead, she winced, shook her head no. But then she went back to her work and ignored his whispered questions. So Bernie stopped asking.

If he could find Suzie, maybe she could answer his questions.

Staring into the Abyss

Finally, Bernie was ready. The manuals read. The rules sort of understood. Potty time, lunchtime, and quitting time all clear. At last, his universe awaited.

Bernie cleared his desk of everything except the desk easel. He selected a large viewing window from his supplies and set it on the easel. Then he opened a jar of Universe Putty and placed it on the desk. He was ready.

Bernie began the process he'd done so often in school. He reached out with his hands and his mind in the way only a god could do, searching through the emptiness. Countless dimensions surrounded The World, each of them an empty void waiting to be captured and bent to the will of the gods. Capturing such voids from the infinite number of dimensions was like grabbing a fish in a tank of slippery fish in a dark room. Finally, Bernie had one in his grip. He kept his concentration as he guided the void to the edge of the viewing window. Holding it with one hand, he used his other to scoop a dab of universe putty with which he bound the void to his window frame. He continued around the edge of the frame until he'd securely attached his void.

While the putty dried, Bernie moved through the window frame and into his new universe. He'd never found a dimension with anything in it, but his teachers said it was prudent to check carefully. He was pleased to see the dimension was a flawless void, extending forever in every direction. *This is perfect*, he thought.

Bernie settled back to consider his next move. Completely unbidden, he heard the voice of his favorite teacher, Beatrice, urging him to *Plan First, Then Create*. He wrote these words on a little sticky and mounted it on the frosted glass of his cubicle. Then he got out a pad and pencil to make his notes.

And that's as far as he got. Hours later, the void was as voidy as ever. No suns. No planets. No inspiration. A plain and simple case of creator's block.

The problem, he decided, was too much freedom. Bernie

had so many possibilities he didn't know where to start. He'd never had freedom like this in school. No one did. No teacher in the history of The World ever told a student to create whatever he wanted.

In school, everything had been done inside a little box. Well, not a box exactly, although a god might think of it that way. For example, if the assignment was to 'create moons on at least four of the five planets in a solar system,' then they gave the students a solar system with five planets already made. They only had to worry about the moons. The planets, where to put them, how fast they moved around the sun, how big they were, or whether they should have atmospheres, were already done for you.

The gods called this modular creation. The goal was to teach one thing at a time. The division where Bernie worked was the one that supplied standardized universe kits to The School. Their job was creating identical universes so each student could focus on learning just one or two tasks. When the class ended, the universes were blinked out and re-voided.

Meanwhile, Bernie, frustrated with his inability to come up with design ideas, started wondering why they were subjecting him to this. After all, who needed to build whole universes by themselves, anyway? Only people who wanted to win awards and stuff. And maybe a few builders in the Research and Development Division. And maybe the Maintenance Division had to know their way around. But other builders, who worked in divisions like this, were specialized. Specializing began to sound like a good thing to Bernie. Life would be simpler if you only had to worry about one or two things at a time, like back in school.

He wondered if his father had this problem. *It's possible,* he thought. *Mom said she'd helped Dad with lots of ideas for his universes.*

In a flash of inspiration, Bernie turned to his building supplies. Searching quickly through the boxes, his expression turned to disappointment when he failed to find what he'd hoped for. There were no pre-built suns, no pre-fab planets, no life-in-a-jar. No kits of any kind. *So much for that idea.* They apparently wanted him to build everything from scratch.

The problem was, if he couldn't come up with ideas for his universe, he certainly wasn't going to make it through his probationary period.

Lunch with Lenny

By lunchtime, not much had changed. The void on Bernie's desk still taunted him. The universe supplies still sat on the floor. And that darn pad of paper remained blank as it waited for a plan. Any plan. Bernie had heard of gods who could build a whole universe in just six days and be home resting on the seventh. Of course, they probably didn't have to spend the first three days reading manuals.

Desperation rather than hunger sent Bernie in search of the cafeteria. He filled his lunch tray without thinking. It was only when he started looking for a place to sit that he thought of Suzie. The cafeteria was large, but he didn't see her anywhere.

"Bernie? Is that you?"

Bernie wasn't used to having anyone talk to him. No one in Final Assembly talked to anybody. Turning to look, he saw a god waving from an empty table. He looked younger than twenty-five—which was the oldest a god ever looked—and his voice lacked the resonating qualities of an older god. The god's unkempt hair was accompanied by a hopeless attempt at beard growing. *That would make him a little older than I am*, thought Bernie. There was something familiar about the eyes. *I'm sure I know him...*

As recognition came, Bernie's expression changed to a smile. "Lenny! How have you been? I didn't recognize you with the beard!"

Lenny had been the first to greet Bernie when he walked into the OWT meeting. Bernie wouldn't have been there at all, except his guidance counselor had urged him to get involved in some extra-curricular activity. 'The Business wants well-rounded people for their builders, Bernie. You need to join some groups or clubs.' When Bernie chose the Off World Technology (OWT) group, the counselor had not been impressed. 'Is that the best you can do? You don't want them to think you're just a geek, do you?'

A quick look at the other eight OWT members told Bernie

he was among his own kind. They all had that gaunt and haggard look you get from staying up all night, playing with computers, desperately trying to avoid social contact, and slapping down energy drinks. They had something else in common: they were all fascinated by the technology to be found on intelligent worlds.

"When did you start?" asked Lenny. "Where are you working?"

"This is my fourth day. I'm in the Final Assembly Division."

"Oh, that's not good. You've got old man Shemal for a boss."

"Why do you say that? He seems okay."

"Everybody hates him. He's fired more people than anybody. You remember Julie? She used to work for him, and he fired four people there before she could get her transfer approved. She said people are so afraid of him they won't even talk to each other. And it isn't just Julie who hates him. Everybody hates Shemal."

"Why? What happened?"

"Final Assembly was getting lots of complaints about their kits from The School. The Board of Directors set up the Quality Assurance Division (QAD) to look into the problem. Before any kits could be shipped, QAD made them pass all kinds of tests so The School wouldn't have anything to complain about. For a while, QAD rejected so many kits, no orders were being shipped at all.

"Shemal claimed it wasn't Final Assembly's fault. He claimed the other divisions were sending him defective suns and planets. So he set up his own QAD to inspect the stuff they sent him. If he didn't like what he saw, he refused to accept the parts. To justify Final Assembly's shipping delays, he sent a report on all the components he rejected to the Board of Directors and blamed the other divisions for the delays.

"So, heck yes, they hate him. They hate the whole Final Assembly Division."

Bernie didn't know what to say. So he changed the subject. "Did you have to make your own universe when you hired in?"

"Sure. Everyone does. What are you working on?"

"I can't decide. Any suggestions?" Bernie tried not to sound desperate.

"Well don't do any of the things you did in school, Bernie. I'm sure most of those will get you fired." Lenny chortled the way geeks sometimes do.

Bernie knew he was being insulted, but he refused to play into it. He would not give Lenny the satisfaction of asking him which screw up he was referring to. Most of his ill-fated endeavors had not received much attention, but the whole school knew about some of them. Billy once claimed the School Board developed a special class called Avoiding Bernards, so they could teach students what not to do. Bernie was pretty sure that wasn't true.

Lenny, sensing his friend's discomfort, went for the kill. "And be sure you don't Bernie-up the life forms. They were never your strong suit."

The sound of geek laughter is never funny when they're laughing at you.

~

Bernie winced. Life forms were much harder than celestial bodies. Well, they weren't hard if you just left them alone. If you left them alone, they were pretty good at evolving all by themselves. But the lab manuals were never content to let that happen. They wanted you to give them certain characteristics. Make them green. Make them tall. Give them scales. Make them fly. Make them intelligent. Make them breathe underwater. Give them yellow eyes. Give them three eyes. Get rid of the tails. Teachers had been teaching so long, there was no end to the things they could think of making students do.

Lenny was probably thinking about Bernie's Advanced Life Design 300 class. The projects were designed in a diabolically clever way. They made you put in writing exactly what you planned to accomplish before they let you start. Wicked Wanda, of course, always did well. But this was one of the most difficult classes for Bernie. He thought of himself as a seat-of-the-pants kind of guy. Go with the flow and all that. An artist, really. It was hard to make things happen just because you had some silly idea a week ago, and they wanted you to stick with it.

That was the class where Bernie decided to do flying things. He had long admired the flying creatures in the Awards Museum, so when he wrote his project paper, he described the beautiful creatures he would make, and how he would gift them with the ability to fly. His project paper was approved, and he began his work.

After a while, it was apparent the life forms were evolving slower than he had hoped. He saw small wings coming out, but they weren't good for much except gliding. He tried moving their food high up in the trees to give them an incentive to fly, but they mostly just waited for it to fall or they ate the tree bark instead. He tried introducing high winds and the occasional hurricane, hoping their airborne experiences would give them the idea. He even thickened up the atmosphere so they wouldn't have to flap their wings as hard, just in case they ever felt like flying. The birds-to-be were totally uncooperative.

In the hours before the project was due, Bernie's solutions became more and more desperate. He heated up the planet's surface, effectively giving all the birds a hotfoot, but it didn't motivate them to spend any more time in the air. He even introduced nasty bird-eating creatures who prowled the ground, hoping to scare them into the air. He tried lots of things. Nothing worked, and he ran out of time.

The teacher gave him a C-minus. The only reason he didn't fail the project altogether was because she noticed during one of Bernie's acts of desperation, specifically when Bernie marched the entire species off a 1,000 foot cliff, that three-percent of them could fly after all.

~

"Well, Bernie, I have to get back to work," said Lenny, dragging Bernie back to the here and now. "Good luck on your universe. Try not to get fired."

"Thanks, Lenny."

Somehow Bernie remembered Lenny being much nicer back in school.

Inspiration

Staring at the void never did much for Bernie. Maybe people like Wanda-the-Weirdo could see things in there, but normal people couldn't.

Then, somewhere deep in Bernie's brain, a small flicker of inspiration took root. It wasn't a big flicker, but Bernie could feel it growing into an idea. *Hmm*... Maybe the reason he had problems in school was because they never let him get good at anything. He was always given something new to do. If he'd ever had the chance to do the same thing two or three times, who knows how good he might have been? All he had to do was think of something he did well in school. Something he could do better the second time.

That was easier said than done. None of Bernie's projects had been impressive. Well, they might have been if Apple-Of-Every-Teacher's-Eye-Wanda hadn't been in so many of his classes. Just being in the same class as her meant the best you could hope for was a C. Everybody did better when she wasn't around.

Back to the subject. Maybe the reason he hadn't done anything great was because they kept making him do such complex things. Building a universe was like building a house of cards—every new level was harder than the one before. But what if you only had to build two or three levels because the bottom levels were already built for you? *Hmm*... An idea had landed and was busy clanging a bell inside Bernie's head, trying to get noticed.

Bernie grabbed the manual and turned to the section he'd read on the pilot program. Yes. There it was. If the employee needed additional supplies, they could requisition them from the Supply Division. Looking through his universe supplies, he found a stack of requisition forms. This was going to be easy!

Wait. Don't forget: Plan First, Then Create, he admonished himself. *I need a plan.* He grabbed his yellow pad and began scratching out a basic universe—not an impressive one, to be sure, but it would provide the foundation he was after. *Let's see,* he mused. *One sun. Let's go with yellow. One planet. Make it a standard rock planet. What about more planets and some moons and comets?* Bernie surprised himself when he decided to not add anything else. He could always add them later. Right now, he had to establish the foundation. It was the most basic universe possible. Nothing complex. Once it was perfect, he would add to it. And he had plenty of time to make sure each new addition was also perfect.

~

The Supply Division proved helpful. They gave him a glossy full-color catalog describing the features and benefits of each product. After some consideration, he chose a beautiful sun-planet combo he'd worked with before. This would help him avoid starting at the bottom of the learning curve again. He hurried back to his desk and laid everything out.

Bernie entered the void and carefully placed his sun in the center. Examining it from every angle, he was convinced he'd made a good choice. Next, he calculated the optimum habitation zone from the sun and positioned his planet in the center before giving it a push into an orbital pattern. After a moment's thought, he straightened the planet's elliptical orbit into a perfect circle. Smiling, he gently twisted the planet, giving it daily revolutions. So far, not even Wanda could have done better. Just to make sure everything went right, he advanced the time lever a full two billion years. And still everything looked good. He pulled the time lever back to the beginning. Time to think about the next steps. *From here on, it gets more complicated.*

And that turned out to be correct. Bernie spent the rest of the day trying to figure out what kind of planet to build. His planet was a blank, and he could make it into almost anything. He considered the big gas planets. He'd worked with them before, but he hadn't done life forms on them, and that was why he set them aside. He liked water planets, because they had interesting swimming things that you couldn't get on a rock planet—although a rock planet with water had possibilities. But again, although he had experience with water planets, he didn't have much experience with life forms on water planets. And everyone knew water planets were his dad's specialty. If he did one too, wouldn't everyone automatically compare his to his dad's award-winning worlds? *That's more pressure than I need for my first universe*, thought Bernie.

As Bernie considered different types of worlds, he listed them on his pad. By the end of the day, he had listed fourteen planet types, and had crossed them all off his list.

When quitting time arrived, he was discouraged. He straightened up his desk, checked to make sure his supplies were stacked neatly in the corner of his cubicle, and headed for the door. He would sleep on it.

Tomorrow he would decide what type of planet to make.

Creation Mechanics 101

Gods create things. It may sound complicated, but, as they say, 'Magic, once explained, is merely science.' The gods do it with three skills. They use *willpower*, *visualization*, and *concentration*. When we explain it, you'll see creating things isn't as complicated as it might sound.

First, consider willpower. Gods have a lot of it. You might not think Bernie received his fair share, but on the scale of gods vs. men, you will find every god has a ton of it. They need willpower to conceptualize the vastness of what they're trying to do. If they didn't have enormous willpower, as soon as they had the idea of creating anything as big as a universe, they would be so overwhelmed, they would just give up. Willpower is essential.

The second thing gods need is the ability to visualize. They must carefully picture in their minds exactly what they're trying to create. It has to be fully three-dimensional. One reason Wanda was good at her creations was her excellent visualization skill, which came from her detailed planning. Bernie, on the other hand, was weak in this area because he often tried creating things before he'd thought everything out.

The third thing a god needs is enormous concentration. Think about what's going on here. With the willpower it takes to create on a cosmic scale, they then have to visualize exactly what they want to create. Every detail of the creation has to be understood and pictured perfectly in their mind. Then they unleash their power of concentration. It is the concentration that makes the visualization real and gives it substance.

Then the god moves on to the next thing he wants to create, carefully repeating the process over and over until his universe is complete.

Now one thing about the nature of universe creation might surprise you. When a god first creates something, it's quite fragile. During the visualization phase, almost anything can destroy the creation. It's like a sculptor creating a statue with soft clay. During the visualization phase the artist shapes his sculpture and makes it look exactly the way he wants. The concentration phase is like baking the clay to make it hard and strong. The gods do the same thing. Until this concentration process is complete, their creations are very delicate. That's why gods have to be careful with their creations until they have a chance to set properly.

Many things contribute to a godly creation being more complicated than any sculpture, but nothing more so than the creation of living things. The gods must imbue their creations with the spark of life. They may even want to define the purpose of that life. Although the spark is instant, it can take a while for the creation itself to absorb the spark and fully understand what their creator wants. If the god doesn't concentrate long enough, you end up with a creation that's alive but has no idea why.

Unfortunately, in today's fast-paced world, the gods never have as much time as they want to concentrate on their creations. Recognizing the problem, the gods discovered an unorthodox solution. They found if they get ten or twelve gods in a room, put a dot on a blank wall, and then have everyone 1) visualize the same dot and 2) concentrate on making it real, something amazing happens. By focusing their combined creative energy on the same thing at the same time, it produces a "creation excess." All around the dot, a wild and mysterious gooey substance begins to form. Soon, there's enough that it starts sliding down the wall and onto the floor, where it's collected and put into containers. They call this 'Universe Putty.'

How is Universe Putty used? Well, during the creation process, the gods use the putty in both the visualization and the concentration phases of creation.

During the visualization process, it is helpful to slap a little putty on your visualization to keep it in place while you are working on other details. For example, as you visualize one side of the object you want to create, you can add some putty to it. This freezes your visualization. Then you can pick it up, turn it over, and work on the other side; you don't have to keep thinking about the first side anymore. You're free to give your full attention to the back side. As you can see, putty is very handy stuff.

The putty is also useful during the concentration phase.

After you complete your visualization, you have to make it real by concentrating on it. If you add a dab of putty, you don't have to concentrate for as long. This frees you to go on to the next part of your plan without having to wait until the last thing you created is completely dry.

As we said before, not all gods are created equal. Some gods have better visualization skills. Others are better at concentration. Because of this, some gods don't use as much putty as others, but everyone uses at least some.

In school, students are taught good workmanship, so they learn to go back periodically and remove any excess putty. First of all, it's expensive. Second, leaving it all over your creation is a sign of slovenly workmanship. But more importantly, too much putty can cause unexpected consequences, so you have to be careful. It is, after all, pure creative power.

And the only really safe place for it is packed away in the jar it came in.

The Problems Begin

The next morning, Bernie's blank pad was still waiting for him. He stared at the paper, willing his pencil to fill the page with answers. What kind of world? What kind of life forms? The pencil did not move.

He glanced into his void, looking for any source of inspiration.

What? His planet was wobbling, like a top slowing down and about to fall over. *It was fine yesterday.* He'd never seen anything like this. He had time-tested his work two billion years ahead. How could it have gone bad overnight?

The planet was no longer spherical. How could it have lost its shape? The planet's crust showed extensive cracking, like a hard-boiled egg squeezed until the shell had cracked in many places. Magma seeped through the cracks, forming small pools of liquid rock.

Bernie instinctively reached out and slowed the planet to a complete stop.

He plunged deep below the surface of the planet, looking for its molten core. The core was the heaviest part of the planet, composed mostly of metals. It looked normal. What wasn't normal was its location. Instead of the center of the planet, the heavy core had shifted to a location near the surface. There, in combination with the natural spinning of the planet, it had caused both the wobble and altered shape of the planet.

Bernie pushed the core back to the center and then remolded the planet to its original shape. Once satisfied, he set it back in orbit around the sun and resumed the gentle rotation of the planet. He advanced his time lever, stopping periodically, checking for wobbles or flaws. Nothing seemed out of the ordinary. Nor did he discover anything to explain what had happened.

Shaking his head, he gave the world another critical look. Although the surface was riddled with extensive cracking, the crust was now thick and stable again. Bernie thought, if no one looked too closely, it didn't look too bad. Good thing there wasn't any water or life on the planet.

Even though everything was restored, Bernie was troubled. This should not have happened.

It shouldn't have happened at all.

Back to the Drawing Boards

Over the next few days, Bernie filled six notepads with ideas and sketches for his universe. Universes, even those with only one star and one planet, require a lot of planning.

As he paused from his writing, he noticed again the sticky on the glass in front of him. *Plan First, Then Create.*

He heard Beatrice's voice saying, "Bernie, you have to do more planning. You're jumping in before you know what you want. Good creations never happen by accident, you know."

He smiled as he thought of Beatrice. He'd taken several of her classes. She treated him as if he had all the ability in the world and just needed to be shown how to use it. Even when she scolded him for being too impatient or not doing enough planning, Bernie knew she was trying to help.

In honor of her, Bernie pulled down his sticky and underlined the words *Plan First, Then Create* three times and stuck it back on the frosted glass. *What advice would she have for me today?*

He remembered the time she had looked over his shoulder, and said, "If you want to solve a creation problem, Bernie, first make sure you're starting at the right place."

"But how do I know where to start?"

"That's easy. You start with the ending." She had gone on to explain *Top Down Planning — Bottom Up Creation.* Beatrice said his plan should be based on his ultimate goal: usually the people he wanted for his planet. Once he figured out the people, then it was time to figure out the animals. When those decisions are made, it was simple to figure out the best environment for them. His decisions about oceans, atmosphere, planet type, sun type and all the rest would follow naturally.

"When your plan is complete," she told him, "then you create everything in the reverse order from the way you planned it. Create your sun, then your planet, then your plants, then your animals. Only then are you ready to create your highest life form."

Before Beatrice's words had stopped echoing in his head,

Bernie jerked up in his chair. He grabbed his pencil and wrote *People, Animals, Plants, Oceans, Atmospheres, Planet,* and *Sun.* He shook his head. He hadn't come close to following her advice. Here he was trying to decide what kind of world to make before he had even decided on the people. Beatrice would call that a beginner's mistake.

First, he had to decide on the life form. What do they look like? What kind of culture do they have? Are they kind or cruel? Are they scientific or artistic? How smart should they be? So many things had to be figured out. Once he made those decisions, he could work his way down, layer by layer, deciding on the environmental elements needed to force his life forms in the direction he had chosen for them. The planning continues downward, addressing issues like atmospheric conditions, planetary composition, and distance from the sun, and anything else that might be related. He wrote out another sticky with the words *Top Down Planning—Bottom Up Creation* and stuck it on the frosted glass.

Bernie thought about this for a while. He didn't want to go back to the Supply Division and ask for a different planet and a different sun. Since he already had them, he would accept this sun and planet as givens. True, this eliminated some life form options, but not as many as one might think. Plus, it wasn't like he was going for the *Exotic Life Form Award* or something.

Bernie reviewed his notes and found them riddled with failure after failure to apply Beatrice's advice. The worst case was his bright idea to make a world with both water and land so he could work on water creatures and land creatures at the same time. He'd reasoned if the land creatures didn't work out, then maybe the water creatures would or vice versa. Then he could add or remove some of the ocean and pretend he'd planned it all along. It seemed like a good plan, but it wouldn't have impressed Beatrice. He needed to put his effort into one high level life form, not two. It was hard enough getting one to turn out the way you wanted, let alone two at the same time. Reluctantly, he tore those notes off the pad.

Looking through his stack of notepads, he was discouraged to see he's made no notes about people. This was the most important decision of all. Nothing made sense until he made this decision. This was his top priority.

Deep in thought, Bernie was startled when he heard a voice behind him.

"Hey, kid. How are you doing?" asked Shemal.

"Well, I'm having a little trouble getting started, sir," stammered Bernie. "But I did read the manuals, like you told me."

"Let me see what you have so far," he said, peering into Bernie's void. Bernie watched as Shemal's face took on the faraway look that happens when a god's awareness moves to another place. Several minutes crawled by as Shemal stared into the void, and Bernie shifted nervously in his chair. Slowly, Shemal's face came back to life, but this time it came with a frown.

"I hope you can do better than this," he said. "All I see is a couple of prefabs. And your planet is all banged up."

"Well, the planet experienced some sort of anomaly overnight, sir. It was perfect before I left the night before."

"Don't they teach you kids anything in school these days? Don't you know how to test for a stable orbit and rotation?"

"But, I did check—"

Shemal interrupted, "You're going to have to do a lot better than this if you want to work here." Then he abruptly walked back to his office.

Bernie's heart pounded so hard, he almost didn't notice the soft laughter coming from somewhere nearby. When he looked up, he saw Billy's face just above the glass of the next cubicle. There was an evil grin on his face as he lowered himself down out of sight. Bernie sighed. It's bad enough to mess up, but to have Billy witness it added to the pain.

Bernie spent the rest of the day trying to complete his design process, but he couldn't get past his creator's block. At the end of the day, he headed home, exhausted. All he could think about was how unimpressed Shemal had been.

Definitely not a good way to start a new job.

Lunch with Suzie

Ever since Bernie started work, Suzie had avoided going to lunch at her normal time. She didn't want to see him. She was still hurt over the way he'd treated her. He could have at least been polite.

Today, she hoped to grab a quick lunch and get back to her desk. She saw him enter the cafeteria. He walked like he always did, deeply engrossed in some thought or daydream only he could see. She put her head down and ate faster than before, hoping she could get away before he saw her.

"Hi, Suzie. I've been hoping to see you here."

"Oh. Hi, Bernie. I'm just leaving," she said as she picked up her tray, most of her food still uneaten. She couldn't avoid eye contact and was surprised to see his disappointment. *What's going on here?* she wondered. *Last time he wouldn't even look at me, now he wants to talk?* "Well, maybe I can spare a couple of minutes." She put her tray back down.

As Bernie sat, she could see him struggling. It was obvious from the way his shirt collar had just turned up into a tight roll. This was the same old Bernie from school. She knew it was best to let him work through this part, because if she rushed him or questioned him, he would insist it was nothing and change the subject. She knew him really well for someone she'd never even held hands with.

Finally, he looked up. "Are you mad at me?" he asked, his voice barely audible.

"No. Why would you think that?"

"When I came to work on my first day, you wouldn't talk to me or even look at me," Bernie blurted. "I thought I'd done something wrong."

"Bernie! You were the one who wouldn't look at me. When you came in, I was going to come over and talk to you, but you saw me and then you ignored me!"

"I did? I am so sorry, Suzie. I didn't mean to," he said, stung by the accusation.

She shook her head. *Bernie may be the dumbest smart person ever to graduate as a builder,* she thought. *He doesn't get it when you're subtle, and when you spell it out for him, he gets scared and tries to run away. If he ever gets married, it'll be because some girl used a net on him. Sheesh.*

"So how's your job going?" she asked, changing the subject.

"Not so well." He sighed. "I've been having problems with my universe. And Shemal took a look at it yesterday and told me it needs to get a lot better or I won't make it past my probation."

"You have to do your best, Bernie. Shemal has a reputation for being harsh. He's fired more people than anyone I know."

"I'm trying to do my best. I just can't seem to get an idea of what I want to do. I have a sun and a planet, but when it comes to figuring out the higher life form, I'm drawing a blank. I feel like nothing I did or learned in school is any help."

"Maybe you should talk to Wanda. She started three weeks before you, and she's already been nominated for Outstanding New Employee of the Month. Apparently she finished her universe in only eight days."

"It doesn't surprise me. She's a planning freak. I don't think anyone can plan like she does. She probably had it all planned before she even started work."

"Actually, that's exactly what she did. Her boss says she showed great initiative and respect for her new job and The Business. Her boss really likes her. You should see the glowing report he put in her file. It almost has a shimmer of its own."

During the pause in the conversation, Suzie sat back and looked again at Bernie. What was it she liked so much about him? He could barely take care of himself—and not just because of his cloud. Back in school it had been a full-time job watching out for him. They were the same age, but, because of his dad, they made Bernie skip a grade. It wasn't fair, really. He had to compete with older students like Billy. Actually, most of Bernie's problems were because of that awful Billy.

The fight was really Billy's fault. He'd picked on Bernie for years, and Bernie never did anything about it—until that day. *Bernie would never have hit him if he hadn't pushed me,* Suzie thought. But why had Bernie done it? He'd no chance of winning, and Billy quickly turned the tables on him. If Bernie's cloud hadn't intervened, he might have died.

The fight changed Bernie. He'd never stuck up for himself before. After the fight, she doubted he ever would again. Bernie was so afraid of hurting someone, she'd seen him walk away from anything that might lead to a conflict. And Billy? It just made him more hateful than ever.

The last incident had been two years ago. Billy was taunting both of them. But several days later, she noticed they hadn't seen Billy recently. When she mentioned it to Bernie, he said, with the smallest of smiles, "I think his schedule got changed."

When she asked him what he knew about it, all he said was "Quite a bit, actually."

Leave it to Bernie to find a non-violent solution to a problem. *Bernie, my hero*, she thought. *Sheesh.*

~

"I just don't know what to do. I can't seem to make my life form choice," he finished.

This wasn't the first time Bernie had creator's block. It happened whenever he had to come up with something on his own, especially if he hadn't done anything like it before. It was time for Suzie to come to his rescue.

"I have a suggestion. Go to The Museum. All the best ideas in the world are right there on display. I'm sure you'll find something to inspire you there."

"That's a great idea, Suzie! The Museum is perfect. I can get a ton of ideas there."

One of her favorite things about Bernie was when he got excited. He was like a child full of enthusiasm and no way to contain it. He spilled excess energy onto everyone in the area, to say nothing of the invisible hand that was now patting her on the shoulder. She savored his enthusiasm for a little longer. It was a shame to send him back into his shell with what she was about to say.

"Well, I have to get back to work now, but I'll meet you at The Museum right after work," she said with a pleasant smile. She didn't bother waiting for him to find words.

Yes, he's a nerd. But he's my nerd, she thought as she headed back to Personnel.

Museum for Ideas

Suzie was waiting outside the main entrance of The Museum. Although it was wasted on Bernie, a more careful observer would have noticed she'd touched up her makeup and let her hair down. Her shimmer showed an inner pleasure not visible earlier in the day.

Bernie, on the other hand, had spent most of the afternoon trying to get over his nervousness. He also critically evaluated the day to make sure it wasn't a dream. It passed the not-a-dream test, which only heightened his anxiety. It was one thing to see Suzie in the cafeteria, but something else to see her outside work. Even back in school, after-school contacts had been infrequent. Bernie prepared for their meeting, but it mostly consisted of practicing things to say and checking to make sure he was wearing clothes.

"Hello, Suzie. Thanks again for helping me," he said, ticking the first line off his list.

"I'm always glad to help, Bernie. Have you thought about what you want to build?"

"I really like graceful life forms, like flying and swimming things. I haven't been too successful with them so far, but I think I want to do something along those lines."

"Well, maybe you'll see something to inspire you while we're here." She picked up two museum brochures and handed one to Bernie. "Where do you want to start?"

Bernie looked at the brochure. All the award-winning worlds were on display. No matter what your major in school, the teachers found something for you to study in The Museum. For builder students like Bernie, a common assignment was to deconstruct a universe and explain how the builder had made it. Teachers never tired of Museum-related assignments. Mercifully, Bernie had never been asked to critique his dad's work, although his fellow students had received the assignment more than once. He was glad; it would have been hard. Yes, his dad's work was good, maybe even great. But did great work make a great god? Bernie wasn't so sure.

"Let's start with the water worlds," said Bernie.

Suzie led the way. As they walked, they paused to look at the universes mounted on the walls. Neatly printed plaques proclaimed the award, the builder's name, and highlighted its unique elements. Suzie said, "I heard the Award Committee puts them in The Museum as soon as they make an award decision. I heard they did it fast so the builder can't do any more tinkering. Is that right?"

"Yes. It's hard for builders to resist the temptation to tweak a little more here and there. They don't let anyone change a universe after it wins an award."

"How do they keep people from changing it?"

"They remount the viewing window. Normally, when we're building a universe, we position viewing windows just inside the edge of the void that makes up that universe. When it's located there, it's easy for us to move back and forth through the window. The instant we move into the void, even by the smallest amount, our powers become active.

"But now, The Museum doesn't want anyone entering these universes, so they remount the viewing window on this side of the void. That keeps anyone from going in, but we can still see everything just fine. We just can't touch or change anything."

"Why are some windows bigger than others?"

"Basically, the viewing window is used to keep the opening to the void in place. The window size doesn't matter much, but it's convenient to have them about the size of a picture frame. If you want to take things out of the universe, you may need a bigger window, but big windows don't stay in place very well. In The Museum, I would guess the larger windows are more to accommodate the number of people viewing them. See how the winners from last year have large windows?"

"Interesting."

Suzie's shimmer suddenly radiated a rainbow of colors. "Oh, Bernie! Have you ever seen Josephine's Universe? She's one of my idols. She changed everything!" Suzie pointed to the second exhibit in the Water World Section.

Bernie noticed the way Suzie deliberately jangled the seahorse earrings she always wore, but, like so many thoughts about Suzie, this was to be another thought that never went anywhere.

"Everything? I know she was the first god to make her females before she made the males, which caused quite a stir. What else did she do?"

"You have to understand why this was so important. They called it the *Male-First Controversy*. It changed the way we view the world. I studied it in my history of building classes."

"I know about the *Male-First Controversy*," said Bernie. "They used to teach everyone to make the male of each species first, and the female was created afterwards as a variation of the male. Josephine decided to do everything backwards and make the females first."

"This is her world, Bernie. She created a race of giant intelligent seahorses. The female produces the eggs, but then deposits them in a specially designed incubation pouch on the male. He has to carry the eggs until they hatch and even goes through contractions to expel them when their time has come. Josephine's world shocked everyone, but it really upset the elder gods.

"She was nominated for a Universe Award, but the Committee rejected her submission. The female builders protested for weeks. Finally, the Committee relented and not only reviewed her submission, but created a new award just for her, the *Unique Sexuality Award*. Her seahorses are a symbol of independence for females. Wherever you find seahorses, you can be pretty sure that world was made by a female builder," said Suzie, almost out of breath.

"Is that why you wear those earrings?" asked Bernie, with an uncharacteristic flash of insight.

"You get an A+ for the day, Bernie." She smiled.

They walked around the exhibits, pausing to look through the windows of the award-winning worlds. With each new world, Bernie quickly oriented himself and easily guided Suzie to the special sights. Someone watching the couple might have commented on how knowledgeable he was about the building process and how quickly he found and pointed out the most distinctive features. The exquisite sights on the winning worlds captivated Suzie, and Bernie was surprised by the discoveries

Suzie made. She saw things he missed every time. It was easy for him to see the moving parts, but he often failed to appreciate the whole. Together, they made many new discoveries.

In the Symbiotic Section they found strange beings living together in unimaginable ways. The winners had been selected for the unique interdependencies between different species that worked to their mutual benefit.

"This is Miriam's Universe. I studied her in one of my history classes," said Suzie.

"We studied her in creative engineering, too. She broke new ground with the way she forced her symbionts to come together."

"What did she do?"

"Miriam created a double pair bond, which had never been done before. She used environmental and emotional forces to bring two species together and get them to bond. She created a planet with bitter cold temperatures at night. She made both species warm-blooded with thick fur coats to resist the cold. She gave the first species intelligence and building skills so they could create shelter against the weather. She gave the second species cunning and hunting skills. She gave both species a cooperative nature, so it wasn't long before they were living under the same roof," said Bernie.

"It was clever to give them inter-dependent skills."

"Yes, but Miriam wanted more togetherness, so she removed the fur from the first species. A perfect move. They had to share body warmth at night to survive, which brought the bonding to a new level. They actually formed double pairs of bonded partners."

"Double pairs? How does that work?"

"At the age of maturity, which Miriam engineered to be the same for both species, they complete their normal male-female bonding within their own species. When this is done, each pair seeks out a new pair from the opposite species to bond with. Once this double pair is formed, they generally stay together for life."

"Look how they're all snuggling together as they sleep. I like how they take care of each other." Suzie smiled.

As they continued their tour, the universe categories shifted toward parasitic relationships. Bernie was jarred when he looked into one and saw a race of intelligent slugs. They made their homes inside a race of big dumb animals. As soon as they entered their host, they inserted a feeding tube into the host's blood stream. Then they spliced into the nerve center near the base of the host's brain so they had complete control over its body.

"Oh, yuck," said Bernie.

"I wouldn't want to be one of the animals. I wouldn't want to be one of the slugs either." Suzie wrinkled her nose in disgust.

Bernie looked up from reading the sign and said, "The animal is still conscious when the slugs take over, but apparently after a few months they give up any attempt at independent thought and just do whatever they're told. The slugs go through three or four of these guys in a lifetime. Oh, double yuck," Bernie said again, in case the cosmos hadn't heard him the first time.

They left the parasite section rather than continue in the direction of even more parasitic relationships. Even a cruel and vicious world could win an award as long as it was done well.

"Oh, look! There's one of your dad's universes."

"That's the one I like best. He captured the grace and smoothness of motion I want to build into my universes someday. And he did it from bottom to top."

Bernie's father, Simeon, had created a gas planet with a dense atmosphere at the bottom that became thinner in the higher levels near the exosphere.

"Look here at the bottom, just above the hard ground. This is where Dad made the gas so thick it's almost liquid. Down here, the intelligent life has fins and a tail, which is perfect for pushing their way through thick fluids. It's dark because the light can't pass through the thick atmosphere, so he gave them full-range radar which lets them stay in perfect formation, even though they can't see each other.

"Now look here. About half-way up from the bottom, the gas is thinner. See how their fins are extending out into wings and the bodies are flattening?

"Now look up here. See how in the thin atmosphere, their fins have fully extended into giant wings? Even their bodies have flattened and are almost completely horizontal. They automatically change form to retain maximum efficiency of movement for whatever level they're on," said Bernie.

Watching them move through the atmosphere was like watching a slow motion ballet. Only a god could see through the thick clouds at the lowest levels, but even there, they swam in small schools where every member matched the twists and turns of their fellows.

"This is beautiful," said Suzie, as she grasped Bernie's hand. "No wonder he won an award."

Bernie felt an electrical shock as Suzie's hand touched his. He didn't know how to respond. Even his cloud was shocked into silence. Her hand felt really soft, and he was suddenly aware of an apricot smell coming from her hair. He felt the warmth of her arm as it brushed against his. And he saw a pinkish color where their shimmers overlapped, creating a soft tickling sensation. He didn't know what to do, so he perspired.

Suzie had planned to take Bernie's hand ever since they'd decided to visit The Museum. But now, she judged, it was time for a merciful retreat before she scared the poor boy to death.

In one smooth motion, she released his hand and turned to face him. With her nicest smile, she asked, "Are you getting any ideas for your universe?"

"Well, ah…" stammered Bernie, who was still thinking about apricots and sweaty hands.

Finally, he caught up to current time and said, "I like the idea of something that can move around in lots of environments. That's where I'm going to focus, I think."

"I know you're going to do a great job, Bernie."

An Idea is Born

Journal Entry

I had a great day today.

I finally saw Suzie. I thought she might be mad at me, but she says she isn't. I don't understand girls. I think she was a little miffed when I looked away on my first day. I guess I did, but it wasn't because of her. My stupid cloud grabbed my shirt and started pulling me in her direction. Someday I'll have to explain it to her. It's so embarrassing.

Suzie suggested going to The Museum to get ideas for my universe. We saw some outstanding life forms. I'm full of ideas, and it shouldn't be hard to pick something. It isn't like I have to win an award or anything. I just need to do a good enough job to pass my probationary period.

One thing bothers me though. I can't explain what happened to my planet. I know I did everything right. The core slipped out of place and wrecked everything. I have no idea why. Maybe they really are making defective parts here. Lenny said they had to create the Quality Assurance Division because of all the problems, and Shemal even set up his own quality assurance program so he wouldn't get bad stuff from the other divisions. Maybe I'll try another planet tomorrow.

Confession: I'm getting nervous about Shemal. He wasn't impressed with my universe. There was no reason for him to be. I'm going to do better. Suzie said Shemal is tough, so I need to buckle down.

Well, time for bed.

~

I got it figured out!

Suzie's idea of going to The Museum was just what I needed. She's so smart I don't know why she changed majors. Last night when I was sleeping it all came together for me. I'm going to write it down before I forget. It's going to be so cool.

I'm going to build the ultimate life form. It will live in water when it's young, on land when it's an adult, and it will fly when it's old. I can hardly sit still. I can't wait to get started.

They'll start out as eggs. Their parents will drop the eggs in the ocean where they absorb whatever nutrients they need until they hatch. When they hatch, they'll have tails and fins and live in the water until they mature. There won't be anything in the ocean except other fish-kids to play with and plenty to eat. They'll be vegetarians, and I'll have plenty of plants for them to eat. No predators anywhere. No school and no parents or teachers telling them what to do. The last thing the fish-kids will do is wrap themselves in a seaweed cocoon and get washed ashore.

The land-people will drag them out of the water and give them a home. They'll emerge from the cocoon with legs and arms instead of fins. The land-people will be telepathic so they can communicate with the hatchlings. In their terrestrial form, they'll be good at climbing and running and getting around on the land. This is where they'll breed and then throw their eggs back into the ocean to hatch. When the land-people get old, they'll go to the top of a high mountain and jump off. But before they hit bottom, they'll shed their skin and their new form will be thin and light and translucent with butterfly wings in a rainbow of colors. And these bird-people will swoop up and live in the air from then on.

I'm going to make them smart and peaceful, so they'll get along with each other. Each stage will get along with the other stages. The youngest ones will respect the older ones. And the older ones will take care of and help the younger ones. They won't have conflicts because I'll make sure they have plenty to eat and drink, and I'll keep their population limited so they don't run out of resources.

Just to be safe, I won't make them too smart either. If they're too smart, it's easy to get into trouble. This way, they can hang out with their friends and do whatever they want. If they get bored, they can take a 'geographic cure' and go live someplace else for a while. It'll be like living on a garden planet. They won't need government or social structures, and they won't be smart enough to develop technology. Oh, I'll make them healthy too, so they don't need physicians or anything.

And I'm going to do something special for Suzie. Yesterday, I got lots of ideas about what she likes. I'm going to make some flowering plants I know she'll love. I'll let her name them, too. This is going to be great.

Woo, woo. Move over, Dad. You aren't going to be the only award winner in the family!

Wow, I just realized something. This means I need oceans, land, and high mountains for my bird-people to jump off. Whoa, Beatrice! I'm beginning to understand the *Top Down Planning— Bottom Up Creation* stuff you talked about in class. It really is the way to go.

Lunch with Friends

Bernie worked hard over the next few days. He filled his notebook with page after page of sketches and design notes. Everything he'd learned in school began making sense. Words from his teachers came back to him as pearls of wisdom just when he needed them, inspiring many stickies that found a home on the frosted glass of his cubicle. He planned and planned. And he planned some more.

He was so engrossed in his design process he missed lunch twice. Today, he barely remembered in time. When he got to the cafeteria, Suzie sat waiting for him. Lenny arrived and set down his tray.

"Hi, Suzie. Have you been skipping lunches, Bernie?" Lenny asked.

"I got wrapped up in planning and didn't notice the time. My design is going really well." Bernie's shimmer echoed his words.

"That's great, Bernie, but you shouldn't skip lunch. It isn't good for you," Suzie said.

Both Suzie and Lenny pretended not to notice the peas on Bernie's tray and their madcap race around the rim of his plate. As the peas approached the mashed potatoes, they tried leaping over the white gooey trap. Green polka dots in Bernie's potatoes stood in mute testimony of those who had failed. Others had already disappeared below the surface.

"What did you decide on?" Lenny asked, trying to ignore the racers, although still curious about who might win.

"Well, it's going to be amazing. My highest life form will spend its youth in the ocean as a fish, and then move to the land where it develops arms and legs, and then, when it gets older, it will grow wings and live in the air. It's so cool," Bernie said without pausing to take a breath.

Realizing Lenny wasn't really listening, Bernie followed his gaze in time to see the last of the peas was about to cross the finish line. "Stop it," he growled, thus aborting the leaps of three finalists, causing them to fall short and add to the greenness of the potato pile.

Lenny laughed. Bernie just shook his head. Lenny laughed some more. As his laughter subsided, he pursed his lips to say something.

"Ow!" he said instead.

Suzie had reached out and smacked Lenny's arm. "Leonard! Stop that. Bernie needs our encouragement, not our laughter."

"Have you started building yet?" she asked as Lenny rubbed his arm.

"No, I only have a sun and a planet so far. I haven't done much except planning. One thing is weird, though. I set up planetary rotation and revolution, double-checked it, and the next morning everything was messed up. The planet wobbled so badly it was on the verge of ripping itself apart. I almost ended up with an asteroid belt. Ever hear of anything like that before?"

Lenny shrugged, "I sure haven't. You hear about quality problems in the divisions, but I never heard of anything that bad. Has it happened again?"

"I don't know. I haven't checked it recently."

"Well, maybe you should report it," Suzie suggested.

"Oh, I wouldn't do that if I were you, Bernie. There's a lot of bad feelings about this quality assurance stuff. If you tell Shemal, then he'll have more ammo to use against the other divisions. They'll blame you for making trouble."

Bernie shook his head. "Shemal already thinks the planet problem is my fault. I don't want to go back and complain about it again. If I have to, I'll get a new planet and start over."

"You may have to," said Lenny. "You can't build advanced life on an unstable platform."

"Words to live by," said Bernie.

The Past Barrier

As soon as Bernie got back, he looked into his void. The sun and the planet were still there. The planet remained in its proper orbit. But when he looked closer, he saw a crater on the planet's surface.

At first he thought it was a volcanic anomaly, but that wasn't it. It was clearly an impact crater from an asteroid strike. And a big one, too. Then he noticed more. Circling the world, he found pockmarks everywhere; his world had been hit repeatedly.

There was no way that could happen. The only things in his universe were a sun and a planet. Nothing else. There shouldn't be any asteroids anywhere.

Bernie moved the time lever forward. He observed the future as one asteroid after another crashed into his planet. He was a billion years into the future and the planet was still taking occasional hits. Where had they come from? How could they have gotten into his sterile universe? There was nothing there except a sun and a rock planet. It made no sense.

He pulled the time lever back to the beginning and started again. As he went forward in time, each time a crater appeared on his planet, he moved the lever back just enough to locate the asteroid before impact. For every future crater he found, he blinked an asteroid into nothingness. He spent the rest of the day blinking them out one by one. Eventually, he cleaned up every asteroid destined to strike his planet in the next billion years.

Bernie wished he could roll his universe back a few days to see what had happened. Had he done anything to cause this? Or maybe it wasn't him; maybe a defect in the prefabs had caused it. If only he could look at past time in his universe, but, of course, the Past Barrier wouldn't allow that.

He didn't completely understand the Past Barrier. One of the Great Mysteries was the gods could alter time for everything else, but not for themselves. Bernie could jump back and forth in time within his universe, pretty much however he wanted. But there was a point in the past denied to even the gods. And that point moved with the passage of god time. They called it the Past Barrier.

~

Phoebe, Bernie's design theory teacher, had said, "Our world has its own time, which we call Real Time (RT). We live inside this time. When you build a universe, it has its own time too, which we call Universe Time (UT). Because you have power over your universe, Universe Time doesn't apply to you. You can move freely back and forth in UT however you want. I know you have all had fun speeding forward in UT, right?"

Chuckles of guilty pleasure rippled around the room as the kids were reminded of their fast forward time experiences. They were supposed to be careful, but what kid hasn't pushed the time lever all the way forward just once to see what it feels like? Going fast and far into the future was a rush, like flying when you know you can't fall, with cosmic winds blowing your hair back as eons rip past. There was no danger going forward as fast as you could. Well, the scenery got a little boring after the sun burned out and all, but there was nothing to fear.

"Yes, I can see everyone here knows what I'm talking about," Phoebe said, as the kids responded with another round of smirks and muffled laughter. She was Bernie's youngest teacher. It wasn't that long ago she'd been sitting in one of these chairs herself. When she said things like this, they could see the twinkle in her eye that let everyone know she'd done the very same thing.

"And I also know some of you have had experience with the Past Barrier, right?"

You could see painful expressions on their faces as they were reminded. Bernie winced as he recalled what had happened to him. He had wanted to see if he could go in reverse as fast as he could go forward. He could, actually. At least until he hit the Past Barrier.

When he regained consciousness, he'd found Phoebe standing over him. "You didn't read your lab manual before you came in, did you, Bernie?" A week later, his head still ached.

"For those of you smart enough to avoid learning about the Past Barrier the hard way, I hope you will remember the lesson someone taught us recently," she said looking in Bernie's direction. The laughter that followed was no surprise to Bernie. *The World is hard on its pioneers*, he grumbled to himself.

"How do you know when you're getting close to the Barrier?" Wanda asked.

Phoebe smiled. "A very good question, Wanda, probably the very one everyone here is asking.

"When you go into your universe, you move into UT. And when you do, the Past Barrier gets set to whatever the UT is at the moment you entered. This means everything in the universe's past is no longer available to you. Otherwise it would be like going back into our own past in RT, which you know we can't do.

"Now this is easy enough to understand, right?" Phoebe, taking pity on the room full of blank expressions, decided to try again.

"Think of it this way. You can go forward and backward in time in your universe. But you can't go back any further than whatever time it was when you entered it. So, say your universe was one million years old when you entered it today, you can go forward and backward as much as you want, except you can't go any further back than the one-million-year mark.

"Now let's say you jumped ahead to the two-million-year mark and then you left for the day. When you go back into your universe tomorrow, it will be two million years old, right? When you enter, you won't be able to go back in time further than the two-million-year mark. That's because the Past Barrier was reset to two million years when you entered your universe today. Is that clear?"

"But how do we go back and fix any mistakes we made?" Bernie asked.

"If your mistake happened earlier than the Past Barrier, then there's nothing you can do about it. That is why it's important to plan carefully, Bernie. As your Past Barrier moves forward, it keeps cutting off more and more of your universe's past to you. That's why you have to be careful the Past Barrier doesn't advance when you didn't want it to."

"This is really confusing," Tommy said. Everyone knew Tommy had been talking about changing majors and trying something less complicated. "Is there anything else we need to know?"

"Yes. Before you leave your universe, think about where you want to leave it. Whatever the UT is when you leave becomes your new Past Barrier. Once you've picked your exit time, bring your time lever to a complete stop. Then you can leave.

"Now there's one little detail you should understand," Phoebe continued. "Even though you suspended time in your universe when you left, if you look close enough the next time you return, you'll see your universe didn't stop completely. It moved ahead no less than the amount of RT that passed for you. So, even if you suspended time when you left, if you come back two days later, you will find time in your universe has advanced by two days. There isn't anything you can do about it. The Barrier just keeps creeping along with your RT," Phoebe finished.

"But if the barrier sets when I go in, and it moves along with my RT, then how do I fix a mistake I made five minutes ago?" Bernie wanted to know all the ways to fix mistakes.

"That's a good question. As soon as you enter your universe, I suggest you move your time lever forward by a few days or weeks before you start work for the day. Then you have extra UT to work with. If you need to undo a mistake, you can go back to the time before you made the mistake and do it over. That trick also comes in handy if you're rewinding from a future task, like a time check; you'll have a little extra buffer before you hit the Barrier."

"This seems quite clear," Wanda said.

Phoebe knew it would take weeks for the class to understand the implications of today's lesson. "If you don't understand it completely right now, don't worry too much. After a while, it'll feel natural, and you'll wonder why you were ever confused about it."

~

Seven years later, Bernie wasn't confused by it. He was just frustrated.

Is It Me, or...

Bernie paced back and forth in the Supply Division's waiting area. He needed answers. He couldn't build anything if problems like these kept happening.

Originally, he wanted to talk with the Quality Assurance Division but Lenny talked him out of it. 'Are you crazy, Bernie? The last thing you want is to start a fight between divisions. If you complain to QAD, they'll start another one of their investigations. Everyone will be upset. Wait until your probationary period is over before you even think about doing something like that.'

Bernie decided to go instead to the Supply Division for answers.

"Hello. My name is Saul. Are you Bernie?" came a soft voice from the doorway

"Yes, sir. I hope I'm not bothering you. I have questions about some components I got from the Supply Division. I hope you can help me out." Bernie struggled to get the words out without sounding too nervous.

"What would you like to know?"

"Well, sir, I picked up a sun and a planet the other day, and I've had problems. I wanted to know if you'd seen anything like it before."

"What division did you say you're from?"

"I work in Final Assembly."

Saul tensed, and his eyes narrowed, "Did Shemal send you here?"

"No, sir. Actually, Shemal doesn't know I'm here. I just hired in this summer, and I'm working on my universe project. I used a couple of prefabs so I could be sure everything started on a firm foundation."

"That sounds like a wise decision. What happened?"

"Well, at first everything went fine. I had a good planetary rotation and revolution, and my future check showed everything was fine. I stopped the universe for overnight. When I came in the next morning, the planet had an awful wobble. The planet's core had shifted off-center and was about to tear the planet apart. I've never seen anything like it."

"How far did you run the time check?"

"Two billion years."

"Well, that's certainly sufficient. Something must have happened between the time you did your time check and the time you found the problem. Are you sure you didn't introduce anything else before you left that night?"

"I'm pretty sure I didn't," Bernie said a little doubtfully.

"You said you had more than one problem. What else happened?"

"Well, I repaired everything, and then I was busy planning for a few days. When I checked again, I found asteroids in my universe. Quite a few had hit my planet."

Saul winced. "Oh, that's really hard on the life forms. Did you lose many of them?"

"Well, no, I hadn't started any yet. It's still just a sterile rock planet. I didn't even have an atmosphere. Except for all the new craters, it was just the way I got it."

"I don't know what to tell you, Bernie. I can see if anyone has heard of something like this, but I know I haven't. Get back with me next week, and I'll let you know what I find out."

Get Started Anyway

As much as Bernie was concerned about problems with the prefabs, he was more concerned about the next time Shemal came to check on his work. He needed to show progress. That was why he decided to put down the next few layers.

Bernie searched through his growing forest of stickies until he found the one he wanted. Reading in reverse order, he saw *Sun, Planet, Atmosphere, Ocean...* Okay, he thought, Atmosphere is next.

Bernie moved into the void where he examined his sun and his planet before deciding everything looked okay. Out of longstanding habit, he advanced time by several rotations before settling down to begin the creative process.

He'd already decided on the type of atmosphere, which, of course, solved the question of where his ocean would come from. As Bernie concentrated, a fog-like structure began forming around the outer edges of the planet. Bernie used some Universe Putty to hold everything in place while he checked his work.

Beatrice said the best way to create oceans was to pull them out of the atmosphere. After some calculations, he decided more atmosphere was required for the amount of ocean he wanted. Bernie focused his creative powers, and the foggy atmosphere responded by growing thicker and extending farther into the space around the planet. A few more splotches of Universe Putty, and everything looked good.

Oh, no, he thought. He'd forgotten to prepare the planet surface. It was a round smooth ball, except for all the cracks and the nasty asteroid craters marking its surface. He had to create lower elevations to hold the ocean's water. Otherwise, when he precipitated the oceans, he would end up with nothing but a shallow puddle covering the whole planet.

Thinking he would have to start over, he realized if he moved the time lever back a couple of days, he could make his topographical changes before the time when he created the atmosphere. So that's what he did.

Bernie selected a planetary model commonly used by students. Beatrice once said it was ideal for people like Bernie—whatever that meant. Bernie carved out a long sausage-shaped continent that extended halfway around the world, wide enough to cover thirty percent of the planet's surface. He designated this as Con-1. This long, thin continent would provide a tight climate range, since everything was located at the equator.

Then he moved to the open ocean basin located between the two ends of the long continent, Con-1. There, he raised up two round circles of land with diameters equal to the height of Con-1. He designated these mini-continents as Lab-1 and Lab-2. They would be his laboratories where he perfected his life forms before transferring them to the rest of the planet. If there were problems, he could wipe everything in Lab-1 or Lab-2 and start over.

Bernie smiled at his work. This was going well. He needed tall mountains for his higher life forms to jump from when they were ready to morph into winged creatures. He liked symmetry, so he created a mountain range that extended along the middle of his long continent. Thinking of the migratory and cultural implications, he flattened the mountains every few hundred miles, effectively creating north-south passages so his life forms could move between the northern and southern halves of the continent. 'Removing unnecessary barriers is good design practice,' Beatrice had said.

He finished shaping the planet's surface, making sure the oceans weren't too deep and the mountains weren't too high. He didn't want his fish-kids getting lost in the depths, and he didn't want his land-people unable to climb to the top of the mountains. Finally, it was ready.

Bernie pushed his time lever forward. After two rotations, he saw the atmosphere he'd created in the future as it began to form. It grew thicker as the right balance of ingredients was added. When it could hold no more, it began shedding its heavy load, allowing a salty rain to fill the ocean basin. After a time, the oceans and the atmosphere found a balance, and the level of the ocean stabilized.

Bernie took a mental bow to his non-existent audience. He

chuckled. *You don't always have to understand the Great Mysteries to take advantage of them.*

His cloud must have liked what it saw. Fortunately, Bernie noticed the small storm cloud as it formed above his head. He was able to dissipate it before the rain started.

"Leave the creating to me, please," he whispered for what felt like the zillionth time.

The next step was to verify the orbit. Moving landmasses around could cause subtle changes in the rotation that later became big problems. Bernie's time check found a few planetary stresses, but they were corrected as he moved through time, fine-tuning the revolution. With the aid of an extra helping of universe putty, he made sure it was stable fully five billion years into the future. Beatrice would have deducted points for using so much putty; she always said better planning requires less putty, but it wasn't a big infraction, so it was no big deal. Most builders took shortcuts to meet deadlines or design requirements. As long as you didn't overdo it, the teachers generally understood.

Bernie was pleased. He looked at his planet and liked what he saw. It was going to be a good world. He had a blank tablet on which to create. In the days to come, he would populate the world with plants and animals. He dialed back his time lever, bringing the time in his universe to a gradual stop.

As he withdrew, his last thought was how wasteful it was to have so much void when he only used a tiny bit of it for one sun and one planet.

It Begins...

Journal Entry

I'm finally making progress. I added atmosphere and oceans today. It feels really good. I made two island labs so I can work on my life forms. I'm going to start with plants—fruits and vegetables mostly. I'm not going to worry about them too much. As long as they're edible, I should be good.

I'm going to scoop out most of Lab-1 so I can put an ocean in the middle. That's where I'll work on the ocean plant life.

Hmm… I didn't think about my plant life on Lab-2. I need to break up the ground and make some dirt for them. I can't grow my plants on rock. If I use the natural method and let meteorological effects hammer those big rocks into sand, I'll use up a billion years of universe time. I guess that's okay. I can't think of anything I need to save the time for.

Once I get the plants made, I'll be more careful with the time. I don't want competitors or predators evolving independently on the planet. I don't want my fish babies alone in the ocean if there's something out there waiting to eat them.

On another note, at lunch today, Suzie said Shemal put a report in my file saying he isn't impressed with me. But he only checked my work once. Next time he stops by, he'll see oceans and continents. That should make him happy, although Lenny says not to get my hopes up because it takes a lot to impress Shemal.

I just had an awful thought: what if I studied and worked so hard and Shemal decided I wasn't good enough? That would be so awful. What would I do? It scares me just to think about it.

Hmm… That's interesting. My cloud is quiet. Usually, when I have strong feelings, it starts doing things. It's never quiet unless I'm studying. He must think writing in my journal is the same as studying.

Let's try an experiment. Think about something I feel strongly about…

That was interesting. I just thought about Dad. Usually that would have him rattling everything in the room. This time, not a peep out of him.

He sees and feels everything I do, but that doesn't mean he's always paying attention. What if I write about it? Will he still ignore it?

Okay, here goes: I don't understand my dad. He left us. He didn't even come to my graduation. We sent him an invitation. But he never even replied.

Nothing… It's almost as if my cloud is sleeping.

This journal is going to come in handy. It'll be nice to have a place where I can talk about things without a certain something getting all riled up.

Payday!

When Friday came, Bernie was thrilled to receive his first paycheck. He'd never had so much money before. What was he going to do with it? A long history of unfulfilled daydreams and fantasies surfaced in his thoughts. But, every time he got excited about something to buy, he wondered what would happen if he failed his probationary period and there were no more paychecks. Not surprisingly, by lunchtime, he hadn't made any decisions. He also hadn't made any progress on his universe.

~

"Hi, guys," said Bernie as he set down his lunch tray. There was a huge pile of macaroni in the center with some chocolate pudding on the side.

"That doesn't look very nutritious, Bernie. Do you want me to get you some greens to go with that?" Suzie asked.

"Naw, I'm good, thanks. I have a question for you both. What did you do with your first paycheck? I got mine today."

"That's great, Bernie. Congratulations," Suzie said.

"I sure remember what I did," said Lenny. "I went to an OWT swap meet, and I bought a ton of really cool stuff. This is one of the best things I got." He pulled a flat, light-blue, oval-shaped stone out of his pocket.

Bernie took the stone from Lenny's hand, turning it over to examine the other side. It looked like an ordinary stone except for the smooth edges and a slight indentation on one side. "What is it?"

"It's a luck detector."

"How does it work?" Bernie asked as Suzie rolled her eyes.

"All I have to do is rub my thumb on the stone while thinking about a course of action. The stone turns dark if it leads to bad luck and white if it's good," Lenny said with pride.

"Gee, that sounds useful, Lenny." There was only the slightest hint of sarcasm in Bernie's voice as he handed the stone back to Lenny.

"You have no idea. It's changed my life. But this is my best one," said Lenny as he pointed to a tiny lump of fur on his shoulder. There was a tiny chain running between the fur ball and a safety pin securely attached to Lenny's shirt. "I call her Sissy."

"What does this one do?" Bernie leaned closer for a better look.

"Sissy's job is to scan the probability universe for me and make whatever adjustments she can to optimize my future. Basically, she tries to bend the rules to give me more good luck and less bad luck. She's my little pride and joy." Lenny gently stroked the little lump of fur.

Bernie couldn't help but ask, "How does she get an ability like that?"

"She comes from a super-dangerous planet. The creator designed the planet so the creatures faced a constant barrage of deadly, near-random events. He made the creatures slow so the only way they could survive was to anticipate these occurrences. That forced them to evolve a limited future-sight. A few of them, like Sissy, developed even more. She can nudge event probabilities in whatever direction she wants."

"So she looks into the future, sees something she doesn't like, and then tweaks it in her favor," said Bernie. Lenny nodded in agreement.

"I don't understand. What kind of probabilities can she change?" Suzie asked.

"Well, let's say she's under a tree, and she foresees a limb that's going to fall and hit her. She can't get out of the way in time. Maybe she notices a squirrel in the tree. She could get the squirrel to jump on the branch, changing the angle of its descent so it misses her. Or maybe she sees a nearby vine and makes the wind blow the vine enough to deflect the branch as it falls. She might even strengthen the branch so it doesn't fall right then, giving her time to get away."

"But how do you know she's doing these things for you and not just for her?" Bernie asked.

"I went to her planet and looked and looked until I found her. We picked each other, really. Isn't that right, Sissy?" Lenny grinned as he dragged his fingers along Sissy's back.

Suzie raised her eyebrows. "Is she purring?"

"Yes. She does that when everything is going well," Lenny said as he continued to stroke Sissy's fur.

"It seems cruel to tie a chain around her," Suzie said.

"Actually, Sissy's holding that end of the chain in her teeth. She's afraid of falling off and getting lost."

Suzie's expression wavered between concern and disbelief. Before she could say anything, Bernie interrupted with "What did you do with your first paycheck, Suzie?"

"I used it to buy new clothes for work, some jewelry, and I saved the rest," said Suzie. "What are you planning to do?"

"Well, I can't think of anything I really need it for, so I'll probably just give it to my mom to pay expenses."

Suzie obviously liked that answer because she said, "Well, aren't you just the sweetest thing!" Lenny was obviously unimpressed because, this time, it was his turn to roll his eyes.

"But you should spend some of your check on new clothes, Bernie. You need more things you can wear for work." When she saw the helpless expression on Bernie's face, she quickly added, "I'll make a list for you," as she got out a pencil and paper.

Bernie Goes Shopping

On Saturday, Bernie wandered downtown, armed with Suzie's shopping list and money from his paycheck. He'd given the rest of his check to his mom, which produced an unexpected outbreak of tears. Bernie never knew what to do when tears started flowing. They mostly made him feel like he'd done something wrong, and the whole world was waiting for him to fix his mistake. But he was never sure what he was supposed to fix, so he mostly tried to get away.

Clothes shopping was a new experience for Bernie. His mom had taken care of it before, except for an occasional T-shirt, which he bought. Fortunately, Suzie hadn't left anything to chance. She even wrote the name of the store she wanted him to visit.

As he entered the store, a sales clerk approached and said, "Can I help you?"

"I need to buy clothes. I have a list."

"Well, let's see what you have there," said the clerk as he took the list. "Do you know your sizes?"

"Sizes?"

"Yes, your pants size, shirt size, shoe size."

"I usually get a large T-shirt," Bernie said, pleased to have at least one answer to all these questions.

"Ho, ho, ho," the clerk laughed.

"What's so funny?"

"I just read your list. It says 'P.S. To whom it may concern: Please help Bernie buy nice clothes appropriate for work. Use your best judgment because Bernie has none.'"

The clerk grinned at Bernie and asked, "Did your mom write this for you?"

~

The next hour began with measurements of various body parts, followed by multiple trips to the dressing room. After Bernie put on each piece of clothing, he reported to the waiting clerk who conducted a careful inspection. A head nod by the clerk meant that article of clothing went into the buy pile. Gradually, the buy pile grew in size, and eventually, Bernie was allowed to leave, carrying his new wardrobe neatly packed in four large shopping bags.

Make It Green...

Bernie spent the day working on sand. Relying on wind and rain to grind rock turned out to be a long process. He got tired of trying to accelerate sand production and ended up grinding part of the mountain range and sprinkling it over Con-1 and Lab-2.

Then he turned his attention to Lab-1. He scooped rock out of the center of the little continent until he had a deep round basin with a narrow rim of land at the edges. He took the rocky material, ground it into sand, and sprinkled it on the land and coastal areas of his three continents. Then he scooped water from the ocean and filled the Lab-1 basin. When he finished, his round continent was a narrow ring of land containing a great inner sea. That was the easy part.

Next, he turned his attention to his small ocean. Using powers only a god could wield, he created new life in the form of a primitive plant. He examined it carefully. He applied putty to hold his creation in place while he instilled a creative urge to bear fruit. Then a bit more putty as he added a directive to be abundant and multiply. And, as an afterthought, he left the slowly moving green things with the urge to seek out many paths, both genetically and geographically. He liked variety in his diet, so he would give it to his people as well.

Lab-2 was next. Here he repeated the process, but he did it on land. This time, he created several different types of plants. One group he gently sent in the direction of vegetables. He pushed a second group to become fruits. A third group he reserved for utilitarian purposes; this group would make homes and shelters and tools. A fourth group was designated for aesthetics, and Bernie gave them the most varied mission of all: Be beautiful. Be graceful. Be a wonder to behold. Bernie smiled because the last group was for Suzie. He had filled several pages with notes and sketches of everything Suzie said she liked in The Museum. He was sure his aesthetic plants would please her.

Bernie moved his time lever forward, watching to see how

his plants responded. They quickly and easily filled both Lab-1's ocean and the surface of Lab-2 with lush new forms of plant life. Bernie tasted the fruits and vegetables, but found several were poisonous. He pulled the time lever back to the start, made adjustments to keep his plants from veering into any toxic directions. Problem fixed. Another future check revealed some plant life had displaced their weaker rivals. Bernie went back and added more direction, telling them to demand little and to mingle easily with each other. And, for good measure, he told them being a plant was the best thing to be, which usually helped keep things from wandering down other evolutionary pathways.

After running more future checks, he determined his plants were properly niched. So he moved his water plants from the Lab-1 ocean to the real ocean, seeding the areas all along the coast of Con-1. From Lab-2, where he had grown his land plants, he took some of every species and placed them on Con-1. When he finished, he moved the time lever forward ten thousand years and was happy to see everything had taken nicely and lush green plants had covered his continent. As he scanned the ocean, he saw his water plants in the shallow coastline around Con-1 and also around Lab-1 and Lab-2. The plants had adapted well and were rapidly covering the ocean floor.

It had been a long day. Bernie had accomplished a lot.

It was good to be a god.

Suzie & Sissy

Suzie was pleased Bernie was over his creator's block. But all this shoptalk made for boring lunches for her. She looked at Bernie and Lenny as they jabbered on about some theoretical aspect of planet building, something about Jacob's Laws of atmospheric composition as it applied to the planet's ability to absorb a range of harmful solar effects. And yada, yada, yada. *When they get like this, I might as well not even be here*, she griped to herself.

Oh, there's Lenny's little luck charm. What did he call her? Oh, yes. Sissy. She's a cute little thing.

Suzie reached over to the small lump of fur on Lenny's shoulder, stopping two inches away. She said in a soft cooing voice, "Hello, Sissy. Do you remember me? My name is Suzie. I think you're cute. Do you like riding on Lenny's shoulder? Are you hungry?"

Neither of the guys noticed or heard anything. They were now talking about some quantum mechanics thingy and the best ways to avoid intermittent shifts in planetary polarity.

Suzie's shimmer flickered with excitement when she noticed two small antennas extend from Sissy's fur and the tiny creature inching closer to her hand. Suzie kept talking, "Oh, my. Are you curious? Are you coming to see me? I won't hurt you. Do you have legs under all that fur?" As she talked, Sissy's antenna cautiously touched Suzie's finger.

"Do you like me? I like you. Do you want to come see me?" Suzie cooed.

Suzie watched, fascinated, as Sissy crawled closer and closer. There was a soft purring, and she felt the vibration as Sissy crawled onto her finger. With her other hand, Suzie began stroking Sissy as she had seen Lenny doing the other day. The purring became louder.

Sissy was still attached to the chain. *Lenny said she was holding it in her teeth because she was afraid of falling off*, Suzie recalled. But was that true? She took a closer look. *Hmm… Sissy's fur is too thick. I can't see anything.*

The guys had shifted topics and were now debating which planetary types were best for producing the most graceful life forms.

Suzie continued cooing and stroking. Sissy continued purring.

"Are you hungry? Do you want some of my lunch? Are you thirsty?"

One of Sissy's antennas pointed at Suzie's unfinished salad. She picked up a piece of lettuce and held it out to Sissy. Suzie watched as Sissy's chain dropped quietly away and back to Lenny's shirt. Sissy nuzzled the lettuce, and when her head came back, part of the lettuce was missing.

Suzie was going to say something to Lenny, but she didn't exist in the Lenny-Bernie World, which was now discussing how to calculate optimum planetary mass for airborne creatures as a function of intended wingspan. And yada, yada.

In the next ten minutes, the two of them discovered Sissy liked lettuce, carrots, cheese, and even croutons. On the other hand, tomatoes and black olives were definitely not food, which was just as well because Sissy now had a distinct bulge in her otherwise sleek shape.

"You're such a cute little thing. We can keep each other company when the boys get like this. I don't think you enjoy being left out any more than I do, do you?"

"Goodbye, Suzie. See you tomorrow," said Bernie, his words breaking into Suzie's soft conversation with Sissy.

"See you later, Suzie," said Lenny as he moved away from the table.

Suddenly, a tiny shriek came from her finger. She felt the skin on her finger rippling as whatever Sissy used for legs tried desperately to get back to Lenny.

"Wait a second, Lenny. You don't want to leave Sissy behind," said Suzie as she held out her furry index finger.

"How did she get there?" Lenny asked.

"Sissy and I have been doing a little bonding," she said as she carefully placed Sissy back on Lenny's shoulder. She brought the end of the chain close to Sissy and the end disappeared into her fur.

Suzie could hear the purring start again as she gave her new friend one last stroke.

Oh, No!

Bernie was excited when he arrived at work. He'd made great progress on his plants this week, and he was eager to continue. Last night he had an idea for an aesthetic plant he knew Suzie would like. She had been impressed by a color combination when they were at The Museum. And he had figured out how to create something very similar.

As he entered his universe, instead of blue oceans, white clouds, and green lands, Bernie found a thick gray cloud blanketing his world. Peering deeper, Bernie looked for his plants only to find shriveled husks lying on the ground. In the ocean, dead and decaying vegetation was everywhere. The thick mottled cloud covering the planet had cut off the precious life-giving energy of the sun.

Where had the cloud come from? Bernie scanned the planet for the source and discovered hundreds of volcanoes all over the planet, each one releasing hot lava from the earth below. The land volcanoes had grown into small mountains erupting with molten rock and spitting volcanic ash into the air. Taller and taller they had grown, all the while releasing a stream of soot and poison gasses into the air.

The ocean volcanoes had used their unending flow of lava to grow above the surface of the ocean. Clouds of black soot spewed from their necks while the ocean at their shores turned to steam wherever the lava found water. And for those volcanoes that had not yet reached the surface, the sea boiled from the turmoil deep below.

Bernie sat in stunned silence. He'd done everything right. These volcanoes should not be here. He'd done nothing to make them happen. Even if he had, they would have shown up when he did his time check. Yet, here they were, and they'd destroyed his plant life and poisoned his world.

He could see no pattern. There were thirty-one volcanoes on his main continent, spewing hot lava. He checked the hot magma under the planet's surface, but it looked normal in every way. There was no unusual pressure under the surface that would cause them to break through.

Examining one of the volcanoes, he saw the lava flowing straight up to the surface. No nearby fault lines had opened and released it. Instead, it looked as if a round hole had been drilled through the crust, and the lava had simply flowed up through the hole. When he checked the other volcanoes, they showed the same pattern.

Bernie thought back to his books. Could there be anti-matter particles drifting in his universe? Had his planet collided with them? The particles could create holes as they passed through the planet. Bernie searched the orbit area of the planet, but found nothing. He widened his search until he had examined the entire void. There was just nothing there.

Turning back to his planet, Bernie went from one volcano to another. At each one, he focused on the lava, reducing its temperature until it became solid rock, essentially corking each volcano. He thought about scrubbing the atmosphere, but since almost all of his life had died, he just moved the time lever forward until the sky was once again clear.

Bernie sat back in his chair, discouraged. Yes, he'd had more than his share of problems in school, but those problems were of his own making. He almost always knew what he'd done to cause them. This was different. He had no idea how this happened. And there weren't any teachers around to ask.

He reviewed his construction notes for over an hour but was no closer to figuring out the problem.

~

"Gosh, Bernie, I haven't seen you so down in a long time. Your shimmer is barely flickering," said Suzie as her friend sat down.

Before Bernie could collect his thoughts, his napkin unfurled over his plate. Lenny and Suzie watched as a hole appeared in the napkin and a gusher of potatoes, gravy, and other unknown foods erupted from below. The mound grew as the escaping food piled up higher on the napkin.

"How does it do that?" asked Lenny.

"You have problems with ants?" asked Suzie.

Bernie just shook his head and pushed his plate away. "No. That was supposed to be a volcano."

Bernie told them about the volcanoes killing his plants. It was hard to get the words out. At one point, Lenny brightened and seemed about to say something, but after stealing a quick glance at Suzie, who gave him an icy stare, he seemed to forget whatever he was going to say and went back to listening.

"And my plants were beautiful. I designed them for different functions, and they were performing great. I had water fruits for the fish-kids and fruits and vegetables for the land people. I created plants for shelter. I even created a class of plants for their beauty, like you suggested, Suzie. And now they're all dead."

"Where did the volcanoes come from?" asked Lenny.

"That's just it. I don't know. Something drilled hundreds of holes straight through the planet's crust, and the magma came up to the surface."

"What about anti-matter particles?" Lenny offered. "If you have a handful of those babies, your whole planet can look like Swiss cheese."

"That was the first thing I looked for, but I couldn't find anything anywhere in the universe. Plus, all of the holes were straight down. If it was anti-matter, some holes would have been at different angles."

"What are you going to do?" Suzie asked.

"There is only one thing I can do. I have to start over."

"From the beginning? That seems extreme," Lenny said.

"What else can I do? There must be something wrong with the prefabs. I'm not doing anything to cause these problems."

"Bernie, I didn't want to have to tell you this," Suzie said as her shimmer's intensity increased and took on a reddish hue. "I've been reading the reports Shemal wrote and sent to your personnel file."

"What did he say now?" Bernie visibly tensed, just as a serving tray rose behind his back, positioned as a shield against some an unseen blow.

Ignoring the tray, Suzie bent forward and said in a conspiratorial whisper, "He said you're indecisive and show poor workmanship. He also said he may have to fire you before you waste any more supplies." Suzie reached out and touched Bernie's hand as she spoke.

"It doesn't sound like a good idea to requisition new stuff, Bernie," said Lenny. "Shemal may see it as more waste. Are you really sure the prefabs are defective?"

"Well, not really. I talked to Saul in the Supply Division, and he's never heard of problems like I'm having. He checked around and said no one else has either."

"Then I agree with Lenny, Bernie. It might be better to work with what you have," Suzie concluded.

"I guess you're right," said Bernie in a dejected manner.

~

Bernie spent the rest of the day and most of the next recreating his plant life. By quitting time, he was satisfied everything was as before. In fact, better. The volcanic ash and the decaying layer of former plant life turned out to be a good fertilizer for his new plants. They grew faster and stronger than the first batch.

But Bernie left work with the uneasy feeling there were more problems on the way.

More Sabotage!

Bernie stormed into the cafeteria, his shimmer flashing angry colors in every direction, leaving a battlefield of interrupted conversations in his wake. For added punctuation, his chaos cloud pushed chairs and overturned napkin holders on the tables as he passed by, sparking more than a few exclamations and protests. Bernie didn't notice any of it.

"I can't believe it," Bernie said.

"Please try to calm down, Bernie. Everyone's looking at you. Your cloud is whipping," Suzie said as she tried to calm her friend.

"What's going on, Bernie?" Lenny asked as he arrived with his lunch tray.

"My world, that's what! It's messed up again."

"What happened?" Lenny glanced nervously at his fork as something bent it into a circle and caused it to roll off his tray.

"Everything was perfect last night when I left. Then, this morning, my beautiful blue ocean is all red!" Bernie struggled to calm his cloud.

"How did it happen?" Lenny asked.

"I don't know. It happened beyond the Past Barrier so I can't find out a thing. I think I've got a lemon world or something," Bernie said. "It looks like a spontaneous generation of red plankton, and it spread throughout the oceans. Now I have to get rid of it all."

"How did it spread so far overnight? Didn't you suspend your universe when you left?" Lenny asked.

"Yes, of course. Not only that, but the Universe Time moved ahead by a million years, which cuts into my—"

"Wait a second, Bernie," Lenny interrupted. "Are you sure you suspended it when you left?"

"Yes, because I had the plants just about right, and didn't want them evolving anymore."

Lenny squinted as he forced his thoughts to the surface, "I think someone is messing with you."

"What do you mean?" Suzie asked.

"If you suspended time when you left, the only way your universe can move forward a million years is if someone went in after you and changed it. The universe can't do it by itself. Only a god has that kind of power," Lenny said.

"Billy!" cried both Bernie and Suzie at the same time.

The Backdoor

Bernie wracked his brain for a solution. There had to be a way to keep an eye on his universe and protect it from Billy. Then he remembered a meeting of the Off World Technology group two years ago.

Bernie checked both manuals and found nothing to prohibit it. So he was going to do it.

He understood the concept very well, and at lunch, Lenny agreed it was a good idea. Suzie had pursed her lips, but said nothing, which Bernie took as permission.

~

"What's a backdoor?" Bernie had asked.

Skeet, who'd waited two weeks for his turn to present his latest discovery to the OWT group, was eager to tell everything he knew. "It's a great way to get into your universe from a distant location."

"What good is that?"

"Well, if you didn't have a chance to finish something on one of your universe projects at school, a backdoor lets you get into it later from home."

"Are you sure that's okay?" Bernie thought it was starting to sound like cheating.

"Well, you don't tell anyone you're doing it," said Skeet. "That's the whole idea behind a backdoor. They're supposed to be secret."

"How does it work?" asked Lenny.

"You create a hole in your universe just like we do when we attach our viewing windows. This time, you hide the hole in a corner where no one would look, and instead of attaching a viewing window to it, you attach something of yours, like an old shoe—anything that's received a good dose of vibes from your shimmer. That lets you find it again later. Then, when you're home, you search among the voids until you find the one with your shoe. When you find it, remove your shoe and put a new viewing window in its place. Use a little putty to hide your second window. You don't want anyone finding it. And that's it. You now have a secret door you can use to get into your universe whenever you want."

At the time, Bernie couldn't think of any reason he would ever need such a thing.

But that was then.

~

Bernie entered his universe, moving with the speed of thought to its farthest corner where he punched a small hole back into the world of the gods. He removed his ring and positioned it in the opening between the two universes. With some help from the putty, he attached his ring halfway between the two worlds. Then, to make sure it remained completely hidden, Bernie added more putty. He didn't want Shemal to find it and tell him it was against the rules.

With his new backdoor, Bernie would be able to enter his universe at any time. If someone was trying to sabotage his world, he would catch them.

~

Bernie rushed home after work, eager to complete his backdoor. In the quiet of his room, he cleared his mind as he reached out into the infinite number of dimensions surrounding his own. Somehow, in the darkness, he sensed the presence of his ring. It was far away, but it was there. Carefully, he reached out until he was able to grasp it. Gently, so as not to dislodge it from the universe, Bernie pulled the ring closer and closer. Next, he removed the ring and replaced it with a viewing window. It took extra time to seal the window because he had no putty at home.

Finally, it was ready. He eagerly entered the universe, finding it just as he'd left it an hour earlier. He saw no changes to his sun or planet. He was so pleased with the success of his backdoor, he almost didn't notice a foreign shimmer on the planet's surface.

As Bernie approached the shimmer, he saw an infection spreading through his plant life. Some sort of fungi was stealing energy from his plants, sucking their life forces, and leaving behind moldy coatings of rust and rotted tissue. He watched in horror as the blight advanced rapidly across the forest, leaving moldering stumps where once great trees had stood. He realized he was observing it in accelerated time. Someone had pushed their time lever forward. Hundreds of years were flying past as Bernie watched. The wilting stain devoured everything, leaving behind rotting memories of his once-beautiful plants. Then time slowed down as someone pulled their time lever to a complete stop.

Before Bernie could overcome his shock at the decimation of his plants, the shimmer disappeared. *Billy! It had to be Billy*, he thought. If he'd stayed any longer, would he have confronted him? What would he have said? It didn't matter now. The real questions now were what had he done, and could it be fixed?

Realizing the Past Barrier was clear all the way back to the moment he entered the universe, even though hundreds of years had passed on the planet, Bernie pulled his time lever back and watched as his plants miraculously recovered from the blight that had consumed them. Bernie moved back until he saw the shimmering figure as it introduced the disease. As the figure began moving forward in time, Bernie stayed where he was. Here, in this time, only a handful of plants had been infected so far. He approached the doomed plants, carefully visualizing both plants and the disease destroying them. He blinked them out of existence. In that instant, the sick plants and the deadly disease they bore were gone. There would be no patient zero here today.

When Bernie blinked the diseased fungi out of existence, he created something teachers hate being asked to explain: a time paradox. He changed the future. Yet the future experienced by the shimmering figure was also real; it just wasn't part of the future Bernie stood in now. Bernie had cut the ribbon that led to that future when he blinked the fungi. Back in the god's world, the shimmering figure may think he had destroyed the plant life in Bernie's universe, but if he were to return, he would not find a world of ruined forests. That world might exist somewhere, but Bernie's action made it inaccessible to any god. Where it went or what happened to it was one of the Great Mysteries. No one really knew.

Bernie was just glad the world of ruined forests was no longer in his universe.

Lenny's Charms

"Where's Suzie?" Bernie asked as he set his tray on the table.

"She hasn't arrived yet," said Lenny, "but that's okay because I have some guy stuff to show you, and I'm not sure she would appreciate it."

"Oh?"

"See that girl over there, the one with the red dress walking down the aisle? Watch this." Lenny opened his hand to reveal a piece of dark wood. He closed his hand again so only a small section of it extended beyond his thumb and index finger. He surreptitiously pointed his hand in the girl's direction. The young goddess came to a dead stop and began looking around as if searching for someone. Unable to find whatever it was she sought, she shook her head and resumed her walk.

Lenny grinned. "Now see that girl over there? The one carrying her tray back to the empty shelves?"

As soon as Lenny moved his hand in her direction, she too stopped and began scanning the cafeteria. Lenny put his head down before she could catch him looking at her.

"What is that thing?" Bernie asked.

"The guy I got it from called it a 'tweaker stick'. The people who invented it use it to send signals to each other across long distances, like a wireless telegraph. It works on us too. About 80% of females and 40% of males so far are sensitive to it," he said as he made two more slash marks in his notebook under the female column.

"What good is it?"

"Well, not much by itself," Lenny admitted, "but if you combine it with other things, I think it'll be very useful. I'm researching several combinations right now."

Bernie couldn't help but ask, "All right. Tell me."

"Think of it as a one-two punch. The first charm gets a girl's attention, and the second one gives them a reason to keep looking."

"What does the second charm do exactly?" Bernie asked.

"They're all different. Today is my first day with this one," Lenny said pointing to a golden stud in his left earlobe. "It's supposed to make me look sexy. So far, it doesn't seem to do much. You find that sometimes. A charm works great for someone else, but doesn't do anything for you, and vice versa."

"How long have you been collecting charms?"

"Gosh, ever since I was a kid. I've got hundreds of pages of notes on them too. If you're going to make scientific progress, you've got to do a lot of testing, you know."

"Have you ever found anything that works?"

"Well, nothing's perfect, Bernie," Lenny said a little defensively. "But I've found a few combinations that show a lot of promise. If you're interested, I know a couple that are practically guaranteed to work for you. Oh, oh—"

Lenny looked up. "Hi there, Suzie. Bernie and I've been waiting for you," he said as he closed his notebook and tucked it away in his pocket.

Shemal Startles Bernie

Although Bernie spent his days working on his universe, he didn't get much accomplished. He was too tired from staying up most of the night, guarding it from unwanted intruders. Despite his vigilance, he hadn't seen the shimmering figure again. During the day, when he looked at Billy's cubicle, Billy seemed busy on his own tasks, apparently oblivious to Bernie or his suspicions.

Shemal made a surprise inspection three days after the rotting fungus incident. Bernie was deep in thought and did not hear him approach. When Shemal touched him on the shoulder, Bernie jumped. His shimmer lit up both his cubicle and the ceiling above him.

"Hey, shimmer down, kid. It's just me," Shemal said.

"Yes, sir," said Bernie as he fought to get his shimmer under control. That wasn't what worried him. His shimmer, after all, was just light. His cloud, on the other hand, could be much more dangerous. He found it busy rattling his wastebasket and lining up paperclips for suicide jumps off the corner of his desk.

"Do you know how to work your dampener?" Shemal reached over to the cosmic dampener installed in Bernie's cubicle. "You have a chaotic bent, right?" he asked as he cranked the dial up from two to eight, thus saving the lives of four paper clips who hadn't yet made the leap.

"No, sir. I didn't find anything about it in the manuals, and we didn't have anything like them in school."

"I had them invented especially for Final Assembly. I wanted to eliminate any quality problems that might be coming from my own people. They work really well. People like you, with a strong chaotic bent, can move things out of alignment when you get upset. This baby tones that effect way down," he said as he affectionately patted the dampener. "It works on order clouds, too. Don't let them kid you, they cause just as many problems when they get out of control as you chaos'ers can. I had one of them cause every planet and moon in her system to come into perfect alignment. We almost had a cosmic episode right there." Shemal chuckled at the memory.

"They teach us to control our clouds, but sometimes—"

Shemal interrupted, "Try it at eight for a couple of days, but don't be afraid to turn it up. It should keep your cloud under control.

"Now, let's see what you've been up to." Shemal peered into Bernie's universe, and his eyes took on a far-away look. His only sounds were an occasional, "Tsk, tsk." and a couple of "What's this?" and one "Oh, my," along with several headshakes. After five minutes, his eyes came back, and he said, "I can see you're getting a bit further, Bernie, but I don't see anything here that impresses me. Tell me, why did you make all those volcanoes and then plug them up?"

He and Suzie had discussed how to respond to these questions. They decided it would not be wise to blame Shemal's nephew for Bernie's problems. They had no way to prove anything. Plus, Suzie said Shemal's reviews of Billy were excellent, and she was sure Shemal wouldn't believe anything bad about him.

"Two reasons, sir. I wanted to make the landscape more rugged looking, and I wanted a good layer of volcanic ash spread around the planet to accelerate plant growth."

Shemal grunted an acceptance of Bernie's answer. "Why are some of the sand and rocks stained red?"

"There were red plankton in my ocean. I… I got rid of them, but… but the coastal areas were badly stained," Bernie stammered.

"Sounds like sloppy work, Bernie. And why don't I see any animal life forms?"

"My higher life forms have very complex elements and interdependencies, so I'm delaying introduction of any animal life until I have everything worked out."

"Work harder, kid," Shemal said as he headed back to his office.

The Putty

Shemal's inspection had not gone well. Bernie spent the rest of the day thinking about the price of failure. He had no doubt Shemal was disappointed with his performance. Shemal wouldn't hesitate to fire him if he thought Bernie couldn't do the job. Creating a good universe was hard enough, but it was impossible when another god undermined your efforts. How could he fight a god with powers as great as his own? Especially a god who didn't play by the rules? Even though he was trying his hardest, he could feel his grip on life as a builder slipping away.

Maybe that was why Bernie, never known for neatness even in the best of times, was more careless than usual. By the end of the day, he was so distraught he forgot to clean up his workspace before heading zombie-like toward the door. That was also why he forgot the jar of putty on the planet's surface.

~

Bernie's scarred and broken world hung like a big blue marble in the black emptiness of the void. The only life forms were the plants on the land and in the water.

The putty didn't have thoughts or feelings as we know them. It was just a translucent gob of goo. But it was aware of the warm sun, and the putty liked the way it felt when the sun shined on it. In fact, the putty liked the sun very much, and wanted to be closer—to reach out and touch the warm bright thing in the sky.

Slowly, small tendrils grew out of the jar and arched upward. You could almost see it stretching, as if waking up from a long sleep. Each tendril shimmered in a kaleidoscope of colors, experimenting until it seemed more and more of the tendrils agreed on green. It liked green. You couldn't call it a plant at this point, because it hadn't really decided what it wanted to be. Right then, it wanted only to be with the sun.

As the sun went lower and lower in the sky, its warmth began to fade. The tendrils reached out farther, searching for the light and the warmth, but it didn't help. The sun was leaving.

As it watched the sun set in the west, the putty didn't like feeling alone. It wanted the bright warm thing to stay. It reached out all of its tendrils and stretched farther, as if beseeching the sun not to go.

And as it watched the sun slip down beyond the edge of the world, the putty reached out so far that the jar, its home, fell over. As the putty oozed from the jar, it yearned for its warm friend.

Ever so slowly, it found a way to move. It moved as a snail would move if it had a forest of arms on its back, each arm reaching toward the sun as its body slithered in the same direction.

If it had words, you might have heard it say, "My Sun... My Sun... Please wait for me."

Billy's Gang

It hadn't taken long for Billy to form a new gang after starting work at The Business. It had been ridiculously easy. All it took was a few choice remarks like, "Gosh, I'm really looking forward to working here. Uncle Shemal and I have always been close, and now we get to see each other every day." Builders were smart people, and they had no trouble reading between the lines of that message.

Billy appraised the people sitting at his table. They were a cut above his lieutenants, RedDog and Butcher, back in school. These young gods were builders. RedDog and Butcher had been just muscle. They followed orders, but they weren't good for much else. Well, they laughed at all his jokes, but that had never been a problem. When you're the king, everyone laughs at your jokes.

Billy didn't delude himself. He knew the young builders at his table were only here because they feared him. He didn't mind. He knew plenty of ways to keep their anxiety levels elevated. From time to time he even threw them little rewards by saying things like, "Gee, that really pleases me. I'm going to tell Uncle Shemal what a terrific employee I think you are." Of course, the real joke was he and Shemal were never close. They only saw each other once or twice a year at family get-togethers.

Jimmy and Candi had been in the Division when Billy arrived. Billy's sixth sense led him to them right away. Although they came across as competent and confident, Billy knew only the first was true. One of his greatest skills was reading the insecurity of others and using it to manipulate them. Jimmy was a basic soldier. He did whatever he was told. It was easy to manipulate him—he just let Jimmy believe serving Billy was the same as serving Shemal. Candi, on the other hand, was different. She had her own opinions and would even voice them. In addition, Candi was strikingly beautiful, which made her headstrong, the way beautiful women sometimes are. But Billy knew how to make her afraid, and when she was afraid, she did what she was told. *After all*, thought Billy, *I don't care about adoration. All I want is obedience.*

The third person at the table was Donald, transferred into Final Assembly seven months earlier. Most people believed Donald had been transferred in the hope Shemal would do the dirty work and fire him. Donald probably believed the same thing, because from the moment he'd arrived, he'd tried desperately to attach himself to Billy. Billy held him at arm's length for a while, knowing it wouldn't help his image if one of his associates got fired. It might give people the idea Billy didn't have as much power as they thought. But after Shemal completed a few reviews without firing Donald, Billy finally let him into the group.

The rest of the table consisted of a person or two Billy invited to stop by for lunch. No one ever refused, because no one wanted to anger Billy. It was the same as angering Shemal, or so they believed.

Today, Billy was talking about Bernie, as he often did. "Yes, poor Bernie is not long for our department. A little birdie told me he's having problems with his universe again."

"Why are you doing this to him?" Candi asked. "He never bothers anyone. What did he ever do to you?"

"Ah, now that's quite a story, dear Candi," Billie said as he casually stroked the hideous scar that ran from his eyebrow to his cheek. He'd seldom met anyone who hadn't fought to suppress a shudder when they first saw him. His gruesome scar reminded every god of his own mortality and the fine line between living forever and death. A moment of carelessness or an act of violence was all it took.

Billy took a moment for the effect to reach its maximum. "It's the tale of a young boy who did not know his place in the world. And even though his betters tried to explain, he resisted his lessons at every turn. Then one day, this foolish boy resorted to violence to the disadvantage of his betters, whose only sin was trying to help him understand his proper place. But do not fear, young Candi, for Fate has a way of setting things right with the finality of a boot in pants and the sound of a slamming door."

Billy's sinister smile lingered. "And who is to be this instrument of Fate, you might ask? Somehow, I suspect Uncle

Shemal has been chosen for that part." Billy laughed. "Although perhaps a little birdie nominated him for that role." At that, Billy laughed more.

That's pretty funny, he thought.

Divine Intervention

The god looming above the planet took time to study it. He saw the continents and oceans of the world resting on a thick shell of solid rock. Bernie had designed the planet to minimize global stresses, but it was easy enough to get around that.

The outer crust of the planet floated on a layer of hot magma. The thick layer of rock protected the oceans and the land from the intense heat deep under the surface, and as long as it remained intact, there was little danger from the inner forces trapped below. The looming god knew this could be changed with a few carefully designed cracks. It wasn't hard at all.

From high above the planet, the god made deep cuts in the crust, giving the pressure below its chance to escape. As he created more cuts in more places, more pressure was released. But carefully, thought the god. It must look unplanned. And so he worked to create a mosaic of fractures around the planet.

Then, to make sure he had planned well, he advanced time to observe his work. By the end of the first million years, he could see the edges of the continents begin to shift. Earthquakes along the fault lines rumbled dire warnings. By the second million years, he knew he had done well.

Jagged edges along the coastline could be easily seen. It would take millions of years to break up the continents. But that wasn't his goal. He didn't want to destroy this world. He wanted a world of mutilations and scars, proof of the incompetence of its creator.

He looked proudly at his work. It was not overdone. Bernie would see it and think he had done something wrong again.

The god smiled as he thought of his enemy. Bernie was feeling the pain. There wasn't enough pain yet; there would never be enough. But this was a start.

And there was so much more yet to come.

The Sun

A long time ago…

The cold night had begun once again. The Sun had set for the day, and everyone was returning home.

The people didn't like the night. They liked the Sun. Each day it warmed them, and it gave them comfort as it had for years beyond counting. But every night, the Sun went away.

For a long time, they prayed for it to stay. But no prayer, no ritual, and no sacrifice ever made a difference. Nothing could prevent the Sun from leaving each night. And so, after a time, they prayed instead for the Sun's safe and speedy return.

So the years passed. Nothing disturbed the peace of this place. They dwelled in a garden, a garden of plenty, where none went hungry or thirsty. It was also a time of learning. They explored the ways of wood, making their homes from the trees in the great forests that covered their land. Later, they discovered stone from the mountains and used it to make strong buildings. The bright stones were perfect for the temples because they reflected the light of the glorious Sun. With it, they built tall pyramids, reaching ever upward in the direction of the Sun. As the population grew, they used their knowledge to build cities. And as their needs became more complex, so too did new skills emerge, and they learned writing and mathematics, which aided in building their perfect world.

Unlike other worlds, these were peaceful people, united in their admiration for the Sun, who nurtured and protected them. The Sun provided plenty throughout the land for everyone.

Although content in their world, they yearned for one thing. They sought to better know their benefactor, the great Sun who had created their world and provided them with such bountiful lives. In this alone, they remained unsatisfied.

And so the years passed.

Not My Fault

Bernie learned to expect bad things to happen every three or four days. Often they happened while he walked home from work. By the time he reached home and checked his world, the damage had been done. Only once more had he caught a glimpse of the shimmering figure, but it disappeared before he could confirm it was Billy.

Bernie began his morning inspection, as he did every day after arriving at work. Something seemed a little off. The first clue came from the plants. They were the right plants, but there were subtle changes. Somehow, they had evolved. Bernie designed his planet for stability, so not a lot of new niches were opening and closing, yet something had given rise to several new species. None of the new species were harmful, nor had they displaced any of his original plants. That, at least, was a relief.

If he wasn't trying to hurt my plants, thought Bernie, then what was he doing? Why else would he have advanced time? Finally, he found the answer to his question—there were hidden cracks all over his world.

By lunchtime, he was still upset.

~

"You're all shimmered up. What's wrong?" asked Lenny taking the seat farthest from Bernie instead of his usual one next to him. His eyes darted around the table, searching for signs of cloud activity.

"I feel like I'm losing ground," Bernie complained. "Every time I do something, Billy messes it up, and I spend the next day straightening it out."

"What did he do?" Suzie asked.

"I knew something was wrong, but at first I couldn't figure it out. My first clue was when I found two new plant species. Billy had advanced time on my world by two million years. But that wasn't the problem. The real problem was he'd gone all over the ocean bottom making dotted-line cuts crisscrossing the planet."

"Why would he do that?" Suzie asked.

"He was making fault lines," said Lenny, who got it immediately. "That's really nasty. Once those things get going, you'll never keep your continents in the same place. Things start drifting every which way."

"After two million years, my main continent started to break up, and my ocean lab had a cracked rim and was leaking into the main ocean," said a very bitter Bernie.

"Can't you just go back and erase it?" Suzie asked.

"No, the Past Barrier was in place. I couldn't go back and fix anything. I fused the fault lines so there shouldn't be any more breaks, but I can't do anything about the continental drift that's already happened. The shifting has stopped, but my planet looks like a war zone," Bernie grumbled.

"Did your plant ecology get disrupted by the unsupervised evolution?" Lenny asked.

"I don't think so, but I'll have to take an inventory later. I have a couple of species that are inclined to wander."

"Hey, Bernie. I have a great idea," exclaimed Lenny. "You remember the OWT device that can jam your time lever? I have one at home. Maybe that's what you need. Then if Billy messes something up, at least he can't run things way into the future where you can't do anything about it."

"Oh, wow! That's really good, Lenny. If Billy can't advance time, he won't be able to do nearly as much damage. Even if he wrecks something, it'll be easier to fix if no time has passed." Bernie's shimmer flashed stronger than it had been in days. "This is really, really good."

That was Suzie's cue to be concerned. "I don't know, Bernie. Sometimes your ideas come back to bite you. Besides, I've never heard of anything that could stop someone's time lever."

"That's easy. You know there isn't really a physical time lever, right? It is just a concept for talking about what we do with our minds—" Bernie started to say as Suzie interrupted him.

"Of course, I know that, Bernie. I took some builder classes too, you know." Suzie sounded a little miffed.

"Oh, yes. Sorry. Well, there was this one universe built by a god who was forever going back and forth in time, to check things out, you know. Mostly, he kept tweaking the culture to force people in the direction of higher technology. But it backfired. His higher life forms apparently didn't like all the back and forth—"

"So they built something that gave their god a nasty headache every time he tried to use his time lever," Lenny blurted out.

Suzie frowned and said, "But that will affect you too, Bernie. How are you going to build if you can't move back and forth in time?"

"That's easy. Technology like this has an on and off switch. I'll just turn it off when I'm working and turn it on when I leave for the day." Bernie smiled.

"Bernie, come to my place after work. I'll lend it to you, and you can install it tonight," said Lenny.

"Thanks, Lenny. That sounds great." Bernie was as excited about being invited over to Lenny's as he was to get the time lever jammer. "I'll meet you out front after work."

The First Expedition

A while ago...

No one was sure where the Sun went at night. Nor did they know why the Sun came back in the east after it had departed in the west. The priests said the Sun traveled under the ground at night so it could return to the east where it rose again every morning. But no one knew why the Sun would do this.

Many years ago, the Senate organized an expedition. They wanted answers to these mysteries. They sent explorers to the west to follow the Sun when it ended its day. The explorers traveled for a long time. They came, at last, to a place where the land ended. Beyond that, there was only ocean. They watched as the Sun sank into the farthest edge of the western sea, but they could get no closer.

The Senate then sent them to explore the land to the east. There too, they found the eastern end of the land. They saw the Sun rising up from the eastern ocean. The expedition reported no discernible effect on the Sun when it rose up from the water, just as they had seen none when it had sunk below the waters to the west. It was theorized there was a place beyond the waters from which the Sun rose in the morning and retreated at night. But no one knew for sure.

Not satisfied with these answers, the Senate ordered the explorers to go beyond the land. And so they built a large sailing craft, the largest ever made. The expedition bravely sailed east to see where the Sun came from each morning.

They did not return.

That marked the first great tragedy the people had ever known. Almost a hundred men and women lost their lives trying to find answers to the most important question of all.

All the world grieved for their loss.

The Central Plaza

Lenny's invitation pleased Bernie immensely. He had school friends, but he had few after-school friends. The builder curriculum had kept him busy, of course, but that wasn't the real reason.

When Bernie's dad left, it marked the beginning of hard times that left deep scars on both Bernie and his mom. She couldn't afford their home, so they were forced to move to a project home on the outer-most edge of town. Bernie had had friends before his parents separated, but he never saw them after they'd moved to the projects. Why had they stopped seeing him? Was it because of the fight with Billy? Was it because Bernie lived in the projects next to the woods? Or because they were poor? Bernie was never sure. He just knew his friends weren't around anymore. He grew up feeling apart from the rest of the group and, somehow, less worthy.

He found Lenny waiting at The Business' main entrance. "Hey, buddy," Lenny called out. Bernie returned the greeting with a big smile.

Central Plaza was a favorite gathering place. The wide-open area allowed the sun to reach every corner. The abundance of sidewalk restaurants and cafés around the plaza were proof the gods loved to spend time there. Evening was also a time for the plaza because, once their work was done, even the gods took time to relax. In the plaza, you always saw people you knew.

In the center, an ancient artesian well formed a water mushroom that fell back into the pool below. The ancient gods created four streams for the water to exit the pool, each stream departing at a cardinal point and continuing in a long outward spiral, eventually circling The Town before cascading off The Edge of the plateau on which The Town was built. A walk from Central Plaza to The Edge meant crossing each of the four streams as they spiraled around The Town.

Important buildings, like The Business, The Town Hall, The Museum, and The School were all located in the Central

Plaza, more formally called the First Circle. Farther out, in Second Circle, were the retail establishments. Most of the population lived in the Third and Fourth Circles, preferring, if they could afford it, the more expensive Third Circle. Only the poorest residents made their homes in Fifth Circle, where the woods battled with the wilderness beyond the plateau for dominance. Bernie lived in the Fifth Circle of the Northeast Quadrant, the very edge of town.

Four quaint little bridges in Central Plaza carried people over the streams as they walked around the plaza. Four larger covered bridges were found at the edge of the plaza, and they were not normal in any way. The gods had made these bridges with the same skill they'd used for their buildings, but instead of using inner space, they used outer space to span greater distances with the bridge, which meant you could travel from the center of town to the outer edge in minutes, instead of over an hour that it would have taken on a normal bridge. Even Bernie, living as far out as he did, had just a twenty-minute walk to work, most of which was the time it took to get from his home to the bridge. It was a good system, and the gods had found no reason to change it. Admittedly, it might take a few minutes longer if you ran into friends along the way and stopped to talk, but the gods considered that one of the plusses.

"Hey, let me show you something cool," said Lenny as they approached one of the plaza's fountains. Each fountain had been brought back, piece by piece, from another world. Fountain figures depicted legendary or mythological beings from that world, and a favorite pastime was speculating about the beings and their stories.

Lenny pointed. "See the life forms on this one? I have a pet universe with creatures that look just like them."

"Did you make them the same on purpose?"

"Nope. I just happened to notice the similarity one day when I was wandering around the plaza. Mine aren't smart enough to have built a fountain. Well, they might be if I let them evolve, but that isn't what they're there for."

"Why do you have them?"

"They're just one of the feeder species I have on one of my planets. My main life form is carnivorous, and it needs to eat a lot, so I transplanted these guys along with a few species from other universes to make sure my carnivores had a healthy diet."

Bernie struggled not to betray the discomfort he felt when a god showed such a callous attitude toward other life forms. He didn't want anything to undermine his budding friendship with Lenny.

~

Bernie never understood the disregard the gods showed for their creations. They considered their own lives precious, but that attitude didn't extend to the life they created.

Several years ago Bernie had made unsuccessful attempts to recruit friends to join him at a "Save the Lookies" rally. A goddess named Agnes had brought one of her creations to town, as most people did from time to time. It was just to show them off, really. Initially, the lookies were very popular because they were cute and playful and fun to watch.

But after a century or two, there were so many lookies, people started complaining. The Town Council issued orders for the Refugee Squad to round them up and dispatch them. By the time the protest rally had any traction, half of the lookie population had been destroyed.

The Town Council gave in to the protestors and ordered the remaining lookies to be captured and turned over to Agnes, who was instructed to return them to their planet of origin.

Although Bernie was not a leader in the campaign, he took some pride in helping save the little creatures.

~

"Bernie! Come here, please." A woman waved at Bernie from one of the restaurants.

Lenny asked, "Is that your mom?"

"Yes," Bernie said as they walked over to her.

Bernie's mom was an attractive woman, slight of frame, with long flowing hair and a light, playful shimmer. It was impossible to guess her age, because like all other adults, she showed no signs of aging. Her voice lacked the resonating qualities she would develop as she aged. She wore a simple dress, and her only jewelry was a pair of earrings.

"I wanted to tell you I have to work late tonight. We're hosting a birthday party. Can you fix yourself something to eat?"

"Sure, Mom. Let me introduce someone," said Bernie. "Mom, this is my friend Lenny. We work together. Lenny, this is my mom, Hannah." He liked the way it sounded when he called Lenny his friend.

"Pleased to meet you, Lenny," said Hannah. "Are you Saul and Ruth's boy?"

"Yes, Ma'am."

"They come in here all the time. Your dad's a good tipper," she said with a smile. "Your mom and I served on some PTA committees together when you boys were in school.

"So where are you off to?" she asked.

"We're going to my place to hang out," Lenny said.

"Please say hello to your parents for me."

"Actually, they'll be gone for another week. They're visiting retired relatives. They haven't made the rounds for a while, so they've got a lot of catching up to do."

"I know how that can be. You have the family album at your place?" she asked.

"Yes. They borrowed it from my Grandpa Titus. It was like pulling teeth. He doesn't like the album out of his hands. He wants to be able to pop in and visit people whenever he feels like it. I had to promise I'd take good care of it and that he could stop by whenever he wanted."

"I understand. Well, run along, boys, and have fun. Nice meeting you, Lenny." Hannah flashed a smile before turning back to the restaurant.

When they got out of earshot, Lenny said, "Bernie, you didn't tell me your mom is such a fox! It was everything I could do to keep my charms in my pocket!"

Bernie looked at Lenny, but he had no idea what to say, so he just shook his head. His shimmer, however, displayed a rare streak of purple and yellow that lasted for almost an hour, and something swirled around his feet, although both boys pretended not to notice.

As they strolled around the plaza, they came to The

Museum. Banners flapping in the gentle breeze reminded people of the submission deadline for the next Universe Award Competition. More banners reminded everyone the new winners would be on display immediately after the Award Ceremony.

"I imagine the Awards are a big deal for you, with your dad being a big-shot award winner and all," Lenny said, nodding in the direction of The Museum banners.

"Well, Dad hasn't won anything for a while now."

"Bernie, he won three awards! Hardly anyone ever wins one, let alone three. Haven't you seen all the books written about him? He's famous!"

"I've seen more of Dad's books than I have of Dad."

"I've seen him several times. Any time he makes a speech about his work, I try to go."

"I think his success went to his head. He never used to wear capes and sequin outfits before he got famous. Mom says his clothes do more shimmering than he does. Honestly, I think it's embarrassing."

"You gotta cut him some slack, Bernie. People like Simeon are supposed to be eccentric. That's what makes them so much fun."

As they strolled along, a large brown mass with two round eyes stared at them with unconcealed fear. If it had arms or legs, they weren't apparent. It had been trying to cross the sidewalk to the grassy section a few feet away but had miscalculated how fast the two young gods were walking. Its movement was too slow to retreat, so it braced itself for impact. This was unnecessary, because no god would have hurt it. Bernie saw its fear and adjusted his course to steer both himself and Lenny well away from the shivering mass, who now had its eyes tightly closed.

Lenny, who was still thinking about Simeon, asked, "What's he like? Does he ever talk about his creations or where he gets his ideas?"

Bernie thought for a moment before saying, "Mom says Dad is a very competent builder, but he is not very creative. The first two ideas were hers, and maybe the third one too."

"I don't remember hearing him say where he got his ideas from, although I remember someone asked him recently what his next project would be. He said, 'I'm still searching for my muse.'"

"He and Mom haven't talked for a long time, so he's probably run out of ideas."

"Well, he shouldn't have any problem finding a new muse. No offense, Bernie, but have you seen the way the girls are all over him? He can have any one he wants." Lenny thought for a moment. "You don't think he's using a charm, do you?"

"No. I don't think so."

"What happened between your parents? Weren't they right for each other?"

"I think they were a good match, but after Dad got the second award, I think it went to his head, and he decided he didn't need us anymore." Bernie pondered whether to say more.

"Hello, Lenny. Hello, Bernie."

Bernie looked up to see Beatrice, his favorite teacher, walking toward them. Every time he was around her, he felt more confident. He smiled, thinking about the stickies in his cubicle. At least half of them were her ideas. Bernie smiled. "Hello, Beatrice."

"What have you been doing since school, Bernie? Did you get a job with The Business?"

"Yes, I started last month. They have me building my own universe."

"That's great, Bernie. Can you tell me about it?"

"I'm still trying to work out the details. It's a lot harder than in school. They said I can build anything I want. With unlimited possibilities, it's hard to know where to start."

"You'll do fine, Bernie. You're more talented than you give yourself credit for. Just do your planning, and everything will be fine." She turned to Lenny and said, "As for you, young man, how have you been? I talked to your mom two weeks ago. She said you're still busy with your OWT collection."

"Yes. I've found some excellent stuff. Lately, I'm focusing on things to make me luckier. I'm going to show some to Bernie tonight."

"You know, Lenny, I'm not a big fan of charms and talismans. It seems to me if you want to be luckier, all you need is good planning and extra effort. I've found that works better than any lucky charm"

"Maybe you haven't found the right charm yet." Lenny laughed.

Beatrice joined in the laughter. "Maybe I haven't. Well, have fun, boys."

Bernie and Lenny paused from time to time to chat or wave at friends as they continued around the Plaza. There were posters everywhere reminding people about the nomination deadline for the Universe Awards.

"Have you ever submitted anything to the Universe Awards?" Bernie asked.

"No. I have a couple of universes that are really good, but the Committee doesn't like anything that involves violent combat. I mean, they have categories for it, but when's the last time you heard of anyone winning an award for their slaughter prowess?" Lenny shook his head. "No. They'd rather give awards for something that's politically correct or based on some silly social issue. They're biased, if you ask me."

"I read the Committee has more people with Building Arts degrees than Building Science degrees. Maybe that makes them favor more artistic things."

"That would explain a lot," said Lenny.

Lenny's Place

Their conversation ranged in many directions as the two young gods found themselves talking about everything other than work. Bernie smiled each time Lenny slowed, knowing he was conducting another experiment was being conducted. A moment later, Lenny would then make a quick note and their conversation would pick up where it had left off. Lenny's notebook added to its wisdom with fourteen new slash marks before the boys completed their first circuit of the plaza.

"Where do you live?" Bernie asked.

"Over in SouthWest-3. We used to be in SouthEast-4, but my parents decided to move in closer."

"Do you like it?"

"Yeah, it's okay. You still live over in NorthEast-5?"

"Yes. But as soon as we can save enough money, we're going to move in too," said Bernie. A fleeting thought reminded him of how he would miss the woods. The woods weren't like the fun house experience of wandering around town, but, for Bernie, they were special, no farther than his back yard. He would miss them.

"This is my bridge," said Lenny as they approached the South Bridge at the edge of the plaza. Traffic on the bridge was light, and they stayed toward the right, avoiding the farthest right, which was for people who wanted to exit immediately. The youths strolled in the center right lane past the Second Circle exit, where mostly stores and other businesses were located. The NorthWest quadrant was an exception. NorthWest-2 contained an exclusive residential section of The Town's elite, which naturally included Bernie's dad. It was also where Billy lived. As they approached the Third Circle exit, they moved to the right, and a few steps later, they exited into Lenny's neighborhood.

~

As they turned the corner, something easily half Lenny's height burst out of the bushes, and raced full-speed at him. Bernie was shocked by the quickness of the attack and unsure of what to do. He looked around for anything to use as a weapon, but there was nothing. All he could do was cry, "Watch out!"

Lenny turned in time to see the furry brute a moment before it reached him. The creature grabbed Lenny's leg with both arms and squeezed hard.

Bernie expected to hear a scream of pain, but instead heard Lenny's laughter, followed by "Hello, boy. Did you miss me today?" A furry head with big eyes looked up at Lenny, nodding an enthusiastic affirmation.

Lenny laughed again. "I call this guy Artie. I don't think he talks, but he seems to understand me. Artie, this is my friend Bernie."

Artie unwrapped himself from Lenny's leg and shook Bernie's hand. When Bernie didn't say anything, Artie shook his hand again.

"Pleased to meet you, Artie," said Bernie. This satisfied Artie, who smiled and nodded his head. He turned back to Lenny, tilted his head, and raised his eyebrows.

Lenny must have understood because he said, "We're going back to my place. You're welcome to come with us, if you like."

Artie smiled and took Lenny's hand. His other hand was for Bernie as he walked down the street between his two best friends. The godly shimmer from the two boys was nearly matched by the joy radiating from their little friend.

Curious plants extended long vines from the safety of nearby gardens to touch them as they passed. Several flowers reached out, offering them smells, which they dutifully sniffed before moving on. Several more creatures waved and even more watched them secretly from hidden places. Both boys enjoyed these encounters as they made their way to Lenny's house. Somewhere along the way, Artie hugged them both goodbye and went off in another direction. A walk through town was always an experience.

"That's my place," said Lenny, pointing to a house set back from the street. From the small yard, to the walls, to the roof, plants of every shape and every color vied for attention. "As you can see, Mom likes her plants." He reached out to clear away the vines blocking the entrance. Interestingly, he didn't have to touch them. They just needed to be reminded they weren't supposed block the entrance. Bernie didn't notice the vines; he was busy staring at the large orange flowers that had been watching him since they'd arrived.

Lenny's house was large on the inside, as were all buildings in town. They entered a great room with three large arched doorways that led to other parts of the house. Skylights brightened the room. An open picture album lay on a flat table in front of the couch. On each page of the large book was mounted an 12x18 inch viewing window. Underneath each window was a neatly written tag with the name of the relative(s) who retired there.

Lenny looked at the open page and said, "It looks like my folks are visiting Samuel today. He's a hoot. I'm not sure what our relationship is because there are so many 'great-great-greats' involved. But he's always on everyone's short list to visit."

"Can I look?"

"Sure. Just don't touch anything. Samuel gets testy if you change anything on his world. Check the second planet in the dwarf star system. If he isn't there, he'll be on the system with the yellow sun, on the third planet.

Bernie slipped into the universe and found the dwarf star. The second planet was mostly land with several large oceans. He'd expected to see a theocracy with Samuel sitting on a large golden throne surrounded by throngs of worshipers. Instead, he found a relatively simple Iron Age culture that seemed to lack even the most basic comforts. When Bernie came back, he said, "I'm not sure I'd want to retire there. What does he see in the place?"

"He doesn't go in for traditional stuff. He has more fun wandering around disguised as a beggar."

"Why?"

"He likes to do miracles. For example, if he goes to a village, and they treat him well, even though he looks like a filthy beggar, the village will find their crops are twice as bountiful for the next few years. Or maybe every illness and infirmity in the village is miraculously cured. He customizes his miracles to the people he meets."

"Do you have to disguise yourself as a beggar to visit him?" Bernie grinned.

"No. He has a huge palace where he lives most of the time. Lives like a king, really. But I guarantee he'll try to get you to go on a mendicant adventure with him."

They both laughed at the thought of a god wandering the world disguised as a beggar.

"Come on back to my room."

Lenny led the way down a corridor until they reached a door with a prominent 'Keep Out' sign. *That sign must be OWT,* thought Bernie. *When I look at it, it makes me want to go away.* As he turned to ask about it, Lenny grinned. "I had some boundary issues with my parents. We're mostly cool now that I'm contributing to the rent." Lenny chuckled as he held open the door for Bernie.

Bernie was surprised to find Lenny's 'room' was actually a five-room apartment, considerably bigger than the home he shared with his mom. Lenny pointed, "That's my bedroom. The one next to it is a kitchen. This room is for hanging out and relaxing. That room is for my OWT collection and my books. And that one is for my universes."

"This is really cool, Lenny. You have a great place here. Show me your collection. I'm dying to see it."

Lenny brightened as he led the way into the collection room. The walls were lined with shelves, and each shelf was full of assorted objects, each with a nametag and detailed notes. Two more long rows of shelves, also full of items, ran through the center of the room. In the corner was a built-in desk where more shelves were piled high with dozens of notebooks like the one Lenny always carried.

"Oh, my gosh, Lenny. This is beyond anything I imagined. How did you ever do this?" Bernie asked with undisguised awe.

"I collected most of these while I was in school. One of these days, I'm going to reorganize everything. I'm going to have to enlarge the room soon anyway. This section is pure technology. The section over here is charms and talismans. That section—"

"How did you get into charms? It doesn't seem very scientific for someone like you."

"Well, it began when I was a kid. I've always been ambi-cosmic. You know how you have a dominant chaotic side? Well, I have equal parts of Chaos and Order. I keep getting hit by one side or the other, usually when I least expect it. It's like a cosmic tug of war with me in the middle. After a while, I found charms to thwart one side or the other. I try to carry enough of both to protect me from whichever side seems to be dominant."

"That sounds like superstitious thinking to me. I never heard you could stop the forces of Chaos or Order from influencing you."

"Of course you have. Think about it, Bernie. You told me about the personal dampeners Shemal installed in everyone's cubicle, right? You've been using it to dampen your chaotic side so it doesn't interfere with your creations, right?"

"Yes. It works really well. And it has a side benefit, too. My cloud usually unravels my clothes, but with the dampener on, I haven't lost anything for weeks."

"Exactly. My charms do the same thing. Some of them have extra benefits, too, so I carry several with me all the time. Cool, huh?"

"Hmm… I guess I hadn't thought of it that way."

"Let me show you what I'm working on now. These are the charms I use to get girls."

"I didn't know you had a girlfriend."

"Well… I'm still working on that part," Lenny admitted.

Lenny sat at his desk and offered Bernie the extra chair. "I've broken it down into its component parts. The first thing you have to do is to get noticed, right? Second, you have to make a good first impression. Then, third, you have to strengthen the relationship. I'm making great progress, but there're lots of variables."

"Like what?"

"First of all, not everything works on everybody. Remember the other day when I showed you the tweaker stick? That one works really well on girls, although not so well on guys. I can get 82% of girls to start looking around. That's the best one I've found so far. I have two others with 75% and 72% reliability. And there are others that are well documented in the literature.

"I worked my way through the best candidates until I found charms that work best for me." Lenny pointed to the long shelf above his desk, where fifteen curious objects were laid out.

"The hardest part is researching the first impression phase—"

Bernie started laughing. "Is that why you keep asking Suzie if she thinks you look any different today?"

"Yes, of course. The problem with this phase of the research is finding girls who will give you accurate feedback on what they're experiencing."

"But, Lenny," Bernie said with a teasing grin, "I've never heard her say she saw anything different about you except for what you're wearing."

"That's your fault, Bernie. She's so hung up on you that some of my best charms just bounce off her. She doesn't see anything else when you're around."

Bernie's heart skipped a beat. "I don't think so."

"Are you kidding? What planet are you living on? Back in school we used to joke about the big crush she had on you."

Bernie thought back to school. Suzie had been a great friend, for sure. But she was smart and pretty and could have any boy she wanted. She certainly wouldn't be interested in him. An irrational bit of hope flickered in Bernie, which manifested as an extra ripple of pink on the outer edge of his shimmer.

"Did you ever hear her say she liked me?"

"No. But everybody knows she likes you."

"Did *anybody* ever hear her say she liked me?"

"No." Bernie's nascent hope died a sudden death.

A heavy sigh was heard. Lenny did a double take, staring at his friend. "Did you do that?"

"No. It was my cloud."

"Wow. I didn't know it could make sounds. What else does it do?"

"It's pretty versatile. I live in fear of the day it figures out how to talk," said Bernie only half joking. "I've heard it make quite a few different sounds. It even whistled at Suzie once. I don't know what was worse, the fact that he did it or the fact that I had to pretend it was me."

Lenny laughed. "I suspect you've had to take a lot of bum

raps in your day."

"Yeah, more than I deserve."

"Hey, let me show you my universe collection," Lenny said, jumping up to lead the way into the next room. "You're going to love it."

If Bernie was impressed with his friend's OWT collection, he was even more impressed with Lenny's universe collection. The L-shaped room had dark walls with viewing windows mounted every few feet. Most windows were the large industrial size, designed for easy viewing. Small plaques gave information about each universe.

"Oh, Great Mysteries," said Bernie. "Did you make all these?"

"Yes," said Lenny, "but it isn't as impressive as it sounds. When both your parents are builders, they start you really young. Plus, they saved everything I ever did. I moved the old stuff to the far end of the gallery when I had the last extension put on. All the good stuff is here." He swept his arm along the left wall.

On the opposite wall, built-in shelves were full of books. Bernie saw familiar schoolbooks, but there was so much more. The small library had everything: geology, astronomy, calculus, geometry, microbiology, physics, time analysis, vector analysis, dimension warping, and on and on.

"Have you read all these?"

"Most of them. Some are from my parents' collection. They moved them into my nursery the day I was born. They used to read them to me instead of fairy tales." Lenny grimaced and shook his head.

A row of supply cabinets stood near the bookshelves with one door ajar. Inside, he saw a collection of building components that rivaled anything The School had. He was surprised to see six jars of universe putty sitting on the shelf. Just one cost a month's pay even for a builder.

Lenny followed Bernie's gaze and said, "Mom and Dad weren't taking any chances about whether I'd become a builder. You can see I always had the best stuff to work with. I had two hours of building-play every day with Mom or Dad. As I got older, they hired a tutor to teach me techniques outside their fields. Did you have anything like that?"

"Oh, no. I had a tutor once, but it was only for a month. We couldn't afford things like that. I have most of my school books though. Mom wouldn't let me sell them in case I ever needed them again. By the time I finished elementary school, Mom couldn't help me with my homework anymore, so having the old books came in handy."

"Do you have a lot of universes at home?"

"Nothing like this. I have four."

"Four! Why so few?"

"Well, it's not so bad. If I want to do something, I make a new solar system in a corner of one of my universes. As long as I put the new system far enough away, there isn't much chance of cross-contamination." Then Bernie laughed. "One of my universes has so many solar systems, it's starting to look like a galaxy."

"Oh, wait here. I want to show you something." Lenny rushed out of the room, returning a moment later with a small gray round object.

"Watch this." As he moved the object closer to Bernie, the little pebble started twitching and bouncing in Lenny's hand.

"What is it?"

"It's the reason we're friends," Lenny said, waiting for Bernie's next question.

"Why?"

"It's a fun detector. Any time I get close to someone who will be fun for me, it starts twitching. I had it with me that first day when you came into the cafeteria for lunch. It was going crazy. That's when I decided we needed to hang out," Lenny said with a smile. "And so far, Bernie, you haven't been boring at all."

Bernie took the little bouncing pebble from Lenny and put it in his own hand. As he moved his hand closer to Lenny, the pebble started jumping around, as merrily as it had a moment earlier. "It looks like it's mutual," Bernie said as they laughed together.

"Actually, Lenny, I really do appreciate all your help. Some days I just want to give up. It's been hard with all the nasty things Billy's been doing. If it weren't for you and Suzie, I probably would have quit by now."

"He's a jerk. He's always been a jerk. He used to give me a

hard time in school too. There's a long list of people who would love to see him get what's coming to him. We'd probably be given the key to The Town or something."

"It looks like you have plenty of things I could use to stop him or at least slow him down."

"Oh, yeah," exclaimed Lenny. "There're lots of choices. For example, we could booby trap your cubicle. I have a trap that can throw him into an unmarked dimension. It will take him a month to find his way back. Or we could hit him with a flash of light so intense it would blind him for a week. Or we could—"

"I don't want to hurt him, Lenny," Bernie interrupted. "I just want to make him stop."

"Sometimes you have to hurt them to get them to stop. You can't be subtle with people like Billy."

Lenny picked up a small device from a shelf and handed it to Bernie. "This is the time lever jammer we talked about. I haven't tested it, but the guy I got it from said it packs quite a punch. All the installation instructions are on the card."

"Thanks, Lenny. This'll be perfect. I'm going to install it first chance I get."

"Now that we got our business out of the way, are you ready to see some really cool universes?"

"Yes. But I'm not up for anything too violent tonight. Do you have something fairly tame?"

"You're going to miss my best stuff," Lenny lamented as he scanned his wall. "Ah, this will interest you. I'm creating a tech farm in this one."

"What's a tech farm?"

"It's where I get a lot of my OWT. I made a race of bright little buggers and evolved them so they have good tech skills. I just tell them what I want, and they invent it for me." Lenny smiled. "I used to pay them in gold, but now they want rare earth metals. It doesn't make any difference to me, of course. I also give them a big bonus when they finish."

"Seems like a slow process."

Lenny laughed. "Maybe for them, but not for me. I just fast forward into their future when they've finished the invention, pay them for it, and then roll back time to the beginning again."

"But, if you keep rolling time backwards, they never get to

spend their bonus money."

"Yes, they do, Bernie. Even though I'm rolling back time, the people in that time line have their bonus money, and they're very happy with the transaction. Besides, I found out I have to do it that way. The first two inventions took a hundred and twenty years to complete. I had to go back twice and re-negotiate with them. The first time, they'd stopped work because they didn't care about the gold I'd offered. They figured out how to make it themselves. I had to keep offering them different things to keep them motivated.

"The real problem with tech farms is keeping them in the optimal tech zone. They need to have the skills to invent what you want, but you have to be able to motivate them. If they get too advanced, they figure out how to make everything themselves, and there's not much incentive for them to do what you want."

"Lenny, you have answers for everything," said Bernie, not sure if he meant it as a compliment.

"I know," said Lenny, who accepted it as nothing less than the truth.

~

As Bernie walked home that night, he felt happier than he had in days. He and Lenny were going to be great friends. There was no doubt of that.

And maybe, just maybe, he could slow Billy down.

The Second Expedition

Not so long ago…

Years later, a group of volunteers came forward and asked the Senate for resources for another expedition. They would make another ocean vessel, bigger and stronger than the last, and it would be provisioned for a long journey. And this time, they would sail west. They promised to return with answers about their beloved Sun. After much debate, the Senate reluctantly granted permission, and the expedition was soon underway.

Their return, after a year and a half, was met with great rejoicing.

Their report, however, was most puzzling. For two months the voyagers had been at sea, no land in sight except three small volcanic islands. Finally, the explorers came to a new continent. It was green and full of life. They saw no mountains of any kind. A landing party found the land rich with fruits and vegetables. Its green bounty extended as far as they could see. The plant life was identical in every way to that of their homeland. They found no sign of people. After gathering fresh supplies, they sailed north around the coast, making occasional stops for supplies and exploration. The plants were always the same, and there was never any sign of people.

The edge of the continent led them to the north as it curved gradually to the west. Before long, they rounded the top of the continent and headed west and gradually southwest. The rounded top of the new land made them think the continent was round—at least the top half seemed to be.

When they came to the westernmost side, they stopped again for supplies. They had two choices. They could continue south around the continent and return home. Or they could turn west, over the open sea again, in search of the Sun's resting place. Their mission was clear, and there was no dissent from the crew. They were there for one purpose: to solve the great mystery of the Sun.

They pointed their ship once again to the west. As the days passed, some of the crew complained no matter how far they went, the Sun never got any closer. And so it went, week after week. For two months, nothing changed the monotony of that endless sea except more volcanic islands. Finally, they came to another continent.

This continent was different. It had no lush forests of green with fruits and vegetables at every turn. They found no people. They discovered instead a desert that extended as far as they could see.

The ship's master sent an exploring party inland. After two weeks of traveling across an empty desert, they reached an inner sea. It was immense, and no one could see the other side. The inner sea was full of green plants and water fruit, of the kind common on the coasts of their own land. Because they could go no further, they re-provisioned themselves from the bounty they found and returned to their ship.

As before, they sailed north around the new continent. Here too, they came to believe the second continent might be perfectly round. And every time they sent out an exploring party, they found desert until they came to the inland sea. The entire continent seemed to be a giant ring of empty desert with an ocean in the center. On their voyage around the northern edge of the new continent, they never found an opening to the inner sea, nor did they find signs of any life.

When they came to the westernmost point of the sandy continent, the curve of the coast beckoned them south, just as it had on the first continent. Once again, they chose the west where they hoped to discover the resting place of the Sun.

Two more months at sea followed. They saw more volcanic islands, but nothing else. Only the empty sea. And in all this time, they were unable to get closer to the setting Sun. Always, it seemed as distant as it had on the first day of their journey.

Finally, they came again to another continent. It looked much like the first continent they discovered with its green forests. On this one, however, they saw mountains in the distance. Another exploring party was sent ashore to gather information and supplies. Imagine their surprise when the exploring party returned to tell the ship's crew they were home.

On that very shore, they found their own people.

The explorers had begun their voyage from the western edge of their land. They had never turned back. At every opportunity, they maintained a westerly course. And yet, they returned to the eastern edge of their land. How was it possible, they wondered, to travel west and end up in the east? It made no sense. And the answer to the disappearing Sun still eluded them.

The Senate convened a special committee to study the report. The committee debated for weeks, but they were unable to draw any conclusions. One group argued the explorers may have started on the same path as the Sun, traveling west, but they must have become confused. Somehow they reversed course. How else could they have reappeared in the east? But the explorers insisted their ship had never strayed from its westerly course.

In the end, the prevailing theory was the Sun simply did not want to be found. And when the explorers had gotten too close, the Sun decided to send them home.

What's Changed?

The watcher with the tiny eyes alerted the others. From her post above the skylight of the young god's home, she had watched the boy as he prepared to leave for the day.

Everyone was concerned about the young god. They talked about it for days before deciding what to do. Something had changed. For weeks now, he had been leaving home earlier and staying away longer than ever before. Even his clothes looked different, and he seldom seemed happy. Worse yet, he never went to the woods anymore. They missed their walks together. And they were worried.

Bowin volunteered to lead a party that would follow the boy when he went into town that day. His bravery in such matters was beyond question. Bowin was the one who had led them when they made their escape to the woods. Brave Bowin was the one who returned to the town again and again, each time gathering as many as he could find, and leading them to the safety of the woods. Finally, he could find no more.

They were never sure what the danger had been. They only knew more and more of their friends had disappeared. Where they went or what happened to them was a mystery. If it was a good thing, why hadn't someone returned to tell others where they had gone? No, they concluded, something bad had happened, for they never saw their friends again.

Some said the gods sent them away. They said the gods brought them here from another world, but had grown tired of them. And now the gods were sending them away. But none of them knew anything about a home world. This was their home. They had all been born here. They did not want to go away. If the only way to stay here was to live in the woods as refugees, then so be it.

But living in the woods had its own dangers. Fierce creatures also lived there. And sometimes these creatures would catch and kill them. So they had to be vigilant. Anything less meant death.

Finally, it was time. The young god closed the door to his home. Bowin took the lead. He glanced behind him. There were four others. He knew he could trust them. Catila, who moved without sound. Renot, fast and smart. Gower, whose courage rivaled Bowin's. And Sibot, who distinguished himself when he saved two children from a hungry Groddix that would surely have eaten them. Bowin smiled; he was pleased with his team. They trusted him and would obey without question.

The first part of the journey was easy. In the outer section of town, woods were thick, and they had plenty of places to hide. Bowin hoped the boy wouldn't go all the way to the center of town, although he knew it was a real possibility. He had prepared his team for any kind of terrain. He even ordered them to sharpen their claws. The sharp claws where not for fighting, of course, but they were invaluable for climbing walls and rough surfaces, especially the wooden bridges they would have to cross. Bowin knew he must lead his party inside the bridge, where they could be seen, so he trained them to scamper along the wooden beams above the walkway of the bridge. Hidden high above, they could follow the boy unobserved until he exited the bridge.

The plan was going well. Bowin signaled for everyone to stay close as they scurried up into the rafters close behind the boy as he entered the bridge. There were other people using the bridge, and although the boy sometimes talked with them, none of them looked up. Finally, the boy exited at the far end of the bridge. It was the same path he had taken when he went to school. It led to the open area in the center of the town.

Now was a dangerous time for the watchers. They must leave the bridge and make it to an area with vegetation or some other cover where they could hide. The Town's Central Plaza was filled with gods and goddesses going about their business.

Bowin signaled for Catila, the stealthiest of the lot, to move to a small grove of red and blue flowers on the corner of the building closest to the bridge. The flowers had wide petals, and Bowin knew they could easily hide behind them. Catila signaled she was in place. Bowin ordered the rest to join Catila and then took up the rear as they rushed across the open space. In his haste to secure cover, Gower bumped into one of the flowers, which reacted with a shrill sound. Immediately, all the red and blue flowers withdrew inside their stalks as they too joined in the screeching sound. The thick lush flowers that were to have provided cover for Bowin and his troop had disappeared. Anyone who looked in their direction would see all five as they crouched behind thin stalks that did nothing to hide their presence.

Bowin ordered the troop to move quickly along the wall to a nearby shrub full of long undulating tentacles. He had no choice. To remain there guaranteed discovery. As they scurried to find cover among the branches of the tentacle tree, they watched in fear as the tentacles reached toward them. Bowin whispered to be calm. He said the trees were just curious and would not harm anyone. It was a credit to the loyalty of the group that they obeyed Bowin. Had they not, there was no place else to run. Several gods already stood by the empty stalks trying to figure out what had alarmed them. They would have been seen.

Bowin ignored the tentacle touching his arm and the other one sliding along his back. He turned his attention to the young god they had come to follow. It was well he looked when he did, because the boy walked into a large building on the other side of the plaza. Bowin did not know the name of the building, but he knew it was important because many people were entering it.

So this was where the boy was going now. As Bowin scanned the area, he saw the other building where the boy had always gone before. Most of the gods and goddesses going into that building were smaller and younger than the boy. For some reason, the boy stopped going to that building, and now must go to the new building. Perhaps, Bowin thought, it's something that happens when they got too big for the first building.

Bowin looked around the plaza. It was a beautiful sunny day. He saw other places they could hide if he dared to move closer to the building, but that would be reckless. He could not enter the building without putting everyone at risk. He must content himself with staying where they were. Bowin prepared his team to wait until the boy emerged from the building. Renot was convinced the boy would not leave until the end of the day, and it turned out he was right.

During their long wait, a pair of air angels discovered them. They measured eight feet tall from the tip of their top fins to the bottom. Their bodies were very thin as they moved silently through the air, as a fish might move through water. Large eyes on each side of their head looked in every direction for anything of interest. One of the air angels saw Sibot's tail and came closer to examine it. The angel tilted downward, looking closer, as Sibot held his tail between his legs and tried to melt into Gower. The angel extended two long antennas, gingerly touching Sibot. Brave Sibot trembled, but did not move or cry out.

Then the angel seemed to lose interest. With a quick jerk of its fins, it joined its mate as they swam through the air on their way to some place of greater interest. Bowin was proud of his people for their courage and for not betraying their position.

Many hours later, when the sun hung lower in the sky, people began leaving the boy's building. The plaza filled with people as friends met friends, and they strolled through the still-warm sun, filling tables in the cafés that lined the open square. Bowin began to wonder if the boy had used another exit when at last they saw him leave.

The young god walked listlessly toward the bridge that would take him home. Bowin didn't understand shimmers, but he knew when a shimmer looked weak and tired. Something in the building was making the boy weary and sad.

They followed the boy back to his home, where he walked inside and closed the door. When Bowin and the others made their report that night, there was much concern. They didn't like what was happening to their boy, but what could they do?

It was beyond them.

The Headache

Billy waited until Bernie left for the day. Things were going extremely well. It was just a matter of time. There was no way Bernie's incompetence could be ignored much longer.

The best part was knowing Bernie felt the pain. It was fun to see Bernie's reaction when he discovered Billy's latest prank. Bernie's shimmer normally extended a foot or two above the walls of his cubicle, so it was easy to see when he had discovered one of Billy's little jokes. The first few times, Bernie had responded with confusion and doubt. For the last week, Bernie's shimmer could barely be seen above the top of his cubicle.

And to make it even more delicious, Uncle Shemal had stopped by to check on Bernie's universe, Billy overheard him comment on how bad it looked and how disappointed he was with Bernie's work.

Bernie will be fired soon now, thought Billy. *Just a few more tweaks, and it will be over. The moron doesn't even know what's happening. He must think his universe is out of control and spontaneously generating random anomalies. Or, even better, he must think it's his own fault.* Billy had heard him lie to Shemal, claiming the volcanoes were part of his plan. *Yeah, right. That's part of my plan, Bernie, not yours.*

Billy decided to hit him hard today. Bernie won't see it coming. He was going to heat up the planetary core, and then move time forward until the heat reached the surface. It would do nasty stuff. The plants would dry up and start burning. The oceans would boil away. By the time Bernie got in tomorrow morning, his planet would look like a burned-out cinder, drifting through space. *Revenge is sweet,* he thought.

Billy was careful not to touch anything as he sat in Bernie's chair. He cleared his mind and slipped into Bernie's universe. He smiled at what he saw. He had ripped and torn Bernie's world in so many ways. Bernie may have stopped the continental drift, but the continental plates looked like a stack of dirty dishes. Billy chuckled as he moved deep into the center of the planet. It was easy work for a god to increase the temperature. He stopped short of anything that might change the physical makeup of the core. He didn't want his tampering to be obvious. Bernie may be a moron, but he wasn't stupid.

Billy returned to the surface, where he would have a better view of his handiwork. His excitement mounted as he thought of the heat moving slowly to the surface, eventually melting the outer crust, and leaving a world of molten rock. All that remained was to push his time lever forward so he could watch it happen.

He reached for his lever and the future—

Suddenly, his vision went white. Blinding pain, more intense than anything he'd ever experienced, crashed into his skull. Black emptiness was the last thing he saw as consciousness left him. The shimmering figure that had hovered above the doomed planet abruptly blinked out.

~

When Billy regained consciousness, he found himself slumped in Bernie's chair, drenched in sweat. Intense pain hammered the inside of his head, slamming him again and again with every heartbeat, threatening a return to the blackness. He couldn't move. He felt some clarity as the drying perspiration chilled his face. He had to move. No one could find him there.

Billy staggered back to his own cubicle, where he rested for several minutes. Finally, he pulled himself upright and lurched toward the door, ricocheting off walls and cubicles alike. He hoped he could make it home.

It would be close.

Billy's Healer

Billy should have stayed home for a few more days. That's what the healer told him. And she was the best, at least according to his mom.

Rachel's office was full of new age stuff like pyramids and crystals, and flute music played in the background. She had long dark hair and wore one of those flowing dresses like you see on water planets. Oh, and beads. They were everywhere. And lots of incense and other smelly stuff, too.

Billy hadn't told Rachel, of course, what he was doing when it happened. He just said he was at work at the time. Even that admission had been a mistake, because his mom wanted him to file an injury claim with The Business. But there was no way he could tell anyone he'd been messing with Bernie's universe when it happened. Fortunately, Rachel didn't seem interested in those things.

She made him stand while she walked around and around him, examining his shimmer and whatever else she had the skills to see.

"Billy, this is just awful."

"It feels awful. Especially my head."

"Yes, I can see that's where it started. But the pain was so strong it made other parts of your body hurt too. I can see it in your shimmer. Do you see how it looks almost normal down by your feet? Around your head, I can barely see anything."

"How bad is it?"

"I've seen something like this before when people crash really hard into the Past Barrier. Your pain is centered in the upper left section of your skull, near your time lever. But I've never seen a case this severe. Were you using your time lever when it happened?"

"Yes, but I was heading forward in time, not back."

"Are you sure? I don't know how this could happen if you were moving forward."

Billy paused to think. Had he become confused and jerked

the lever backward instead of forward? He didn't think so. But he couldn't remember exactly what happened, except the blinding white pain.

"How can you tell this from looking at me? I don't know much about shimmers."

"Well, that doesn't surprise me. Boys don't seem to care about such things. When I was your age, there were never any boys in my shimmer classes."

"I don't think that's changed. I don't know any guys who took those classes either. We don't care about how we look as much as girls do."

"Well, it's not just about how you look. Shimmers are a lot more than just what color your aura is. They tell us a lot. I use them to see how you are feeling and to diagnose problems."

"Well, I don't care about that stuff."

"There's more to shimmers than just medicine, you know. Lots of people have to learn to control them. An actor, for example, needs to make his words and his shimmer line up. No one will believe what he's saying if his shimmer is telling a different story. Models have to manage their shimmers so they don't detract from the clothes they're wearing. Even a sales person has to manage it if he wants to be good at selling."

"What does it have to do with sales?"

"If someone is trying to sell you something, but they're thinking about the bad day they had yesterday or an errand they have to do after work, then that's what their shimmer will show. Most people, when they see distracted, unfocused shimmers, don't want to buy anything. The sales person seems insincere.

"Your shimmer, for example," continued Rachel, "is very tight and controlled—not necessarily in a good way. You carry it around like a shield, keeping your real feelings hidden."

"So I already know how to control my shimmer. I don't need any classes." Billy made a crooked grin.

"That's only part of what they teach you. Yes, there are times when you want to control it, but it's usually more important to let it flow. For example, if you're happy, you want your shimmer to show it. If you're curious, it is okay to shimmer your curiosity. It's a way of emphasizing what you're thinking or feeling. Your shimmer is like an extra facial expression. You can use it to smile, frown, show happiness, or even show anger. It helps you communicate with people because you're telling them how you feel and what you want."

"I think I would rather keep my secrets," Billy said, as his shimmer tightened a little more.

Astrology Says...

Bernie spent the morning planning life forms. Although he had most of the details worked out for his Fish2Birds, the secondary animals continued to trouble him.

He wanted companion animals for his Fish2Birds, but, so far, the secondary animals he designed had numerous potential conflicts with his people. For example, if he created an airborne creature as a companion for his people-birds, what was to stop it from deciding his fish-babies were more appetizing than the plants? His secondary animals required more thought.

As Bernie considered the problem, he thought back to his dad's universes. Simeon hadn't created companion creatures. He said in his book he didn't want any distractions for his primary life forms. That didn't feel right to Bernie. *Shouldn't there be a higher purpose than just looking good? Isn't it important for creations to enjoy living? Shouldn't they have meaning in their lives? A purpose of some sort? What else was living for?* He knew most gods would laugh at him for wasting time on such questions. But still, the questions troubled him. He wanted his world to make sense. He wanted his people to understand their place and to live happy lives, content knowing they are fulfilling a divine plan.

He spent the morning thinking about higher purposes and companion animals. By lunch, he had no answers, although he was confident he was asking the right questions. As long as he did that, the answers would come.

~

"Hi, Bernie. I see you're in a better mood today," Suzie said.

"Yeah, my world was fine again this morning," he said. "I've had a chance to do some planning."

Lenny arrived a few moments later. "Hi, guys." He lowered his lunch tray, scowled at the tapioca pudding, and asked, "Is there a way to tell if this stuff is alive?"

"Well, you could plant it on a sterile world and return later to see if it had babies," Bernie suggested.

After they settled in, Bernie said, "I'm trying to work out some issues with my animals. Can I bounce some ideas off you both?"

"Sure. Animals are one of my specialties," said Lenny, his tapioca suddenly forgotten. "For my universe project, I made giant armor-plated reptiles with horns, sharp teeth and a bellow that could knock you over. When they fought, it was like thunder and earthquakes. And when—"

"That's not what I'm looking for, Lenny. I don't want anything that will hurt my higher life forms."

"For goodness' sake, Bernie. Why do you care about that?" Lenny asked with unconcealed confusion.

"I just don't like it when they hurt each other."

"So what? You can always make more of them." Lenny was still confused.

As Bernie struggled to find an explanation, Suzie responded, "Bernie is a gentle soul, Lenny. You know that. He doesn't have to make animals that hurt each other if he doesn't want to."

"I know," said Lenny. "I just can't figure out why anyone would want to. It's so boring."

"Have you named your higher life form yet?" Suzie asked, guiding the conversation toward easier ground.

Bernie looked gratefully at Suzie. *Still defending me after all these years,* he thought. *Someday I will make it up to you, Suzie. I promise.*

"I think I'm going to call them Fish2Birds. Either that or Pod People."

"Pod People?" said Suzie. "I don't understand."

"Well, you know how the fish-kids go from eggs to a cocoon?" asked Bernie. "When they hatch, they become land-people. Then when the land-people get old, they jump off the mountain, shed their skins, and become bird-people. I'm having trouble designing a fast enough metamorphosis for the bird-people."

"It's hard to mix morphological processes in the same species," said Lenny. "If you're going to multi-morph them, it's easier if you keep the morphing process as similar as possible. If you're going to use cocoons for the first transition, then keep it the same for the second one, too. Have your land-people climb the mountain and spin a second cocoon up there. Then after they hatch, they can grow wings and fly away in bird form."

Bernie nodded. "That makes a lot of sense. Thanks, Lenny."

As Bernie considered the materials his people would need for their second cocoon, Suzie asked, "I've been thinking about your universe, Bernie. Have you added any moons or planets yet?"

"No. I was thinking about not adding any. It just gives Billy more things to mess up."

Lenny shook his head. "That's not a good idea. You need planets and moons."

"Why?" Suzie asked.

"Because if you don't have any other planets or moons when you add your animals, it's really hard on higher life forms. They end up listless, without any sense of purpose," Lenny said.

"That's just an old god's tale," said Bernie. Turning to Suzie, he said, "Some people think planets and moons exert control over your life forms like puppets on strings. The distant planets make them happy or sad or bring them luck or take it away. It's dumb."

"No, it's not! Didn't you take Creation Astrology?" asked Lenny. "Ester said it's really important. She says never to use fewer than three planets. You should put your life planet in the middle of the group, and at least one planet should be a gas giant. And if you want more diversity in your animals, then you need more planets."

"Well, I don't want much diversity. I want my higher life to swim in schools and eventually to fly in beautiful formations. I don't want a bunch of individual thinkers in the group."

"Well, regardless, you'd better have at least three planets," Lenny insisted.

"What about moons?" Suzie asked.

"You'd better have at least one," Lenny said, more to Bernie than to Suzie. "Honestly, Bernie, you need to read this stuff before you go any further."

"Does the color of the moon matter?" asked Suzie. "I was always partial to yellow moons."

"Okay, you win, Lenny. Two more planets and one yellow moon," Bernie said.

More Planets

Bernie borrowed Lenny's textbooks on creative astrology. He hadn't taken the class because it was an elective. His creation sociology teacher had talked about the astrological aspects of culture management, but she hadn't suggested any further reading.

Bernie had doubts about this astrology stuff. He'd never heard of any physical laws explaining how a planet could affect one creature on a different planet without affecting others on the same planet in the same way. But he knew one thing for sure: he couldn't afford more problems in his universe.

He worried about going back to Supply and asking for more prefabs. He didn't want Shemal thinking he was wasting supplies. But surely no one would begrudge him a couple more planets and a moon. Lots of people made complicated universes with more than he had used so far. Suzie said Wanda's universe had two twin star systems with over a dozen planets in each one. *What a show-off.*

The Supply Division was helpful. If they knew Shemal thought Bernie was wasting supplies, they didn't show it. They got out the glossy catalog with detailed technical descriptions for each planet. They seemed genuinely disappointed when he only selected two planets and a moon.

Bernie chose a gas giant for the outer orbit and a metal planet for the inner orbit, the minimum configuration suggested by Lenny's astrology book. A major portion of the book was devoted to planetary orbits. Interestingly, the book was more concerned with how the orbits appeared when viewed from the life planet. *This makes things complicated,* thought Bernie. *It's hard enough to manage celestial bodies when all you have to do is make them revolve around a sun. But to design something from the viewing perspective of one of the planets? Now that's a challenge.*

The book also suggested he delay many of his building tasks until the planets were lined up just right. To do so would require burning up hundreds of thousands of years of universe time waiting for the right alignment. *That's not going to happen.* He would add the planets and the moon, but he wasn't going to waste time on the rest of it.

He glanced in the direction of Billy's cubicle. He hadn't seen Billy for several days, which was undoubtedly why there hadn't been any recent sabotage. Billy must be taking a few days off. Bernie shook his head. So far, Billy's damage had been repairable, but that could easily change. If Billy wanted to destroy his world, all he had to do was blink it out. There would be nothing Bernie could do. Well, tonight at least, he didn't have to worry about that.

Bernie entered the void of his universe. He placed the giant gas planet into an outer orbit, and he put the smaller planet in an orbit close to the sun. He watched them for a while as they looped around the sun. The idea of planets having an effect on his life planet bothered him. The book said distance didn't matter, as long as the planets were visible from the life planet. So he changed the orbits. He pushed the gas giant farther away from his planet, and then he pushed the small heavy planet closer to the sun. If distance didn't matter, then he would keep them as far away from his planet as possible. That way, if Billy exploded one of them, he'd have more time to clean up the debris before it hit his world.

Bernie reached for his moon. He thought of Suzie as he placed it into an orbit around the planet. He liked the moon. He liked Suzie. She was always trying to help him. Lenny said she liked him. Maybe she did—

Hey, stay focused, he admonished himself. He glanced around to see if his cloud had done anything during his momentary lapse. Finding nothing, he turned his attention back to his work.

The moon was completely smooth. Not a mark on it, unlike the planet it circled. Suzie wanted a yellow moon. Bernie gathered his creative power and directed it toward the surface of the moon, willing it to become yellow. And as he willed it, so it became.

Suzie will like this moon, he thought.

A Gift from the Sun

Not everyone saw the night sun in the same way. Zardok, the high priest, believed it was nothing less than a gift from the Almighty Sun to his beloved people. Others, however, weren't so sure. Why was there no warning of this event? Some said even Zardok was surprised by its arrival. And what of the two small suns that could only be seen at night? What were they trying to tell them? Some said they were the Eyes of the Sun, watching over His people.

Zardok called together the most learned of his inner circle. They deliberated behind closed doors, coming out only at night to observe the night sun and the two little suns, as did everyone else.

It was on the third night people noticed something happening to the night sun. Part of the night sun was being consumed. It began as a sliver, but each night after that the night sun grew smaller and smaller. The priests had no answers for why this might happen. Something wonderful was being destroyed. There could be no good explanation for such a thing.

Again, they asked the priests to explain, but they were told the signs were not yet clear. "Be patient," the priests said. "We will know everything soon."

But the interpretation did not come soon enough, so the people took it upon themselves to find their own answers.

They came to believe the Sun was angry. 'The message is clear,' they said. 'See how the night sun denies its light to the people at night? So too shall the Sun deny His light to the people during the day.'

The threat was clear. But what did the Sun want them to do to avoid this fate? That was not so clear.

Lord Rigel stood among those who sought answers, and he spoke thus, "You know I venerate the Sun above all else. But I am one who questions whether Speaker Zardok is the best person to lead us in these uncertain times. Even now, Zardok waits for answers when the truth is perfectly clear to the rest of us."

"Lord Rigel, what should we do?" the people asked.

"It's obvious," said Lord Rigel. "The Sun, through the night sun, has shown us what will happen. If we ignore His warning, the fate of the night sun will be our fate. We will be cast into unending darkness from which none shall return. We must ask the Senate to demand answers. We must discover what the Sun wants from us. And we must do it quickly, before it's too late."

So spoke Lord Rigel.

In the face of such logic, the people had to agree. And so, Rigel set out at once to petition the Senate for an audience.

Shemal Stops By

"Okay, kid. What have you got for me today?" Shemal asked from the doorway to Bernie's cubicle. Shemal watched for any sign of Bernie's cloud and was pleased to see none. He also noticed the dampener turned to its maximum setting.

"Hello, sir. I don't have much new. I'm still doing a lot of planning. My animals are very complicated, and there are a lot of things to work out." In testimony to his claim, Bernie's desk and walls were thick with sketches and layers of stickies.

Shemal said, "Well, I have something else to talk to you about anyway. I heard you were asking the Supply Division about defective parts."

"Yes, sir."

"Why didn't you come to me about this if you thought there was a problem?" Shemal asked.

"Well, sir, ah…"

"Just spit it out, son."

"I heard you took a lot of flak because you demanded high quality parts from the other divisions. I didn't want to cause more problems for you."

That was not the answer Shemal expected. He looked carefully at Bernie. *Loyalty?* he wondered. *You don't see much of that these days.*

Shemal asked, "What did Supply tell you?"

"They said they hadn't heard of any similar problems."

Shemal laughed. "That's what they told me before I started documenting everything." He looked at Bernie and, in a soft voice that belied his age, said, "Let me give you some free advice, kid. No one ever made the perfect universe on their first try. Stick to the basics. Put together something that works. And, for goodness' sake, don't try to get too fancy. I've seen lots of kids fail because they tried to do things they weren't ready for."

"Thank you, sir."

As Shemal walked away, he thought about Bernie. The kid seemed conscientious and hardworking, and he was sure he meant well, but when he looked at him, he just didn't see a builder.

He was going to have to think about making a tough decision.

Billy Returns

Billy came back to work after four days. Bernie caught a few glimpses of him. Billy's shimmer looked weak, often flickering, as if about to go out. Bernie had never seen anything like it.

Bernie stuck his head around the corner into Billy's cubicle and whispered, "Is everything okay, Billy? You don't look so good."

He was surprised by Billy's angry reply, "This isn't over, Ber-Nerd."

When Billy didn't say anything else, Bernie slipped back into his cubicle. *How can Billy be mad at me?* he wondered. *Billy's the one doing all the damage here.*

I'm the one who should be mad.

Zardok Explains

Speaker Zardok had been high priest for the Sun Temples as far back as anyone could remember. His absolute devotion to the Sun made him the natural choice for the position. A host of other talents kept him in the position.

From the beginning, he was a tireless worker who recruited talented men and women to the service of the Sun. Almost singlehandedly, he turned a simple practice of Sun worship into a formal religion, practiced by the entire population.

But it was his second talent that made Zardok unique. Time and again he demonstrated a deep understanding of both the secular and the religious realms. Although he had countless opportunities to acquire secular power and evolve the Temple into a theocracy, he chose not to do it. He believed it would detract from his real and only mission: to serve the Sun and, through such service, to serve the people.

Zardok, like all lords, stood tall. His physical height marked him in a crowd, as did his clean-shaven head. He wanted no barriers between himself and his beloved Sun, which also explained the deep tan of his greenish-brown skin.

Zardok took pride in the loyalty of his priests and priestesses who had also taken to shaving their heads, although he had never asked them to do so. One could easily recognize members of the Temple by their bald heads and yellow robes. Even lay people, as a declaration of their faith, often went about with shaved heads and yellow robes.

Today, Zardok was not pleased. One of his unending challenges was keeping unhealthy ideas from corrupting the minds of the faithful. There was always some new group with wild ideas about something or other. Lately, because of the emergence of the night sun, there were more than ever.

"What now?" Zardok asked with no attempt to conceal his irritation. "Who are they?"

"Well, no one really. Their leader is Lord Rigel. They've developed their own theory about the night sun, and they're urgently petitioning the Senate for an audience," said Lord Winson.

"I know Rigel. He's a believer, although he tends to have his own way of interpreting things. Do they have any allies in the Senate?" Zardok asked.

"Lord Rigel petitioned for a hearing through Senator Grenwy, whose influence is weak, at best."

"Very well. Contact Leader Gondal for me. Tell him we have important news about the night sun, and I wish to inform the Senate."

"Yes, Speaker. It will be done."

"Oh, Winson. Make sure we are on their agenda at least two days before Rigel is able to address the Senate. There's no point in letting Lord Rigel get everyone upset before we have a chance to explain what's going on."

"Yes, sir."

Gaia? Already?

"Are you sure, Bernie? That doesn't sound right." Lenny's brow wrinkled in thought.

"Yes, I'm sure. I saw her aura this morning."

"I don't understand. What's this 'gaia' you're talking about?" Suzie asked.

Bernie explained, "Gaia is something that happens when life forms reach a critical mass on your planet. It's like a brand new life form that starts all by itself. No one understands it completely. Gaia is a life force made up of all the other life forces on the planet. And they have minds of their own, too. They don't like conflicts or disruptions, so they're always trying to get the life forms into a homeostatic state."

"Just like a mother for the whole planet," exclaimed Suzie. "I like them!"

"You wouldn't like them so much if you were trying to do something, and they fought you every step of the way," Lenny said.

"Why would they fight you?" Suzie asked.

"I can give you lots of examples," said Lenny. "I have a dragon universe at home. I tried to make the male dragons fiercer, so they'll fight more often. Just as I was making progress, my gaia deliberately reduced the oxygen content in the atmosphere to make them sleepy and less combative. Another time she reduced the male birth rate and increased the female birth rate. The males were so busy with all the new female dragons, there was nothing I could do to get them to fight. They were too busy giving each other high-fives over their cool harems."

"How can she do that?" Suzie asked. "Those are god-powers."

"Well, she can't do it quickly. Sometimes it takes her generations to make it happen, but if there's a way to do it, she will. She's very tricky," Lenny said as he shook his finger in a scolding manner.

"So why is the gaia a problem on your world, Bernie?" Suzie asked.

"Well, she hasn't done anything yet. But that's not the thing. The thing is she shouldn't be there at all. My planet is nothing but a bunch of plants. There are no animals. Have you ever heard of a gaia emerging on a planet with just plants?" Bernie asked Lenny.

"Yes, but it isn't common. It usually takes both plants and animals to get one going, although if you wait long enough, even plants can produce a gaia."

"I've only had plants for two million years," Bernie reminded him.

"That's not very long. I was talking about at least a billion years," Lenny said.

Bernie's brow furrowed in thought as he considered anything else that could have contributed to the early emergence of his gaia.

"I can tell you how to kill her if you want," Lenny offered.

"Lenny!" Suzie said, clearly shocked.

"I don't think that's necessary," said Bernie. "So far she hasn't given me any trouble."

A Divine Event!

The high priest stood on a wooden platform in the center of the Senate's Great Chamber, a large amphitheater that faced the front of a two-story building where the offices of the Senate were located. The amphitheater seats were filled with five hundred senators and lords who had assembled to hear the words of the high priest. A thousand more seats in the upper levels of the Great Chamber held citizens who wished to attend. All the seats were full.

Rearing up on magnificent stone pillars, the Senate Building displayed exquisite carvings and statues along the front and sides of the building. The second floor was set back from the first, creating a wide ledge over the first floor, which overlooked the center stage. A grand door on the second floor gave access to the platform.

Sitting on the viewing platform on a raised dais were thirteen men and women. They sat behind a long, curved wooden table that faced the center stage. Twelve were ministers of the Senate. The thirteenth, a man named Gondal, was their leader, and he sat in the middle.

The Senate was justifiably proud of their Great Chamber. Constructed from beautifully carved stone, it had taken decades to build. The seats of the amphitheater were supported by tall pillars of marble carved from the Central Mountains and transported hundreds of miles on carts pulled by men and women. The Senate Building was made of the same stone and decorated by statues on the top and all around the sides. No one could enter the Great Chamber without being moved by its grandeur. The ornate carved Office Building was matched only by the splendor of the Great Chamber and its thousand seats, all open to the sky.

Leader Gondal snorted as he looked at the wooden platform where Speaker Zardok stood in the center stage. It was designed to raise Zardok to a level equal to Gondal as he sat behind his table on the raised dais. It had begun as a serious issue between them, but evolved into a mere matter of protocol. Lord Zardok, High Priest of the Temple, and Speaker for the Sun, would not allow anyone to see him as subordinate to any person or secular institution, even if it was the Leader of the Senate. So, whenever Zardok agreed to appear before the Senate, Gondal was forced to have his workers rebuild the wooden platform for him. Zardok would not address the Senate without it.

Leader Gondal listened as the Speaker for the Sun gave the Senate his news.

"It is a divine event! Nothing like it has ever happened before," the high priest shouted to the sound of people stamping their feet and shouting, "Hear! Hear!"

"But what does it mean?" the Leader asked.

"It means the Sun has answered our prayers," the high priest said in a knowing way.

"Please explain."

"Certainly, Leader. Everyone knows we have prayed for the Sun not to leave us at night. For reasons we do not understand, He could not stay. But because of our prayers and our devotion, He created a small Sun to light our night. We call it the 'night sun'. In this way He shows us His love." The stamping of feet and shouts of approval echoed through the amphitheater.

"But what of the two tiny lights in the sky?" one of the senators asked.

"Our priests are studying those lights. We think they may be smaller Night Suns held in reserve in case they are needed," the high priest said.

"But what of the night sun itself? Every night a larger part it is consumed by the darkness," the senator persisted.

"There is no cause for concern, Senator. We believe, even if the night sun should disappear completely, the Sun will create a new night sun from the two that remain. There is no evidence the smaller suns are being consumed in any way," said the high priest with confidence.

"What about the flooding?" asked Minister Landor, who was responsible for the port facilities. "The cities on our coast have reported ocean waters rising and falling every day. Our docks and nearby buildings are flooding and the moorings for our ships have become unusable. Is the night sun the cause of this?"

"Minister, would you not agree that a little flooding is a small price to pay for the night sun?" asked Zardok. "Just move a few buildings and build your docks a little higher."

Minister Landor didn't think it was an even trade, but he knew few would agree with him. Even the coastal cities had rejoiced upon the arrival of the night sun.

"Well, I'm still concerned," said Landor, as he turned to the Leader. "Has anyone asked Lord Alcandor for his opinion?"

"That is completely unnecessary, Leader," bristled the Speaker. "Our interpretation is obviously correct. There is no need for any second opinion."

"At this time, I think religion provides the answers we need, Minister," said leader Gondal. "If we find their explanations wanting, then we shall turn to Lord Alcandor's science."

Billy Is Sick Again

This time it was much more serious. Billy had been barely able to crawl back to his cubicle before passing out. The cleaning staff found him and arranged to get him home. His mother called Rachel, the healer, who came straight to the house.

Billy lay very still, barely breathing. Rachel walked around his bed, observing him from every angle. Finally, she turned to Billy's mom and dad and asked, "Can you think of anything that might have caused this?"

"No, nothing at all," Billy's dad said.

His mother said, "We asked him when it happened the first time, but he wouldn't talk about it. We thought he'd just been careless and was too embarrassed to admit it."

"Is he going to be okay?" Billy's father asked.

"Oh, he'll recover. I don't see any permanent damage," said Rachel. "But these episodes take a lot out of him. If they keep happening, and he isn't able to fully recover his strength, there could be serious problems."

As Billy's parents watched, Rachel drew arcane symbols at the head and foot of their son's bed. She took stones from a pouch by her side, selected three, and placed them around Billy's head. Finally, she assembled a large pyramid frame over his bed.

"These will help him recover his strength. He will sleep for a day at least. Let him. That's the best medicine right now. When he wakes up, call me. I'll stop back and see him then."

~

"How are you feeling, Billy?" Rachel asked.

"Better, thanks. Will I live?"

"Yes, but you may not survive many more of these. Are you ready to tell me what happened?"

"All I know is it has something to do with the time lever. But it doesn't seem to happen all the time."

That was only partially true. Billy had been thinking about

it since he regained consciousness. The last thing he remembered was being in Bernie's universe.

~

His plan had been simple, really. Melt the polar ice cap. It was thick from two million years of accumulation. A fast melt would send a massive tsunami rushing to the equator, where it would overwhelm Bernie's sausage-shaped continent.

Billy had planned it carefully. He would create a large vertical wave, called a bore, to come rushing in with water churning at its front. He wanted it large enough to drag a wave train of lesser waves behind it. The elevation of Bernie's continent was not high, except for the mountain range in the middle of the main continent, and he was curious to see how far inland he could send the tsunami.

After he saw what the northern ice cap could do, he would make any needed adjustments, melt the southern cap, and see if he could do better. Everything had gone perfectly on the northern cap. He melted everything, creating mountains of water surging toward the equator.

Knowing it would take time for the tsunami to reach the continent, Billy decided not to wait. He wanted to enjoy watching the tsunami as it made landfall. So he moved his time lever ahead. That was when something went wrong.

Billy thought back to when he'd overheated the core of Bernie's planet. He had no problems until he tried to move forward in time so he could observe the destruction as the oceans boiled away. That was when he'd been struck down the first time. Yet, he'd used his lever many times that very day on his own projects without any problems.

Then a thought occurred to him. Bernie was geeky enough to have figured out how to lay a trap in his universe. It had to be something like that. *Bernie has figured out how to stop me from advancing time in his universe. Hmm... I have to give Ber-Nerd some credit*, he thought. *He's a bit slow on the uptake, but he hits back hard.*

~

"Why are you smiling?" Rachel asked.

"I just figured out a problem from work," said Billy. "Speaking of which, when can I go back?"

"You'd better stay in bed for a couple more days. Get your strength back. You can go back on Monday."

"That'll be just fine."

Ring of Emptiness

Bernie got home, went to his room, and entered his universe through the new backdoor. He'd done the same thing every night. While Billy had been gone, there were no new problems, and Bernie had enjoyed the respite. His conversation with Billy today made it clear Billy was angry. It was a good thing he checked his world when he did, because he was barely in time.

At first, the universe looked okay. The sun, the planets, and the yellow moon were just as he'd left them. But something was wrong on the planet. As he studied it more closely, it finally registered: the northern polar icecap was missing. The southern icecap remained, but in the north, there was nothing.

The ocean at the top of the planet was hot. Very hot. The water temperature at the South Pole was cold, as it should be. What had Billy done? The thick mantle of ice covering the North Pole had been melted. *Polar ice mixing with ocean water shouldn't be too harmful. There has got to be something more. What was Billy trying to do?*

He flashed to his main continent to see if his plants were okay. That's when he saw the problem.

All around the planet, in an ever-widening ring, was a wave of surging water. A huge tsunami raced toward his continent. He might not have noticed but for the volcanic islands scattered across the ocean. The tsunami had devastated island after island on its surge toward the big continent.

Bernie's mind raced as he tried to think of a way to stop this giant wave from washing over his land. As the wave moved closer, he could see it begin to rise up as it approached the shallow waters near the northern shore.

A quick solution was not easy. Creation is not a fast process, and Bernie had no putty at home. That left only one option. He must use his power to destroy. Yet if he wasn't careful, he could destroy more than he intended. He had to act quickly.

Bernie visualized a latitude line that circled the planet twenty miles north of the long northern shore of his sausage-shaped continent. He pictured in his mind a strip of water five miles wide and two miles deep that continued around the world. This ring that existed only in his imagination was where he would make his stand.

Bernie held his visualization as the giant wave entered his ring, rearing up higher and higher as it neared the land. Then, before the wave could escape the ring, he blinked. He blinked all the water in his five by two mile ring into nothingness. All around the planet was an empty trench where the water used to be.

An oncoming wall of water from the north rushed to fill the empty channel. Water from the landside was also drained to fill the trench. As the trench filled, the tsunami prepared to resume its assault on the land. Bernie blinked again. And the water disappeared.

He repeated this until the tsunami faded at last. Only then did he let the ocean fill his ring.

"Oh, Chaos," he said. "That was a close one."

Tragedy at Sea

Reports had been coming in for several days. Gondal, Leader of the Senate, had called a meeting of his ministers to review what they knew. It was Landor, the minister responsible for ships and port facilities, who spoke first.

"There are two vessels past due. The *Sun Seeker* has a crew of forty-two and sails the northern coast between Calidona and the Capital. The *Sea Breeze* has a crew of fifty-three and sails the northern coast between the Capital and Surinex. They're both engaged in textile shipping."

"What effort has been made to find them?" Gondal asked.

"We launched four ships to look for them, but so far we've heard nothing."

"Tell me about the anomaly that was reported," Gondal said.

"People claim the water along the coast just disappeared. An hour later it was back to normal."

"Disappeared? That doesn't make sense," said Minister Nottag demonstrating his famous scowl.

"They claim the water just drained away," said Landor. "They could see the ocean bottom for miles in every direction. Ships in the harbor lay at anchor on their sides."

"Where did this happen?"

"Everywhere—at least along the northern coast. There are no reports like it from the southern coast," Landor said.

"Were there any ships at sea that observed this phenomenon?" Gondal asked.

"We only know of the *Dawn Joy*. The captain says when the water went out, his ship was beached on some rocks. Otherwise, he says his ship would have been drawn out to sea with the rest of the water. They saw a dark line out in the ocean. He claims it was miles wide, and it kept appearing and disappearing. After a while, the water came back and lifted his vessel again. He sailed immediately to the nearest port. We located him in a bar near the waterfront. He and his crew had drunk themselves into a stupor."

"I don't like this at all," said Gondal. "What precautions have you taken?"

"I've called all the ships back to port for the next five days. The only ships I have at sea are searching for survivors."

Gondal nodded his approval and turned to the rest of his ministers. "Can anyone here offer an explanation?"

"I asked Speaker Zardok about it," said Minister Tonst, the official liaison between the Senate and the Temple.

"And?"

"He said he will consult with his senior priests and advise us if they uncover any explanations."

"I talked with Lord Alcandor," said Branton, the science minister. "He couldn't explain it either, but he said something interesting about the ocean."

Gondal nodded for Branton to continue. "He said there's a relationship between the depth of the sea and the position of the Sun. He said twice a day, the ocean reaches its highest point. The first is when the Sun is directly overhead and the second is when the Sun is halfway between setting and rising—"

Minister Nottag interrupted Branton. "He's known that for a long time. Alcandor called them 'tides' or some such. This isn't new information."

"If I might be allowed to finish, Minister? Alcandor has also been studying the effect of the night sun on the ocean. The night sun also makes tides twice a day. He says instead of making the ocean rise by inches, as the Sun does, the night sun makes the ocean rise by several feet."

"That's impossible," said Tonst immediately. "Nothing is more powerful than the Sun."

Although there were murmurs of agreement from the ministers, Gondal asked, "What proof does Alcandor have for this claim?"

"He's been using measuring sticks in several ports along the coast," said Branton.

"With all the other strange things happening lately, why is he studying the water?" Nottag asked.

"I can answer that," said Gondal. "We asked Alcandor to study it. You remember the reports of flooding when the night sun arrived? We wanted to know if it was temporary or if we should abandon the areas that keep flooding."

Branton continued. "I think when Alcandor makes his report, he'll tell us the night sun flooding will continue. He said it's so regular he can predict exactly when it will happen each day."

Landor groaned. The Senate's building fund would have to be tapped again. Gondal steered the conversation back. "Does Alcandor see a connection between the flooding and what happened here?"

"He's looking into it. He said it may be another manifestation of the flooding phenomenon. Some sort of inverse correlation, whatever that means," said Branton.

"What's his best guess?" Gondal asked.

"You know how Alcandor gets." Branton shrugged. "He has lots of theories, but when I pressed him for answers, he told me he just doesn't know yet."

"Until we know more, I think keeping your ships in port is a good decision, Landor. Let's continue that for now. If there are more unusual events, let me know right away, and we'll reconvene," Gondal said.

If he'd been able to see the future, Gondal would have shuddered. Nothing in his life had prepared him for the unusual events yet to come.

A Favorite Bookstore

Tonight felt different. For the first time since Bernie installed his backdoor, he didn't feel the need to rush home and protect his universe. Billy had been absent for two days.

After work, he meandered around the Central Plaza until, after crossing one of the bridges, he found himself in front of his favorite bookstore. When he worked for Good Shimmer Imports, his job was keeping their bookshelves stocked. Isaiah, the owner, was a gregarious god who always had a kind word for young Bernie. Life had been much simpler when all he had to do was keep books on shelves.

Isaiah shop carried a full range of books. The new titles, prominently displayed at the front of the store, included *Building for Fun and Profit*, *Building in the Zone*, and *The Top 100 Destination Universes*. Bernie, like most builders, was drawn to the award winners section with its parade of new titles. Among the current best sellers, he found: *This Year's Award Winners: Why They Won*, *The Top 50 Awards of All Time*, and *What Does It Take to Win?*

As Bernie read the new titles, he drifted into the biographies section. The shelves were full of stories about current and past award winners and what they had done to make their universes special. It was a popular section, since everyone wanted insight into any tricks or gimmicks the winners had used to put them over the top.

Bang! Thump!

"Stop it. Just stop it," Bernie muttered under his breath. His cloud ignored him as a third book fell to the floor. Once again, he calmed himself before reaching down to pick up the fallen books. He wasn't surprised to see the books were about his dad. He was usually more careful in this part of the store. The first book was titled *Simeon Claims Number Three*, a perennial best seller. The second book was an autobiography he had once borrowed from Isaiah called *Simeon Tells All*. At first, Bernie had been excited to read about his dad, but his excitement turned to disappointment when he found no mention of his mom or himself. Simeon talked plenty about his childhood and the rest of his life. But, neither his wife nor his son had merited any comment.

"Hey, Bernie. I guessed it had to be you throwing your dad's books around again." Isaiah grinned as he waved to Bernie from his tall stool near the register.

Bernie shook his head. Fortunately, none of the books had been damaged. The last thing he wanted was to have to pay for one.

He wandered instinctively to the Self-Help Section, where he had purchased more than a few books. One title that caught his attention was *How to get Along at Work*. When he saw several chapters about difficult bosses and unsupportive coworkers, he decided it was a good investment.

On his way to the checkout, he passed through the Occult Section. The best sellers here included: *Good Luck or Bad Luck: It's Your Choice*, *Bending Probability to Your Advantage*, *What's Happening in the Parallel Dimensions?* and *Does Magic Work in Our World?* Bernie thought again of his friend. *Lenny's a bright guy, and he loves this stuff. I understand OWT, but this is over the top for me.*

At the checkout, Isaiah asked, "How have you been, Bernie? We haven't seen you for a while."

"I'm fine, thanks, Isaiah. I got a builder job with The Business. They've been keeping me really busy."

"That's great, Bernie! Congratulations. So when do you think we'll have some books with your name on them in the awards section?" Isaiah asked with only a hint of teasing.

"Well, it might be a while. I found out it isn't as easy as it looks."

"You'll get there, Bernie. You've got Simeon blood in you. It's just a matter of time."

A Garden Universe?

Two more days passed. Billy still hadn't shown up to work.

It was a productive time for Bernie. He worked hard on his animal designs. He'd set a goal to create a companion animal for his pod people, but the complexities of creating companion creatures with the same morphing ability as his pod people was proving exceedingly difficult.

By the end of the day, the best he had come up with was two overlapping companions. The first companion would be a tadpole-like creature living with the fish-kids in the water. Eventually it would grow legs and become like a slow dog and live on land. When it died, halfway through the land period, the pod people would get their second companion. It would be a Rite of Passage for them. The second companion would resemble a flightless chicken. When the pod people were ready to leave the land, the chickens would develop strong eagle-like wings, just in time to follow their companions into the mountains to begin their new lives in the sky.

That kept things tidy. No left over companions.

~

"Bernie, I think you're working way too hard at this," Lenny said, more than a little exasperated. "Interesting life will develop all by itself if you just give it a chance."

"But I'm trying to create a very specific type of higher life."

"I know, but if you can't figure out what you want or how to do it, in the end, you're going to end up with nothing. Then you're really screwed."

"What would you do?"

"I'd probably just do a Big Bang. That works pretty well."

"What's a Big Bang?" Suzie asked.

"Basically, you create a huge mass in the center of your void, apply pressure and heat, and let it explode. Then you advance time about fifteen billion years and see what you've got. If you do it with a big enough mass, there's sure to be all kinds of interesting things that come out of it," Lenny said.

"I don't think that will convince anyone of my builder skills. Even if I get something interesting, everyone will know it was just random chance."

"Then try a garden universe," Lenny suggested. "I read a study that one of every four worlds that achieve gaia will develop advanced life forms."

"I remember gaias," Suzie said. "You said they happen when the life on your planet reaches a critical mass. A gaia comes alive and starts looking after the planet, right? But what's a garden universe?"

Lenny liked it when he got to explain things. "That's where you plant every kind of seed you can think of in your universe. Then you sit back and see what happens."

"What kind of seeds?" Suzie asked.

"For example, you pick five types of suns. Then you pick five types of planets. Then you pick five types of orbits. You keep adding more variables, like atmospheric composition, the number of moons, and so on. Once you have your variables, then you create one system for each possible combination."

"But that could mean thousands of worlds," Suzie said, as she considered the permutations.

"Yep. You have to plant a lot of seeds in a big field if you want a good crop. The purists would frown on it, Bernie, but you could even seed your worlds with a good dose of primordial soup. That would kick-start the slower ones. Then all you have to do is jump ahead three or four billion years and see what hatched. Make sure you have a good star chart, so you can keep track of which systems didn't take. Then, when you go back, you can try something different on your duds," Lenny said.

"How many of these worlds will generate higher life forms?" Bernie asked.

"It all depends on your variables. Some are more likely than others. If you throw in some soup, my guess is you could get thirty to forty percent. Out of that group, you should get something you like."

"Hmm... So with 1,000 systems, I might get 300 to 400 worlds with higher life forms. That sounds pretty good. What do you do next?" Bernie asked, warming to the idea. His shimmer confirmed his excitement by adding two new colors to its display.

"I'd pick the 5-10 most interesting, blink out the rest, and then—"

"What?" Bernie interrupted. "Why would you destroy the rest of them?"

"Well, you don't want one of these other systems contaminating your chosen systems. What if somebody develops space travel and starts messing with your good systems? Or what if some of them start evolving into spiritual beings? A lot of those spiritual types end up as missionaries, trying to turn everyone in their neighborhood into spiritual beings too. It's hard enough to make life forms take the path you want without a bunch of meddlers trying to send your people someplace else. It's better to eliminate the competition."

"I don't think I can do that," Bernie said as his shimmer lost the two new colors and a third one as well.

Candi Comes Calling

Bernie was the first to see her as she approached their table in the cafeteria. Her long light-brown hair, mixed with her golden shimmer, made her look like a slow motion comet heading straight toward him. Her shapely legs, the slow sway of her hips and arms as she moved were as hypnotic any cobra that ever existed. Whatever thoughts Bernie might have had turned into perspiration and were lost for all time.

Still, she had not yet revealed her super power. That came when she looked into Bernie's eyes. Her gaze stabbed deep, and he found himself in a dream sequence, aware of oncoming danger, but powerless to move out of its path. Having pinned her victim, she readied her final strike—the lethal smile. It began with her lips, but soon joined forces with her eyes until the look and the smile fused into a laser beam so powerful it vaporized any male thought within a fifty-foot radius. It apparently also worked on clouds.

And so it was to a blank-eyed, slack-jawed, empty-headed Bernie that she said, "Hi, Bernie. My name is Candi. May I join you?"

It appeared Bernie was at least three to four minutes away from coherent words, let alone complete sentences, so it was probably a good thing Lenny spoke first. "Don't trust her, Bernie! She's one of Billy's henchmen!"

The stunning goddess slowly turned in Lenny's direction, taking her super-weapon with her. Those same eyes stabbed out, capturing Lenny as easily as she had captured Bernie moments earlier. And, totally unnecessarily, she threw in the smile for good measure. She bent close to him and twirled her finger in what Lenny's friends generously call his beard. "Now, Lenny," she said, batting her long eyelashes. "Do I look like a hench-*man* to you?"

Lenny's eyes darted back and forth, searching desperately for some means of escape, but the only thing that escaped was an unintelligible gurgle. Later, Lenny would refer to this as a lost-time episode.

"Y-y-yes," Bernie said as he fought to regain control.

Candi turned back to Bernie with some confusion on her face. "You think so? That wasn't the effect I was going for at all."

Candi noticed Bernie's hand extended in the direction of an empty seat at the table. "Oh," she said realizing that Bernie was responding to earlier request. "Thank you," she said as she put her tray down.

Suzie, who hadn't uttered a word, was saying plenty with her shimmer. And it was definitely not in the PG range. With eyes narrowed, jaws tightened and shimmer flickering, she hissed, "Why are you here?"

"That's pretty direct." Candi looked hurt.

"You must admit, Bernie hasn't been welcomed with open arms in your division," Suzie spat.

"I know, and I feel badly about it. And I'm not the only one who feels that way."

"Why would you care?" Suzie asked, still suspicious.

"We know what's been happening to Bernie." Candi's voice softened to a near whisper. "Billy told us what he's been doing. He's not going to stop until Bernie gets fired. There's nothing we can do about it, but we had to tell you we don't like what's happening," she said turning her gaze back to Bernie, this time careful to hold down the intensity.

"But why? Why's he doing this?" Bernie sputtered. At a table somewhere behind Bernie, someone cried out as their glass of orange juice turned itself upside down.

"I don't think he'll ever forgive you for the scar you gave him. I've never seen him so determined to get someone fired before," Candi said.

Bernie felt again the guilt that came whenever he was reminded of the fight. Although he rationalized the incident, there was nothing that could justify the price Billy paid for his near-death experience and the scar that would always remind him of it. No matter how many years passed, Bernie would regret that day.

Candi broke Bernie's reverie when she whispered, "Did you have anything to do with Billy being sick?"

"He's been sick? I thought he was just taking time off."

Lenny perked up and said, "You don't suppose he's sick because—

"Ow!" Lenny rubbed his leg where Suzie had kicked it. "Why do you keep doing that?" he grumbled at Suzie, who made it obvious she had no intention of answering the question.

"If there's anything I can do to help, I will," Candi said to Bernie.

"You and your friends could report what Billy's doing," Suzie said.

Candi shook her head. "That would make things worse. Billy would get a reprimand for foolish pranks, but the rest of us would be systematically harassed and fired. Shemal likes Billy, and anyone who makes trouble for his nephew will end up dealing with Shemal. If I learn something that can help, I'll try to get a message to you. I can't promise more than that."

"Thank you," Bernie said.

Suzie was still withholding judgment. Lenny, on the other hand, was busy formulating a question. Finally, he said, "How do you know our names?"

"We all know Bernie's name. Suzie's name wasn't hard to find because we know she works in Personnel. Your name, Lenny, took some detective work. But one day, I just got determined, and I asked around until I found out."

"What day was that, exactly?" Lenny inquired.

Candi gave Lenny a quizzical look and said, "It was last Thursday."

"Do you remember what time, exactly?"

"Lenny," said Bernie and Suzie at the same time.

"This is important," Lenny pleaded.

"Well I guess it was when I saw you at lunch that day. Yes, that was when I decided to find out your name," Candi said.

"Excellent," said Lenny, as he began paging through his notebook looking for last Thursday. "It must have been the star-crossed tawalla seeds," he announced with a happy smile.

"They always worked pretty well for me," Candi said slowly as she looked again at Lenny, as if for the first time.

Lenny and Candi stared at each other for so long, it became uncomfortable for Bernie and Suzie. Finally, Lenny said, "We should talk."

"I couldn't agree more," Candi said as she picked up her tray.

Lenny picked up his tray and followed her to an empty table.

"It looks like Lenny's charms are finally working," Bernie said with a smile.

"Or else hers are," Suzie observed with considerably less optimism.

Burn, Baby, Burn!

The first thing Billy noticed after his return was Bernie had begun staying behind as the others left for the day. He pretended to be working, but he was just making sure Billy left before he did. That didn't mean Billy couldn't come back later, of course, and that was exactly what he did.

When he got his first look at Bernie's world, he couldn't help but smile at the big trench that circled the globe just above the coast of the main continent. *Bernie must have done that to stop the tsunami. It must have worked; because I don't see any evidence the water reached the continent.*

Surprisingly, Billy wasn't disappointed. He liked seeing the gashes and gouges on Bernie's planet. It showed Bernie was sloppy and careless, which he knew were two things Uncle Shemal would never tolerate.

Although Billy would never admit it, he was nervous. Spending the last week in bed made it clear the stakes in this game were higher than anything he and Bernie had back in school. He was convinced Bernie had done something to prevent him from using his time lever. Who knew what other tricks Bernie may have set up? He would have to be careful.

Very careful.

~

It had taken time for his plan to mature. For several days now, Billy had returned to the office late at night. Each time, he removed all the moisture in the atmosphere above Bernie's world. That was why it hadn't rained for days. That was also why the forests were so very, very dry.

Tonight, the young god was ready for something different. Tonight, he was ready to make the cloud. He could have made it easily by creating a volcano, but he wanted no trace of his handiwork. He began by warming the air above the surface of the planet. At the same time, he created a thick layer of moisture high in the sky. As the hot air rose, it mingled with the moist air. He smiled as it swirled and thrashed as competing forces fought with each other.

Billy made more adjustments, each time adding to the powerful forces of his new creation. Soaring thousands of feet above the ground was the largest pyrocumulonimbus cloud that had ever formed on the planet. Billy tweaked the churning cloud to keep it from touching the ground, and once more to keep it from releasing the moisture from which it drew its energy. He wanted none of its strength lost through rainfall.

As the cloud's power grew, lightning and thunder lashed out in all directions. Billy forced that destructive energy back inside. The cloud turned inward, feeding on itself until its fury nearly matched the anger of the god who had created it. Then it was ready. And Billy released it onto the world.

Lightning tore from the angry cloud downward, seeking the tallest of trees in the forest below. When it struck, it was not a smoldering branch that it left behind. Instead, an entire tree was engulfed in flames. And those flames reached out hungrily for nearby trees.

That was exactly what Billy wanted. So he made more. When he finished, seventeen fire clouds raged above the long continent. Before Billy withdrew, each cloud had proven its ability to bring fire to the world below.

And they were just getting started.

Candi and Lenny

Candi looked forward to lunch. She was eager to show Lenny her new talisman. For days now, they'd been sharing their greatest discoveries. She never dreamed of discussing this with anyone. First of all, gods didn't talk about lucky charms, and, even if they did, no one would ever admit to believing in them. Second, she'd put much effort into finding charms that worked. Why would she ever tell someone else? Let them figure it out for themselves.

But Lenny was different.

That's funny, she thought. *Calling Lenny 'different' is the biggest understatement of the year. Lenny is the most fascinating god I've ever met. One thing for sure, though, a charm-based relationship is an interesting dilemma. We'll have to talk about it someday.*

As she set her lunch tray down, she carefully positioned herself so Lenny would view her from a westerly angle. She also gave her bracelet a quick glance to make sure her bonny charm was properly displayed. She smiled. She was ready.

Lenny sat down moments later. He was smiling too.

"Wow! That one packs a punch. I want to jump over the table and ravish you. Is it the barrette?"

"No. It's the bonny charm here on my bracelet." She pointed to the cause of his intensified infatuation.

"Is there anything you can do to control the intensity? We could get written up for unprofessional behavior in a public area," he said with a rakish gleam in his eye.

"Oh, I suppose I can tone it down for you, Lenny. I wouldn't want you to forget to eat," she teased.

Lenny looked different today. He had gone from ectomorph to mesomorph overnight. His normally thin body showed strong, well-defined muscles. Even his shirt seemed stretched tight over his chest.

"That's very impressive. It looks like you're about to burst through your shirt."

"I'm glad you like it," said Lenny. "It's a pocket charm. Works from every direction too. It works on 60 percent of females," he said as he took out a small green walnut with a yellow feather hanging from it.

"I'm hearing a strange sound again. Is that coming from you?" Candi asked.

"Oh, that's Sissy. I don't know what's wrong with her lately. When she gets upset she makes a clucking sound. It usually means she's warning me about something, but lately, she's been doing it all the time. None of my other prognostication charms are sensing any danger, so I've been ignoring her. She usually stops after a few days."

Candi bent forward and looked closely at the small fur lump with the golden chain on Lenny's shoulder.

"Hello, Sissy. How are you? Are you taking good care of Lenny?" Sissy's clucking continued. Candi moved her finger closer to Sissy, only to find Sissy backing away and the clucking sound becoming louder.

"Don't take it personally," said Lenny. "She doesn't like females. The only women I've ever seen her friendly with are my mom and Suzie."

"Well, I'm sure someday we're going to be great friends," Candi said to Sissy, but the sounds coming from the little creature didn't suggest any imminent Kumbaya moments.

They ate in silence for a few minutes. There was a big question on both their minds. Neither of them wanted to talk about it. But silence has a funny way of bringing up things that are otherwise content to remain hidden. Finally, it was Candi who broke the code of silence.

"Have you ever wondered what I'm really like?" she asked. She'd used charms for so long, she wondered if even she knew the answer to that question.

"Ah… Yes," said Lenny, knowing where this conversation was leading, and doubly afraid because of it.

"We both know we're not the people we appear to be," Candi said as she stroked Lenny's well-muscled arm. "But when I look at you, I can't tell the difference. I know tomorrow you may or may not have muscles or you may be taller or shorter than you are now. Or you may have a hypnotic gaze or a way with words you don't have today. I know it isn't real. What I don't know is whether it should matter." She looked questioningly at Lenny.

Lenny looked back, reached deep inside, and pulled up his own confession. "I'm afraid I'm manipulating you. I know you wouldn't like me if it weren't for my charms. And I'm using them to make you see someone else. It's just an illusion. Whenever I do something that makes you happy, I feel like I've tricked you, and it's all going to unravel. And when you see the real me, you'll be disappointed and angry."

"I have the same fear, Lenny. If you knew the real me, you wouldn't want me either."

"That's crazy! I like everything about you. You're smart and beautiful and fun and lots more besides."

"But, Lenny. I have a charm for every one of those. What if you saw me without any of them? What would you think then?"

As they thought their own thoughts, the only sound heard above the silence was a soft clucking.

It was Candi who moved them both forward. "If we left our charms behind, and we got to know each other, I'm not sure what that accomplishes."

Lenny looked at her and cocked his head in a quizzical way.

"Our charms are part of who we are. They make us unique. I'm not sure what purpose would be served trying to figure out what we're like without them. I don't intend to give mine up, do you?"

"No."

"Then we're charm-people, Lenny. One package. You have to take me as I am, charms and all."

"You don't feel like I'm manipulating you when I make you think and feel things you shouldn't?"

"Not at all. Do you feel like I am manipulating you?" Candi asked back.

"No," said Lenny. Then he added, "But, I think you could if you wanted to."

"That has nothing to do with my charms, Lenny. That has to do with being a girl." She batted her eyelashes at him. To demonstrate her point, she caught the eye of an unsuspecting young god walking by. She turned the full intensity of her smile on him. Her victim, unable to break his gaze, stumbled into a chair, returning him to reality just in time to avoid dropping his tray. Candi hid her giggle.

Then she turned back to Lenny and patted his arm as she said, "Don't worry, Lenny. Where you're concerned, I promise to use my powers only for good."

A World Ablaze

"Where?" Gondal asked, trying to keep his voice even.

"Everywhere," exclaimed Minister Wadov. "Come see for yourself." He led the leader of the Senate to the nearest window.

The tall billowing clouds had not been there the day before. Although they looked like large thunderclouds, in these times, it was hard to trust anything to be normal. Lightning flashed across the sky, illuminating nearby clouds, followed by the rumbling sound of thunder in hot pursuit. No rain fell. From the giant cloud high above, the sky lit up as a bolt of lightning emerged and struck a group of trees less than a mile away. Moments later, they felt the boom of its thunder.

"Did you see where the lightning hit? Do you see the flames? The tree is burning. Now, look over there," said Wadov, pointing to the southeast. "Do you see the column of dark smoke? The lightning struck the forest near Lantor an hour ago, and now it burns. Look there and over there. There are at least four more fires."

"How widespread is this storm?"

"When we noticed the clouds forming, we asked for reports from nearby cities. They all reported the same cloud formations and the freakish lightning. We have to assume it's widespread."

"What do you recommend?"

"I don't think we can hope for rain to put out the fires. These clouds don't seem to have any. We have to tell people to flee. I think they should head in the direction of any large body of water or toward the coasts."

"I agree," said Gondal. "Get the word out quickly. We must save as many as we can."

~

The savage clouds hovered everywhere. Every time the lightning touched the land, it found things to burn, and the sky grew darker with the smoke of burning forests. The town of Fonnzet, located in the foothills of the Central Mountains, was the hardest hit. Residents saw the forest burning below them, and though they tried to escape, the fire consumed the town and pursued the survivors up the mountainside. The lucky ones died from the smoke. The dead totaled 2,362 people, including fourteen children.

Fires hit eight other towns. In some, the people saw the fire coming and were able to flee. The fires left only the stone buildings, destroying anything made of wood. In these towns, the devastation was beyond imagining. The death count was estimated at 6,740 people. Although the count was not complete, at least thirty-four children were known to have died. And two lords perished in the flames.

Only one town escaped the fate of the others. The town of Sadoban found itself surrounded by two fires. They were forced into the center of town, where the Temple stood. In His infinite mercy, the Sun protected them in the stone Temple where they sought shelter.

Yet, it could have been much worse. The Sun surely watched in great dismay as His land and His people burned. Hundreds of fires raged all over the continent. Then, by some miracle, one by one, the fires flickered and died. Fire after fire was extinguished by some unseen hand.

Gradually, the lightning and the crashing thunder began to fade. Slowly, the blue sky appeared again. For several days, a haze in the sky remained to remind everyone of what had happened. Then, even that disappeared.

It was a very angry god that saved these people. The god wasn't angry at them. He didn't even know about them. He was angry at another god.

A god named Billy.

Billy Scares Candi

It started as a beautiful morning. It didn't last. As Candi headed down the corridor to her desk in Final Assembly Division, Billy came up next to her.

"Candi, we need to talk."

"Sure. What about?" Candi asked, pretending a calmness she did not feel. She'd been spending lunch periods with Lenny instead of sitting at Billy's table. She knew Billy would not ignore it for long.

"We'll talk at lunch."

By lunchtime, Candi was nervous. There wasn't much she could do except listen to whatever Billy said and try to respond as best she could. She had long ago given up trying to find a charm that worked on him. He remained closed and controlled. People like him were always hard to influence.

Candi saw Lenny enter the cafeteria and waved him off. She sat down with Billy, who had chosen an empty table and was waiting for her. She waited for him to speak. Billy looked at her and shook his head as one would with a misbehaving child in need of a gentle scolding.

"Candi, I'm disappointed in you."

"Why?"

"I've told you Bernie is a short-timer here. People like him are social misfits. They have a kind of disease, Candi, and if you aren't careful, you can catch it from them."

Candi stiffened. She had talked to Bernie only once. Had someone told Billy? She had to be very careful now.

Billy continued, "You must know Lenny and Bernie are friends. It doesn't reflect well on you, to be seen with one of Bernie's known associates. After all, since Bernie is a misfit, it follows that Lenny and Suzie are also misfits. Hanging out with either of them raises doubts about you. Doesn't that make sense?" he asked in a mock-fatherly way.

"I don't know about Bernie and Suzie, but I like Lenny. He's interesting, and we've become friends."

"Ah, Candi, Candi, Candi… Maybe I need to explain this differently," Billy continued. "Think of this as a battle between our side and their side. Bernie doesn't have a lot of people on his side. At most, just Suzie and Lenny. Our side has an army, including you and me and Uncle Shemal. Very soon, our side will deal a deathblow to their side, and Bernie will not survive. Other people on their side may also get hurt. When that happens, you don't want to be standing close to any of them. Does that make it easier to understand, Candi?"

"Yes," Candi said, feeling trapped.

"Oh, and one more thing…" Billy's eyes hardened to a piercing stare.

"What?" Candi's heart pounded in her chest.

"You never want me to wonder whose side you're really on," Billy said, his voice dripping with menace. "I'm pretty sure you wouldn't survive that."

Bloody Moon

Billy saw a continent with thousands of acres of scorched earth. The fire clouds had done a great job. They started fires everywhere. *Bernie must have stopped them though, or they would have destroyed everything.* Billy smiled as he examined his work. The whole planet looked bad. *Too bad they don't have a Universe Award for Most Incompetent Builder, Bernie. You'd win it hands down.*

As Billy looked at the other two planets, he didn't see much he could do. They were just prefabs. Bernic hadn't done anything with them. The pretty yellow moon, on the other hand, begged to be the next target. Bernie must have changed the color for a reason.

In Billy's visualization, he pictured the surface of the moon, but in his picture, it was not a soft yellow, but a bloody red. And as he concentrated, it became as he wished. Billy smiled at the discolored moon.

Stay tuned, Bernie, he thought. *You ain't seen nuthin' yet.*

Wake Up!

"Wake up, Speaker! You must see this!"

Zardok, speaker for the Sun and high priest of the Temple, had been roused from a deep sleep. When he recognized Lord Winson, he grumbled, "Why have you awakened me?"

"Please, Lord, come to the window quickly. You must see it with your own eyes," Winson urged the groggy Zardok.

As Zardok made his way to the window, he prayed it was not another fire. Even before he got there, he could tell something was wrong. The night looked different. It was not dark, as it had been before the night sun arrived, but also not light, the way it should have been this evening. The night sun should have been at full strength, making it easy to see. Yet the outside was barely visible.

"Oh, my Sun," said Zardok as he saw the blood-red color of the night sun. "When did this happen?" he demanded of Winson.

"Just moments ago. The night sun was bright and yellow and almost full, just as we predicted. But then it started changing. It got darker and darker until it became this color. What should we do?"

"Call the Council together. Do it now! Tell them to meet in my conference room. We must have answers before tomorrow. The Senate has been listening to other voices of late because they offer quicker answers. We must not let this happen again," Zardok said as he rushed to his wardrobe closet to dress.

~

"Wake up, my Lord! Something awful is happening," his aide said.

Leader Gondal, normally a deep sleeper, had not had a good night's sleep in a long time. Thousands of people had died, and he slept with the guilt of his failure to prevent it.

"What is it?" Gondal asked as the knot in his stomach

tightened.

"The night sun—it's covered in blood," Tuderon exclaimed.

Gondal rushed to the window. Just as Tuderon said, the night sun stared down from the sky, tainting everything a dark, bloody red. This was not good. What did it portend? At a minimum, it would terrify the people. There were many already who distrusted the night sun. He needed to get ahead of this before the rumors started.

"Quickly, Tuderon. Fetch Lord Alcandor at once. Tell him I have urgent need of his council. I will await him in my office," Gondal said as he put his hand on Tuderon's shoulder, urging him along all the faster.

He's a Wimp

Suzie sat alone at their usual table in the cafeteria.

"Where's Bernie?" Lenny asked as he took a seat.

"I don't know. I didn't see him yesterday either," Suzie added with concern.

"He's probably just working on his universe. Nothing to be worried about. When you're in there, it's easy to lose track of time."

"I haven't seen much of you lately."

"Candi and I've been spending time together. At least we were. Lately, the whole world is conspiring against us."

"What's been happening?"

"At first it was little things, like messages not getting delivered, and then it became things that forced us to cancel our plans. Then my boss changed my schedule, which made it harder to get together after work. Then, to top it off, Billy gave Candi a hard time about hanging out with me. He says she should know better than to be seen with any of Bernie's 'known associates.' Candi suggested we cool it for a few days. I can't believe these things keep happening."

Suzie wasn't really listening. She had something on her mind. This was as good a time as any to say it. "Lenny, I have to say something. I'm worried about Candi. I'm afraid you will tell her things that could get back to Billy. Something Billy might use against Bernie."

"Don't worry about that. I'm pretty sure my charms are stronger than her charms," he said as he patted his pocket. "I'm the one in control of the relationship."

Suzie politely stifled a laugh. *Oh, Lenny*, she thought, *you're as girl-savvy as Bernie. Both of you spent your lives studying building science. The only thing you know about girls is what you read in a book. You're as vulnerable as you are clueless.*

"And do you agree with that, Sissy?" she asked as she stroked Sissy's fur.

Sissy's response was not the purring she expected. Instead,

Sissy made a clucking sound. "What does that mean?" Suzie asked, somewhat concerned.

"I don't know. She does that when she's upset about something."

As they ate their lunch, Lenny's thoughts drifted to important things, like figuring out how to see Candi again. When Lenny got like that, he didn't notice anyone else.

Sissy waved her antenna in Suzie's direction.

"I'll bet Lenny hasn't been listening to you either, has he? All he wants to think about is Candi," Suzie cooed as she stroked her little friend.

More clucking sounds came from Sissy.

"Are you worried about Candi and Lenny?" Suzie asked.

More clucking sounds.

"Maybe it would be better if Lenny and Candi didn't see so much of each other."

This time a purring sound came from Sissy.

"Lenny, I don't think Sissy likes your girlfriend."

Lenny looked up from his plate of macaroni. "She gets like that sometimes. Just ignore her, and she'll be fine in a few days," he said, which solicited a new round of clucking.

Suzie looked at her little friend. *Is there something you are trying to tell us, Sissy?*

Before she could say anything, Lenny interrupted, "I have a question for you."

"Are you going to ask me what I think of you today?" Suzie asked politely, although on the inside she was shaking her head.

"No. I want to ask you about Bernie. I really like the guy, but I don't understand why he's such a wimp."

"A wimp?"

"You know. He's always afraid of hurting things. When he came over to my place, he didn't even want to see my best universe because it was too violent. How did he ever make it through school like that?"

"I know he had problems in some classes because he didn't like to blink things out. They were going to kick him out of the program, but his mom got them to change their minds. After that, he studied extra hard so he would pass even if he flunked an occasional lab assignment for not destroying the life forms."

"How could he get through school if he wouldn't blink anything? It's an essential builder skill."

"He can blink most things. It's the higher life forms he has trouble with."

Suzie remembered a conversation with Bernie when they were in middle school. "Is there a rule against talking with higher life forms on your planets?"

"Yes, there's a school rule about it. It's a pretty strict rule, actually. They can kick you out of the building program if they catch you doing it."

"Bernie told me about it once. He couldn't figure out why they were so adamant. I said they probably didn't want you getting attached to your life forms."

"That's exactly the reason," said Lenny. "Why did he have a problem with it?"

"He said it didn't make sense. The teachers told the kids not to think of their life forms as real. They said created life doesn't have feelings or souls, like we do. The rule was there to encourage a certain detachment from them."

"That's true."

"Bernie said a punishment as severe as being expelled from the building school didn't make sense. He said the rule was there to scare you. He was convinced they were hiding something."

"What did he think they were hiding?"

"He thought maybe life forms really do have feelings and maybe even souls," said Suzie.

"No way. You have to think of the stuff we make as toys. We make them one way, and if we don't like it, we take them apart and make them a different way. And if we don't like that, we just blink them away and start over."

"What about feelings and souls? Do they have them?"

"Absolutely not," Lenny said.

"Not even feelings?"

"Nope."

"What about Sissy here? She comes from a created world, right? Are you saying she doesn't have feelings?"

"She doesn't have feelings. You have to have a soul to have feelings," Lenny declared. "Everything you see in a creation like Sissy is an instinct or a learned response that mimics emotions.

They don't feel a thing."

Sissy responded with even louder clucking sounds.

"I don't know, Lenny. It sounds like Sissy's upset with what you said."

"Nope. It's not possible. She has intelligence, but definitely no feelings. I can show you the books to prove it."

Suzie reached over to stroke Sissy. "What do you think, Sissy? Do you have feelings?" Sissy's clucking changed to purring.

"I don't think we agree with you or your books, Lenny."

"It's called anthropomorphism. Untrained people like you make that mistake all the time. You're projecting your own feelings onto something that doesn't have any. Builders are highly trained to avoid that mistake," said Lenny with finality.

Sissy clucked. Suzie shook her head.

"I think Sissy and I agree with Bernie," she said.

We Must Explain

The inner circle of priests and priestesses had assembled with great haste. No one dared to keep Speaker Zardok waiting. Especially not lately.

"Members of the Inner Council, these are evil times," Zardok began as he called the meeting to order. "Evil is everywhere. It has killed our people, destroyed our cities, burned our forests, and now it corrupts our night sun. This evil must be fought. As long as it remains unchallenged, our people pay for it with their lives. We cannot allow this foul power to continue its advance against us or against the people we serve in the name of the Sun.

"This evil has spawned another evil, and we must be equally vigilant against it. It is an evil from within. Everyone suffers from confusion and doubt, but some have chosen not to cast these demons out. Instead, they embrace them. Some defectors have claimed our temples and begun teaching distorted versions of the truth.

"We may be powerless to stop them, but we must not allow this to happen again. If the Temple and the people we serve are to survive, we must preserve our resources and strength. We cannot allow things to be taken by defectors and splinter groups who think they have found answers when we cannot.

"I submit these groups formed because we were slow in giving direction and interpretations to our people, and without answers, they fell victim to false beliefs. Henceforth, we must respond more quickly, so people see us leading in the battle against evil. Can I assume this is clear to everyone?"

No one challenged his statement.

"Then let us discover answers in the matter of the night sun," said Zardok. "Who wishes to begin?"

Lord Noseter was the first to stand. "I think we can make some suppositions. The bloody color of the night sun tells us it has been grievously hurt. This much is obvious. Also, we can see, in spite of its hurt, it still shines. From this, we have proof it yet lives. The unresolved question is whether it has been struck a mortal blow or whether the night sun can recover. If it's possible for the night sun to recover, we must consider any actions we can take to aid its recovery."

As Lord Noseter took his seat, the Lady Eonis stood. "I see this differently, Lord Noseter. It is not blood I see on the face of the night sun. It is anger that we see. We have done something to displease Him. If you need further proof, consider the light He bestows on us. It has been muted. In His anger, He denies us the full gift of His light."

The next to stand was the Priestess Ximow, long noted for her wisdom and her ability to see clearly. Ximow said, "Honorable members of the Council, I believe we're approaching this question in the wrong way. Consider: we've already determined the night sun is a gift from the Sun. It is a thing created by our Sun and nothing more. If it appears different to us, we should not ask 'What is wrong with it?' We should ask instead 'What is the Sun trying to tell us?' I believe the Sun has a message for us, and He's using the night sun to deliver it. Our task is to understand the message."

Zardok scanned the room. Ximow's words had resonated with the Council. "Let us consider Ximow's argument further. Ximow, please continue."

"Yes, Speaker. Please consider the night sun for a moment. It's a source of light that chases away the darkness. This alone makes it a wondrous gift. But I believe it's more. I believe the night sun is a tapestry upon which the Sun paints his messages.

"We've already seen one message. Tonight's message is the second. The first message was delivered as we watched the night sun being consumed night after night until it wasted away to nothing. There have been many interpretations, but I submit the Sun is showing us the future. I believe He's telling us His light will soon be extinguished. I believe He's using the night sun to show us—"

The Council was not ready to hear these words. Protests broke out from all quarters. Zardok sat stunned. Finally, he said, "No. I reject this idea. The Sun is immortal. Nothing can harm Him."

"Speaker, if you order it, I will say no more. But I pray you let me continue. If, Sun forbid, I'm correct, the Sun may not survive without our help."

In ordinary times, Zardok would have wasted no more time on Ximow's preposterous idea. But these were not ordinary times. It was hard to deny the parallel between the Sun that lights the day and the new night sun that lights the night. Perhaps the Sun did create the night sun to deliver its messages. It arrived before any of the disasters. *Perhaps the Sun has been trying to warn us*, he thought, *and we failed to listen.*

Zardok had no choice. He held up his hand to silence the others. "I feel a fool for listening to these ideas, Ximow, but I concede if there is even the smallest chance you are right, we must consider your thoughts."

"Speaker, I assure you I take no pleasure in putting these ideas forth," Ximow said.

"Continue." Zardok steeled himself for her unwelcome ideas.

"As I said, the first message was to tell us the Sun may be consumed. I believe these disasters have led to a weakening of the Sun. I believe the red color is His way of telling us He fears grievous injury."

"Why is the injury something that has not yet happened?" asked Zardok. "You theorize our Sun can be harmed. If this is true, then surely He has been harmed already by one or more of the tragedies we've already suffered."

"I believe the messages speak of things yet to come. Consider the first message. We saw it portrayed on the face of the night sun before the disasters began. So too, I believe the blood tells us of something yet to be."

"Do you have any further interpretation for us?"

"Just one more thought, Speaker. I ask this question: Why would the Sun tell us of things yet to be? He must believe telling us can make a difference, that we can help in some way. But I have no idea what that could be," said Ximow, her voice trailing off at the end.

"Ximow, I thank you for your thoughts. You were right to speak them," said Zardok.

He turned to the full Council and said, "I caution everyone to keep these words inside this room. If the people heard them, nothing good could come of it.

"So where do we go from here? I remind you, we must have answers before dawn," said Zardok.

"Speaker, I counsel caution," said Lord Spekon. "There are no answers we can provide by dawn that will satisfy the people. Already, they whisper about why the Sun has not staved off these disasters. If we tell them our Sun is in mortal fear for His life, there will be panic everywhere."

The Lady Eonis stood and said, "You are right, Lord Spekon. May I suggest we tell the people something easier to accept? Let us tell them the red night sun is a sign our Sun has begun fighting the evil forces. Tell them it's His promise that He will keep us safe as He always has. This will give the people reason to hope. It will also give us time to find answers."

"I do not like deceit, Lady," Zardok said with a frown. "But I fear what would happen if the people lost hope."

Zardok sat in silence as he considered. Finally he turned to Lady Eonis and said, "We will tell the people your story, Lady, though I do not like it. We will do it because we must not let the people lose faith in the Sun. Meanwhile, this Council will unravel the mystery of what the Sun is really trying to tell us.

"If He needs our help, we must not fail Him."

Getting Discouraged

Journal Entry

It's Billy's first day back from vacation, and he's already back at it. This time, he turned Suzie's moon red. I can't find anything else he did. I changed it back to yellow.

I can't think of a way to stop him. There has to be something. Suzie believes confronting him will make him more destructive. She's usually right about that stuff. That leaves me with only defensive strategies, which is almost impossible. Building is complex. The more advanced I make my world, the more ways there are for Billy to destroy it—my job gets harder while his gets easier.

It's been days since I've done any real building. I can't concentrate. Every time I think of something, I think of how easily Billy can wreck it. How in the world can I stop someone who is as powerful as I am?

Honestly, I'm discouraged. I'm afraid I'm going to get fired. Nothing I've done is going to impress Shemal. Why should it? My universe wouldn't get a passing grade back in school. I can't let it end like this. There's got to be something I can do.

You know what bugs me the most? It'll break Mom's heart. She's sacrificed everything for me. If I fail, what's it all been worth?

Maybe Isaiah will give me a job at the bookstore.

A Little Breeze

The time lever jammer had been hard on Billy. It had taken days to get his strength back. However, as his strength returned, so too did his anger. And with new anger came new ideas.

He routinely visited the Lab-1 and Lab-2 continents to see if Bernie had been working on anything new, but all he ever found were the plants. So he contented himself with tormenting every green thing he could find.

Bernie's lack of creativity when he chose a simple model for his world made it harder. If his land mass was more spread out, instead of being a flat little sausage around the equator, Billy could have used it to generate some wicked water and wind currents. But Bernie didn't want those variables in his world. It meant a little more work for Billy, but he didn't really mind.

High above the atmosphere, Billy pushed and pulled the air below him. Even Billy was affected by the beauty of the swirls and twists of the air as it churned below. He was the conductor of an orchestra, gesturing with his arms, warming it here, chilling it there, as he performed his tasks. His arms were not needed for this work—everything he did, was with the power of his mind. But it was simple work, and he enjoyed the feeling of potency as the whirling clouds seemed to obey his hands.

He grabbed and twisted the storm in an ever-faster counterclockwise direction as he prepared it for the northern coast. Above the swirling center of his storm, he chilled the air above. With downward motions of his hands, as if directing the brass section of an orchestra, he sent cold air down the funnel of his storm toward the ocean below. When it arrived, he did not wait for the warm ocean to heat the cold air. Instead, he turned his palms upward and, with swift jerking motions directed at the trumpet section of his mind, he heated the air himself. It was short work to produce this monster storm. It was even shorter work to nudge it toward the waiting coast.

The conductor god continued his symphony through three more movements, changing the tempo of each movement as he created the next storm. Each one was a masterpiece of destruction. By the time Billy reached the finale, he was exhilarated by what he had done.

Each of the four great storms would gather ever more strength as they spiraled toward landfall. His only regret was not being able to use his time lever to observe the damage.

He would have to leave that fun for Bernie.

Oh, Do Tell...

Suzie was only half listening as Bernie and Lenny talked about design strategies for Bernie's universe. She liked to make suggestions when she could, but it was hard when you only understood one of every three words. It was a welcome distraction to see Sissy's antenna waving at her.

"Well, hello, Sissy. How have you been?"

The small lump of fur made a clucking sound.

"Are you still upset, Sissy? Do you want to tell me what's wrong? I'll listen to you." She cooed as the little piece of fur crept closer to her. Sissy dropped the little chain that kept her attached to Lenny and arched her head and wiggled her antenna.

Suzie held out her finger as Sissy crawled on. "You want to come talk to me, Sissy? I'll be happy to talk to you. The boys don't even know we're here right now, do they? We might as well have a little girl time," she cooed.

Suzie heard the clucking sound change to purring as Sissy crawled onto her hand. Suzie smiled. "Yes, Sissy. I like you too. We'll have a nice little talk while the boys talk about boring stuff, okay? You know, I think you're getting cuter every day, Sissy. Did you know that? Yes, I think you are," Suzie declared as the purring continued.

"Do you want anything to eat? Last time, you liked the vegetables a lot. Do you want some today?" Suzie was surprised as she heard Sissy's purring change to a popping sound. She reached over for her salad and offered it to Sissy, who continued to make a soft popping sound. Sissy made no movement toward the food.

"Okay. It looks like you aren't hungry. What do you want to talk about? Can you make other sounds? I know you can purr and Lenny said you make the clucking sound when you're upset. And now you made a little popping sound. Can you make other sounds?"

Sissy responded with a very soft, hard to hear, "*Ye-ye-ye.*"

Suzie's eyes widened. "Are you trying to talk with me,

Sissy?"

"*Ye-ye-ye.*"

"Does that mean yes?"

"*Ye-ye-ye.*"

"Does that mean no?" Suzie asked, expecting to hear the *ye-ye-ye* again.

"*Pop-pop-pop,*" said Sissy very softly.

"Oh, my. Can you understand me, Sissy?" asked an astonished Suzie as she raised Sissy closer to get a better look at her.

"*Ye-ye-ye.*"

"Lenny, can Sissy talk?" Suzie asked. She had to ask again before she was able to break into the intense conversation going on. *Apparently, when someone is discussing geothermal design, it makes them partially deaf,* she thought.

Lenny rolled his eyes, clearly miffed at the interruption. "No. She makes different sounds, but they're random, except for the purring and clucking," he said as he turned back to Bernie.

"Is that right, Sissy?" Suzie asked.

"*Pop-pop-pop.*"

"You really do understand me, don't you?"

"*Ye-ye-ye.*"

"Can you tell me why you've been upset?"

"*Ye-ye-ye.*"

"Are you mad at Lenny?"

"*Ye-ye-ye.*"

"Is he hurting you?"

"*Pop-pop-pop.*"

"Do you like Lenny?"

"*Ye-ye-ye.*"

"Do you like Lenny a lot?"

"*Ye-ye-ye.*"

"Is it something Lenny is doing?"

"*Ye-ye-ye.*"

Suzie thought for a moment. She asked, "Are you upset about Candi?"

"*Ye-ye-ye.*"

"Is Candi doing something to harm Lenny?"

"*Pop-pop-pop.*"

"Is Candi doing something to harm Bernie?" Suzie asked suspiciously.

"*Pop-pop-pop.*"

Suzie looked at the tiny lump of fur on her hand. She recalled Lenny's frustration because plans to see Candi were running into problems. She also remembered Sissy's power to change, if ever so slightly, the probability of future events.

"Have you been trying to keep Lenny and Candi apart?" she asked in as even a tone as she could.

"*Ye-ye-ye.*"

"Sissy. Are you jealous?"

Silence. Then, "*Ye-ye-ye.*"

Suzie drew in a long slow breath as she looked at the tiny creature in her hand. "I have a very important question, Sissy. Are you sure Candi is no threat to any of us?"

"*Ye-ye-ye.*"

"Then, Sissy, I think I should tell Lenny about this. If he understands what's going on, maybe he can make it better. Is that okay?"

Silence. Then, "*Ye-ye-ye.*"

"Lenny, we have to tell you something," said Suzie. Although she tried to interrupt, it was clear the best theoretical model for conceptualizing particles as they fell into black holes was more important. She had to poke Lenny to get his attention.

"What?" he exclaimed, blinking as if suddenly discovering himself in a brightly lit room.

"Sissy can talk," said Suzie. She watched as Lenny began his eye-roll again. "No. Listen to me, Lenny. Sissy and I have been talking. She makes a '*ye-ye-ye*' sound for 'yes' and a '*pop-pop-pop*' sound for 'no.'"

"I told you she makes random sounds. They don't mean anything," Lenny insisted. It was clear he wanted to get back to black holes and string theory.

The problem with these guys, thought Suzie, *is sometimes you have to smack them really hard to get their attention.* So she said, "Sissy has been keeping you and Candi apart."

Suzie watched Lenny's expression go from impatient indulgence to full attentiveness in less than zero point four milliseconds. After all, Lenny already knew Sissy could affect his life.

"That's nuts. Why would she do that?" Lenny asked doubtfully.

"She's jealous of Candi."

"How can she be jealous? She doesn't have any feelings to be jealous with."

This produced an alternating string of clucking and popping sounds. Lenny stared at the little piece of fur as he held stubbornly to his position.

"Lenny, you have an open mind about so many other things," said Bernie. "Why can't you believe she has feelings?"

"If you want to see Candi again…" Suzie's voice trailed off. She knew she didn't have to finish the sentence.

"I… I need to think about this," Lenny said as Sissy crawled back on his finger.

And so he did. A lot.

Wicked Winds

Their world had no seasons. No extremes in temperature. No ocean currents flowing from the frigid north to the temperate zones. The ingredients needed to spawn hurricanes did not exist on their world. Only the power of a god could have created such terrible forces.

Now the wild winds released their fury against an unprepared world. Before this day, protection from the elements had been unnecessary. Buildings were designed with open courtyards because it was important to let the Sun shine in. In a world where property crimes were unknown, entrances seldom had doors. Walls were built with multiple windows for the sunlight and the gentle breezes. There were no fierce winds to shutter out or keep at bay.

Many buildings were built of stone. Those buildings survived. The wooden buildings did not fare well. Nor did the people who sought shelter in them. They were the first to die.

The people had no experience with such things. As the great storms approached, people thought they were thunderstorms. Getting wet was inconvenient, but nothing to be overly concerned about. And it was good for the plants.

By the time the first of the storms was upon them, the roaring winds, unlike anything known before, flattened people and buildings alike.

A mother, rushing across the street to reach her young daughter, watched in horror as her little girl was blown over by the wind. As she ran to rescue her child, she herself was hit by flying debris and died instantly.

A family, sheltering in their wooden home, was crushed when a nearby tree was uprooted and crashed through their roof.

And so it began.

No one had ever seen winds so fast or so strong.

Nor did the deaths come from wind alone. The winds brought high water levels and mass flooding to the lower elevations of the coast. Many people huddled in their dwellings as the flood waters rushed down the main streets of town. They drowned in their own homes.

~

Leader Gondal banged his gavel and called out, "The Senate will come to order."

Grim expressions were everywhere as the Senators took their seats in the crowded amphitheater. Perspiration still beaded the faces of some, due to the haste with which they'd traveled. They were desperate to learn anything the Senate had discovered about the wild winds that had ravaged the land.

"Thank you for coming on such short notice." Gondal, knowing the importance of setting appropriate expectations, said, "We have only one item on our agenda. Before we start, I will tell you now that we do not have many answers. Do not expect today's session to result in decisions and action. We will instead recount recent events so you understand what has happened. Minister Wadov will begin."

Wadov, seated behind the table on the raised dais, stood to address the crowd. "Thank you, Leader. I've tried to put these events in chronological order, but the breakdown in communication and the distances involved makes it difficult. I've done the best I can.

"The first sighting of the wind storms was made in Kazonit, located on the northeastern coast. Far out at sea, they saw a massive cloud front approaching. By the time it reached them, the sea had become extremely violent and huge waves crashed against the shore. The storm brought heavy, stinging rain driven by howling winds. The winds were so strong, they ripped up the wharves and blew them away. Several ships were capsized by the winds. The ocean itself rushed inland and flooded several streets. The southwestern section of town, which had many wooden structures, was demolished. Flying debris inflicted further damage, including damage to stone buildings around the town. There were fifty-three lives lost, including one child," said Wadov amidst a number of groans and laments.

"The storm continued inland to the town of Globet, fifty-five miles southeast of Kazonit. Reports from Globet indicate they suffered heavy winds and some damage, but no flooding, and nothing like the intensity experienced by Kazonit on the coast. Thank the Sun, no lives were lost there.

"Later the same day, the village of Maris on our southwestern coast was hit by a different storm. Their storm also came from the ocean, and they reported similar events. The town is smaller than Kazonit. There were thirty-one lives lost, including three children," said Wadov. This time the groans were even louder.

"Less than a day later, on the northeastern coast, the town of Rabinit was hit by a third storm. It began the same as the others. The wooden docks were destroyed almost immediately. Town officials moved people away from the coast and into the natural shelter of a large cliff which protected them from the direct force of the wind.

"Suddenly, the wind stopped, the rain stopped, and the clouds disappeared. Minutes later, the day was clear and normal. The storm just ceased to be. There appears to be no explanation.

"We believe at the same time a fourth storm was bearing down off the south-central coast, near Guntamin. As soon as they saw storm clouds approaching, they began preparing for the worst. However, before the storm made landfall, it just disappeared. They claim it was the Sun who saved them because as the storm clouds dissipated, the Sun broke through and warmed the land," Wadov said.

"Were there other reports?" Gondal asked Wadov.

"There was one report from a small village on the eastern coast. They saw a massive storm moving directly toward them at dusk, but they did not get the bitter weather they expected. It may have passed them by, but it was too dark to see what actually happened. We believe it's possible their storm disappeared at the same time the storms at Rabinit and Guntamin disappeared. The timing was very close," Wadov said.

"Have there been other reports or sightings?"

"No, Leader. All four sightings happened within two days of each other. There have been no new reports in the last three days."

"Thank you, Minister Wadov. Are there any questions or comments from the other ministers?" Gondal looked toward both sides of the long table where the ministers were seated. "No? Then I turn to the Senators. Are there any who would ask questions or who wish to make a statement?"

"Yes, Leader. I am Senator Anitol. I represent the south-central district of Vigiton. I would ask three questions. First, what caused these hellish winds? Second, what can we do to prevent them from happening again? And, if we cannot prevent them, my third question is what can we do to minimize any loss of life?"

Wadov stood. "Until we know the cause, the best thing we can do is be prepared. If another storm is sighted, keep your people away from wooden structures. Shelter them in your strongest stone buildings. Keep them away from low areas that could flood. And, if you have advance warning, move inland as far and as fast as you can. These storms appear to be strongest at the water's edge. If you can't escape the storm, then seek shelter and wait it out."

Branton, the minister of science, stood next and said, "With respect to discovering the cause of these storms, we've asked both Speaker Zardok and Lord Alcandor for their thoughts. At this time, we have no answers from either. Until we know what caused these wind storms, it is pointless to speculate on what we can do to prevent them in the future."

~

The Senators left the meeting with few answers. And little hope. Their world was falling apart. People were dying. No one knew what to do about it.

An Understanding

"Hey, Lenny," Bernie said.

Lenny smiled as he took his seat at their table.

Suzie noticed immediately the kaleidoscopic green and orange elements in Lenny's shimmer. "You're in a good mood."

"I should be. Candi and I have a date tonight," he said as he stroked Sissy's fur.

Suzie laughed. "Did Sissy have anything to do with that?"

"Yes, quite a bit actually," Lenny admitted.

"You must tell us everything." Suzie wiggled in pleasure.

"I wasn't sure you and Sissy were talking," Bernie said.

"We had a long talk. It might be more accurate to say, I had a long listen. Sissy had a lot to say. There's a lot more to her than I thought," Lenny said as Sissy purred.

"What did you talk about?" Suzie asked.

"Well, you were right about her, Suzie. She was jealous of Candi," said Lenny. "She'd been doing things to keep us apart. I think I convinced her she doesn't have to worry about that."

"How did you do that?" Suzie asked, not willing to let Lenny off the hook so quickly.

Lenny's face turned red as his shimmer added two new colors to the mix. "We talked, like I told you."

"Do I have to ask Sissy what you said?" Suzie teased.

"Okay. I told her no matter what happens with Candi, I will still like her."

"*Pop-pop-pop*," Sissy said.

"Sissy says that isn't exactly right, Lenny." Suzie was grinning.

Lenny sighed as he said, "Okay, okay. I told Sissy it was okay for her to love me because I love her too. I told her no matter what happens with Candi, I will always love my little Sissy."

Suzie watched as Bernie's jaw dropped. They were both hearing words they never thought would come from Lenny's mouth. Suzie tried not to laugh with delight.

"Is that right, Sissy?" Suzie asked her little friend.

"*Ye-ye-ye*," came the sounds from Lenny's little fur ball.

"We're going to be better than ever. This morning, Sissy told me to get to work three minutes early, and when I did, I bumped into Candi. That's when we made our date for tonight."

"This is very interesting. If Sissy can tell you what to do, she'll be a lot more helpful, won't she?" Bernie asked.

"*Ye-ye-ye*," Sissy said proudly.

Sauna, Anyone?

Billy found it increasingly difficult to get into Bernie's universe. The idiot simply refused to go home before he saw Billy leave for the day. This forced him to come back late at night or early in the morning to get his swipes in. Today, he'd come in early.

Sitting at Bernie's desk, he reviewed his plan. It was a good one, both simple and subtle, although the visualization was large in scope.

From his vantage point far out in space, Billy visualized the planet and its moon. Carefully, so as not to disrupt any of the relationship parameters, he dragged both the planet and its moon closer to the sun. He made all his calculations earlier, so it was quick work to move everything to the new position.

Not too much closer. I don't want Bernie to suspect anything. At this distance, everything on the planet would come to a slow boil. By the time Bernie figured it out, everything would be dead.

Say goodbye to your plants, Bernie.

Suzie Intervenes

Ezrah read the memo from Shemal again. He'd been expecting it for some time. But still, he was sad to see it.

Shemal's memo described Bernie's poor performance on his universe project. Shemal claimed he had never seen anything nearly as bad, and, recently, there had been no progress of any kind. Shemal said he was making the recommendation with some regret, because Bernie was a likeable fellow with some positive traits. But, he concluded, there was no reason to believe anything would improve in the near future.

Ezrah called Suzie into his office. He knew she would be upset, but there was no point in putting it off.

Suzie came in with the pot of coffee, filled Ezra's' cup, and returned the coffee pot before sitting down.

"What's up?"

"Suzie, I just received a termination recommendation for Bernie. Shemal says he's given Bernie every opportunity to prove himself, but he doesn't believe Bernie is the kind of employee we're looking for. I know he's your friend. I'm sorry to have to tell you this, but I'm going to approve the termination."

"Oh, no! This isn't fair, Ezrah," Suzie said as her shimmer displayed colors and patterns he'd never seen before. "Bernie's work has been sabotaged from the beginning."

"What are you talking about?" Ezrah asked, more concerned with calming her down than what she had to say.

"Do you know Billy?"

"Yes. We hired him last year. I've seen excellent reports on him." Ezrah thought for a moment before asking, "He and Bernie had the big fight, right?"

"Yes. Back in school, Billy always picked on him, and he's doing the same thing here. He's been sabotaging Bernie's universe."

"That doesn't make sense, Suzie. If Bernie had a problem, he would just go to Shemal and tell him. I'm sure Shemal would have looked into it."

"No, he wouldn't. Billy is Shemal's nephew. I've seen the good reports Shemal has written about Billy. He would never believe Bernie over Billy," she said. "I told Bernie not to tell Shemal, because I knew Shemal wouldn't believe him."

"You shouldn't have done that, Suzie," said Ezrah as his own shimmer flickered. "Bernie should have gone to Shemal right away so it could be straightened out. Shemal might have solved the problem. Or we might have intervened and transferred Bernie to another department. It's too late for that now."

"Oh, Ezrah. Please don't let this happen. Bernie is a great employee. He's making a great universe in spite of what Billy's done." Ezrah pretended not to notice the teardrop that fell on the corner of his desk.

"How can you say that, Suzie? Shemal has seen his universe, and he says it's the worst thing he's ever seen."

"Please, Ezrah, Bernie just needs more time. Give him a chance to show what he can do."

"I don't know, Suzie."

Ezrah was struggling. On one hand, he wanted to support Shemal, who was in the best position to evaluate Bernie's work. Normally, there wouldn't be any question about accepting his recommendation. On the other hand, Suzie—from his own department—talked Bernie out of having his claims of sabotage investigated. That wasn't good. She should have told Bernie to report the problem so it could be properly investigated. She'd given him very bad advice. Was it fair to punish Bernie for doing the wrong thing? Especially when that bad advice came from someone in his own department? This cut into Ezrah's sense of ethics and fairness. He wasn't sure what to do.

It was Suzie who tipped the scales when she said, "What if he won a Universe Award? Could he stay then?"

"Well, of course, but I don't see how that can happen."

"We can nominate anyone we want. The Committee dropped off the nomination forms yesterday. I'll nominate Bernie. If he wins, he stays. Okay?" Suzie begged.

Ezrah shook his head and said, "Suzie, I don't like any of this. I think Bernie should go to Shemal and tell him whatever he thinks Billy has done. If Shemal finds Billy has sabotaged his work, he'll be reprimanded, and Bernie will be re-evaluated."

"Answer me honestly, Ezrah. You know Shemal, and you've seen his evaluations of Billy. You also know how quick Shemal is to fire people. Do you believe Bernie will get a fair review?"

Ezrah pondered her question. "Probably not. Too much time has gone by. He should have reported it when it first started happening," Ezrah admitted.

"Then, please, give Bernie a chance to save his job by winning an award. You can tell Shemal Bernie has been nominated, and you want to delay any termination decision until the Committee has a chance to see his work."

Ezrah avoided looking at her. It was bad enough imagining the tears in her eyes without having to look at them.

"Well…" Ezrah began, although the argument was over. Suzie would get her way, and Bernie would get a second chance.

Use your time well, Bernie, he thought.

Gee, It's Hot

"Gondal, we need to talk," Nottag, the minister of building projects, said from the doorway to Gondal's office.

"Certainly. Come in," said Gondal as he gestured to a seat.

"It's the heat. No one remembers anything like it. I'm afraid it's the beginning of another catastrophe."

"It is bad. Have you sketched out any scenarios?"

"There is only one scenario. Not to be overly dramatic, but there's only so much heat we can take. We're getting reports from several project sites of people collapsing. Others are having respiratory problems. The heat is too much."

Gondal started to ask which projects, but with all of the rebuilding going on, they were too numerous to mention. Even the Senate building had suffered damage.

"What action have you taken?"

"We changed the work schedule," said Nottag. "We've got people coming in before dawn, and we're sending them home before noon. We have a second shift coming in the late afternoon and working until after dark. That lets them avoid the heat of the day—"

Gondal had stopped listening. He didn't move. He didn't blink. He couldn't. His brain had stopped the moment he grasped the implications of Nottag's statement. The people were succumbing to the heat at mid-day, when the Sun was at its height. If this was true, then everything was lost. How could they survive if the danger came from the Sun itself? They were doomed.

"Leader, are you okay?" Nottag asked. Nottag's hand was on Gondal's shoulder, shaking him gently.

Seeing his minister's concerned expression, Gondal instinctively hid his fear. He had to remain strong, even among his Council of Ministers. They could not see their Leader filled with doubt. So he did what he always did, and reached down inside himself for still more energy, though he felt his fingers scrape the near-empty bottom. He calmed his breathing as he collected his thoughts.

"Thank you for your report, Nottag. I agree with your decision to change the schedule. Will you please send Minister Tonst and Minister Branton to me? I have a matter to discuss with them."

"Yes, Leader." Nottag left in search of the ministers.

~

As Gondal waited for Tonst, his minister of temple affairs, and Branton, his minister of science, he considered his options. He needed answers. Lately, answers from the Temple had not been helpful. Worse, the Temple's credibility had suffered from the recent events. Take the night sun, for example. The Temple claimed it was a gift from the Sun, but it had become associated with all the troubles that happened since it arrived. Some claimed the night sun itself was the cause of their problems.

The summoned ministers arrived within minutes of each other. Gondal knew the two ministers had once been friends, and, perhaps could be again someday, but for now, their respective ministries put too great strain for any friendship to flourish. Some said it was because religion and science don't always agree.

Gondal had appointed both men to their positions. Zardok had endorsed Tonst for the minister of temple affairs position, and since Tonst was well qualified, Gondal had accepted his recommendation. Branton's experience came from having taught in one of Alcandor's learning centers before the lord left to pursue his own studies. He and Alcandor had maintained a good relationship over the years, which made Branton a good choice for minister of science.

"Ministers, please be seated," said Gondal as he gestured to two empty chairs. "I want to know what you can tell me about this oppressive heat. People are experiencing serious health problems, and I want to get ahead of this before it becomes our next crisis."

"I made an inquiry to the Temple to see if they had any thoughts on it," said Tonst. "The Inner Council is working on this very question. They promised to inform us as soon as they finish their analysis."

"And you, Branton?" Gondal asked, hoping for a better answer.

"I just got back from meeting with Alcandor. He's also working on the same question."

"And what did he say?"

"He's been taking measurements for several days," said Branton, "and the heat is definitely increasing. The plants are being affected and some, especially the fruits, may be harmed or killed if the heat continues."

"Does he know the source of this heat?" Gondal asked, although he dreaded the answer.

"He said he didn't want to speculate because he's still considering various theories. It wasn't easy, but I got him to tell me some of his theories. After he did, I understand why he doesn't want to discuss them. I promised him I wouldn't say anything until he completes his research."

Gondal's patience, worn thin by weeks of desperation and uncertainty, exploded, "Branton, I want answers! If Alcandor has some, I want to hear them now!"

Branton, chastised by Gondal's anger, promptly said, "He claims the most obvious heat source is the Sun. He showed me his experiments. He believes the Sun has grown slightly larger than it was just a few days ago. It's not enough to detect without instruments, but Alcandor says the bigger Sun is giving more heat and more light than before."

"That's preposterous! Everyone knows the Sun is unchanging. It's a Universal Truth," Tonst exclaimed.

Gondal's full attention was on Branton as he asked, "Does he know why this is happening or what we can do about it?"

"No. Right now he's just trying to understand it. He thinks if we understood more, maybe we could fix it."

"How can you even say such things?" exclaimed Tonst, who couldn't believe what he was hearing. "You talk about 'fixing' the Sun? That's blasphemy! It's the Sun that protects us, not the other way around!"

"Minister Tonst," said Gondal. "There are times when we must not be afraid to ask any question nor seek any answer. We're responsible for too many lives. Anything less is dereliction of our duty."

Gondal was disappointed. Meeting with the ministers had yielded no solutions. He had to force things along.

"Minister Tonst, please inform Speaker Zardok his presence is urgently requested at a meeting of the full Senate tomorrow afternoon. We await his explanation of this heat and any recommendations he may have to reduce the damaging effects," Gondal directed.

"Minister Branton, you will give Lord Alcandor the same message," Gondal said.

Both ministers were surprised. It was Tonst who said, "Leader, I may not be able to get Speaker Zardok to attend if he knows Lord Alcandor will be present. You know there is some animosity between these two men."

"Then tell Zardok I will greatly regret his inability to appear, but the meeting will be held. We will listen instead to Alcandor's thoughts on this urgent matter," Gondal retorted.

Gondal knew forcing Zardok to this meeting would come with a price. But it would be nothing compared with the growing heat outside.

The Deal

Bernie had been glum since Shemal's last inspection. He'd told Lenny and Suzie it had not gone well. They'd been supportive and tried to keep his spirits up, but it wasn't easy.

Today, when he sat down at the lunch table, he could see something was wrong. Bernie, though untrained in shimmers, knew they were both upset.

"What's wrong?" Bernie wanted to know.

"I'm really sorry, Bernie," Lenny said as he put his hand on Bernie's arm.

"There's no easy way to say it," said Suzie. "Shemal recommended your termination. But—"

Bernie interrupted, "Oh, no... I've been afraid of that..." Bernie said as his words trailed off, swallowed by the silence of impotent frustration.

His impotence didn't include an angry cloud that pushed a stack of dirty lunch trays onto the floor, eliciting yells from several gods who now sported splashes of pea soup on their clothes. Around the lunchroom, several gods looked in the direction of the commotion but quickly lowered their heads, hoping to avoid becoming the next target of the unseen force.

Bernie was unaware of any of this. He was wondering how he would tell his mom that he'd failed. A black hole opened beneath his feet, and he felt himself being sucked into it. Maybe it was better to keep falling. Maybe the end of the fall would be easier than the nightmare he found himself in. How could he tell Mom?

What had he done wrong? He'd tried hard. He hadn't hurt anyone. Well, except for Billy. Billy had been hurt in the fight. Somewhere inside, a fierce denial surfaced: it was not his fault! He hadn't told his cloud to hurt Billy. Billy was the one who started the fight. If Billy hadn't hurt Suzie, none of it would have happened. Wasn't it okay to defend a friend? Even The School hadn't punished him for what his cloud had done. Still, his dad had left. His friends had left. The fight changed his life. Did he have to pay forever? It wasn't fair.

Chaos clouds don't think in terms of fair. It's far too subtle for them. Powerful emotions, like anger and fear and hurt are what they understand. And they don't like those feelings at all. That's why Bernie's cloud was on a rampage. Food was flying from the serving line while nearby gods held trays like shields against globs of potatoes and carrots flung in their direction.

"Bernie! Bernie!" It wasn't Suzie's words that broke through Bernie's thoughts. It was Lenny shaking his shoulder that forced him back to the present. Then he heard Suzie's urgent whisper, "Get control of your cloud, Bernie!"

As the cafeteria returned to normal, people looked around for the source of the chaos. Bernie's friends pretended to be as clueless as the rest of them, while preventing Bernie from jumping up and apologizing to everyone.

Suzie glanced at Bernie. He had the appearance of a puppy who'd been kicked again and again. She was torn between the desire to hug him or to go find Billy and give him a new scar to match the one he already had.

"I thought I had six months."

"Six months is the maximum. If they can make a decision sooner, they do," Suzie said softly.

"Thank you both for everything. I know you tried to help," Bernie said. He stood up to go, although he had no destination in mind.

"Wait, Bernie. It isn't over yet." Lenny put his hand on Bernie's arm and pulled him back into his chair. "Suzie worked out a deal for you. Tell him, Suzie."

"I told Ezrah about Billy. I told him Billy has been sabotaging everything, and it's not fair to judge you because of what Billy did. I told him you could build a great universe in spite of Billy."

"What did Ezrah say?"

"Well, he was upset with me for telling you not to go to Shemal. He said you should have gone to him right away and told him what was happening."

"And now I've got you in trouble, too," Bernie said as his shimmer dropped to its lowest intensity that day.

"Don't worry about me."

"Tell him about the deal, Suzie," Lenny urged with growing impatience.

"I told Ezrah you could make a great universe in spite of Billy. I told him you could win a Universe Award because it's going to be so good. You just needed more time. I told him I would nominate you for a Universe Award. Ezrah agreed that if you win an award, then you can stay."

Bernie tried to feel gratitude. But all he heard was that, instead of building a universe good enough to pass his probationary period, he now had to build one so outstanding, it exceeded the best effort of all the gods before him. And he had to do it while keeping Billy at bay. He shook his head.

"It's impossible. I give up."

"No, it's not," said Lenny trying to show enthusiasm he didn't feel. "We'll help you, won't we, Suzie?"

"Absolutely. Don't give up, Bernie. The Awards Committee won't be doing reviews for several weeks. That's a lot of time. I know you can do it."

Bernie wasn't sure. Not sure at all.

The Hot Senate

The heat in the Senate's amphitheater was uncomfortable, but the tension was worse. Leader Gondal was not the only one who knew having Zardok and Alcandor at the same meeting could prove explosive. The whole Senate feared that very thing.

There were no empty seats, and several Senators were forced to take seats in the high section, with the other citizens.

Gondal said, "Senators, Lords, and Citizens, I welcome you to this emergency session of the Senate. Many of you have come from distant regions, and we appreciate your attendance on such short notice. Although others are en route, matters are so dire, we cannot wait for their arrival.

"I invited Speaker Zardok and Lord Alcandor to join us today. It is my hope they can shed light on the latest crisis." Leader Gondal gestured to center stage, where Speaker Zardok stood on his raised platform, and Lord Alcandor stood next to him, on the ground of the Great Chamber.

"Everyone is aware of the heat. It's been getting hotter every day. You may not be aware of the problems it's caused. It's become nearly impossible for exertions of any kind, and we've been forced to suspend all public works projects. The people on the coast tell us the ocean temperature is also rising. Inland cities near the Central Mountains report higher temperatures, although not as high as here.

"Our streams are drying up, and several rivers and lakes are shallower than ever before. Our freshwater is disappearing. Several varieties of plants have shriveled, and no longer produce food. Plants closer to the central mountains are showing greater hardiness, although this may be due to the lower temperatures reported there."

Gondal looked around the room. There was good reason for the fear he saw in their eyes. Unless they found a quick solution to the growing heat, there wouldn't be more meetings of the Senate, or any other body, for that matter.

"I pray that Speaker Zardok and Lord Alcandor can share

new information to help us with this crisis. I will first offer the floor to Speaker Zardok. Do you have any opening statements you wish to make?"

"Yes, thank you, Leader Gondal, I do have something to say." Zardok turned to face the Senators in the amphitheater surrounding him.

"Senators, I know you are concerned. And you are right to be. These are dangerous times, and there has been grievous harm thrust upon us. Thousands of people have died, including many of our precious children. And now we are visited by yet another disaster. The awful heat steals our water, kills our plants, and threatens our lives. It is but one of many trials we have faced in recent weeks.

"Senators, I hesitate to tell you this, but there are more trials to come," Zardok said as the Senate broke out with boos and hisses.

"Yes, Senators, it is true," Zardok insisted. "And why, you might ask, are we facing such trials? The answer is simple. It is because the Sun, our great benefactor, has lost faith in us."

Senators responded with shouts of "No!" and "It isn't so!"

Zardok continued. "Yes, the Sun has lost faith in us. Why, you ask? It is because He believes we have lost faith in Him."

The senators continued with cries of protest and denial, but Zardok kept talking.

"The Sun has seen many who have questioned Him, doubted His motives, and even doubted Him. Who among you would give your utmost for such an ingrate?" Zardok looked around the suddenly silent Senate. "Neither will the Sun!" he thundered.

A senator in the front row stood and shouted, "Give us the names of these faithless, that we may root them out!"

Another senator shouted, "We want our covenant with the Sun restored! We will not allow the faithless to force the faithful to pay such a price!"

"What can we do to make amends?" shouted another.

Zardok, Speaker for the Sun and High Priest of the Temple, said, "You must be vigilant. When you recognize the words of the faithless, you must reject them and their polluted ideas. You must do this over and over until the Sun is persuaded the great majority of His people can and do maintain their faith. Only then will He pick up His mantle and restore His protections. Only then will we see an end to this great apocalypse.

The Senate responded with outcries of "Let it be so!" and "Aye!"

Gondal suppressed any sign of the anger he felt. *Nicely played, Zardok*, he thought. *I'm sure you believe every word, but how can I introduce Alcandor after that? He will be cast as one of the 'faithless' and shunned by all the true believers. Alcandor will say whatever he believes to be the truth, and that could be dangerous. It might also discredit the one person who might be able to save us all.*

And so his decision was made.

"Thank you for your rousing words, Speaker Zardok. We shall adjourn for today so we can consider everything you have said. Again, I thank all of you for coming on such short notice."

Gondal pounded his gavel and dismissed the Senate.

Shemal Talks

"Bernie, will you come to my office, please?" Shemal stood in the entry to Bernie's cubicle.

Bernie had been dreading contact with his boss since Suzie revealed Shemal wanted him fired. But Suzie said Ezrah had not approved the recommendation. *Has Ezrah changed his mind? Am I going to be fired after all?*

Bernie struggled to master the feelings raging inside him, otherwise as soon as he moved beyond the range of his dampener, his cloud would be free to cause trouble. *Oh, my shimmer too*, he thought. He willed it to neutral colors, although he knew it seldom obeyed.

More than anything, he must not betray Suzie. She would be in serious trouble if anyone learned she'd told him what Shemal said.

As Bernie turned to follow Shemal to his office, he saw Billy grinning at him. Billy slid his index finger across his throat and grinned again. Even Billy thought he was about to be fired.

"Sir, you wanted to see me?" Bernie asked.

"Close the door and take a seat, Bernie."

Bernie sat as the sound of his heart pounded louder in his ears. He noticed his shoelaces twitching on the floor and willed them to stillness.

"Bernie, I have to be honest with you," Shemal said with sadness in his voice. "I don't think you have what it takes to be a builder. I've watched your work for weeks now, and it just doesn't measure up to our standards."

"But…" Bernie began.

Shemal held up his hand to stop Bernie. "Let me finish. My job is to make the best decisions I can on behalf of The Business. These decisions can be very hard because they usually affect people. At the same time, you've shown conscientiousness and loyalty since you arrived. Frankly, I wish more people had these traits. However, you have not demonstrated the skills of an effective builder. That's why I recommended your termination."

"But... Sir..." began Bernie as Shemal held up his hand again.

"I recommended terminating you, Bernie, but the Personnel Department did not approve my recommendation. They decided to give you more time. I have no idea why, but Ezrah said your work has been submitted to the Universe Awards Committee. The Committee will come here to review your universe in a few weeks.

"You should think of this as a reprieve, Bernie. It's a second chance to earn a place here. If you convince the Committee to grant you an award, then I will consider it proof I misjudged you. In that case I will approve your probationary period. If you are not successful with the Committee, then my original opinion remains unchanged. Do you understand?"

"Yes, sir. I... Thank you, sir. I really appreciate this," Bernie said.

That Billy!

Shemal called me into his office to tell me he wanted to fire me. It was just like Suzie said. Shemal said my only hope is if I can win a Universe Award. My little cloud was so scared, he hid behind my back and shook the whole time.

I almost told Shemal about Billy. But what good would it do? I have no proof. All I have is suspicions. Even if I caught Billy in the act, it would be my word against his. Candi and her friends are too afraid to say anything. She said Billy never comes right out and says what he's doing. He just makes innuendos that could be interpreted different ways. Suzie's right. Shemal would never take my word over Billy's, especially when he already thinks I'm doing a bad job. He'd just assume I'm trying to blame my problems on someone else.

I feel trapped. I'm in some crazy game. Now I have to win a *Universe Award*. Give me a break! How can a new builder just out of school do that? It's impossible. Even if I had an idea for a winning universe, how could I do it? No matter how good I am at building, Billy is better at un-building. I spend days working on something; he wrecks it in minutes.

I wish I could ask Dad. He knows all about building winners. But what good would that do? Even if he gave me the answer, how could I build it with Billy tearing everything down?

I'm still upset about Billy's last trick. I knew something was wrong because Gaia's aura was really stressed. It turned out my plants were getting weaker. It took me days to figure out they were suffering from too much heat. The whole planet was getting hotter. But I couldn't find the reason. Finally, I realized Billy had moved the planet closer to the sun. I only spotted it because I rechecked my biosphere calculations to see if I'd made a mistake. There was no mistake in the calculations. But my planet wasn't where it should have been. If I hadn't figured it out when I did, everything would be gone.

I can't imagine what he'll do when I put animals on the planet. They're more vulnerable than plants.

I hate him. I just hate him!

Let's Try Faster

Billy had no idea why Uncle Shemal hadn't fired Bernie yet. When Shemal called Bernie into his office, Billy had been sure that was the end. After all, Bernie's world was so wrecked it bothered even him to look at it. Apparently Shemal needed more convincing.

Bernie is obviously stuck on his higher life forms. There's still no sign of animals on either of the lab continents. No matter. Plants were vulnerable to lots of things. And Billy had another idea for them. He doubted Bernie would notice.

With power beyond imagining, Billie grasped the world in his mind. And he gave it a twist, making it spin faster. It was only a little faster, but it was enough to make a difference.

"Oops. I pushed too hard. This end of Bernie's continent got a bath," Billy said in mock dismay. He laughed as the ocean waters swept over the east coast.

"It's subtle, Bernie, but I think you'll like it."

He left the office and headed home. It was late, and he needed his sleep.

Little Friends

Billy had changed tactics. He would leave at quitting time, but then return at random times during the night to do his mischief. Fortunately, Bernie had the backdoor that let him check his world every few hours. But the strain of constant vigilance was showing. For weeks, Bernie had made little progress. All his time was spent in defense and rebuilding. He was tired and frustrated and desperate for relief.

He checked his universe, relieved to find nothing had happened in the time it had taken him to walk home. Wearily, he prepared himself for more checks throughout the evening and the two or three more times he would wake up during the night to check again. It was exhausting.

Then he brightened. How could he have forgotten? Back in school, when he was stressed, he would go for a walk in the woods. It always helped.

Maybe that's why I'm upset lately; I haven't been to the woods, he thought.

~

As Bernie closed the door behind him and turned in the direction of the woods, the tiny observer smiled, knowing she would have the honor of telling the others the boy was moving toward the woods. The swift relay of her silent signals brought the tribe together to hear Catila's report. Bowin was pleased. It had been a long time since the boy god had ventured out. He motioned for the group to proceed quietly as he led them along the path the boy had taken.

~

The sun hung low in early evening sky, and dipped lower with each moment. Bernie stumbled over an exposed tree root. Cursing, he knew he couldn't blame his cloud. He was tired and being tired made him clumsy. It had been so long since he'd had a good night's sleep. Up ahead, Bernie saw his favorite place, an opening in the trees with soft, moss-covered ground, where he had solved some of the world's greatest problems. Well, not really. But it had felt that way at the time. Those problems seemed so minor now.

He sat down to think. Maybe he would just close his eyes and rest them for a few minutes…

~

Even though it was light and they had observed no other movement in the woods, Bowin posted sentries. It was good that he had been cautious. If he had not, there would have been no warning of the approaching nazark.

The first report came from Shelda, who spotted the ferocious nazark from her tree at the edge of the clearing as it climbed up the side of the plateau from the wild country below. Bowin signaled for everyone to retreat. He would take no chances. This evil creature had killed and eaten far too many of his kind. Nothing could compete with the long claws and venomous bite of the fierce monster. Their best hope was to get away before they were noticed. Then he thought about the boy.

The young god had fallen asleep in the clearing. The nazark lifted its head and sniffed the air. From its reaction, Bowin knew the black beast had discovered a scent and knew it wasn't alone. The deadly creature looked around for the prey he knew was there. Bowin held his breath, hoping the nazark would not notice the boy. But it did.

Bowin watched the nazark lower its head and bare its fangs as it crept toward the sleeping form. What could Bowin do? None of his kind could hope to defeat a nazark. Many of his friends had died trying. Even if he called everyone together, they could not prevail. And yet, he could not let the boy come to harm in this way.

But the boy was a god. Perhaps the nazark could not harm him. Perhaps the boy would awaken and laugh at such a puny creature that intended him harm. As Bowin struggled with what to do, he realized he had already made a decision. He was moving full speed toward the boy and the approaching nazark.

Bowin gave his fiercest battle cry as he raced forward. He bounded onto the boy's stomach to awaken him, and his forward rush carried him further still. He landed on his feet between the young god and the snarling nazark.

He yelled his fiercest threats, but the monster bared its fangs and stood its ground. Then it began moving closer. For Bowin there was no possible retreat. No means of escape.

Bowin thought of the way they would remember him. 'Bowin, the bravest of the tribe,' they would say, 'had died trying to save the boy god.' It was a fitting epitaph.

Without warning, a deep shout rang through the woods. The nazark looked up at something behind Bowin and snarled, again exposing his deadly fangs. Bowin could not risk taking his eyes off the nazark to see turn around. His first moment of inattentiveness would be his last. He continued his fiercest yells and held his ground. He heard his friends shout from their hidden places around the clearing. The hungry nazark backed up two feet. The snarling continued, but the shouts grew louder and from more directions as the rest of the troop joined in. Suddenly, the nazark turned and slunk back into the wilderness from which it had come.

Bowin watched without moving as the dark figure retreated. He lingered in his own thoughts, numb to the idea he had survived.

"Thank you," came a sound from behind him.

Bowin whirled around to see the young god standing high above him. The boy moved slowly, careful not to make sudden motions as he sat down. He held out his empty hands in front of him. Although Bowin did not understand the boy's words, the meaning was clear. A gesture of friendship.

~

"I think you saved me from something awful," said Bernie. "It took a lot of courage. Thank you."

Bernie looked around the clearing and spotted more of the little creatures. "I didn't know there were any of you left."

He sat calmly, as a dozen little creatures emerged from

behind bushes, crawled out from under leaves, and lowered themselves from tree branches. They watched for any sign of disapproval from Bowin over their approach, but he gave none.

Bernie found himself surrounded by new friends he hadn't known he had.

Something Is Very Wrong

"We will begin with a report on the tragedy in the eastern province," Leader Gondal said to the Senate. "Branton, our minister of science, will review this for us. Minister, if you will, please."

Branton stood and faced the assembly. "You all know about the giant wave that killed 1,347 citizens sixteen days ago. Three villages were wiped out when the ocean, without any warning, surged over the land. The only thing that stopped it was the Central Mountains.

"At the same time, people all over the country reported feeling dizzy and unstable on their feet. There was some speculation they may have felt the deaths of the people on the east coast, although there were no similar reports during the horrendous forest fires that killed even more.

"A few days later, Lord Alcandor brought more news. Apparently, the giant wave was not the only occurrence on that day. Lord Alcandor is here to present his findings himself." The crowd shifted in their seats as they prepared for more bad news.

"Thank you, Minister," said the Leader as he turned to the man in the center of the stage. "Lord Alcandor, thank you for coming. Before we start, I will tell the Senate that Speaker Zardok was also invited to attend this meeting. His aide informed me the Speaker has pressing business elsewhere and cannot attend."

Some members of the Senate made a booing sound and a few more stomped their feet. Gondal held up his hand for silence. "Please give your attention to Lord Alcandor."

"Thank you, Leader." Alcandor turned to face the Senate. "I've discovered disturbing things. Before I start, I must tell you, I don't have answers to the questions you're going to ask me."

"Get on with it," shouted one of the senators.

"Very well. We've known for a long time how long it takes the Sun to go from sunrise to sunrise. It never varies. But, sixteen days ago, this changed. It used to take ten candle marks for the Sun to rise, make its trip across the sky, and pass under the world to where it rises again. But now it takes nine candle marks. For some reason, the Sun is moving faster."

Gasps from the crowd echoed the shock in the heart of every person present. The greatest constant in the world, the immortal, unchanging Sun, had changed. This was indeed terrifying news.

"Where is Zardok? Does he know?" a senator called out.

Leader Gondal said, "I informed Speaker Zardok of Alcandor's findings four days ago. He offered no comment on them. Lord Alcandor, please continue."

"I've also been closely observing the night sun. As I reported two months ago, the night sun goes through a cycle that repeats every thirty-two days. It shows its full strength at the beginning of each cycle, gradually giving up more and more light until it becomes dark on the seventeenth day. Then it grows in strength, adding more and more each day until it reaches its full strength again on the thirty-second day. We've charted four complete cycles since the night sun arrived. But since the giant wave, there have been changes. The night sun has been slowed. The night sun's cycle of thirty-two days now takes thirty-five days."

The Senate made few sounds. The news was too shocking.

Gondal, though he had heard this before, knew he needed to guide the discussion. "This is incredible news, Alcandor. The Sun is moving faster, and the night sun is moving slower. You're sure of these measurements?"

"Yes, Leader. We also used a water clock to confirm the measurements. There is no mistake."

Alcandor seemed lost in thought. The Leader had to prod him by asking, "Lord Alcandor, can you tell us why this has happened?"

Alcandor blinked, and said, "What? Ah… No, not really. I think we can say with certainty the events are connected. Whatever caused our Sun go faster is the same thing that slowed the night sun, and I believe the flooding was a side effect of that same force."

"How can you say something affected the Sun? It's never been affected by anything before," said Minister Tonst, the liaison between the Senate and the Temple.

"That's a fair question," said Alcandor. "Consider the calamities that have befallen us in recent months. We've seen the creation of night sun and the two tiny suns. We've had unprecedented worldwide disasters, including forest fires, hurricanes, flooding, and most recently, the terrible heating. No one has ever experienced a time like this. All these things tell me our world is changing."

"We must wait for Speaker Zardok," insisted Minister Tonst. "He will explain these things to us. Even now, he consults with the Inner Council to find answers."

Minister Nottag flashed his famous scowl at Tonst and said, "It makes no sense to wait for answers from the Temple. They're in chaos. They haven't had answers for a long time."

Numerous voices were raised in protest to Nottag's words. The most common cry was, "Prove it!"

Minister Nottag stood up and looked around the Senate. "Who here has not heard of the divisions in the Temple? It's no secret many temples have been taken over by priests and priestesses who challenge Zardok's leadership. Have you heard of the Temple of the Moon? Priestesses there claim the night sun is a new god sent to hold back the darkness. They claim when something evil attacked the night sun and turned him red, the power of the night sun was so great he healed himself.

"And what of the group who claims the night sun is evil? They claim our ill fortunes began with the arrival of the night sun. They would vanquish the night sun and send it away. They too have claimed temples in the west and call themselves Soldiers of the Sun.

"Every one of these splinter groups, and more besides, claim they know the truth. Some claim we have to change our ways. Others claim we're being warned. Others claim our end is near. I don't know what the answer is. I do know it's a bad idea to wait for the Temple to come up with answers. We must find our own," Nottag thundered at the crowd.

This time, the Senate responded with, "Hear! Hear!"

Leader Gondal stood and uttered the ritual words, "I hear the will of the Senate, and I will obey."

Gondal turned to Alcandor and said, "The Senate will seek

its own answers. And you, Lord Alcandor, shall be our instrument. I charge you to return here in five days with answers to these questions and any others relating to the troubles that have befallen us."

Lord Alcandor started to protest, but his words were drowned out by the senators who cheered the mandate he had been given.

Someday, He Will Pay

Journal Entry

I feel like crying.

Billy has caused so many problems. I can't get anything done. He practically burnt my world to the ground, and then he hit me with hurricanes and flooding. I was going to advance time and give the forests a chance to recover, but what's the point? Billy will just do it again with something else.

And lately, it's getting harder to spot what he's done.

Last week, I noticed one of my plants had stopped producing fruit. It was starting to hibernate, which it shouldn't do on this planet—because conditions never change. It took me until today to figure out Billy had spun the planet faster and skewed all my circadian patterns.

I'm supposed to be making an award-winning universe. What a joke! Even if Billy went away today, there's not enough time left to do anything that will impress the Committee. I haven't even had time to create a single animal yet.

Mom asked what I thought about moving closer into town. I told her we shouldn't do anything until I complete my probationary period.

I didn't have the heart to tell her anything else.

Blame the Night Sun

Speaker Zardok, as head of the Temple, was used to respect and deference when he addressed the Senate, but the unprecedented death and destruction had not helped the decorum of the Senate.

"You're the one who claimed the night sun was a gift from the Sun. But ever since it arrived, we've been cursed with death and destruction. We've never had anything like this before. How can you claim it's not the fault of the night sun?" Senator Blantor shouted at Speaker Zardok as he stood on his raised platform in the center of the amphitheater's stage.

The audience in the stands shouted, "Hear! Hear!" and stomped their feet.

Zardok seethed. He didn't like being challenged. "Senator Blantor, let me understand. You are complaining about the problems that have befallen us, and you blame our Sun for sending the night sun?"

"You are twisting my words, Speaker. I'm not saying the Sun would send destruction to us. I'm suggesting the night sun may not be the gift you say it is. It may have come from another source, and it may be the cause of our problems," said Blantor, amidst more, "Hear! Hear!" from the audience.

Minister Landor, responsible for the ships and the ports, said, "The ocean has been out of control since the night sun arrived. It rises and falls. Some ports flood every day while others lack enough water to float their ships. We had to evacuate several coastal towns because of flooding. I don't see much good coming from this night sun."

"And who is your authority for blaming these problems on the night sun?" Zardok asked with contempt.

"Alcandor has researched these matters for us. We've reviewed his findings and are satisfied with his conclusions," said Branton, the science minister.

"Then perhaps you should ask him to come before the Senate and explain these things to you. You obviously do not want my explanations," Zardok snarled with unconcealed fury as he descended from his raised platform and stormed out of the Senate.

Lookies!

"You'll never guess what I saw in the woods last night."

Suzie scanned Bernie's food choices before joining in Lenny's quizzical look.

"Lookies," Bernie said, unable to contain his excitement. Instead of responding to Bernie, everyone's eyes were drawn to the movement on his tray. His fork and spoon were standing upright on the plate. The fork bent forward in a deep bow to the spoon before grabbing her and twirling the two of them around in some sort of silverware happy dance. "Stop that," he hissed. The unheard music seemed to end, and the fork lowered the spoon gently back to the plate before falling over himself. Bernie scowled as he examined the fork, trying vainly to bend the tines back into their original position. "Now I have to pay for that."

Lenny brought them back. "Lookies? I thought they were eradicated years ago."

"They were one of the refugee groups you tried to help, weren't they?" asked Suzie.

"Yes. The Town Council decided the lookie population was out of control. They declared them a public nuisance and ordered them exterminated. They were catching them and throwing them into a waste dimension. We protested, and they changed their policy and sent them back to their world of origin instead. I still have my 'Save the Lookies' T-shirt," Bernie said with pride.

"Where did you see them?" Suzie wanted to know.

"I'd gone for a walk in the woods, and I sat down to do some thinking, but I fell asleep. I woke up to find one standing between me and a nasty looking beastie that had crawled out of the wild. The lookie was squealing at it, trying to chase it away."

"It was protecting you?" exclaimed Suzie as she clapped her hands together with delight. "That's wonderful."

"I doubt that," Lenny responded. "Why would it try to save you? They don't have…" Lenny's voice trailed off as he desperately tried to avoid another double lecture from Sissy and

Suzie.

"I managed to scare the beastie away. When I stood up, I think it decided I was too big to eat."

"How many lookies were there?"

"When I sat back down, they started coming out from all over. I counted fourteen of them. I think the one who tried to protect me is their leader. I couldn't understand them, but they seem to communicate with each other.

"You know what's funny?" Bernie continued. "They followed me home. When I left for work this morning I noticed several of them watching me leave. I waved at them, and three of them waved back."

Alcandor Offers a Theory

Alcandor sat in Gondal's private office in the Senate Building. He'd come early at Gondal's request.

"I want to talk with you privately before I convene the Senate today, Alcandor. I want to make sure you understand the importance of this meeting."

"You think I'm unaware of the global catastrophes threatening our very survival, Gondal?" Alcandor asked with some irritation in his voice.

"No, of course not. You are a good thinker, Alcandor, probably the best we have, but even you need some advice in this matter."

"Please continue." Alcandor appeared somewhat mollified.

"You think in ways that can be difficult for others to follow. You must consider your audience today. If they do not understand you, they will not ask you to explain. They will turn to other explanations. I cannot allow that to happen. I no longer believe the Temple has the answers we seek."

"But I've come today with hypothesis and theory, not answers. Finding answers takes time."

"We don't have time for long studies, Alcandor. You must convince the Senate you understand what's happening. And you must convince them to give you the resources you need to solve the problem. We're out of time."

~

"We want answers, not theories! That's what," shouted the minister at the end of the table.

There was a chorus of, "Hear! Hear!" from the senators.

"We've been getting better theories from the idiots on the street," shouted one of the senators. She was also greeted with a chorus of "Hear! Hear!"

Lord Alcandor stood alone in the center stage. He felt chagrin, knowing Gondal's warning had come true. The senators were scared and in no mood for theory. They wanted answers, just as Gondal predicted.

"Senators, please listen to me. This is important." Alcandor pleaded, fearing they'd lost their willingness to listen. The crowd confirmed his fears with more boos and hisses.

"Silence! Silence, everyone," shouted Leader Gondal as he pounded his gavel. As the crowd quieted down, Gondal decided to invest more of his personal and political capital in Alcandor. The meeting was too important to end without decisions.

"Senators and Ministers, everyone knows we are desperate for a way to deal with these disasters. I believe Alcandor offers an answer. Not a complete one, perhaps, but one we must consider. Please hear him out.

"Continue, Lord Alcandor. You have the floor." Gondal stared the crowd into silence.

"Thank you, Leader," said Alcandor. "Let me summarize the things we all agree on. We are experiencing the worst onslaught of major catastrophes in our history. We've seen massive flooding, forest fires, threats to our food supplies, wicked windstorms, brutal heat waves, tidal waves, and numerous problems that have caused thousands of deaths. On this, we can all agree. We can also agree these disasters are becoming more frequent and more deadly.

"What we may not agree on is the cause of these disasters. Yet it's critical we find the cause. If we can't find the cause, then we'll never find a solution. Most people will agree with this logic," he said to a soft response of "Hear! Hear!"

"Let me turn to the different theories to explain what is going on." As the audience groaned, he said, "Yes, yes. I know you've heard them before. Please indulge me.

"One prominent theory is our world is coming to an end. The proponents of this theory show that not a month goes by without some large-scale disaster. And, by all accounts, the disasters are getting worse. Some argue the night sun, which goes dark every thirty-two days, is but a portent of the end of our Sun. They argue the world is unstable and total annihilation is around the corner. If this theory is true, there's nothing we can do about it. It will happen. The only thing we can do is prepare ourselves for the end.

"Another popular notion is the karma theory. This theory says we are being punished for something we've done. These disasters, they say, are retributions for our sins. If this theory is correct, we must find what we've done wrong and stop doing it.

"Another speculation suggests the presence of a new divine being. In this theory, a god is trying to communicate with us. Some say the god is trying to teach us something or warn us of something. It's not clear. If this theory is correct, we must figure out what this god is trying to tell us, so we can comply before worse disasters befall us.

"My concept is different. I believe we have a protector. We all know the horrible disasters we've suffered. But they could have been much, much worse," he said to an outbreak of boos and hisses.

"Wait. Wait," Alcandor shouted back at the crowd. "Think about it. Please. In almost every case, we've been rescued at the last minute. Something has intervened to prevent the disasters from becoming even worse. Remember when our forests burned, but on a single day, all the fires were suddenly extinguished? Remember, the hurricanes all ended on the same day. Don't forget the heat wave that was destroying our plants and threatening all of us. It, too, ended suddenly. And what about the shorter days? Who knows what might have happened if things hadn't suddenly returned to normal? There are many more examples.

"In my theory, there is a divine being watching over us and working to prevent or minimize these disasters. I call Him the Great Protector. If my theory is correct, then we must find a way to communicate with Him. He is the key to everything. If we can just talk to him, He could warn us about future disasters. We may even be able to tell him about problems so He can resolve them more quickly."

The room went silent as the senators considered his words.

The Leader bent forward and said, "Tell us, Lord Alcandor, why do you propose the existence of a Great Protector? Surely if anyone has saved us, it would have been the Sun. Why would you suggest something else is involved?"

Alcandor raised his hand to silence the crowd. "This is the hardest part to understand. You must listen carefully," he said with a soft voice that forced the senators to listen more closely.

"Almost all of the disasters lasted several days before suddenly ending. I ask you, if the Sun had the power to stop them, would He have waited so long? Would He have delayed his mercy for days as He watched His people suffer? I submit He would not. Therefore, I know it was not the Sun who intervened. It was instead the Great Protector."

Gondal had difficulty accepting the argument when Alcandor first introduced it. It was hard to accept that the Sun had been powerless to help. The senators struggled now with the concept. Yet, if the Sun could intervene, it was impossible to believe He would have delayed so long before doing everything He could.

When Gondal judged the senators had enough time to consider, he asked, "Why should we believe your Great Protector theory instead of the others?"

Alcandor paused as he collected his thoughts. "Leader, that's an excellent question. Consider this.

"If the world is ending, there is nothing we can do about it, so I submit, for purposes of discussion, let's not waste any time with this theory. Each of us will have to prepare for the end in our own way.

"For the karma theory, we must consider any sins we may have committed that would justify such horrible punishments. I find nothing to justify this. We are a gentle people. We do not harm anything, except the food we eat. This has not changed since the beginning. We have done nothing to justify being treated in this way. And for that reason, I reject this theory.

"The divine being theory is also flawed. To my way of thinking, if there is a divine being who wants to talk with us, surely he can find a better way than sending a flood or a tidal wave to get our attention. We are more than willing to listen. Any being this powerful can surely figure out a better way to communicate.

"This leaves me with my theory. If there is a benevolent god out there trying to protect us, then it makes sense to communicate with Him. Our existence depends on it. We must figure out how to do this. We must tell Him we're grateful for His help. We must tell Him when we see other problems. And we must listen to His warnings of any disasters He cannot prevent. Only by establishing communication with this higher power can we hope for safety," Alcandor finished.

"Let us assume for a moment, Lord Alcandor, that your theory is correct," said the Leader. "What would you have us do?"

"The first task is communication. But there are several things to consider. For example, the Protector may be acting on behalf of the world. He may not be aware we even exist."

These words triggered an outcry from all sides. Loud shouting and shaking of fists were everywhere. It took three minutes before the Leader could restore order.

One senator summed up the crowd's sentiment, "How can He not know about us? This is our world! We've been here since anyone can remember!"

"Some of my observations," began Alcandor, "suggest the Protector is not omniscient. If he was, these disasters would not have progressed as far as they did. He clearly doesn't want them to happen, yet if He was omniscient, He would have stopped them before they got started. And something else: He isn't all-powerful either. If He was all-powerful, and He didn't want these disasters, then He would prevent them or even make them unhappen. From this, I conclude our Protector, as powerful as He is, has His own set of limitations."

"If He actually exists, how do you propose to communicate with this Great Protector of yours?" asked a senator from the southern mountains.

"The main problem will be getting His attention. Considering what He can do, He may be massive in size, and if that's true, He may not have noticed us. Therefore, we have to give Him some sort of sign that we're here," Alcandor said.

"This is ridiculous! If He's that big, surely we can see Him. Please point Him out to us, Alcandor," said the senator to a quick response of "Hear! Hear!" from the crowd.

"He might not be visible to us. But He's here! I'm convinced of it. And it's essential we figure out how to communicate with him," Alcandor persisted.

The Leader shook his head. This was becoming harder to accept than the first time they had talked. "I don't know, Lord

Alcandor. You want us to believe in an invisible being, who may or may not be willing to help us, if He only knew we were here. Is that about right?"

Lord Alcandor sighed. "Yes, Leader. That's about it."

For the next hour, debate raged on. The Senate was desperate to take action to deal with the crisis. In the end, they voted to give Lord Alcandor the manpower and resources he requested. Very few were satisfied with this decision. But no one offered any better alternatives.

And, as crazy as Alcandor's idea sounded, at least they were doing something.

One Bright Spot

Journal Entry

The one bright spot of this whole week was seeing the lookies again. They must have been living in the woods for a long time. It's been years since the Town Council tried to get rid of them.

When I have time, I'm going to see if they'll come out again.

I wonder if they've had anything to do with all the lost things that kept showing up on my doorstep over the years. I always thought it was my cloud, but it never made sense. My cloud isn't the type to find lost things.

He's the type that loses them in the first place.

Senate's Progress Report

"Every time you call me to testify, you delay my progress," Alcandor fumed.

"Yes, we understand that," said Gondal. "But surely you understand we need to be kept informed of your progress. If your attempts are not successful, we must explore other measures." Senators expressed their approval of Gondal's words.

Gondal knew there were few 'other measures' waiting to be explored, but they were desperate for news. They were all upset and worried. He had to balance the Senate's need for information against Alcandor's need to work uninterrupted.

"I apologize for my outburst, Leader. I apologize also to the Senate," said Alcandor as he bowed his head to both. "I know everyone is concerned. Please, let me start again."

"Proceed," Gondal said.

"Let me review what's happened since the Senate charged me with contacting the Great Protector. The greatest challenge is finding a way to get the attention of such a being. We're fairly certain He is not all-knowing or all-powerful because, in spite of His apparent desire to keep us from harm, He's not always able to do so. And yet when He does make an appearance, His powers are immense. From this, I conclude He's distant from us at least part of the time. This means we can't just speak with Him because He may not be around to hear us. We have to wait for him to come to us.

"Think of Him as someone who sees an unending forest. If we want to be noticed, we must draw His attention to a tiny clearing in one small part of that forest. How do we do this? We must do something a forest cannot do. We must make some sort of sign, one that makes Him curious enough to investigate.

"I chose fire for the sign, because fire is not natural to the forest. And we know large bonfires at night can be seen across long distances. Admittedly, our initial attempts were not successful, so we began forming patterns with the fires. We set

the fires in locations to form triangles, squares, and pentagons.
We also varied these patterns by creating greater distances
between each of the fires—" Alcandor said as one of the
ministers interrupted.

"But none of this has worked," exclaimed Minister Terwin.
"If it isn't working, why are you still making fires?"

"I still believe fire is a good signal. As I said, we've varied
the signal in several ways. Our next effort will be to make the
signal stronger and more noticeable."

"But Lord Alcandor, we're running out of forests," said one
of the senators, which produced the first laughter heard in the
Senate in many days.

Even Alcandor chuckled. "Fear not, Senator. I'm doing
something different this time."

Leader Gondal said, "Please continue."

"You've all seen lanterns with a mirror-side built into them.
The mirror is used to reflect and amplify the lantern's light and
send it in a specific direction. I'm currently building fifty large
mirrors that will be used to direct the bonfire's light upward,
where I believe the Protector will notice it. This will make the
light brighter and more visible than anything we've done
before."

"Where do you plan to do this?" Minister Terwin wanted
to know.

"That's something I need to talk about," said Alcandor. "I
want to do it on top of the highest temple in the highest
mountain we can find. The Temple at Fernwod would be
perfect, and I was hoping the Senate could prevail on the
generosity of Speaker Zardok to make it available."

Gondal took a quiet breath. That would not be easy. Gondal
felt, once again, the enormity of trying to bridge the gap between
Speaker Zardok and Lord Alcandor. Those two had been at
odds as long as he could remember. They were as different as
two people could be. The Speaker's entire belief system was
based on his unswerving faith in the goodness and beneficence
of the Sun. Alcandor, on the other hand, didn't take anything for
granted. It angered the Speaker when Alcandor challenged
things the Speaker believed should be beyond questioning. Yet,
that was the very thing that made Alcandor's science so valuable.

He made them see things they couldn't see before.

"I'll make the request, Lord Alcandor," said Gondal. "You'll be informed as soon as I have an answer. Before we adjourn, can you tell me if you have other ideas if your mirrors do not work?"

"Yes, I'm working on something with glass. When light passes through glass of varying thickness, it changes the intensity of the light. I think it can be used to force the light of the bonfire into a more intense pattern that can be seen from farther away."

"Thank you, Lord Alcandor. On behalf of our people, I urge you to make great haste."

IIow Can This Be?

It was late, and Bernie needed rest. Just one more look around the planet, and then he would get some sleep. Everything looked fine as he scanned the planet. Then he noticed something that should not have been there. The main continent was on the dark side of the planet, but there, near the center, he saw a flicker of light. Bernie groaned at the thought of more damage from Billy. What was it to be this time?

Bernie zoomed down for a closer look. High on the ridge of the central mountain range, thick jungle had been cleared away. In the center of the clearing stood a large stone pyramid, rising two hundred feet above the ground. The pyramid did not extend to a point, but rather had a flattened top, fifty feet wide. A large bonfire burned in the center.

A ring of mirrors surrounded the bonfire, each at least ten feet tall. They had been tilted backward to reflect the firelight upward, in effect sending a beacon of light straight up into the sky. This was what Bernie had seen from so far away.

A man stood next to the fire, watching as flames leaped high in the sky. A long line of men and women trudged up and down the steps of the temple, carrying firewood. When they reached the top, they threw their burden onto the flames and turned back for another load.

Bernie was flabbergasted. *Impossible. There's no life here. Plants, yes, but no animals and certainly no higher life forms.* Bernie knew he had to be dreaming. *I'm exhausted. This has to be a nightmare, nothing more.*

The man standing at the top of the great pyramid looked more concerned with searching the sky than the progress of the flames. He kept calling out as he scanned the sky above him. Bernie opened his mind and listened. Then, through power only a god could wield, the man's sounds melted into words.

"I call out to the Great Protector. Please listen to me. We desperately need your help. Great Protector, are you there? Please speak with me," the man cried out.

Bernie hovered near the man, wondering how a dream could be so vivid and contain such detail. Without warning, the man turned from the sky and looked directly at Bernie. His words gushed forth, "Great Protector, you have come at last! Please hear me. We're in great danger, and we desperately need your help!"

This was too much for Bernie. He popped back into his room and spent the night under his covers. Nothing good ever started with seeing things that weren't there. And when they started talking to you, the last thing you wanted to do was have a conversation with them.

First Contact Protocol

The first thing Bernie did when he arrived at work that morning was go straight to his world, back to the place he'd been the night before. In the center of the cleared jungle, he found the stone pyramid. The ashes of the great fire were still smoldering. There was no sign of the man. Near the base of the pyramid, Bernie saw people gathering another large pile of wood. They apparently planned a repeat of last night.

As Bernie looked around, he discovered more buildings and more people. Most were dressed in togas and sandals. Some wore jewelry, consisting mostly of necklaces, bracelets, and anklets. Except for the slight greenish color of their skin, they looked just like the gods at home.

Streets, lined with buildings made of wood and stone, led to other parts of the city. One road led away from the city, and when Bernie followed it, he was shocked to discover it led to other cities.

How had he not noticed this?

And, more importantly, how did they get here? Bernie hadn't created them. His Pod People were still on the drawing board. There shouldn't be any animals of any kind on the planet.

Plants? Could they be the result of a wild plant that jumped one evolutionary path in favor of another it liked better? It couldn't be. Billy had destroyed his plants two million years ago. He'd had to start over. There was no way higher life forms could evolve in just two million years.

Could it be another trick of Billy's? If so, it was unlike anything he'd tried before. Plus, Bernie saw no evidence the people were causing any harm. But still…

At no time did he hear any suspicious laughter coming from Billy's cubicle.

~

"You're kidding," said Lenny. "How could you not know you

had people on your planet?"

"Lenny, I didn't make any people," Bernie said defensively. "There wasn't any reason to think they were there. Do you go around looking for things you know aren't there?"

"But there had to be signs. What about air pollution? That's a good clue something's going on," Lenny persisted.

"They aren't that advanced—nothing more than bronze era. They aren't doing much to impact the planet."

"How could they get there if you didn't do it?" Suzie wondered aloud.

"It had to have been Billy," said Lenny. "He's the only one who's been messing with you."

"I thought so, too, at first. But I can't see they're doing any harm. The only thing they seem to want is to talk with me."

"I thought you were supposed to avoid contact with your creations," Suzie said.

"That's just when you're in school," said Lenny. "Everything's different now. We can talk to them all we want."

"Well, maybe I should see what they want. They've gone to a lot of trouble to talk to me."

"Can't hurt as long as you follow the protocol," Lenny said.

"Protocol? What protocol?" Bernie asked.

"The First Contact Protocol, of course. You can't just go down to see them wearing torn jeans and a dirty T-shirt, Bernie. You have to dress for success if you want to impress them."

"I don't want to impress them. I just want to find out what they want."

"Trust me, Bernie. It's easier if you impress them first. I'll bring in my notes on how to do it."

"Okay. Meanwhile, I'll take a closer look at their world and see if I can figure out what's going on."

A Cultural Assessment

Journal Entry

I've been studying the planet for two days now. The people there look just like us. I have no idea how they got there. I definitely didn't make them. They have a greenish hue to their skin, which made me think they might have come from the plant life, but that doesn't make sense. All my plants are accounted for. There are no missing links anywhere.

At first I thought they were something Billy did, but I don't think so anymore. The race is peaceful. There's no sign of weapons or soldiers.

One thing I noticed is they don't seem to die. The population increases over time, but it's very slow. I calculated how long they've been around by looking at their population growth. It's hard to believe, but they may have been here for at least a million years.

The race is definitely intelligent. They have a written language and a system of mathematics, which seems well known throughout the population. They don't have much technology. I would put them squarely in the bronze era. They use mechanical devices like looms for manufacturing. They work collaboratively on their buildings, which they make out of carved stone they mine from the mountains and transport to their building sites. They don't have animals, so they do the hauling themselves on long carts made for that purpose. Their favorite buildings appear to be meeting places, temples, market places, and large living areas. Many buildings are made without roofs or doors.

They use a simple bartering system that involves the exchange of personal time for goods or services. I observed one example where the state owns a large textile plant that manufactures clothes. The people acquire their clothes in exchange for promising a certain number of hours of work. This promise is recorded and then cashed in at some later time. The work promises can be bought or sold to others.

I found what appears to be their capital city in the central northern coast, about fifty miles inland. The population is greater than in the other cities, and the buildings are larger too. I spent most of my time there. They have a central government, with representatives from other cities. The capital city is where the largest government offices and the largest temples are located.

Their religion is basically sun worship. It looks universal, and everyone participates in prayer services at dawn and at sunset. There is another service at high noon, which appears to be mostly performed by the priesthood.

Most of the population lives in smaller cities scattered around the main continent. They have a good system of roads between the cities. I still can't believe I missed seeing them. But they don't really have a very big footprint. I just never thought to look for advanced life.

I've been watching the guy who first caught my attention. His name is Alcandor. He lives in the capital city. He has a large stone building with over twenty rooms. It looks like a cross between a laboratory and a library, filled with equipment and books. They're doing a lot of work with glass. One room is probably where they made the bonfire mirrors. In another room they're currently building glass lenses. I suspect they're trying to intensify the light of the bonfire. They're obviously serious about getting my attention.

I've decided to meet with this Alcandor. I looked over Lenny's first contact protocol notes, and it looks okay. Lenny says it's no problem to change my appearance on the planet. I can look like whatever I want as long as I keep concentrating on it. The protocol suggests I dress in a flowing white robe, with a long gray beard and hair. Apparently, most life forms associate gray with age and wisdom. And I'm supposed to make myself three times bigger than they are. Oh, and my shimmer should be golden, but I need to turn it down by at least 50% or it can sometimes hurt their eyes.

Well, I guess I'm set. We'll see how things go tomorrow.

Meet Your God

Bernie waited until he got home to make first contact. He didn't want any interruptions. Sitting in his room, he realized he was procrastinating. Frankly, he was nervous.

He'd never talked to one of his creations before. In school, they had strict rules against it, and Bernie always tried to obey the rules. Even though this rule hadn't made sense, he wasn't about to lose his chance of becoming a builder by disobeying.

Now he had the chance to taste that forbidden fruit.

As Bernie slipped into his universe, he moved his time lever ahead by two days. He felt silly doing it, but if he made a bad impression and messed everything up, he wanted the option to roll back time and try it over again.

He went to the capital city, where he had last seen Alcandor. He dimmed his shimmer as much as he could. Lenny said some life forms could see shimmers even if the god hadn't taken corporeal form, which probably explained why Alcandor had seen him at the bonfire. This time he would not be seen until he was ready.

Bernie found Alcandor in his building, in a room filled with hundreds of books. He was seated behind a carved wooden desk, writing rapidly with a brass-tipped pen that he periodically dipped into a nearby inkwell.

Bernie looked at the height of the ceiling. If he made himself three times Alcandor's height, he would not be able to stand up inside the building. He could sit on the floor in front of Alcandor's desk, but how dignified was that?

Bernie compromised by sitting cross-legged while hovering three feet off the floor. Then he allowed himself a corporeal presence. He remembered the long hair and beard at the last second and quickly put them in place. Then, he allowed his shimmer to come up to a soft golden color. Perfect. He was ready.

Alcandor was so preoccupied with his writing, he didn't lift his head. Minutes passed. It was Bernie who blinked first.

"Ahem…" said Bernie.

Alcandor looked up. His whole body jerked, and his eyes grew wide with shock. His mouth moved, but no words came out. He closed his eyes and composed himself. When he opened them again he had the confident look of the man Bernie had seen on the temple top as the bonfire burned away.

"Great Protector, you have come at last. I… I thank you," Alcandor said.

"Tell me, Alcandor, why have you called out to me?" Bernie said in a deep bass voice that filled the library. Bernie was proud of the reverberating echo he'd added to his voice. It was his idea to add that little touch; it made him sound like an elder god.

"Our world is in trouble, Great Protector. Terrible things have been happening. We cannot withstand much more. We beg to know of anything we may have done to deserve this. And we beg for your continued assistance."

Only the smallest tremor in Alcandor's voice betrayed the emotional turmoil inside the man as he addressed the god hovering before him. Bernie tried to imagine what he must be feeling as he faced a being more powerful than anything he could possibly imagine. Somehow, he had deduced Bernie's existence and called out to him. *How had he known?*

"Tell me, Alcandor. How is it you know of me?"

"I didn't know for sure. But when I looked at the things happening to us, I realized they could have been much worse. Something kept saving us. For some things, it might have been luck, but over time, it became clear our world was being protected by a great power. That is why I knew you had to exist."

Bernie thought back over the last few days, which could have been weeks or even months here, on the planet. He cringed internally when he thought of what they must have gone through. Billy had caused tsunamis, earthquakes, hurricanes, forest fires, and more. Bernie realized even some things he'd done might be on Alcandor's list of disasters.

"Please, Great Protector, can you tell us why these things are happening to us?"

Bernie thought for a moment. Well, he certainly couldn't tell him these problems are because a god named Billy had a grudge against him from back in school. That would definitely be too much information.

"An evil force has discovered your world, Alcandor. And this evil force seeks to do great harm."

"What have we done to bring this evil force down upon us?"

"This evil is not here because of anything you or your people have done. It has reasons of its own you would not understand."

"Great Protector, I have so many questions. There are many things we need to know. Are you here to help us? Is there anything we can do? Why is—"

"Your questions will have to wait, Alcandor. For now, I will tell you this. I do not want the evil force to harm your world in any way. And I will do what I can to undo any evil I discover. Let this promise be enough for now. We will talk again," Bernie said, as his image began to fade.

"Thank you, Great Protector. Thank you." Alcandor sank to his knees, just as he did at the beginning and the end of every day when it came time to thank the Sun for His gifts of light and warmth.

A World to Save a World

Bernie told Suzie and Lenny about his first contact with Alcandor. Lenny was impressed, and Suzie was proud.

"That's really great, Bernie. A textbook encounter. You impress them, answer a few questions, and then leave them wanting more. Perfect in every way," Lenny said.

"And I liked what you did hovering above the floor," Suzie added.

"But it makes everything more complicated," said Bernie, who'd had time to think about it.

"How so?" Lenny asked.

"Well, for one, how am I supposed to keep working on my universe when I have to work around an existing life form? They have a complete civilization there. What am I going to do with them? I mean, they don't look like they would hurt my Pod People, but it cuts into my creative options."

Lenny rolled his eyes. "Bernie, just get rid of them! You've got to keep your priorities straight. You need to build a universe so you can keep your job. If these guys interfere with that, then they have to go!"

Bernie didn't have to say anything to make it clear that was not an option for him. His shimmer flickered with disapproving colors. Lenny just snorted.

Suzie said, "Maybe you can move them someplace else. Why don't you make another planet for them or move them to a different universe?"

"I suppose I could try that," said Bernie, as he felt yet another load fall on his shoulders.

"It doesn't work that way," said Lenny. "You can't just move a world into a different universe. It's way too big. Although, you might be able to find a portal to let you move between two universes. I heard about them at an OWT meeting once. Portals aren't very big, but if you can get everyone to walk single-file through the portal to the second world, it might work."

"That's a great idea, Lenny," said Bernie. "I'll make another universe for them. I have all my notes, so I can make it really close to what they have now. And Billy won't ever know about it."

"Okay. Then I'll see if I can find us a trans-universe portal somewhere," Lenny said.

~

In the quiet of his cubicle, Bernie placed an empty frame on his desk. Capturing a void didn't always happen quickly, but this time, Bernie got lucky. He found his slippery fish and attached the void to the frame. He had never been able to do it this quickly before. He told himself it was because he was getting better all the time, and even imagined he used less putty than usual to hold the window in place.

As the putty dried, he examined the new universe. It was pure emptiness in every direction. Hovering in the very center, he began to visualize a sun. He would use no prefabs this time. He worked faster and with more confidence than ever before. When he finished, he saw a beautiful yellow sun equal to any prefab he could have requisitioned from the Supply Department. Next, he created his life planet and gave it the same yellow moon Suzie liked so much. Next, he added two more planets, to keep Lenny's astrological forces content.

Only then did he pause, amazed at how much he'd accomplished. He couldn't help but think of Beatrice, who'd told him so many times to *Plan First, Then Create*. Having a plan probably was the reason Wanda made things look so easy. He promised himself again for the umpteenth time he would spend more time on the planning side of things.

During this pause, he thought of the people on the planet who were going to lose the only home they'd ever known. The planet might look the same from far out in space, but the people moving there would see a world with none of the unique characteristics that marked their own. As he thought on this, he decided to do more.

He would make this world the same in every way.

~

Over four days, Bernie made many trips between his two universes. He recreated feature after feature, including Billy's meteor craters, volcanic islands, stacked-up continental plates, and even the ring around the world he had created to stop the tsunami. Every detail was as perfect as he could make it. He'd kept good notes, and they served him well.

When he finished, he had a near-perfect duplicate of his original world. Only two differences. The new planet had no buildings. And, of course, the gaia on the new planet would not be born for millions of years. Otherwise, the lush green land and the plant-filled oceans were identical.

The only thing needed now was Lenny's portal. Then Alcandor could lead his people to the Promised Land.

You Want Us To Go Where?

Bernie found Alcandor working in his library. This time, when he materialized, Alcandor seemed to have been expecting him.

"Great Protector, thank you for returning." Alcandor lowered his gaze as he waited for the Protector to speak.

"Alcandor, I have considered the evil that has invaded your world, and I have considered my promise to do what I can to keep you safe. There is one thing I can do."

"Please tell me."

"I can move you and your people to another world—a world hidden from the evil force. You will be safe there."

Alcandor stood for a long time. Finally, his voice quivering, he spoke. "You can do such a thing?"

"Yes, I have already created the world. You will cross from this world to the new one through a special portal, which will be ready soon."

Alcandor gasped. "You created a world? A whole world? How is this possible?"

"Well, it's not really that hard. Your system is pretty simple. I just had to make a sun, three planets, and a moon. It was—" Bernie stopped when he saw Alcandor lost in thought. Then he realized he'd been careless. This was not the time to impress the locals with his creative powers. That would just confuse them.

"When can you and your people be ready to go?"

When Alcandor finally replied, it wasn't an answer to Bernie's question. Instead, he asked in a hushed voice, "You made a Sun? Truly, you made a Sun? You can do such a thing?"

Bernie wasn't sure how to get the conversation back on topic. Somewhat exasperated, he said, "Alcandor, stay with me here. When can you and your people be ready to go?" Bernie's shimmer flared a bit, and red flecks could be seen in the gold glow.

"I can't make that decision. For something like that, the Senate and the Temple will both have to agree. We'll have to talk with them."

"Then make this happen, and quickly."

"Great Protector, you ask the impossible. I'm the only one who has ever seen you. If I make such a request, no one will believe me. I need your help to convince them. We must talk to the Senate and the Temple together. Once they are convinced, they can convince the people."

"I have important things I must do and little time left. This is not an easy thing you ask of me," said the god.

"I'm sorry, but I see no other way."

"Tell me about these others," said Bernie. "Who are they? What must I know of them?"

Alcandor paused to collect his thoughts. "The Temple is led by Speaker Zardok. He's a selfless man who dedicated his life to bringing all of us closer to the Sun. His devotion to the Sun is second to none. And when he speaks, the people listen. For several reasons, he and I do not get along well."

"What is the reason for this discord?"

"In our land, Zardok is well-respected, and he speaks for the Sun and the Temple. I've developed a modest reputation as a seeker of knowledge. There are times my knowledge is at odds with the dogma and tenants of the Temple. I think such debate brings us wisdom and more knowledge, but Zardok believes it undermines the people's faith in our Sun."

"I see. Is there anything else?"

"Yes. But it's personal."

"I would hear it and judge for myself."

Alcandor drew in a slow breath. "Very well. Many years ago, there was an amazing woman. Her name was Vianna, a free spirit who charmed everyone with her intelligence and her beauty. She loved the Sun, as we all do. Almost as much, she loved the pursuit of knowledge and the thrill of discovery. Zardok and I both fell in love with her. Zardok loved her for her devotion to the Sun. I loved her thirst for knowledge. We each sought her hand. Finally, she chose Zardok. In truth, he's an honorable man, and she made her choice freely.

"I had proposed a great expedition to seek knowledge of our Sun. The Senate approved the expedition but would not let me lead it. Instead, they chose Vianna. The expedition was lost.

No one ever returned. Zardok was heart-broken, and he's never forgiven me for my hand in it." Alcandor's voice trailed off as he added, "Nor have I ever forgiven myself…"

"I understand," said Bernie. Unsure of what to do with the feelings he had exposed, he merely said, "Thank you for telling me."

Bernie waited a few more seconds and then said, "What can you tell me about the Senate?"

"The Senate is made up of 500 elected representatives, called senators, from all over the country. They come here, to represent the interests of their district. The Senate elects a leader, who then appoints twelve ministers to perform the tasks of governing. The Senate is led by Lord Gondal, an able leader who has held the position a long time. And, of course, any lord or lady who wants to attend has the right to vote with the senators."

"Who are the lords and ladies?"

"They are the oldest of our people. There are 117 of us now. Zardok, Gondal, and I are three of the lords. It's an honorary title given to the oldest of our people; no one remembers when we were born.

"How do you suggest we approach the Senate and the Temple?"

"For the Temple, the only one we need to talk with is Zardok," said Alcandor. "Whatever he decides will be law throughout the Temple. We should talk with him first. The Senate is more complicated because there are more people with less power. If we can win Zardok's support, it will be easier to convince the Senate."

"That makes sense. When can you arrange to meet with Zardok? It should be in a place where we can talk privately."

"I can try to arrange something in two days. We should go to him, I think. Zardok does not trust my science and if we met here, he might think you are some sort of trick."

Bernie couldn't stifle a small laugh. "Well, if he thinks I'm a trick, it won't be hard to convince him I'm anything but."

"Great Protector, how shall I let you know? Is there a way we can communicate?"

Bernie looked around the room. He saw a large rock Alcandor was using as a paperweight. He pointed to it and said,

"If you need to speak with me, take that rock and move it to the other corner of your desk. I will know, and I will come to you when I am able."

"Your powers are amazing, Great Protector."

Bernie smiled. It wasn't much of a trick. All he had to do was stop by and see if the rock had been moved. If it had, then he would look for Alcandor. If it hadn't, then he would do a fast forward with the time lever until he arrived at the time when Alcandor did move the rock. Alcandor was a bright guy, but he would never understand this time travel stuff. Better to keep it simple: if you want your god, move the rock.

Meeting with Zardok

Bernie suppressed his shimmer and stayed incorporeal as he followed Alcandor through the Temple's long corridors. Three times, they met workers clearing broken stones and shoring up walls against further damage. After several unavoidable detours, they arrived at a small waiting room, where a priest stood next to a large set of doors. As the priest recognized Alcandor, he bowed his head slightly.

"Welcome, Lord Alcandor. Speaker Zardok is expecting you. Please go in."

Alcandor acknowledged him with a slight bow of his own head.

The chamber beyond was large. The man at the far end of the room stood as Alcandor entered the room and walked forward to greet him.

"Alcandor, you said you had urgent news. Have you found this Protector of yours?" Zardok asked, in a mocking tone.

"Actually, Zardok, I've done exactly that."

"Surely, you jest. You know I give no credence to such theories. There's no need to hypothesize a new god to explain what has been happening to us."

"Perhaps we can avoid our usual debate, if I just introduce you to the Great Protector and let him speak for himself."

Zardok shook his head, but said, "Please do."

"We should stand over here," suggested Alcandor. "He's quite large."

As they moved back, Bernie positioned himself as before, hovering cross-legged in the center of the room. He went through his checklist: beard, long gray hair, white robe, muted golden shimmer, reverberating voice. *All set. Now, slowly become visible.*

If Bernie was going for shock and awe, it clearly worked.

Zardok stood speechless, staring at the godly figure before him. Moments later, the high priest seemed to have a 'weak-knee' moment. Alcandor grabbed a nearby chair and guided the speaker onto the seat only to discover Zardok had been trying to get on his knees.

"Just sit, Zardok. The Protector doesn't expect us to kneel before him. In fact, you're going to find him different from anything you may have imagined."

"I never imagined him at all," croaked Zardok.

Bernie was overwhelmed by this display. He was just 'Bernie' at home, at school, and at work. Here, he was so much more. *Being a god is a rush,* he thought. Composing himself, he looked directly at Zardok.

"Zardok, I come with terrible news. Your world is in grave danger. Although I've tried to protect you, the evil forces are very strong. I no longer believe I can keep you safe."

Zardok gave the Protector a quizzical look. "The Sun will keep us safe. He has protected us since the beginning of time. He will continue to do so."

Bernie shook his head. "The evil I speak of is more powerful than your Sun, Zardok."

"That is not possible. Nothing is more powerful than the Sun," Zardok said with confidence. Straightening in his chair, Zardok asked, "Did the Sun send you to talk with me?"

"No."

"Then where do you come from? What are you doing here?"

"I have always been here, Zardok. I was here before your world. I was here before your Sun. I have always been here. I will always be here."

"How can this be true? Nothing is greater than the Sun. Nothing existed before He did."

Bernie, sensing the conversation heading in the wrong direction, tried to get back on topic. "Zardok, you know what has been happening to your world. You know things are getting worse. The only safe place for you and your people is on another world."

"What? The Sun will protect us. We have no need for another world. This is our world."

"Please, Zardok," said Alcandor. "Listen to Him. I believe He offers us our only hope."

"I have never heard of another world. Where is it? What is it like?" Zardok struggled to regain his composure.

"The new world is much like this one. It has a sun, a night sun, and two tiny suns," said Bernie, trying to use terms Zardok would understand.

"Another world with another Sun? How can there be another Sun? Surely it must be a false-Sun."

"No. It's just like the Sun you have now," Bernie said reasonably.

"That is not possible. How can you claim such a thing?" asked Zardok, his voice rising.

Bernie shrugged and said, "I know because I made it."

"You made a Sun?" Zardok asked with disbelief all over his face. "There is only one Sun."

"No, there are lots of suns. I've made quite a few, actually."

Zardok stood and glared at Bernie. "You are a deceiver and a blasphemer! Your words are false beyond doubt. In the name of the Sun, I cast you out. Take your minion with you. I will hear no more of this!" Zardok shouted.

"Well, that didn't go very well," Bernie said to Alcandor.

~

And neither did the next eight times Bernie tried to redo the meeting. He used his time lever to return to the start of the meeting. Although he tried different approaches and different arguments, it still ended up the same.

Zardok believed in the Sun. He didn't believe in Bernie.

A Dead End

Bernie materialized in Alcandor's study. Rather than wait for Alcandor to return from their meeting with Zardok, Bernie moved forward through time until Alcandor arrived. During the hour it took him to walk back, Alcandor been thinking about the failed meeting. Bernie, on the other hand, was still fuming over all eight of the failed meetings which, for him, had happened just moments ago.

"I'm sorry, Great Protector. I'd hoped he would show more wisdom."

"Maybe meeting with the Senate will go better."

"Even if the Senate is in complete agreement, the split between the two will mean many people will not leave."

"Oh, Chaos! This whole thing makes me so mad I could just spit," Bernie growled.

Bernie noticed the shocked look on Alcandor's face. He blurted out, "Well, you know, I just get upset sometimes. I try hard to help, but no one wants to listen."

Alcandor didn't seem to be listening. He was staring behind Bernie. A number of his books had jumped off their shelves and were leaping about the floor like fish on dry land.

Looking in the direction of Alcandor's gaze, Bernie said, "Oh, sorry." The books came to rest.

"Great Protector, what's happening here?"

"Oh, nothing. It's too hard to explain," Bernie murmured, forgetting to put the echo in his voice.

"Alcandor, let's call it a day. I need to think about this. Please give it some thought. We'll talk again soon, okay?"

Alcandor bowed his head and said, "Yes, of course, Great Protector."

Bernie winced. "And that's another thing. I don't feel much like a Great Protector. Maybe you should just call me Bernie. That's my name."

"Ber-Nee? Lord Ber-Nee?"

"No, just Bernie."

"Very well, my Lord. I shall address you as Bernie. But I suggest we call you 'Great Protector' in public," he said. "It will be easier for people to understand."

"Good night, Alcandor."

"Good night, Gr— Bernie."

Lenny Gets Upset

"So this Zardok won't agree to anyone leaving the planet?" Lenny asked.

"No. He practically threw me out of his office," Bernie admitted. He immediately regretted his words. Lenny had criticized him more than once for not behaving like a professional builder and doing what needed to be done. Bernie braced for the tirade he knew was coming.

"Then just get rid of him," Lenny said through gritted teeth. "When he's gone, the others will do what you want. I suggest finding a good public place and turning him into a pillar of fire. That will get everyone's attention."

"I can't do that, Lenny." Bernie's shimmer radiated with the seldom-seen colors of firm resolve.

"Well, you'd better figure out how to do it, or you're going to get fired," Lenny said in an infuriated tone.

"Come on, Lenny. You're being too hard on him," Suzie said, not for the first time.

"No, I'm not," growled Lenny. "He's throwing his life away for no good reason! He should have cleared off that whole planet and started something new weeks ago. Instead, he's letting time run out, and it's going to be for nothing."

"Alcandor and his people aren't nothing, Lenny. They're as real as you or I," Bernie insisted.

"No, they're not! They're just created beings. They don't matter! What matters is keeping your job." Lenny was angrier than Bernie had ever seen him.

Then, without warning, Lenny picked up his tray and moved to another table. The only other sound was Sissy's clucking as he moved away.

305 Bernie and the Putty

What's He Like?

Alcandor tossed and turned all night. His thoughts were dominated by his experience with the Great Protector. He had many questions.

Alcandor's logical mind pieced together everything he knew.

First of all, he thought, *He's incredibly powerful. The things He's done to save our world make that clear. Anyone who can stop giant waves, put out forest fires, stop hurricanes, change the color of the night sun, is more than just powerful.*

But He's not all-powerful. He can't undo things that have already happened. He can't make Zardok do something he doesn't want to do. He thought He could convince Zardok to go to the new world, but He was wrong, which means He can't tell the future. He's willing to fight on our side against the evil forces, but He isn't sure He can stop the evil, which means the evil may be more powerful than the Protector.

I can't believe He said He made a Sun for the new world. Is it possible He's more powerful than our Sun? And even if He's more powerful, why hasn't He talked about seeking help from our Sun? Surely the Sun would be a great ally in this fight. It's as if He doesn't think the Sun can help Him against the evil forces.

And why does the Protector have a name? That's another mystery. Why would anyone need a name, unless there were more than one of them? And if there are more Protectors, why haven't we heard about them? Surely there would be many unexplained events if other gods were living on our world. If he doesn't live here, then where does he live exactly? Does he just float around in the sky?

I didn't expect Him to have emotional reactions either. He was genuinely upset after the meeting with Zardok, and it caused my books to fall off their shelves. He didn't even know He'd done it. Can you imagine what would happen if there are lots of gods someplace, and they ever got in a fight about something? It could tear the world apart.

I can't shake the idea He's hiding something. He seems sincere about wanting to help us, but when He got upset, His voice changed, and He sounded like one of us. That makes me wonder if His deep echoing voice is real. If He's changing the way He sounds, then what else is He changing? If He wants to look like us, why didn't he make the color of His skin and His hair the same as ours? I understand him being bigger. To do what He does, He's undoubtedly a lot bigger than He seems. If anything, He's probably making Himself smaller than He really is, just so He can fit in our buildings.

Oh, Lord Bernie. What a mystery you are…

Alcandor Tells Gondal

Alcandor had no choice. He had to tell Leader Gondal about the Great Protector. And he had to do it soon.

The failed discussions with Zardok could not be ignored. Zardok was undoubtedly already making plans to discredit them both. That was insanity, of course. The Protector was the only thing capable of saving their world. Alcandor could not allow Zardok to discredit the Protector. The only remaining hope lay with Gondal and the Senate.

That's why he asked Gondal for a private meeting.

~

In his office in the Senate Building, Gondal waited for Alcandor to arrive. It had been several days since he'd heard anything from Alcandor.

"Welcome, Alcandor. I hope you have some good news," Gondal said pointing to a seat.

Alcandor paused to brush fallen masonry off the chair. He looked up, saw a crack in the ceiling, judged no collapse to be imminent, and sat down. They had known each other more years than either could remember.

"I found Him," said Alcandor simply and calmly.

Gondal looked at his friend. Over the years, Alcandor had accomplished impossible things and made startling discoveries, but this was, without doubt, the most astonishing discovery in the history of the world. Gondal had prayed to the Sun that Alcandor would be successful, but he'd prepared himself for failure.

"What's He like?" Gondal asked with an equally calm voice that revealed none of the excitement he felt inside.

"He looks like us, except He's much bigger. When I first saw Him, He hovered in front of me surrounded by a golden shimmer. The only thing different about Him is His pale skin and gray hair and beard. He has an echo in His voice as if He's speaking in a tunnel."

"So much like us…" said Gondal. "How is it possible?"

"Actually, I think He can change the way He appears."

"Really? What makes you think so?"

"When He gets upset, His voice changes and His shimmer does, too."

"Upset? What happened to make him upset?"

"We met with Speaker Zardok. The meeting did not go well."

Gondal shook his head as worry lines appeared on his forehead. "Maybe you should tell me what happened."

"The Protector appeared in my office four days ago. I looked up, and there He was, floating cross-legged in the air, three feet above the floor. He wanted to know why I was trying to contact Him. I started to tell Him what was happening here, but He seemed to know already. He said a great evil has discovered our world. He said He would try to prevent it from doing further harm, and then He left.

"Two days later, He appeared again. He said the evil was too strong, and He couldn't protect us. He said He made a new world for us, one where the evil couldn't find—"

"What? He *made a world*? How is this possible?" Gondal interrupted, unable to hold back his disbelief.

"I had the same reaction," said Alcandor with a smile. "I asked Him about it, and His answers were so unbelievable I hesitate to repeat them. You'd believe them less than I did."

"Try me. What did He say?"

"He said the new world is just like ours."

"Is it far away?"

"I think so. He said He made a new Sun for the new world, too." Alcandor waited for Gondal's reaction.

Gondal's mouth fell open. "He claims to have *created a Sun?*"

"Yes. And He didn't think it a 'big deal' because He said 'your system is pretty simple', whatever that means."

"Alcandor, this isn't easy to believe. The Great Protector claims to have created another Sun? What did He say about our Sun?"

"Actually, He didn't say anything about our Sun. But there is more to tell about our meeting with Zardok."

"Why didn't you come to me first?"

"I told the Protector the only way our people would leave this world is if both the Temple and the Senate recommended it. We decided it would be easier if we could convince Zardok first. But it didn't go well."

"What happened?"

"Zardok is a stubborn man. He refused to accept the idea the Sun needs any help. When the Protector told him He'd created another world for us, with a different Sun, it was too much. He accused the Protector of being a deceiver and a blasphemer, and he kicked us out."

"Oh, my. What did the Protector do?"

"He became very angry. I feared He would give up on us, but He still wants to help."

Gondal thought for a while. "If the Temple opposes the Protector's plan, I don't think the Senate can convince the people. Some, maybe, but I doubt we could get even half to leave our world. Is He sure that's the only way?"

"He said the evil is so strong that He cannot prevail. That's why He wants us to go to a place where the evil can't find us."

"Do you have any idea of how powerful He really is? Can he truly help with these problems?"

"I'm convinced His powers are formidable, but He does have limits. For example, He can't force someone to do something or He would have made Zardok listen. I don't think He can see the future, and I'm pretty sure He can't change the past. He seems to have a code of conduct He follows or else He'd just pick us up and move us. And there are some other strange things I haven't figured out yet."

"Strange things? Like what?"

"Well, when we got back from meeting with Zardok, the Protector was upset. His voice sounded different, and He had a problem controlling some of His powers. The books on my shelves started jumping all over until He noticed and stopped them."

"What do you make of that?"

"Honestly, it's like when I used to teach in school. You know how when the children didn't get their way, they sometimes have tantrums? Almost like that."

"I sure hope that isn't what's going on. We have deadly problems, and we need adult solutions."

Still Best Buds

"I'm sorry," said Lenny.

"I'm sorry, too," said Bernie.

"You're my best friend, Bernie. I don't want to lose you. But if you blow your universe project, you won't be able to work here. I don't understand what you're trying to do."

"I'm not sure I do either," Bernie admitted. "I'm spending all my time worrying about what Billy's going to do next. Even when he's not doing something, I'm afraid to add more life, because he'll just kill it. Now that I've met these people, I can't let anything happen to them. Honestly, I don't know what to do."

Bernie looked at his friend, expecting to be told to blink out anything that got in his way. Then he heard Sissy's soft clucking. Whatever Lenny had been about to say was apparently forgotten.

"It sounds like Sissy has an opinion on this." Bernie didn't try to hide his smile.

"I'm finding she has opinions on a lot of things. She spent last night telling me most of them. I was better off when I didn't know she could talk," he said with a grin.

Sissy must have understood the joke because she made a putting sound.

"Hello, guys," said Suzie. "I wasn't sure I would see you together after your argument yesterday. I'm glad you patched things up."

"That's what best friends do," said Bernie.

We Must Agree

"Why must you be so stubborn?" Alcandor shouted.

"Why must you always question everything?" Zardok shouted back.

"Gentlemen, please. This isn't solving anything. We have to work together. The people are depending on us," Gondal pleaded.

He shook his head at the two men glaring at each other. Sitting back wearily in his chair, Gondal felt if they had been locked in the same battle since the beginning of time.

And maybe they had...

~

The Lords were a small group of men and women, originally numbering 152. The three of them had always been at the forefront of events that moved their world.

Zardok had led them out of the time of darkness, the time that no lord could remember. He led them to an understanding of the Sun and His ways. Zardok's dedication and commitment led to the creation of temples throughout the land. His strength and charisma attracted men and women to the new priesthood where they devoted their lives to the service of the Sun.

Gondal's earliest memories were of helping Zardok bring the message of the Great Sun to their people, but as the world became more complex, their paths diverged. Zardok never wavered from his commitment to the Sun, but Gondal left the priesthood to serve the world of men. Yes, the people needed spiritual guidance, but they also needed a roof over their heads and food in their bellies. Each man knew the other was essential. Neither wanted the path the other had chosen.

And both men knew Alcandor well. He had helped them both often enough with countless challenges over the years. It was impossible not to respect Alcandor's problem solving skills. His gift for creative and independent thought could be counted on for new insights into any problem. Gondal knew, as an administrator, to do his job well, it was essential to surround himself with people like Alcandor.

Zardok, on the other hand, had not sought Alcandor's help for a very long time. Alcandor's ability to find solutions where others failed stemmed from his unsettling propensity to challenge even the most basic of assumptions—including assumptions about the Sun—which angered Zardok. While Zardok might concede Alcandor was often correct, he believed challenging important doctrine was upsetting to the people. Better to avoid such things.

And then there was Vianna. It was no secret both Zardok and Alcandor had fallen in love with her. Her beauty was very real, but her charm and her wit were what made her unique. Neither of the men had ever married. So great were their obsessions with their work, no one had ever been able to divert them long enough to get them interested. But Vianna was different.

When Alcandor met her, she was the newly appointed minister of science. Alcandor had petitioned the Senate for resources for a great expedition beyond the land and across the ocean to search for the Sun's resting place. The idea was not popular with the Temple, although the Senate was eager for the undertaking. Vianna became the diplomat shuttling between the Temple, the Senate, and Alcandor.

Vianna mediated months of debate between Zardok and Alcandor. During this process, both men fell in love with her, wooed her, and wanted her hand in marriage. It has been said Zardok, to win her love, gave up his objections to the expedition. It wasn't long afterward, Vianna accepted Zardok's proposal, and they were married. But Zardok's joy was short-lived.

And Alcandor was to be disappointed yet again. The Senate refused to let him lead or even accompany the expedition.

Gondal himself had said, "You're too valuable to us, Lord Alcandor. We cannot let you take this risk."

Instead, the Senate appointed Vianna to lead the expedition. As minister of science, she was a logical choice. Zardok and Alcandor had both protested, but no one, not even Vianna, had listened. And so she left.

Never to return.

~

"Gentlemen, please," Gondal said yet again. "Can't we agree on anything?"

"Not if Alcandor keeps saying the Sun has no ability to help us. Without the Sun, we would not be here. Our Sun has kept us safe since the beginning. He needs to show Him more respect," Zardok stormed.

"All I'm saying is we need all the help we can get right now," Alcandor persisted. "If the Protector can help, why would we refuse it?"

"If your 'Protector's' solution is to leave our Sun and our world and go to another place, that is reason enough to reject Him and His solution," Zardok growled.

"Did the Protector say this is the only solution?" Gondal asked.

"No. He said this is the best solution, but He didn't say it was the only one."

"Then let's ask Him about other options," Gondal said to Alcandor. "Perhaps He knows something we can all agree on."

"The Protector gave me a way to contact Him. I can ask Him to meet with us, but it won't do any good if Zardok refuses to listen."

"He's right, Zardok. You must control yourself. We need all the help we can get."

"I am willing to listen," Zardok said reluctantly.

Gondal knew this was the closest Zardok would come to an agreement. He could never admit the Sun was powerless. He looked at Zardok and then back to Alcandor.

"Then I'll contact the Protector and ask Him to meet with us."

They agreed to meet again in Gondal's office in two days, subject, of course, to the availability of the Great Protector.

Alcandor Learns More

When Alcandor returned to his study, he thought again about the Great Protector—the god who wanted to be called Bernie. He needed to learn more about Him. If he knew more about Bernie's powers, he might be able to suggest ways to avert these devastating calamities. Well, the first step was to contact Bernie. He braced himself for the otherworldly contact.

Bernie said to pick up the rock and move it to the other side of the desk. The rock had been brought back by the second expedition from one of the volcanic islands they discovered as they searched for the Sun's resting place. Alcandor had kept it in the sentimental belief Vianna might have found such a rock on her ill-fated first expedition.

Alcandor had detected no change in the rock after Bernie had said it could be used to summon him. It looked the same as before. Just one of the mysteries he hoped to understand soon. He picked up the rock and moved it to the other side of his desk.

No sooner had Alcandor moved the rock, when the room filled with a golden shimmer, and he felt the presence of the god. No one can ever truly prepare for such an experience, which is why Alcandor, in his surprise at the quickness of the Protector's appearance, blurted out, "Yikes! Were you just sitting there, waiting for me to move this rock?"

The Great Protector, hovering before him, began to laugh.

~

Bernie couldn't stifle his laughter. It burst forth as it had not for many days. It felt good to laugh. It had been so long since he had seen the humor in anything. And when his laughter finally subsided, he noticed Alcandor's expression of uncertainty.

"Alcandor, I am sorry. I don't mean to laugh at you, but it's been a long time since I've laughed at *anything*."

"I'm glad I was able to lighten the gravity of our situation for you," Alcandor said with some hesitation. "Perhaps you will tell me what you found so funny."

Bernie thought for a moment. This man was his only ally. What could it hurt to explain a little to him? Plus, Alcandor seemed pretty sharp. Maybe if he told him a little more, he could actually help.

"I wasn't waiting for you. I don't have the luxury to wait for anything."

"But if you're busy, how is it that the instant I summoned you, you were able to come so quickly?" asked Alcandor.

Bernie smiled. *What a sharp and inquisitive mind you have, Alcandor,* he thought. *Let's see how well you handle more information.*

"I can move through time on your world. When I arrived on your world, it was less than one day after we last met. I came to your study and moved forward through time until I saw you move the rock. That's when I appeared."

Alcandor was unable to suppress a gasp of astonishment. "But, Great Pro... err... Bernie, if you can move through time, why don't you go into the past and prevent these awful things from happening?"

"It doesn't work that way." *Alcandor might just understand.* "I can never go further back into the past than the time I entered your world. In this case, it was one day ago. Beyond that, I cannot go."

"If you moved ten days into the future before I moved the rock, then you would be able to go ten days back?"

"Exactly."

"If you can go into the future, why don't you go and discover the next problem we'll face? Then you can come back and prevent it from happening."

Bernie smiled. "That's excellent thinking, Alcandor, but there's a problem with it. Think of the future as a tree with infinite branches. Every choice we make means one branch taken and another possible branch abandoned. In this way, there is really only one tree and only one branch because we have never taken the other branches. Yet if I come back with knowledge of the future and use that knowledge to take a new branch, then the tree has two branches. This has to be true because how else could I have learned of a different future?"

"So if you have future knowledge, and we use it to take a

different action, there is still a version of us who didn't take the action that saved us?"

"Precisely. We'll have saved ourselves, but our other selves on the other branch will be doomed to suffer the mistake we avoided," Bernie explained.

Alcandor looked at Bernie, and said, "Such great power you have. Yet even you have limits."

"Tell me, Lord Alcandor, why you have summoned me."

"I met with Gondal, the Leader of the Senate. We then met with Speaker Zardok. We both tried to convince him to move to your new world, but we were not successful. I want to ask if there are any other options for us to consider."

"It's good to consider options. The portal I hoped to use to transport your people may not be available."

"What happened?" he asked, surprised by Bernie's failure.

"The portal may not exist. I thought it did, but we couldn't find one. My friend said he would keep looking, but he wasn't optimistic." Seeing Alcandor's expression, Bernie realized he'd once again said too much.

"You have friends?" Alcandor blurted out. "How many more of you are there?"

Bernie wasn't sure how to close the door he'd opened. *Should I tell him more? What good would it do? Alcandor can't stop Billy. I can't even stop Billy.* But Alcandor certainly had a stake in the outcome. He might understand if he had all the facts. *But it's embarrassing. All his problems are really my fault. If I hadn't fought with Billy, he wouldn't be doing this.*

How could Bernie tell Alcandor he was the reason his people had died? How could he tell him his whole world would be destroyed because he wasn't a good enough builder to keep his job? Bernie was about to lose his job, his friends, and everything that mattered to him. But Alcandor was about to lose his life and the lives of everyone he knew. Hopelessness overwhelmed Bernie and sent him to a very lonely place.

A hand placed on his arm startled Bernie and brought him back from that dark place. "Bernie, I would help you if I could," Alcandor said softly.

That caught Bernie off guard. Anything else he could have handled. This offer of help was so genuine, so heartfelt, it opened the floodgates inside him, and he found himself powerless to hold back the feelings that spilled forth.

"It's all Billy's fault. He's doing this, and I can't stop him. I tried and tried." Bernie knew gods weren't supposed to cry, but he couldn't hold back the tears. He didn't want these people destroyed. And with each sob, more words came out. "My friends are helping me, but we can't stop him. And if we can't, they're going to fire me, and then they'll destroy your world. And there's nothing I can do about it."

The sobs continued.

~

Alcandor watched in speechless fascination as the great god sobbed and his words spilled forth. The anguish Alcandor had sensed in the god had caused him to instinctively reach out and touch Him. Watching now, his hand still on the god's arm, he witnessed the extraordinary changes that followed. Bernie's gray beard and long hair faded away, as did the white cloak, leaving the god dressed in pants and a T-shirt. Next, the god's sandals turned into shoes with long, untied laces.

Yet the greatest change of all was to see the massive god shrink. With each sob, He became smaller and smaller until He was no more than Alcandor's height. Alcandor was mesmerized by the sight. Suddenly, it all made sense. So many questions were answered. Alcandor realized Bernie was a youth. More powerful than anything he could imagine, but still a youngster.

Bernie looked so small and so helpless. Alcandor was so moved, he reached out with his arms and embraced him. Bernie, for the first time in his life, felt something his father had never given him. He felt the strong arms of a man consoling him. Somehow, it filled an empty place.

Actually, it filled an empty place for both of them.

I Blew It

Journal Entry

I can't believe what happened. So much for 'Master of the Universe'. I'm so embarrassed. I can't ever tell Lenny or Suzie about this. Lenny will say I broke every rule in the First Contact Protocol Handbook.

I know what Dad would have said if he'd seen me. "How can you be so stupid? Get out of my sight!" Then he would have blamed Mom for everything and made her cry.

Alcandor is so different.

I can't imagine what he must have thought. Here I am, the most powerful thing in his universe, crying my eyes out. He didn't laugh or anything. He held me in his arms. I never felt that before, and it made me cry even more. My dad would never have done that.

Afterwards, we talked for a long time. I told him everything. I told him about Billy and what he's been doing. I told him how I've been trying to protect his world. I even told him what will happen if I fail. I know I shouldn't have told him any of this, but I'm glad I did. At least he knows I've been trying.

I really like him. He told me a lot about himself, too. He's never been married nor had kids. The only woman he ever loved was Vianna. When she married Zardok, he was heartbroken. He still blames himself for not demanding the Senate let him lead the expedition. But he knew Vianna wanted it, so he didn't protest. He still regrets that decision.

How is it possible to love someone that much? I don't think my dad ever loved Mom like that. If he did, I never saw it. I feel sorry for Mom. She deserves better.

It's too bad Alcandor never had kids. He would be a terrific dad.

Astronomy 101

Bernie had begun visiting Alcandor in the evenings as soon as he got home from work. They talked of many things.

Every time, Bernie saw the awe in Alcandor's eyes. "You humble me, Bernie. Your knowledge has no limits. I've spent my life trying to learn, but all of my knowledge is nothing to yours. And most of my knowledge is wrong."

"You're being too hard on yourself. My knowledge comes from books. They made us read thousands of books in school. Each of those books has the combined wisdom of hundreds, if not thousands, of others. I'm only repeating what I learned from them."

"But how can they know such things? Their insights are truly amazing."

"Remember, you have disadvantages they didn't have."

"How so?"

"I created an extremely simple system here. The only thing you ever saw was your sun. Most people see multiple suns and sometimes even galaxies. In most universes, there are lots of planets and moons. Because things change all the time, people look for explanations. Eventually, they figure it out.

"You lack any of these. You have no celestial landmarks to gauge the passage of time. You only have one sun. Until I made the moon and the other two planets, there was nothing to be seen in your sky. All of your days are the same as the next."

"I think I understand. Even now, people are starting to refer to past events in terms of the number of cycles the night sun has completed, instead of the number of days."

"Exactly. And if you had seasons, you would probably count the number of times the most important season had happened. This would give you the concept of years. Now, not to get too technical, but if you lived on a world that..." continued Bernie.

~

"We live on a sphere? How can this be?"

"Yes. Your world and the sun both have the same spherical shape. It is—"

Alcandor, in his enthusiasm, interrupted. "The Sun is not flat? Our earth is not flat?"

Bernie waited for him to absorb that information.

"But how can anything survive on the upside down part of the world?"

"It's just like here. There's a force that holds everything down. They don't experience being upside down."

~

Bernie was fascinated by how quickly Alcandor grasped new concepts. Everything Bernie said shattered and re-shattered Alcandor's concepts about his world. Alcandor paused long enough to grasp each idea, incorporate it into his new world-view, and then rushed eagerly to the next question.

~

"But what of the great voyage? If our continent stretches along the equator of our world, as you said, then our voyagers traveled along the equator."

Bernie watched as Alcandor tried to visualize their world, waiting for his *aha* moment. It came quickly. "They sailed west and returned from the east! That's how it happened. They circled the world and arrived back where they started! We never understood how that could happen."

Alcandor thought back to the larger question, the reason the voyage had been launched in the first place. They had failed to find the resting place of the sun.

"The Sun must travel around this equator too. We never discovered where He rested at night because He does not rest. He stays high in the sky and does not come down at all. Every day He makes the same journey our explorers made. This is why He departs to the West and He returns in the East!"

~

"Bernie, is it possible the monthly wasting of the night sun is just a shadow? That would mean our night sun has no light of its own but is illuminated by our Sun," said Alcandor as his thoughts raced onward.

~

"Bernie, if our Sun doesn't move, then our planet must be turning all the time so it just looks like He's the one who is moving. This makes so much sense." Alcandor thought through the implications.

"Is it possible the night sun revolves around us? I could calculate this to see if I'm right. I should be able to calculate the tiny suns, the ones you call planets, to see if they revolve around us or around the Sun. I'm guessing they revolve around the Sun too…" Alcandor said as one insight after another exploded in his brain.

~

Bernie enjoyed watching this amazing man hurtle through concepts that normally took centuries to discover.

He wondered if he had done any kindness here. This knowledge had forever changed Alcandor and made him different from the others on his planet. Some people already resented Alcandor's fearless search for truth and his willingness to tell the world whatever he found. *Such things can get you killed,* thought Bernie. *Perhaps it's time to temper his enthusiasm.*

"I'm concerned your new knowledge could be harmful."

"How can knowledge be harmful?"

"Many people become attached to their view of the world. If you challenge it, they can get upset." Bernie watched as Alcandor turned his mind to this new question. Bernie had no doubt of Alcandor's ability to see down this road as he had seen so clearly down the other roads of knowledge.

Alcandor paced back and forth. Several times, he appeared about to speak, but his thoughts raced onward, leaving him no time to voice earlier thoughts. Finally, he said, "I begin to understand. The things I know undermine everything we believe.

"We believe the Sun is our benefactor, the giver of everything we hold dear. To discover our Sun is not a god would be calamitous news. How can we trade our loving god for a ball of fire with no special powers or sentience or caring?" Alcandor took a deep breath and then said, "You're right, Bernie. I can't share this knowledge. Not at this time. We all need something to believe in.

"And right now," said Alcandor, "we desperately need our god."

Zoology 101

No matter how busy he was, Bernie made time to visit Alcandor every day. Alcandor enjoyed their visits every bit as much as he did.

"I still can't figure out where you came from," Bernie said one day. "I never put anything on this world except plants. I was going to add animals, but I never got that far."

"Animals? Do you mean people like us?"

Bernie wondered how to explain animals to someone who had never seen any. "Well, think of it this way. There are two kinds of life on this world, plants and animals. In the plant category, out of an unlimited number of possibilities, I created eighty-seven types, mostly selected for their food value. In the animal category, there are also an unlimited number of possibilities. But here, there's only one type, and that's you. Usually the animals look very different and most of them are not as intelligent as we are."

"Hmm… You're intelligent. We're intelligent. We look like each other. Is that just a coincidence?"

"That's one of the mysteries I haven't been able to explain. You have no knowledge of any place before you came here?"

"We've always been here. No one remembers anything else. The Sun has always been here. Some of us can even remember when we learned to make fire, built our first shelters, and learned to gather food from the sea. Some lords claim to recall the time before we had a spoken language."

"Sometimes people come from other worlds, but since there are no other worlds here with any life, that doesn't explain your situation," said Bernie, "although sometimes, life can start by itself."

"Perhaps that's what happened with us."

"The problem with that hypothesis is there just wasn't enough time. To evolve to a higher life form like yours takes millions of years. Billy destroyed all the life on this planet two million years ago. That's when I reintroduced the plant life. Even if you got started then, it wouldn't be possible to evolve into people in two million years. Look at the plants. They are still very close to the way I created them."

"One difference between you and me, Bernie, is my green skin, which is the same color as the plants. Perhaps there's a connection between us and the plants?"

"That gives me an idea. Can you tell me about your children? Do they look like you when they're born?"

"Yes, they're small versions of us. They have green skin. They have fingers and toes like us. There's a 500-day gestation period."

"Where can I find women whose gestation period is just starting?"

Alcandor's green skin showed a hint of red. "That might be a little awkward."

"That's not what I meant," said Bernie. "I'll be right back."

~

Bernie moved 600 days into the future. He scanned the city until he found a newborn baby. The child's form looked just as Alcandor had described. Bernie was looking for something else.

With unsupervised evolution, life moves from primitive forms to more advanced forms as the life form develops increasingly specialized survival skills. His teachers said you could figure out how it evolved by doing phylogenetic analysis. You just watch the embryo from its fertilization to the time it's born. Interestingly, life forms retain their evolutionary history in their cells.

Bernie recalled one creation lab experiment where they observed the gestation process of an organism whose earliest embryo looked like a fish, changed to an amphibian, then to a reptile, and finally to a mammal before it looked like its parents and was finally born. This was what Bernie wanted to observe now.

The young god moved his time lever backward as he focused on the newborn baby. Just before birth, the fetus looked like every parent wants their child to look: fully formed, with all its fingers and toes and no abnormalities. Bernie pushed back in time, eager to see what it would look like. Would the early embryo resemble one of Bernie's plants? Maybe its progenitors were plants living deep in the ocean that survived when Billy destroyed the other life on the planet. The child's form remained stable for quite a while. Finally, he saw it begin to change. Bernie observed all the way back to the point of fertilization. Well, not quite that far. Bernie was a little uncomfortable with that kind of stuff. He'd studied it in school and all, but he didn't really have any firsthand experience with it.

Now, Bernie moved his time lever forward and watched again as the zygote began its process of mitosis. The new cells divided over and over again until they looked like a large translucent gob. The gob stayed gob-like for days; the only noticeable change was taking on a light green color. Finally, the gob began shaping itself into the form of a child. Yet it was still translucent, and no bones or internal organs could be seen. Slowly, organs formed and bones materialized inside the gob.

Bernie saw no evidence the child's ancestors had once slithered across the ground, swum in the sea, or walked on all fours. The bones that formed were complete and ready for upright walking. By the end of 100 days, any hint of an evolutionary ancestor was lost.

Bernie ran his time lever forward and back several times, each time observing different aspects. He didn't have to do that. He did it without thinking as he tried to absorb the inescapable explanation to his mystery. Alcandor's people had not come from another planet. They had grown up right there. There was only one place they could have come from.

Bernie returned to Alcandor, allowing a five-second interval between his disappearance and his reappearance. Otherwise he would have to explain that he actually left and returned in what Alcandor would experience as no more than the blink of an eye.

"I found the answer," Bernie said with excitement.

Alcandor's expression changed to one of surprise and something more. Shaking his head, he said, "We must be fools. We've been baffled by this question from the beginning, yet you answer it in seconds."

"You could never have guessed this answer," said Bernie as he composed his thoughts. "Something we use to help us in our creation process is called Universe Putty. The gods combine their creative energy to make the putty. It's very powerful. It can become anything."

"Are you saying we came from this putty?" From his expression, Bernie suspected Alcandor had hoped for a different answer.

"Yes, I'm sure of it. The putty has a history of making unexpected things happen. This wouldn't surprise anyone."

"But, putty?"

"Think about it. Everything ever created in the universe bears the fingerprints of its creator. The gods created this putty. If you evolved from the putty, it makes perfect sense you would look like us."

Alcandor considered this.

Bernie added, "It also explains why you live so long."

"We live so long? What do you mean?"

"Most animals don't live very long. We're taught to add a death directive when we create life forms because it helps them evolve and stay adapted to their world. I put directives in the plants. Gods don't have one. That's why we live so long. You don't have one either."

"But we do die, Bernie. You've seen it."

"So do we, but not because we get old. Neither of us age. If a god dies, it's from accidents or something that hurts us on our world."

"Why do we have green skins?"

"I don't have an answer to that. Maybe it's because there are no other animals here. You might have some special connection with the plants."

"We believe our skin is green because the Sun loves green. The green is His promise to us that He will always be here for us."

Bernie wasn't paying full attention to Alcandor. He was still thinking about the putty.

"You know what else this means?" Bernie said, grinning.

"No."

"We're related!"

Quakes and More

Billy scowled. He didn't know why Bernie had built the mountain range. It wasn't part of what they'd learned in school, so he guessed it was intended for whatever higher life forms Bernie was planning. He could see regular breaks in the mountain range to allow north-south movement. *Bernie's such an optimist. After I'm done, there wouldn't be any life forms who want to live on this planet.*

The mountains had given him the idea. There was a lot of planetary stress underneath them. Bernie had sealed the tectonic plates earlier, but the mountains were a perfect place to hide new fault lines.

Billy systematically began work on the crust beneath the mountains. He cut lines at different angles and depths. He created fault lines designed to weaken and eventually give way. He used the height and mass of Bernie's mountains to leverage the pressure. Then he created more fault lines on the ocean floor, to make the slippage easier.

He could have stopped here and let the earthquakes happen at seemingly random points in the future, but Bernie hadn't been advancing time on his world. And, because of Bernie's booby trap, Billy didn't dare to use his own time lever. Yet he didn't want to wait forever for his plan to begin. So he deepened the faults and applied more pressure, until he knew the damage was but hours away.

They wouldn't be big quakes, to be sure—nothing like half the continent falling into the ocean. But quakes would be just the beginning. He had created a little surprise for Bernie—a series of little surprises, actually, that would keep on giving. He grinned, thinking of the effort it would take to undo what he had done. *You get three-for-the-price-of-one today, Bernie.*

Had he stayed to watch, Billy would have been pleased. But by the time things started happening, he was home in bed, fast asleep.

Command Performance

As the hour of the meeting drew close, the Senate's amphitheater was filled beyond capacity. Every seat was occupied, and the aisles were jammed with yet more people. The only place not crowded was the center of the amphitheater, where one man stood alone. Everyone waited anxiously for the meeting to begin.

Gondal understood their anxiety. This would be the most important meeting in the history of their world. They were about to meet the Great Protector. Gondal wiped his sweating palms on the side of his toga and tried to control his breathing.

Everyone was waiting for him. He could delay no longer.

"Senators, Lords and Ladies, and citizens, as Leader of the Senate, I thank you for your attendance. Everyone knows the events that have befallen us. In all the history of our world, there has been more death and destruction in any week of the last five months than all the time before. We have never known such sorrow.

"With respect to those who sought answers, I remind you, just a month ago, we had none. Our only hope lay with Lord Alcandor, who spoke of a Great Protector. He believed such a being existed and urged every effort to contact Him. He believed such a being, if he existed and could be found, would be our salvation.

"The Senate charged Lord Alcandor to use every means possible to find and communicate with the Great Protector. By now, all of you know he succeeded. Lord Alcandor found the Great Protector. Everything Alcandor hypothesized about Him is true. The Great Protector was the one who interceded time and time again to save us from the worst of the disasters.

"On behalf of the Senate and our people, I asked Lord Alcandor to invite the Great Protector to appear before us. It's fitting He receive our thanks for all He's done to prevent our fate from being worse.

"I turn the floor over to Lord Alcandor, who will tell us

more." Gondal gestured to the man in the center and took his seat.

~

Lord Alcandor appeared solemn. He'd kept his head down while Gondal was speaking. Slowly, he looked up at his audience. "Everyone here has lost loved ones in recent months. Each of us has shed tears over such wanton death and destruction.

"Let me remind you how I knew the Great Protector must exist. I knew it when I realized the disasters we've suffered could have been much worse. Remember the drought that threatened to destroy the very food we need to survive? It ended when the gentle rains came. Remember the forest fires that ravaged our world, killing thousands of people? Suddenly, they were extinguished. Remember the hurricanes that brought the floods and brutal winds? They suddenly ceased. Remember the recent heat that threatened us? That too suddenly ended. All of these things are common knowledge. These are but a few of the things our Protector has done to stop the evil that threatens our world."

It was the custom of the Senate to give their feedback with cries and foot stomping. Today, with the gravity of what was being discussed, the only responses to Alcandor's words were scattered cries of "Hear! Hear!" and the sound of a few stomping feet. The rest of the audience devoted their full attention to his words.

"I have the honor of introducing you to the great and benevolent being who has chosen to aid us." Alcandor selected his words carefully, avoiding any reference to the Sun. They decided it would be best not to suggest any relationship between the two. "Great Protector," Alcandor called out with his arms raised high. "Please appear before us. We beg the opportunity to speak with you." As Alcandor spoke, he moved to the side of the center stage.

As the people held their collective breaths, a bright golden shimmer appeared and took the form of a giant who sat cross-legged, hovering six feet above the ground. The being had long gray hair and a full beard. Dressed in a bright white robe, He looked like them, except for the gray color of His hair and the pale color of His skin. There was no sound and little breathing as the Great Protector looked around the crowded amphitheater. It was a measure of His godly power that each person thought the Protector looked directly into their eyes.

There was a rush of sound as hundreds of people moved from their seats to their knees before the Great Protector.

"Please," said the deep reverberating voice of the Protector, "I require no such observances. Rise and be as you were."

Leader Gondal was slow to rise from his knees, but it was his duty to lead discussions with the Great Protector, and he knew what he had to do.

"Great Protector, I welcome you on behalf of the Senate," Gondal said with a shaking voice. "Lord Alcandor has told us of the many times you helped us. On behalf of the Senate and all of our people, I thank you. We are forever grateful for everything you have done."

"Thank you, Leader Gondal. I regret not being able to do more. I know your people have suffered greatly." Everyone felt the sadness in the words of the Great Protector.

"Great Protector, Lord Alcandor has told us of your great power. I must ask, on behalf of our people, do you have the ability to bring back those who have been lost to us?"

"Alas, Leader Gondal, that is beyond my power. I cannot change what is past."

"Can you tell us why this is happening to us? Can you tell us what we've done to deserve this fate? Or what we can do to make it stop?" Gondal knew these were the questions in everyone's mind.

The Protector lowered His head, and then raised it again. "I know your people, Leader Gondal. You are good and kind. You have done nothing to deserve this. This is the result of an evil force that has discovered your world. I have done everything in my power to stop this evil, but it is very powerful. And I am not always successful."

"Is there anything we can do?"

"For now, I know of nothing. If you need me, Lord Alcandor can reach me, although it may not be as quickly as you wish."

"Great Protector, there are others who would ask you questions. Will you speak with them?"

"Yes, Leader Gondal, but please be brief. There are other demands on my time."

Minister Tonst, the liaison between the Senate and the Temple, stood. "Great Protector, your presence here comes as a great surprise to us. We are curious to know how you fit into the cosmology of our world. Are you an agent of the Sun? Are there others like you yet to be discovered?"

Alcandor and Bernie had anticipated this question and knew to avoid it. Any attempt to provide answers would lead to controversy and divisiveness. Bernie said, "Minister Tonst, I understand your curiosity, but I have no time for such discussions. I have spoken of these matters with Lord Alcandor. I will let him answer your questions at another time."

Senators were not used to having their questions deflected. Several responded with boos. Almost immediately, there was dead silence as they realized what they had done. The Great Protector frowned at the senators who had booed him.

"What am I to make of this discourtesy?" The Great Protector's displeasure was clearly written on His face.

Gondal responded, "Great Protector, please forgive us. It is our custom to respond to our speakers in this manner. No disrespect is intended. I beg you to think of it as nothing more than an expression of disappointment."

The Great Protector turned to the Leader. As He did so, Gondal shrank from the steely gaze of the giant god who faced him. Suddenly, the ground began to shake.

Every senator and lord felt terror as they braced for the unknown fury of the Great Protector. Senators and lords scrambled to their knees. Cries from every corner beseeched the Great Protector for forgiveness.

Only one lord was confused. Alcandor knew Bernie would not harm them. What then, he wondered, was happening? He and Bernie had talked about the skepticism of the Senate and the possible need to demonstrate his power. But this was not part of the script.

"Alcandor, something is happening," said the Great Protector to the only man still standing in the Senate.

"Can you tell us what it is?"

"I can show you."

The Great Protector's image transformed into a giant image of Alcandor. As the small Alcandor looked up at the giant Alcandor, the giant also looked up. It took a moment to understand.

"We're seeing the world through the eyes of the Great Protector," Alcandor called out, shocked at the enormity of it all.

Alcandor's image disappeared, replaced by a rapid series of new ones as the Great Protector sought the source of the shaking earth. People saw images of their world from high in the sky. There were views of the coast and then close-up views of waves from far out in the ocean. When the view changed again, they saw a long and wide strip of land with ocean on both sides. Far below, the clouds looked like tiny puffs of smoke. Green forests covered the land, except for swatches of destruction left by fires and hurricanes. In the middle, they saw the Central Mountains.

Everyone watched, unable to tear their eyes away, as the Great Protector searched for the source of the disruption. Forests and mountains flew by, and they saw the end of their land. Only one man among them truly understood what they saw.

Moments later, far out on the ocean, they saw a round continent. If Alcandor had any reason to doubt the science lesson Bernie had given him about the shape of the world, those doubts were forever banished. From Bernie's height above the planet, Alcandor saw the softly rounded edges of his world.

Image after image flashed before them, none lasting even a second as the Great Protector searched at the speed of thought. Quickly, another continent loomed ahead. With a flash of insight, Alcandor recognized the course traveled by the Great Expedition. Viewed from above, it was easy to see the explorers were right. The entire continent was a ring of land completely enclosing a small ocean.

The god was moving fast, and the Sun was left behind as more images of western lands were seen. It might have been complete darkness, but the god's vision shifted into a new spectrum and the visibility remained clear. Finally, as He rounded the planet and came to the eastern coast of their land, the light of the Sun could be seen again.

Another vibration shook the Senate building, knocking several senators from their seats. *Please hurry, Bernie*, thought Alcandor.

Without warning, everything began shrinking, until it appeared the land and the oceans had been painted on the outside of a child's ball. The eyes of the god turned from the painted world and the night sun appeared. In an instant, the night sun went through a full cycle of light and dark.

Then, in the distance, they saw the Sun, surrounded by black instead of blue. In a flash, the great Sun loomed larger than anything imaginable. They could almost feel the heat as enormous columns of flame flickered and shot upwards from the surface of their god.

Just as quickly, they saw their world again. This time, the view was from high above the Central Mountains. Smoke and gas were escaping from a large fissure near the top of one mountain. The images came more slowly now, although harder to describe. It was as if the god had entered the mountain and was looking at the pressure and heat changes deep below the surface. Alcandor sensed Bernie's desperation to find and correct the problem before it was too late.

Before Bernie could do anything to release the pressure, the top of the mountain exploded. The mountain peak, once covered with white snowcaps, disappeared as pieces of rock and magma flew in every direction. Immediately, red hot magma gushed from the open wound and flowed down the mountain, igniting everything in its path. The images changed again as the Protector scanned the area for nearby cities or towns. He found none.

The Protector's view shifted back to the emerging volcano. And then it ceased. In the center of the Senate, there was only emptiness.

The crowd was silent as they tried to absorb what they had seen. Here and there could be heard soft whispers as people tried to understand the un-understandable.

"Was that real?" one of the senators shouted to Alcandor.

"Yes. Without a doubt."

"Why didn't we hear or feel anything when the mountain exploded?" asked another.

"It's very far away," said Alcandor as he considered the distances involved. "We probably won't feel anything for a while. It will be even longer before we hear it."

Gondal asked, "How dangerous is this?"

"Anyone living close to the mountains is in great danger. The quakes might be able to reach us even here. The danger will come from the quaking earth, fires, and maybe flooding. I've seen stone buildings knocked down—"

Gondal didn't wait for Alcandor to finish. He shouted to the crowd, "We must leave. It's not safe here. Seek protection in open areas. Stay away from the water. Watch out for fire. Tell others. Go! Go, now!"

No one needed to be told again as they made their way out of the Great Chamber. Just twenty minutes later, seismic waves rippling through the earth reached them. Two massive columns on the eastern side of the Senate Office Building crumpled, and a large section of its roof fell to the ground.

It was two hours more before they heard the sound of the explosion.

The Rest of the Story

During recent weeks, Bernie had developed an inspection routine he used when he thought Billy might have done something. When the quake hit, he automatically launched into his routine. It took several minutes to realize his mistake. It had been careless to let the Senate see him viewing a world they believed was flat, or checking out the sun and the moon. He had no time to think about that now. He would have to trust Alcandor to contain the damage.

Finally, he'd found the problem. It was a volcano and not a simple one either. It was a supervolcano, capable of wiping out life on the planet with its lethal combination of toxic fumes and cloud cover. In just days, the clouds could fill the sky, cutting off the sunlight his plants needed to survive.

He stopped sending his vision back to the Senate. He needed his full attention to deal with the problem. They would have to use their imaginations from here.

Then he remembered the quake damage could easily reach the Senate and beyond. Did he dare go back and make sure everyone was safe? No. This was the priority. The volcano had to be stopped before it killed thousands of people.

Bernie watched in horror as the earth trembled yet again. He hadn't expected Billy to have made more than one. Within minutes, a chain reaction along the Central Mountains gave birth to four more volcanoes. Three of the four were supervolcanoes and the fourth showed potential. Each arrival was accompanied by an explosion and massive quakes, opening giant fissures and unleashing billowing clouds of dark gases, volcanic ash, and more red-hot magma to flow down the mountain.

As Bernie tried to gauge the full extent of the problem, he saw three hot spots in the ocean, where clouds of steam and gases bubbled up from the ocean's floor. Potential tsunamis sprung into his mind. Meanwhile, the new volcanoes were spreading fire to the beautiful green hills as the new smoke and ash darkened the once-blue sky.

Bernie focused on the active volcanoes. He'd had plenty of practice when Billy created over 200 of them. Two million years ago, Billy's volcanoes had wiped out his plant life. *After you plug your two hundredth volcano, you start getting good at it*, Bernie thought with some sarcasm. *Thanks for nothing, Billy.*

Bernie began by cooling the magma at the mouth of each volcano to stop the flow and to seal it. He moved rapidly, cooling the magma everywhere he found it. In this way, he corked one volcano after another.

Next, he focused on getting the fires put out. On a planet with an abundance of plant life, there was no shortage of oxygen in the air, which fed the rapidly burning forest fires. Bernie had extinguished Billy's forest fires before by changing the air to carbon dioxide. But he couldn't use that solution again. The heavy gas could easily flow into nearby valleys and kill the people there. For the same reason, he couldn't snuff the fires by removing the oxygen.

Instead, he created massive thunderclouds above each raging fire and let them deliver sheet after sheet of torrential rain. And, for good measure, he created storm fronts and sent them to chase the volcanic ash and poisonous gases that had already been released.

As Bernie started to catch his breath, he felt the earth tremble again. It didn't take long to locate the new epicenter, close to the site of the second volcano. A fifth volcano, another supervolcano, had exploded. He saw gases escaping and knew magma would soon follow. His first thought was to plug it as he had done with the first four, but a fifth volcano meant something else was going on.

Billy must have created a network of fault lines under the mountain range. If he plugged this volcano, it would just build up pressure until the next one blew. He needed to fix the real problem.

Bernie spent three more hours searching the earth under the mountain range. He found the fault lines and fused them one by one. In addition, Billy had created a continent-long strip of hot magma just below the mountains. Every time a quake opened a crack, the magma was ready to emerge. It wasn't until he cooled the magma under the mountains that things began to quiet down as the number of quakes gradually subsided. There had been no new volcanoes for two hours.

Bernie was so exhausted, he almost forgot about the fault lines in the ocean. He found them on both sides of the continent. Bernie fused those lines as well, but by now he was drained; all he wanted was sleep. Even gods pay a price for using their powers.

Oh, no! Alcandor! Was he okay? Bernie sped back to the Senate. The sun was nearly down, and people were milling about in the street. Some wept, while others wore expressions of hopelessness. Everywhere, buildings had suffered from the quakes. The side of the Senate Office Building had collapsed, along with part of its roof. Bernie's heart pounded as he scanned the wreckage, but he found no bodies.

Moving to Alcandor's home, he found the building buckled in one section. Inside, he found Alcandor pacing in his study.

"Alcandor! Thank goodness you're safe," Bernie exclaimed as he materialized. There was no longer any pretense between them, and Bernie appeared as his true self.

"Bernie, I'm so glad to see you. You've been gone so long. I... I was worried about you too," Alcandor said, as they embraced.

"What happened?"

Bernie explained the supervolcanoes and what he'd done to stop them. He explained the superheated magma below the mountains, the fault lines he repaired, and the forest fires he extinguished. When he finished, he asked, "Tell me about the people. Did we lose many?"

"We were lucky. Gondal had the wits to send everyone out of the building before it collapsed. We used our signal system to tell people in nearby towns to keep out of the buildings during the quakes. So far, it appears we have injuries, but no known deaths."

"Thank goodness."

"You put on quite a show," Alcandor said with a twinkle in his eye.

"I'm sorry about that," said Bernie. "I didn't think about what people would be seeing when I looked for the source of the problem. I hope it won't cause difficulties for you."

"I don't think many people understood what they were seeing. In any case, leave that to me. It looks like you could use some rest. In fact, I think we could all use some rest," Alcandor said wearily.

"I agree. I'll see you tomorrow."

Bernie was exhausted, but the relief he'd felt when he found Alcandor unharmed had taught him a valuable lesson. He must do whatever he could to keep Alcandor safe. That was his greatest priority. And he would find a way, no matter what...

As he began to fade away, Alcandor's voice sounded in the background.

"Good night, Bernie. And thank you again for saving our world."

A Time of Peace

The fallen stones and rubble had been cleared away, but the Great Chamber didn't look 'great' at the moment. Nevertheless, all the seats of the amphitheater were filled. Gondal stood on one side of the center stage and next to him stood Alcandor. The Great Protector hovered in the center.

Gondal bowed his head to the god and then said, "Great Protector, again, I thank you for your service to our people and to our world. We saw the volcano you dealt with. Alcandor told us of the others and explained how they caused the earth to quake, which caused so much damage."

"I am glad I could help, Leader Gondal. I am sad to see what this has done to you and your people. I wish I could do more."

Gondal lowered his head and said, "The only thing that can help us now, Great Protector, is time. We need time to heal. Time to nurse our injured back to health. And time to rebuild our buildings and our society. Can you grant us that, Great Protector?" Gondal asked of the god who hovered above him.

The Great Protector's eyes looked sad as the god lowered his head. Then he abruptly lifted his head, as a half-smile spread to his lips. "Actually, Leader, that is something I can do. I can grant you a time of peace and it shall last for 1,000 days. But, when that time is over, the evil will still be here. Perhaps you can use the time to heal and to rebuild."

Although the senators should have learned their lesson, there were more than a few who could not resist calling out "Hear! Hear!" and stomping their feet.

"Thank you, Great Protector. Thank you. We will make good use of your gift," said Gondal as a lump rose in his throat.

Alcandor Makes a Request

"Bernie, if you grant us this 1,000 days of peace, won't that mean we won't see each other for a while?" asked Alcandor.

"Yes. That's the way it works. When I advance time in your world by 1,000 days, it will prevent Billy from being able to get to you. But it also means that time is lost to me. I won't be able to see you until it's over."

"As I understand it, there won't be much time that has passed for you, is that correct?"

"Yes. Only one day will have passed for me."

"You once offered me the chance to visit your world. I would like to do this when the time of peace has passed."

Bernie brightened. "That'll be great! I can introduce you to my friends. I know they'd love to meet you. And there is so much for you to see. You're going to love The Museum."

"But how will I communicate on your world? I know you learned our language, but isn't that because of the special powers you have on my world?"

"Yes. On my world, no one will be able to understand you, not even me."

"You said you still have your old schoolbooks. Are they something I could use to learn your language?"

"That's a great idea. I'll bring some books and a dictionary too. You might find some of the books boring, though."

"Why?"

"Most of the reading primers are Dick and Jane and Spot. Things like 'Look, Jane. See Dick build a universe. Good, Dick. Come, Spot. See Dick's universe.' and stuff like that."

Alcandor started laughing. "I guess that proves we're related. We have Dick and Jane, too."

"I'm not sure that proves anything." Bernie chuckled. "Dick and Jane are one of the Great Mysteries. They seem to pop up in universes everywhere."

"Still, it'll be like seeing old friends again," Alcandor said with a smile.

Not Cool

Bernie viewed Alcandor's world from outer space. Even from that distance, the scarred landscapes were clearly visible. It was fortunate he'd been on the planet when the volcanoes started. If he'd arrived later, it would have been much worse. Still, the volcanoes had done plenty of damage with the quakes and the fires.

Bernie prepared himself to grant the time of peace. Moving a universe 1,000 days into the future was a simple thing. The challenge was to make sure you weren't forgetting anything, because, once done, it couldn't be undone.

He asked Alcandor to help by using the rock in case he discovered problems before Bernie did. Bernie opened part of his mind to the rock in Alcandor's study. Another part of his mind he reserved for the gaia.

Well, thought Bernie, *I guess I'm ready.*

"Hello, Gaia. How're you feeling today, girl?" Bernie had not studied shimmers or auras, but it didn't take training to see the distress in the gaia's aura. Normally, a gaia's aura was a soft blue-green color. "Hmm... That doesn't look good," he said as he looked at the weak aura. "I don't like those flecks of red either. Those volcanoes were hard on you, weren't they, girl?

"It looks like you could use a little time of peace too," he said as he gently moved his time lever forward. Slowly, as the days flickered by, Bernie watched her aura grow brighter as Gaia regained her strength. With another part of his mind, he watched Alcandor's rock. Day after day, the rock stayed where it was. Bernie allowed himself a smile, taking vicarious pleasure from the gentle days that passed below. Each day that passed became closed to Billy. As soon as Bernie left the universe, the Past Barrier would cut it off to both of them.

Then, several days passed when Gaia's soft aura did not improve. Bernie slowed time to observe more closely. More days passed. Gaia's aura seemed weaker than before. Something was wrong. Bernie suspended time. Nothing anywhere in the universe moved. Only Bernie was exempt from this.

He scanned the world. The northern polar ice was slowly rebuilding. Hints of new green could be seen where the fires had raged. He saw people in the towns and villages frozen as they went about their business. He even saw Alcandor reading one of Bernie's schoolbooks. Bernie allowed himself a smile when he noticed Alcandor was now reading at a fifth-grade level. Nowhere did he find anything wrong.

In School, they classified the gaia as one of the Great Mysteries. The gods didn't do anything to create them. They were an independent creation that would, in their own good time, come into being on almost any living planet. Efforts to transplant them or create them on demand had proven unsuccessful.

Bernie had learned to trust this gaia. She'd given him warnings before when things were not right. She alerted him when the planet's rotation had been accelerated. She had tipped him off when Billy moved the planet closer to the sun. No words were required—if her aura was weak, then Bernie looked for problems. When her aura became stronger, he knew he had resolved the problem. What was she trying to tell him now?

Cautiously, he advanced time a few more days. More red flickers in her aura told him of additional suffering. "Yes, Gaia. I can see you're trying to tell me something," Bernie slowed time to a complete stop.

Gaias weren't entities that existed solely within the biosphere, he recalled. They extended into the atmosphere, the hydrosphere, and even the pedosphere. Bernie scanned the atmosphere for any differences from his original design specifications. He found none. He repeated the process with his ocean. Again, nothing out of the ordinary there, other than a high presence of toxins in the ocean, caused by the recent volcanoes. Still, it should not bother Gaia. Finally, Bernie looked to the earth. It didn't take him long to find the problem.

Not far below the surface, he found the heat. As he went deeper into the planet, he found greater and greater temperatures, far beyond anything he had planned. The planet's crust was slowly melting from the inside. Billy had overheated the planet's core, and the heat was radiating upward, layer by layer, on its way to the surface. As it got closer, oceans would evaporate and every living thing on the planet would fry.

Bernie closed his eyes as he took the anger he felt and moved it once again to another place. He could fix the problem, he knew. But sooner or later, he would miss something and arrive too late. With his anger safely tucked away, the only thing he felt was sadness.

Billy, Billy, Billy, he thought. *You are such a bad boy.*

The Kids Prepare

"It's hard to believe they look that much like us, Bernie," said Lenny. "Are you sure there isn't more?"

"I don't think so. The only thing that's different is the greenish tint to their skin. They don't age, so there's no gray in their hair."

"Then all I need to do is to bring my makeup kit and lighten up his skin," said Suzie. "But what about communicating? Even if you gave him books, how is he going to know how to pronounce anything?"

"I left him a dictionary with pronunciation guides, and I borrowed a voice recorder from Lenny's OWT collection and used it to record myself reading one of my books out loud. He can use the book and the recording to figure out how to pronounce things."

"That's expecting a lot, Bernie," Suzie said.

"He's really smart. You'll see. I can't wait for you both to meet him."

A soft clucking sound reminded Bernie there weren't just two people who wanted to meet Alcandor. "You too, Sissy," he added, which turned the clucking into a purr.

"When are you pulling him out?" Lenny asked.

"Today's Friday, so I'm going to bring him out tonight. Then we'll have the whole weekend together."

"Where's he going to stay, Bernie? Have you told your mom about him?" asked Suzie.

"I told her a friend is coming to spend the weekend. She's going to cook dinner for us."

"Did you tell her where he's really from?" Suzie asked.

"No, I just told her he's someone I met through work."

Lenny chuckled. "Well, that's true."

The Extraction

Bernie tingled with excitement. Suzie met him after work, and they strolled together to Bernie's home. Twice, Suzie had taken Bernie's hand. And once, when she laughed at something he said, she gave him a playful bump in his side with her shoulder.

As they approached the edge of town, Suzie became nervous about being that close to the woods. "There's really nothing to be afraid of."

"All my life, I've heard about wild beasts and dangerous things in the woods. I can't help being afraid." She held Bernie's arm with both hands.

~

As Bernie approached his home, he was observed by tiny eyes. This was something different. The boy had never brought anyone home before. Who was this girl? Why was she with him?

Maybe he would come to the woods again, and they would find a way to ask him.

~

Suzie, like other gods, had heard things about the project homes in Fifth Circle. When she entered Bernie's home, she was relieved to find it neat and clean. She guessed Bernie's room wasn't that way, but it was good to know Bernie's mom kept a tidy home. The few decorations had been chosen with taste and an eye to usefulness. Obviously, Bernie's mom didn't have any money to waste.

Bernie left Suzie in the family room/dining room/kitchen while he disappeared into his room. He returned carrying the viewing window that led to Alcandor's world.

"This is exciting. You've talked so much about your universe. This is the first time I've ever seen it." She bent closer to the viewing window and let her awareness enter the universe.

"Oh, Bernie. I'm so sorry," exclaimed Suzie as she saw the world before her. "I see why you're so upset with Billy."

"Let's not talk about him. I don't want to think about him at all this weekend."

"That's a good idea."

Bernie positioned the viewing window over the couch. "He's going to be heavy once I pull him through. I want to make sure he has something soft to land on if I can't hold him. Plus, my viewing window isn't as big as the ones at work, so it'll be a narrower fit for him. Ready?"

"Oh, yes. I can't wait to meet him."

Bernie moved close to the window, as he had many times before when he worked for Good Shimmer Imports. This time, instead of fetching books from another universe, it would be a person. Not so much different, but definitely heavier.

Bernie's head and arms disappeared as he reached into the viewing window. Then, in one smooth motion, Bernie pulled out and back from the window. As he did so, he brought a man with him. The extra weight of the man unbalanced Bernie, and they both fell backwards onto the couch. Before Suzie could start worrying someone was hurt, she heard both of them laughing.

It was an infectious laugh, and soon Suzie found herself caught up in it as well.

"Don't worry. Going back is easier, because I'll have all my powers on the other side."

They untangled arms and legs until two distinct people stood in front of Suzie. She smiled at Alcandor and did a small curtsy. "Welcome to our world, Lord Alcandor. I trust your journey here was a pleasant one."

Alcandor flashed a delighted smile and bowed back, "Thank you, Lady Suzie. I can truly say I have never traveled so far in so little time. Nor have I ever been greeted at the end of my journey by a more beautiful young lady."

"I understand you perfectly," said Suzie. "I was worried you wouldn't be able to learn our language from Bernie's books," she said as the rest of his words sank in, which caused her to blush.

"I told you he was smart."

Alcandor beamed with the compliment.

Bernie watched as Suzie and Alcandor looked at each other. Alcandor had never seen another god besides Bernie. Suzie, for her part, was considering what she needed to disguise Alcandor. Suzie spoke first.

"Bernie told me you look just like us, but this is remarkable! You look like a distinguished gentleman from the Second Circle district of town. I was worried about explaining your lack of a shimmer, but you have one! I've never seen an off-worlder with a shimmer before. Your shimmer not only looks normal, but it's well-defined and very sophisticated."

Alcandor grinned as he turned to Bernie and said, "Your girlfriend is delightful, Bernie. I can see why you like her so much."

This produced another red complexion outbreak. Bernie said, "I… Ah…"

"Well… Ah…" said Suzie.

Alcandor laughed again, and soon everyone was laughing.

~

It didn't take long before Alcandor's transformation was complete. Suzie brought clothes for him, and, with the makeup in place, he could go anywhere without arousing suspicion.

"Is there anything special you want to do?" Bernie asked his guest.

"Everything. I've read about wondrous things here, and I have no idea where to begin. Perhaps I should leave you in charge."

"I'm sure you would like a tour around town. And we have to take you to The Museum," Suzie suggested.

"And there are people you have to meet. Lenny would've been here tonight, except he has a hot date with Candi. He wants to see you tomorrow. My mom's cooking dinner for us. I'm so pleased you're here," Bernie said in a gush of words.

"So am I."

~

Bernie's mom arrived with an armload of groceries for dinner. Alcandor stood as she entered, while Bernie rushed to put everything away.

"Thank you, Bernie. We can put them away later," said Hannah as she relinquished her bags to Bernie. "Hello, Suzie. I'm glad to see you. In fact, I hope to see more of you in the future," she said in the special way females communicate with each other with multiple layers of meaning.

"Bernie, are you going to introduce me to our guest?"

"Sure. Mom, I would like you to meet my friend Alcandor. Alcandor, this is my mom, Hannah."

"I'm very pleased to meet you, Lady Hannah," he said as he gave a courtly bow of his head.

"Well, thank you, kind sir." Hannah returned his bow with a slight curtsy of her own. Even Bernie noticed the pleasure his mom took in the extra courtesy Alcandor showed. *He must have read the etiquette book too*, thought Bernie.

"I don't think I've seen you before, Alcandor."

"I've spent most of my time off-world. Coming here is like a new experience for me. I'm eager to see everything," said Alcandor truthfully.

"Well, I'm sure the kids will have no trouble showing you around. But if they don't do a good enough job, let me know. I can always find time for distinguished off-world visitors," she said with a girlish smile.

Suzie noticed Alcandor's blush remained hidden by her makeup. She'd used one with a strong foundation, and if it didn't let green through, then red had no chance.

"Is there anything I can do to help?" offered Alcandor.

"Well, you can open this bottle of wine," said Hannah. "I think we can let the kids have a small glass, don't you?"

"Well, I guess that would be okay. As long as we maintain strict adult supervision." The twinkle in Alcandor's eye told Bernie Alcandor was amused to discover the Great Protector was not old enough to drink intoxicating substances.

When dinner was served, Suzie observed a pattern. Alcandor paused long enough to observe the others. Eating utensils must be different on his world, she realized, and something like this wouldn't have been in any of Bernie's schoolbooks.

"I recognize all of this," said Alcandor, referring to the food on the table. "This frosip is excellent. And so is the wonreg. I've never seen them prepared in this way."

"I decided to make Bernie's favorites. I'll give you the recipes, if you like," Hannah offered.

"That's a wonderful idea, Hannah. I'm sure a lot of what I eat is on Bernie's list of favorites," he said as Bernie stifled a laugh.

"Well, you make what you love..." Bernie said just loud enough for Alcandor to hear.

~

After dinner, Bernie walked Suzie home. Bernie liked it when Suzie held his hand tightly. He enjoyed being her protector, even if there wasn't anything she needed to be protected from in the woods.

"Alcandor is amazing! He adapts to whatever is around him. I would never guess he wasn't one of us," she said when they were out of earshot from the house.

"I know. It surprised me too. Sometimes things on other worlds seem cool, but when you get them back here, they don't seem as exciting. He's not like that. If anything, he's more interesting."

"Your mom sure seems to think so."

"Yes. They hit it off well, didn't they?"

"Do you think Alcandor will be okay alone?" Suzie asked.

"I can't imagine any problems. He and Mom were having a great time, and we never get any visitors out here."

They walked along in silence for a while.

At last Suzie asked, "What are you thinking about?"

"I was just thinking about my mom and Alcandor. What if they got together? That would make Alcandor my stepdad." Bernie wasn't sure how he felt about his mom getting married again, but if she did...

Alcandor as Dad... I would like that, he thought. *I would like that a lot.*

What Are Those?

The next morning, Alcandor was up and ready to go by dawn. Bernie, who would normally have grumbled about having to get up this early, was right there with him. Since there was time before they had to leave for Lenny's house, Bernie couldn't resist taking Alcandor for a walk in the woods.

"It's beautiful here, Bernie. I've never seen such stunning plants."

"Well, I wasn't really going for aesthetics in my plants. I was—"

Alcandor said, "I meant no criticism of my world, Bernie. I just never imagined all the diversity that's possible."

Bernie chuckled. "You ain't seen nuthin' yet. Wait until you see the animals." Bernie looked around, but his little friends were nowhere to be seen.

The walk was taking a long time. Alcandor stopped every few feet to examine each new plant he encountered. "All these plants were created by the gods?"

"No. Many of the plants in the woods are indigenous. We'll see more created life when we get into town."

"Indigenous? You have a term for life you did not create?"

"Of course. We don't know much about indigenous life forms. Come over here, and I'll show you." He led them to the edge of the plateau. "This is the edge of the plateau where we live. Down there is the wilderness. It just goes on and on. No one ever goes down there."

"Why not? Aren't you curious about what's out there?"

"People think it's too dangerous."

"Dangerous? What could be dangerous to a god?"

"We have no real powers in our world. Everyone stays in town, where it's safe."

"If it's dangerous, why do you live so close to the edge?"

"After Mom and Dad got divorced, this was all we could afford. We're saving money to get a better place, but I talked Mom out of doing anything for now." Bernie saddened, his very real problems surfacing despite his effort to only think positive thoughts. If he didn't keep his job, they would just have to move back again.

"I understand."

They walked along in silence. Suddenly, Alcandor exclaimed, "What's that?"

"That's a flying animal. We call them birds." Bernie held up his arm with his finger extended and gave a shrill whistle. The bird looped back and swooped in for a perfect landing on Bernie's finger.

"Alcandor, I would like to introduce you to Platus. Platus, this is my friend Alcandor."

Alcandor looked at the beautiful blue and red feathers. The bird had a long mane of loose yellow feathers, which it shook as it turned to face Alcandor.

Alcandor's eyes went wide with wonder as he said, "I... I'm pleased to meet you, Platus." Alcandor waited patiently for a response before asking, "Can you talk?"

"No, he doesn't talk. Most animals, including Platus, are intelligent. They understand a lot of what's going on. He likes it when you talk to him, and he even lets me scratch him. Do you want to hold him?"

Alcandor nodded and held out his finger. Bernie continued talking to Platus as he moved his finger closer to Alcandor's. Platus stepped onto Alcandor's extended finger. "This is extraordinary. What makes him fly?"

"You can see he's light and when he pumps his wings, he generates enough lift to overcome gravity. He uses his wings and tail to steer through the air. Fish use their fins to do the same thing in water."

"What's a fish?"

"You'll see a lot of those later at The Museum."

As they talked at the edge of the clearing, Bernie looked for his little friends. He was afraid Alcandor's presence would keep them from revealing themselves, but he had not counted on Bowin's courage. Bernie spotted Bowin standing at the edge of the clearing. It was his way of telling Bernie, 'We are here. Summon us if you will.'

"I have someone else I want you to meet," Bernie said with

muted excitement. As if on cue, Platus chose that moment to depart. Alcandor couldn't tear his eyes away from watching the bird as it soared into the sky. Not until Platus disappeared over the treetops did Alcandor remember to breathe.

"We have to move slowly now," said Bernie. "We'll sit here and let them come to us. They're quite shy." He and Alcandor sat on the soft grass just a few feet from Bowin.

Bowin stood on his hind legs and walked forward until he stood in front of Bernie. Bowin's tiny eyes shifted between Bernie and Alcandor, looking for any sign of danger. He found none. The young god's friend looked as gentle as the boy.

Bowin signaled for Renot to come out of hiding. He trusted Renot, who had demonstrated both strength and caution in the past. If anything went wrong, Renot could take care of himself. Renot emerged from behind a tree and cautiously approached the young god and the stranger who sat next to him.

One after another, they came forth. This time, there were nine. Alcandor sat spellbound. He looked from one to another, noting slight differences in appearance and mannerisms. The smallest of the nine had not taken her eyes off Alcandor since emerging from the foliage. As each minute passed, she crept closer until Renot moved to block her way. She was in no danger; Alcandor couldn't have moved if he wanted to.

Renot walked to Alcandor and touched his knee. Alcandor did not move. Renot touched it again. Still Alcandor did not move. Twice more, Renot touched the stranger's knee. Then Renot hopped onto Alcandor's leg and looked him in the eye. Bowin crept closer in case he should be needed.

A soft whisper came from Alcandor. "You are amazing."

Renot was so intrigued by the stranger that he didn't notice when the young one crawled up Alcandor's leg to stand next to him.

Very softly, Bernie said, "Hello, everyone. This is my friend, Alcandor. He's happy to meet you."

"Can they understand us?"

"I think they have their own language. I communicate with them mostly with my hands and tone of voice. The tall one there is their leader." Bernie pointed to Bowin. "The little one on your knee is quite young. It's a rare treat to see their young. They usually hide them away."

"What are they called?"

"We call them lookies. They were brought here by their creator. The gods loved them, but after a while, the lookies started breeding so much the Town Council declared them a nuisance and ordered them removed. They rounded them up and sent them back to their home world, but some of them escaped to the woods and became refugees. The Town Council doesn't know about them, and I'm not telling them."

"Why don't they want to go back to their home world?"

"They were born here. To them, this is their home world. But they can't live in The Town because they'll be captured and sent away. Yet it's very dangerous for them in the woods because there are things here that prey on them."

Alcandor looked at the little creatures scattered around him. "I wish I could take them to my world. My people would love them. But I guess that could be more dangerous than just staying here."

Bernie felt a twinge of guilt. Alcandor was right. Even though they finished a time of peace in their world, only one day had passed for him. And when the weekend ended, Billy would be back at it again.

What Bernie didn't know was that, at that very moment, Billy was planning his next move. He had tired of playing games. He was ready to end it all.

This Is Lenny

Bernie should have allowed more time for the trip to Lenny's house. Dragging Alcandor across town had been a daunting task. Every time Alcandor encountered something new, he simply stopped walking. Coming from a world with only thirty-seven species of plants, no animals of any kind, and a completely different culture, it was easy to understand how everything was new to him. And everything had to be explained before they could move on. Finally, they arrived at Lenny's home and were ushered inside by an impatient Lenny.

"Sorry we're late, Lenny. I had to explain everything we saw between my house and yours. It took longer than I planned." Bernie shrugged his shoulders, offering a smile and an expression of mock helplessness.

Instead of responding, Lenny walked around Alcandor, looking him over from top to bottom. "The makeup looks okay. I don't see any green. How did Suzie get him to shimmer? It's really quite good."

"Lenny, you're being rude."

"Huh?" said Lenny in genuine surprise. A distinct clucking sound was heard as Lenny cocked his head, listening to something the others could not hear.

"Oh... Oh, sorry. Where are my manners?" Lenny turned to Alcandor and carefully enunciating each syllable, as if talking to a child, said, "I am pleased to meet you, Alcandor."

"I'm pleased to meet you too, Lenny. I've done a lot of gawking myself recently," Alcandor said with an easy smile.

Lenny tried not to show it, but Bernie could see his friend had not expected Alcandor to speak their language. Lenny was burdened by generations of builder training that insisted created beings, such as Alcandor, were just constructs. To treat one like a real person was a foreign idea, especially since no construct had ever before spoken the language of the gods. Bernie smiled as he thought of Sissy, who had been the first to open Lenny's eyes. That wasn't to say his friend didn't need to be reminded occasionally.

"Would you like to see some of my universes?"

"Oh, yes. Very much," said Alcandor with eagerness. "I've been amazed by everything I've seen today."

"Alcandor seems especially interested in the animals. I never got around to putting any on his world," Bernie reminded Lenny.

"It is hard to imagine such a variety of creatures. Each of them is so different. My favorite, so far, are the lookies."

"Well, I have some animals that will blow them away." Lenny led them to his wall of viewing windows.

"No carnivores, please, Lenny," Bernie said. Lenny, who had stopped in front of one window, pouted as he led them to a different window.

"Okay, but you're missing some of my best work."

Alcandor was eager to see everything. No matter what Lenny talked about or showed him, Alcandor wanted more. Two hours later, Lenny showed no sign of slowing as he dragged Alcandor from one room to another, showing him treasure after treasure. No matter what Lenny talked about, Alcandor was interested, asking questions and making relevant comments. Lenny treated him to a display of universes with stars so thick they looked like clouds, worlds where the animals looked like rocks, a flying machine from his Off World Technology Collection, and even the star-crossed tawalla seeds he'd used to capture Candi's attention. They were having such a good time, Bernie hated to interrupt them.

Finally, Bernie said, "We're going to have to leave now or we'll be late meeting Suzie at The Museum."

The disappointment on Lenny's face was a memory Bernie would relish all day.

Time to End It

Billy had grown frustrated, and very angry. His street cred had been questioned.

At lunch last week, Donald had the impudence to ask, "What's taking so long to get rid of Bernie?"

It was a fair question. Billy had asked it himself often enough. Uncle Shemal had never hesitated to pull the trigger before. The formula was simple. Plant evidence of the person's incompetence, and Shemal's quality assurance systems would find it right away. It never took long for Shemal to throw them out. It had been easier to get Ronny and Chrissy fired, and they'd had excellent work records, at least until Billy decided to go after them.

What was different now? Maybe Shemal was influenced by Bernie's big-time dad and giving Bernie the benefit of the doubt. Maybe Suzie had influence in the Personnel Department and was doing something to keep him around. Whatever it was, it was frustrating. Billy had done enough to Bernie's universe that no one could see anything there except gross incompetence.

That was when it hit him. Bernie was different. He wasn't part of the quality assurance system. His work, unlike everyone else's, wasn't being measured and recorded every day. If Bernie messed up, it didn't show up on Shemal's production record at all.

Billy growled. He was being entirely too subtle. If Uncle needed to see he was wasting his time on Bernie, then it was time to take things to a new level. No more little mistakes and minor disasters, it was time to demonstrate how inept Bernie really was. It was time to unleash an apocalypse. And, as everyone knew, a good apocalypse had to be done with style. Just blinking something out wasn't good enough. When you do an End of the World, it was a lot more fun if everything went out in screaming pain.

And that became his plan.

The Museum

Suzie was waiting outside The Museum when Bernie arrived with Lenny and Alcandor. "I'm sorry we're late. Alcandor had to stop and see everything along the way. I think he's enjoying himself."

"That is quite an understatement." Alcandor grinned at Suzie. "How are you, my dear?"

"Fine, thanks." Suzie returned Alcandor's grin with a hug.

"Get ready to be amazed," Bernie said in anticipation of Alcandor's response to The Museum.

"I don't know how I can be more amazed than I am already."

"Everything in here has won an award. Each new winner has been judged better than the last winner in that category," said Lenny. "You can't get into The Museum without being extraordinary."

"I would think there would be fewer new winners each year," Alcandor said.

"You would think so, wouldn't you?" said Suzie. "But people keep rising to the challenge. Each year they average fifty winners from over a thousand submissions."

Alcandor was indefatigable. He asked questions about everything. Bernie and Lenny, both trained in Building Sciences, and Suzie, who minored in History of Building, did their best to answer his questions.

Long before Alcandor ran out of questions, The Museum staff told them it was closing time. The afternoon had gone so quickly no one had noticed.

"But there's so much more to see," Alcandor protested.

Bernie laughed. "They have less than one percent of the universes on display. We could spend years here."

As they were ushered out of the museum, Alcandor asked a final question. "To save your job and to save my world, your universe has to be judged worthy of a place in that museum?"

The question remained unanswered, and they walked home

in silence.

Billy Destroys the World

Hovering high above the planet, Billy shook his head. "This time, I'm going to give Shemal enough proof of Bernie's incompetence that he won't be able to ignore it anymore. Look at this stupid planet! It's a builder's nightmare. Everything about it is messed up. When I'm done tonight, Uncle, you won't have any choice but to fire Bernie."

Bernie's planet rotated slowly as it continued its journey around the sun. The sausage-shaped continent, lush with its green plants and central mountain range, could be easily seen. The two lab zones on the equator waited for the next spark of life. The deep blue ocean sent gentle waves to lap the shores. North of the continent was a deep ocean trench that circled the world.

Billy barely glanced at the world. It wasn't the planet's surface that concerned him. Instead, he moved deep into the inner core of the planet. It was there, in the very center, that he did his work.

He visualized a network of fibers extending from the inner core to the upper mantle just below the planet's hard surface. Billy concentrated as he made the twisting and turning fibers a reality. He then began another network with more fibers that twisted and turned near and around the fibers of the first network. But the elements with which he constructed his fibers were never meant to coexist. If they touched, the result was catastrophic, just as he wanted it to be. And then he made more. He riddled the interior of the planet with his network of deadly threads. There could be only one outcome.

Finally, Billy knew he'd created sufficient destructive force to accomplish his plan. He paused to admire his handiwork. The planet's own forces would take it on a suicidal path to an unalterable outcome. The planet's molten core would bring the elements of Billy's deadly network together, mingling the elements that must never touch, and igniting his galactic fuse.

Moments later, it began.

This time, he would not leave before it was finished. He would not return the next day to find Bernie had somehow found a way to minimize or undo the damage. No. This time, he would see it through. This time he would watch everything to the bitter end. And so he did.

Billy rose above the planet in time to see a section of its outer shell outlined by the light from an explosion deep below. The highlighted section included a third of the sausage continent. The detonation unleashed a force so colossal the land was thrust upward, breaking it into multiple pieces with such force that some fragments would never return to the planet. The rest slowed as gravity overcame inertia and the shattered crust fell back into the open pit of red molten lava below.

The lava pit churned as it consumed everything that had fallen back. Lava that was not red hot was white hot. The pieces of land did not float long. One by one, they were dissolved by the red-white hot fluid. Along the edge, waters from the ocean cascaded into the pit, turning momentarily into steam before disappearing altogether. Nothing survived. Everything that had ever lived on that land died instantly.

Could a planet survive such a blow? Could it heal from such an open wound? Billy knew the answer. He had planned too well.

The oceans went first. They were drained into that unquenchable cauldron as the world's water was turned into scalding steam. The planet was enveloped by thick clouds. The polar ice from the southern pole vaporized as it hastened to follow the path of the oceans.

Billy had no trouble seeing the destruction he caused, for nothing can be hidden from a god with the will to see. He watched the wall of hot steam racing across the world, boiling the life that had been lucky enough to escape the first blow.

Then came the fires, consuming anything that could burn.

The crust of the world had cracked like an eggshell from the first horrific explosion. Now Billy watched as the ultra-hot magma seeped through the cracks, widening them as it ate away at the remaining surface of the world. The floating pieces melted one by one in the searing heat.

Finally, nothing was left except the molten mass of a once-living world.

Billy looked at what he had done. And he was pleased.

Damn You!

Bernie was still on a high from the terrific weekend he'd spent with Alcandor. Their time together was everything he'd hoped. Even Lenny had been impressed. Actually, everyone had been impressed—even his mom. None of this was a big surprise to Bernie, who'd been impressed with Alcandor ever since they'd met. The only disappointment was when the weekend ended, and he had to return Alcandor to his world.

Bernie was full of energy when he arrived at work. The trip to The Museum had given him ideas for his planet. As Bernie settled in, he glanced at Billy's cubicle. Billy seemed busy with his own tasks. Bernie had been so preoccupied with Alcandor's visit, he hadn't thought about Billy all weekend.

Bernie grasped the viewing window from its holder on his desk and began to lower it to its place beside his desk. He was proud of his little subterfuge. For over a week now, he'd been using his duplicate universe as a decoy. Why not? Zardok didn't want it. Maybe it would be of some benefit after all. As he lowered the viewing window, he saw something he didn't expect.

What he expected was a planet with green continents and blue oceans. What he saw was a mass of red and white hot magma roiling and bubbling where his planet had once been. The planet had been destroyed. There was nothing left. *Nothing.* Bernie blinked in disbelief.

Maybe on another day, he would have handled it differently. But after months of torment, the special place where he put his anger was full. He could not shove any more in. He jumped to his feet and dashed into Billy's cubicle. He grabbed him by the shoulder and spun him around.

"How dare you!" Bernie shouted, shattering the silence of the office. Immediately there was a sound of thunder and a flash of lightning, courtesy of an unseen cloud that was just as upset as Bernie.

Billy looked at him with feigned shock and surprise. "Why, Bernie, whatever are you talking about?" Billy made no attempt to conceal his evil smile.

Bernie, more than anything, wanted to hit Billy—like he had in school. He wanted Billy to suffer the way he was suffering. Billy's smug smile represented everything Bernie was about to lose. But he couldn't. He couldn't risk another fight.

The only reason Bernie hadn't lost everything was because Billy had attacked the wrong universe. Everything Bernie cared about was being destroyed by this evil, twisted boy who sat in front of him. The rage Bernie felt was rivaled only by what was happening on the surface of his destroyed world. He was dimly aware of thunder as it rumbled even more loudly, followed by the arc of electricity that came from nowhere to strike Billy's desk.

"Damn you!" he said with a hatred that would have burned holes through anyone else. With Billy, it made him smile all the more.

"Did something happen to your little world, Bernie?" Billy asked with sickening sweetness.

"What's going on here?" thundered the deep voice of Shemal.

"Gosh, I am not sure, Uncle. I think Bernie was expressing his disappointment over some ineptitude or other. I really have no idea," Billy said with such innocence that Bernie wanted to hit him all over again.

"Well?" Shemal stared at Bernie.

"Nothing, sir," Bernie said between tight lips.

"If it's nothing, then I suggest you get back to work. The Universe Committee will be here in just a few days, you know."

Back at his desk, Bernie reached down and picked up the window with his real universe. As he placed it in the cradle on his desk, he was relieved to see his world still intact. As he breathed a sigh of relief, he felt eyes on his back and turned in time to see Billy staring at his universe.

"I don't know how you did that, Ber-Nerd, but you won't fool me again," came an angry whisper only Bernie could hear.

The Booby Trap

"But it's getting worse all the time. He tried to destroy everything. I don't know how I can stop him. Thousands of people have died because of Billy. I can't let this continue. I have to do something."

"Then it's time to talk about my ideas," Lenny proclaimed.

"I don't like where this is heading," Suzie said.

Lenny scowled. "Billy is playing mean and dirty. It's time he was stopped."

Bernie heard the animosity in Lenny's voice. Perhaps it was justified. Billy wasn't just hurting him. Lenny and Suzie had met Alcandor, and they had a better understanding now of the stakes. Plus, Lenny had an extra reason to hate Billy: he had tried to break up his relationship with Candi.

"What do you have in mind?" asked Bernie. A glance in Suzie's direction caused him to add, "Remember, we just want to stop him, not hurt him."

"Well, that cuts down on a lot of options, you know." Lenny didn't hide his disappointment.

Lenny closed his eyes as he did a mental inventory of his OWL collection. "I have just the thing. It's a very small explosive device. You attach it to anything you don't want opened. When they open it, the blast will knock them across the room. It has a guaranteed thirty-foot blowback radius. It'll be perfect!"

Suzie, who didn't like the idea as soon as she heard the word 'explosive', said, "Lenny, that could hurt someone. You can't do that."

Lenny, looking for support, did not find any in Bernie's expression either. After more thought, he said, "I have another one that could work. It detects any movement within a defined radius, and when it finds it, it makes a siren noise, alerting everyone in the area."

"That sounds perfect," Bernie said.

~

It turned out there was something about Lenny's booby trap he'd forgotten to mention. It might be more accurate to say he 'neglected to mention' in the presence of Suzie. The booby trap did indeed generate a shrill piercing sound, intended to draw everyone in the area to investigate. It also generated an intense flash, rendering anyone in the blast zone temporarily blind. That was to prevent them from running away before the authorities arrived. That was why the tag next to it described it as a 'Flash Bomb.'

It might have worked well on Billy. As it turned out, it also worked very well on cleaning crews.

And Shemal was not happy. Not happy at all.

"Bernie, why did you do this?" Shemal fumed.

Bernie, whose immediate response was to tell the truth, knew he could not reveal the whole truth. "I'm so sorry, sir. I didn't mean for this to happen."

"Why, Bernie? Why?" Shemal repeated with an even deeper timbre in his voice.

"I... I... Someone has been messing with my universe, sir. And I wanted them to stop. I thought if they were surprised by the noise, they would run away and think twice before they tried to sabotage it again."

"What makes you think someone is messing with your universe?" Shemal glared.

"Every few days I find something else wrong. I know it wasn't me, and it takes hours to fix the problems. Sometimes I don't see the problem right away, and when I finally notice it, even more things have gone wrong."

Shemal had heard every excuse by now. And this one wasn't even original. Some mysterious 'other person' did it. This excuse had become common lately; the last several people he'd fired had all used it. Shemal bit back his first response, which would have been to call such an excuse pure poppycock.

Instead, he said, "It's a poor workman who blames problems on other people, Bernie. You have to take responsibility for your mistakes, make an extra effort to fix them, and then do whatever it takes to prevent them from happening again. Is that clear?"

"Yes, sir."

"I forbid you to do anything like this again. Someone could've been hurt. As it was, you scared everyone. This can't happen again. Do you understand?"

"Yes, sir."

"Remember what I said, Bernie. Take responsibility for your mistakes, and work harder to make sure they don't happen."

As Bernie walked back to his cubicle, dozens of eyes watched him. Each one expected Bernie to begin clearing out his desk. Only one person was disappointed when Bernie sat down, cleared his workspace, and began work for the day.

That one, of course, was Billy.

Go Home, Bernie

As much as Bernie desperately wanted to win a Universe Award, he knew it wasn't going to happen. All he wanted was to make sure Billy didn't destroy his world. Every time he looked at the viewing window of his duplicate universe, he shuddered. The whole world had been reduced to a molten mass, devoid of any life. Billy had destroyed it all.

Shemal had forbidden Bernie to use any kind of booby trap in his cubicle. That left him with only one thing he could do to keep Billy away. He had to guard it personally.

Bernie had slept in his cubicle for the last four days. He never left it, except to use the bathroom. When he got hungry or thirsty, he dipped into Alcandor's world for something to eat. When he couldn't stay awake any longer, he draped himself across the viewing window, so no one could get into it without waking him. There were only two more days before the Universe Committee arrived. So far, the plan was working.

"Bernie, we need to talk," Shemal's deep voice broke into his thoughts.

"Yes, sir."

"Have you been sleeping in your cubicle at night?"

"Ah… Yes, sir."

"Bernie, I won't have it. I don't mind people working over or coming in early, but this is not acceptable. Do not do it again. Do you understand?"

"But, sir, I—"

"Do you understand?" Shemal's tone made it clear he did not want to repeat himself.

"Yes, sir."

Billy's Threat

"I can't believe the Universe Committee is wasting their time on Bernie's universe. It's an abomination. Anyone having anything to do with them coming tomorrow is going to look bad." Billy growled with such intensity, even the people at his table were uncomfortable.

Candi felt trapped, and she wasn't alone. Jimmy was just as afraid of Billy as she was. Had it been only a year since Billy had arrived? So far, nine people had lost their jobs all because Billy decided he didn't like them. He didn't do the firing himself, but he made it happen. Bernie would be the tenth.

When Billy gets like this, thought Candi, *it's best to say nothing. You don't want to give him a closer target for his anger.* And so, Candi and Jimmy remained silent. Donald, oblivious to the danger, said, "When the Committee sees how bad it is, they're going to be upset."

"That's right, Donald. They are," said Billy as he raged against the unfairness of the world. "I tried to save everyone from this embarrassment the other night, but it didn't work out."

"What happened, Billy?" Donald asked.

Billy looked at the people seated at the table. Candi knew Billy didn't consider them friends. They provided an audience for him, but there was only one reason for that: they were all terrified of him. She had requested a transfer months ago, but with all the people trying to get out of Final Assembly, it wouldn't happen soon. She needed to keep her head down while she waited.

"Let's just say I tried to remove all doubt about Bernie's incompetence."

"That was good, Billy. Why didn't it work?"

"Bernie created a fake universe in his spare time. And the idiot made it exactly like his real universe. He re-created every screw up and every mistake. Basically, I wasted my lesson on a fake universe," Billy admitted, clearly unhappy about it all.

"So what are you going to do now?"

"When someone doesn't get it the first time, Donald, what do you have to do? You repeat the lesson, of course."

"But the Committee is coming tomorrow," Donald said.

"I know," Billy said with grim determination.

The Last Goodbye

Alcandor was sitting at his desk, a vacant stare on his face, as Bernie appeared. A pile of untouched and unanswered correspondence was stacked on the corner of his desk.

"This the last night, isn't it?" Alcandor asked in a quiet voice.

"Yes. The Awards Committee is coming tomorrow morning," Bernie said softly.

"You're sure there's no hope, Bernie?"

"You've seen The Museum, Alcandor. I've done nothing here that will convince them to give me an award for anything. I'm so sorry. If I were a better god, things might be different." Bernie narrowly succeeded in suppressing a sob.

"I do not blame you, Bernie. No one here blames you. You've done your best. It's time for us to accept our fate."

Bernie sat in the chair next to Alcandor. They shared a few minutes of silence. Bernie looked at the man next to him. In spite of his youthful appearance, he'd lived thousands of Bernie's years. Why was he so ready to accept death? Was he weary of living? *No, that's not it,* thought Bernie. He was a Lord, one of the original beings formed from the universe putty, evolved over eons into the man who sat there. He was very strong.

Alcandor was not thinking of strength. When he finally spoke, he asked quietly, "Can you tell me what it will be like, this end of days? How will it happen? Will our people suffer?"

"No. It's not like that," Bernie said, unable to look directly at the man he had come to love. "Someone will just blink everything out. It will be as if it never was. It's instant. There is no pain," Bernie said as his eyes clouded with tears.

"That's good, then."

Another period of silence followed.

It was Alcandor who spoke first. "My one doubt, Bernie, is whether I should tell the people the fate that awaits us. Don't they have the right to know? And yet, if there's nothing we can do, if our end is certain, then isn't it better to shield them from this knowledge? On this question, my wisdom deserts me. I've found no answers."

Bernie could only think of one thing, and he began again with more conviction than ever. "Alcandor, please don't stay here. There is still time to save you and some others. I can't save everyone, but I can save many. Surely that's better than certain death."

"Ah, Bernie. Thank you. But this is my world. These are my people. I cannot desert them, even at the end. But I thank you."

"Alcandor, you must let me do something. I don't want this to happen. It's wrong. There has to be something I can do."

"I know of nothing, Bernie. Nothing at all. After all, it's not a perfect world."

"I know that all too well," Bernie said as his eyes filled with tears.

"I meant no insult by that, Bernie. I know you did the best you could." Alcandor placed his hand on Bernie's shoulder.

Bernie tried to hold back his tears. No god he knew cried over his creations. But this was different. These people were honest, and they cared about each other. They'd worked hard to build a good life. They weren't much different from the gods. In fact, they were a lot like them. *Some of them are even better, I think. They love their families and their children, and they would give anything for them. They're as worthy of living as anyone on my world.* But they were all going to die. They hadn't done anything to deserve it. Their only mistake had been to live on the world of a builder so incompetent he couldn't even save his own job, let alone their world. Someone would just snuff them out. And it was all his fault.

"Bernie, I want to tell you something." Alcandor gently drew Bernie to a standing position. "I've never had children; there never seemed to be the right time for a family. That's my only regret in leaving this life. I will tell you this: if I ever had a son, Bernie, I would want him to be just like you."

Bernie reached out to Alcandor and hugged him tight. Alcandor held back nothing with his embrace. As Bernie's tears flowed down his cheeks, they mingled with the tears of the man who held him.

Billy's Lesson

It was after midnight when Billy stole back into the office. Doors in town didn't have locks, so getting in was never a problem. The cleaning crew had finished and was long gone. He wanted no interruptions. He walked quickly through the corridors. Numerous nightlights in the corridors and the moonlight through occasional skylights illuminated his path. Even in the moonlit room, he had no trouble seeing, as he strode confidently to the cubicle next to his.

Billy saw Bernie's fake universe leaning against the corner wall of his cubicle. He glanced inside and saw his handiwork. The planet was still a red and white-hot molten mass, seething in the black void that surrounded it. Billy took a moment to admire his work. Finally, he said, "It was the right lesson, Bernie. We just have to repeat it until you get it."

Billy stepped up to the viewing window of Bernie's universe. "This time, I won't be fooled by some fake world."

As Billy moved into Bernie's universe, he found himself filled with resentment. "I wouldn't have to be here in the middle of the night if it weren't for Uncle Shemal," Billy grumbled. "I don't know why he's so thickheaded when it comes to Bernie. I got him to fire Wendy and Stacey and the others easily enough. I just tweaked a few things to make them look bad on Uncle's Quality Assurance Reports. He couldn't wait to get rid of them. Well, no matter. When the Committee comes tomorrow and leaves in disgust, Uncle will have to take action. If he doesn't, then somebody higher up is going to start questioning whether he should keep his job," Billy said scornfully.

"Let's see now. It looks like Bernie's world," he mumbled as he searched for more proof. "Ah, there's Bernie's gaia. The first time I saw her, I was surprised, because they don't usually come so quickly. If I'd thought to look for her the other night, I wouldn't have been fooled by Bernie's fake."

Billy drifted closer to the planet, determined not to be tricked again. "I can't imagine what you've been working on all this time, Bernie. It's just a banged-up world with nothing but plants. It may be the most boring planet ever. No seasons. No range of temperatures. No vertical continents to alter ocean currents or global temperatures that make interesting weather conditions. I had to make the hurricanes and bad weather by myself." Billy laughed, "Maybe you could win an award for the *Most Boring Universe.*"

As Billy scanned the surface of the planet, he saw the ocean trench Bernie had created to stop his tsunami. The northern pole was still missing. Numerous volcanoes dotted the ocean. There were large swaths of forest across the planet where hurricanes and tornados had knocked trees flat for miles and miles. There, along the top of Bernie's central mountain range, he saw evidence of his supervolcanoes. The fires had spread for miles before Bernie extinguished them. Billy smiled as he considered his handiwork. "This is a masterpiece of proof and more proof of Bernie's incompetence. What's wrong with Uncle Shemal that he can't see the evidence in front of him?"

As Billy turned away from the fire-scorched earth, he caught something out of the corner of his eye. In the middle of one fire-blackened area, there was a glimmer of white. Out of curiosity, he approached for a closer look. He was surprised to see stone buildings in the center of a town. Fire had consumed the nearby vegetation that would have otherwise hidden it.

"Oh, my goodness. You've been holding back, Bernie. You have people on your planet." Billy moved closer.

Billy was shocked to see people that looked just like the gods—except for their green skin. "So you weren't completely wasting your time. Interesting... Well, no matter," said Billy immediately discounting what he'd seen. He wasn't there to admire Bernie's world. He was there to destroy it.

Billy cleared his mind and prepared for his descent to the center of the world. The network of explosive fibers he'd created for Bernie's fake planet had worked well. Destruction had been total. Unfortunately, the effort was wasted on Bernie's fake. "Not wasted, actually. It was more of a dry run for what's about to come next."

He took a final glance at the people as they walked along their streets, talked with their friends and neighbors, oblivious to their imminent destruction.

"Goodbye, little people," Billy said casually as he began his descent to the center of the world.

When he reached the inner core of the planet, he cleared his mind. He visualized the network of explosive fibers that would riddle the planet from its inner core to its upper mantle. As soon as those fibers were in place, nothing could stop the planet from complete and total destruction.

But something was wrong. Something was interfering with his concentration. There was pain. Pain? From what? He was a god. Nothing could harm him here. But the pain became greater, and his visualization was spoiled.

What was happening? The pain was coming from the side of his head. Had Bernie left another trap? Billy had never experienced this before. The pain was coming from his ear. It was as if his ear was being pinched in a vice, and it was pulling at him. And it hurt. Oh, how it hurt!

Billy felt himself dragged away from the planet's inner core. He rose above the surface of the planet and continued upward.

Still the pain continued. The planet and the sun dwindled in the distance as he felt himself dragged faster and faster to the edge of the universe. Something powerful was pulling him out of the void. By his ear.

"*Uncle Shemal!*"

Committee Arrives

Nothing about this day could be good. Bernie and his friends had delayed the inevitable for as long as they could, but the inevitable had finally arrived.

Bernie would have been fired weeks ago if not for Suzie. She'd bought time for him. Lenny had offered every trick and device in his OWT collection. And they'd tried many. But that ended today. Today there was no more time, no more excuses, and no more second chances.

There were days when Bernie desperately wished the Committee would come before Billy could do more damage. At the same time, he knew his broken world was not, and never would be, worthy of an award.

Only minutes remained before his own world would begin collapsing. All the consequences were set up like a row of dominoes. The Awards Committee would reject him. Next, Shemal would fire him. And, worst of all, they would then destroy the universe along with Alcandor and his people. Thousands of innocents would die. And it didn't stop there. He wouldn't see Suzie or Lenny anymore. His mom would be crushed. Billy would be happy, of course. But he was the only one.

Bernie saw three people drifting like ghosts toward his cubicle. They wore the white ceremonial robes of the builder, with gold braids and bright insignia. Wearing somber expressions, they looked neither right nor left, but instead glided silently toward him. Heads raised above cubicles to watch the procession as the judges made their way to Bernie's cubicle.

The woman leading the procession was tall, and her shimmer so strong it reached into the cubicles as she passed. Bernie didn't know the protocol for greeting a Judge. Few people did. With piercing eyes, she looked at Bernie and said, "You are Bernie. I am Judge Jazelda. My companions are Judge Thomas and Judge Michael. We will conduct the initial evaluation. If we find your submission worthy, we will take your universe with us for further evaluation by the full committee. Is this clear?"

Bernie, who was still trying to figure out if he should bow, managed to say, "Yes, Ma'am. Er... Yes, Judge." It was almost impossible to do anything other than obey the powerful voice of an elder god.

"During our evaluation, we will be communicating orally with each other. Do not interrupt us during this process. Is that clear?"

Bernie put on his bravest smile and said, "Yes, Ma'am. Uh... Ma'am, before you start, there's something I need—"

Judge Jazelda held up her finger to silence him. "No comments allowed, young man. We will draw our conclusions exclusively from what we see in your universe."

The three judges stood shoulder-to-shoulder in front of Bernie's universe. One by one, their expressions went blank as they moved into the void.

~

"It looks like the sun and two planets are just prefabs. Nothing going on there I can see. I suggest we focus on the middle planet," Judge Thomas said, with some disappointment.

"It's a student continent with two lab continents. Not very fancy," Judge Michael muttered.

"This place is a mess! Look at the asteroid strikes all over the planet," said Judge Jazelda. "I haven't seen anything this untidy in a long time."

"What about these volcanoes? See the round holes? He deliberately created them and then plugged them up. It probably caused a nuclear winter and wiped out all life on the planet. Why would he do that?"

"Is this some kind of a joke?" Thomas asked.

"Look at this. It looks like more deliberate destruction. Why would he do that?"

"This is strange. It looks like he intentionally caused continental drifting. See the perforations along the ocean floor? Then he accelerated it, and then he froze it in place. Why would he do that?"

"More of the same over here."

"You're sure this is Simeon's son?" asked a doubting Thomas.

"I'm sure," Judge Jazelda said. "He must have had some reason. Look more closely."

"It's a wonder he managed to get any life going at all. It looks like the gaia has suffered a few near-death experiences. Do you think he was trying to kill her?" Michael asked with some disgust in his voice.

"There's a fossil record here. It appears he developed plant life, spread it throughout the world, killed it off, and then started it again. What's weird is I don't see any difference in the fossils from his first plants compared to the plant life he has now. Why would he do that?" Michael wanted to know.

"There's a strange ring cut deep into the ocean just north of the main continent. It goes all the way around the planet. What's that all about?"

"I can explain that. The ice at the northern pole is gone. He melted it rapidly and caused a massive tsunami. He used the ring to control the level of flooding as waves reached the shore."

"Now will you look at this? For some reason, he overheated the planet's inner core but then cooled it before the heat reached the surface and destroyed everything. He obviously didn't intend to kill the life forms, but why would he do it? Only reason I can think of is to create extreme planetary stress for the gaia."

"Is there any animal life here?"

"I can't imagine it. Even if something was here once, it isn't likely to have survived all of this."

"I found where he shifted the planet's orbit closer to the sun. There were helium traces left in the closer orbit. It looks like he kept it there long enough for the planet to overheat. Then he moved it back. Why would he do that?" Jazelda wondered.

"None of this is rational. What in the world was he trying to accomplish? Is he crazy?" Michael asked, clearly disgusted by what he was seeing.

Bernie could do nothing but stand helpless as the three judges continued their review. For every criticism, Bernie had condemned himself more than once. How could he have let these things happen? He should have stood up to Billy. He should have confronted him in the beginning. Anything would have been better than this. At least he would go out with some dignity. This way, he would be out, but it would be because everyone thought he was incompetent.

"Look at the gaia. Poor thing. She looks half-dead. I still think he was trying to kill her."

"Maybe. The planet is covered with vegetation, but you can see where he set dozens of forest fires and burned off thousands of square miles. Then he put them out before the whole continent was consumed. That would have caused the gaia a lot of pain."

"That isn't all. Look at what the hurricanes did. See the trees that have been knocked flat?"

"And tornados too. See the smaller twisting paths they took? They're all over the continent."

"All of this was deliberate. Simple continents like this can't produce weather conditions to create hurricanes and tornados. He had to make these conditions himself."

"I've been looking at a string of volcanoes along the central mountain range. He used fault lines to make them, and at least four were supervolcanoes. Can you imagine the quakes when these babies started popping?"

"But there isn't much lava. He stopped them before they really got started."

"I've been thinking about the gaia. Given the age of the planet, I'm surprised there's a gaia here at all."

"I hate this! It's just awful. I vote to terminate the evaluation. There's nothing here except the product of a sick, sadistic mind. We need to move on," Michael fumed. His disgust had turned to anger.

"I agree," Thomas said. "Let's go."

Bernie had been bravely listening to their words. He tried to pretend they were talking about something else. Someone else. But he knew they were not. He wanted to shout at them. He wanted to tell them he had saved the planet. That he would never do these awful things. But instead, he stood motionless as tears streamed down his cheeks. He hadn't seen Billy that morning. That was the only thing missing: for Billy to see him crying.

"No," Jazelda said without enthusiasm. "We need to finish

our evaluation. Has anyone seen any animal life?"

"If there is any, I'm sure they're hiding under a rock somewhere. This is not a safe place to live," Thomas said grimly.

"Oh, my. Come over here," Michael said with surprise. "I found a city. It's quite advanced. A lot of stone structures. It looks to be Bronze Era. A lot of their buildings are being repaired."

"It surprises me they even try, given how often this kid keeps knocking things down."

"Yeah, they're resilient little buggers," Michael said.

"Hey! Look closer. They look a lot like us," Thomas said, suddenly very interested.

"What? How can this be? The man in the toga looks just like my Uncle Joshua," Jazelda said as she moved her presence closer. She examined the man closely, and finally said, "That's really impressive."

"The lady in that doorway looks like my mother. The resemblance is striking. Except for the light green skin, they could pass for us." It was hard for Michael to deny his senses and resist the temptation to call out to her.

"I don't believe it. Do you see what I see? They have shimmers," Jezelda exclaimed. "How can this be? No one has ever been able to reproduce our shimmers. Builders have been trying for millennia. Is it possible this Bernie has done it?"

"The kid's a genius," Michael said.

Thomas said, "They look like miniature gods."

"Does anyone need to see any more?" Jezelda asked.

"No. I have seen more than enough," Michael said.

"I'm satisfied, too," Thomas said.

Bernie quickly wiped the tears from his face. The gods' eyes gave up their far seeing and returned to their bodies. Each of the judges looked at him and flashed him a smile.

Judge Jazelda said, "The contest rules require us to take your universe with us, Bernie, but don't worry. We will take good care of it. I can tell you we're very impressed. We're going to submit your universe to the full Committee. Your people are amazing, and the Committee will want to see them."

"This was well done, son. Very well done," Judge Thomas said as he gently lifted Bernie's universe from the cradle on his desk.

"This is the best thing I've seen in a long time, Bernie. And that's what I am going to tell the Committee," Judge Michael added.

The Terrible Swift Sword

After the Committee left, Bernie collapsed in his chair. He thought about what the Judges had said. Was it possible? Did he dare hope the Committee would give him an award? The award, of course, was not what mattered. The only thing that mattered was saving a world and a man who lived there who was closer to Bernie than any father he had ever known. *Don't get your hopes up,* Bernie cautioned himself. He desperately needed to talk with someone.

He stood and looked in the direction of Shemal's office. Maybe Shemal would have answers. But the office was empty. In fact, he hadn't seen Shemal at all that day. He hadn't seen Billy either. He'd been sure Billy would be there, making snide comments about getting one step closer to being fired. But even his enemy wasn't there.

Bernie noticed dozens of heads above cubicles looking at him. Everyone in the office had seen the judges come and go. In this small office, they probably heard what the judges had said. Actually, it would be hard not to. The judges were elder gods, and their voices could be heard from far away.

Bernie heard a distant sound. And then the same sound from another direction. Understanding was slow, but as he heard more and more of the sounds, he realized it was the sound of clapping. What were they applauding? One god after another joined in until the sound came from every cubicle. Everyone was smiling and looking at him. Then a cheer broke out. And another. Bernie wasn't sure what was happening, even when some of them were pounding him on the back and shaking his hand.

Finally, he dared to hope.

~

As Bernie walked into the lunchroom, he discovered the news had preceded him. People rose from their seats and began clapping. Bernie gave an embarrassed grin and did his best to send thanks in every direction. His cloud got into the act, throwing handfuls of confetti—made of shimmering light—in all directions. Bernie didn't even try to stop him, knowing the cloud wouldn't listen. And his audience laughed and clapped even louder as the confetti of light filled all corners of the room.

Bernie was too excited to think about lunch, so he went straight to his table, where he found Suzie, Lenny, and Candi standing and applauding him.

Suzie ran up and embraced him. "I'm so proud of you, Bernie. I knew you could do it!" Bernie returned the embrace. He liked this hugging stuff. Maybe he and Suzie could practice it again later without all the confetti. It would probably also be easier when your best friend wasn't thumping you on the back.

"Way to go, Bernie! You were outstanding," Lenny said enthusiastically.

Bernie could even hear Sissy making "*Ye-ye-ye*," sounds as loud as she could.

Candi, who stood next to Lenny, said, "Congratulations, Bernie. You did a fantastic job!"

"I think they really liked it," Bernie said. "They said they're taking it to the full Committee to review."

"That's excellent," said Suzie, who had actually read the contest rules. "They reject almost all of the universes during the first review. When they bring one back, it's a great sign."

Bernie was immensely relieved. Here, among his closest friends, he allowed his anxiety to turn to excitement. "Do you know what impressed them?"

Lenny, as blunt as ever, said, "Not really."

"They were impressed because my people looked so much like us. The judges said they felt like they were seeing people they knew. And when they saw the shimmers, they got really excited."

"See! I told you the shimmers were important," Suzie said as she wagged her finger at Lenny.

A moment of quiet peace followed as the group reflected on everything that happened in the last several months. Each of them had a stake in Bernie's success. They all felt real pride in his accomplishment.

Suzie was the first to break the silence. "I have some news.

I know I shouldn't say anything, but this is one secret I can't keep."

"What is it?" Bernie asked.

"Billy's in trouble. Big trouble. Shemal wants to fire him."

"What?" said Bernie and Lenny at the same time. Candi raised her eyebrows.

"Billy came back late last night. He was going to destroy your universe, Bernie. Everything. Just like he did to the duplicate universe you made. But Shemal caught him in the act and kept him from doing any damage," Suzie said in a conspiratorial whisper.

"Oh, Chaos! That would have been awful." Bernie shuddered at the thought. "Shemal stopped him?"

"Yes. When Ezrah and I got to work this morning, Shemal was waiting for us. He suspended Billy and sent him home, but not before he got Billy to confess to lots of things. Shemal was so angry when he was telling us about it, his shimmer set a chair on fire. We had to find a metal chair for him." Suzie struggled to keep a straight face.

Bernie felt the weight come off his shoulders. Was it possible? After everything Billy had done, would he finally get what he deserved?

Lenny scratched his head and asked, "Why was Shemal there in the first place? It doesn't make sense he would come back in the middle of the night to stand guard over Bernie's universe."

"I can answer that question," said Candi. "At lunch yesterday, Billy told us what he was going to do. I… I couldn't let that happen. So I went to Shemal and told him what Billy was planning. Shemal asked me a lot of questions. He said he would look into it."

"Thank you, Candi. I know that was a brave decision for you," Suzie said as Bernie and Lenny nodded their heads in agreement. Even Sissy chimed in with, "*Ye-ye-ye.*"

"There may be others who will benefit from this," Suzie continued. "Shemal and Ezrah are reviewing all the termination decisions he's made since Billy got here."

"I'll bet Ezrah insisted on that," said Lenny, who still had doubts about Shemal.

"No, no. It was Shemal. He even insisted on working through the lunch hour so they could start contacting people right away. I think Shemal's going to hire them all back."

"Hmm... Maybe I misjudged him," Lenny admitted reluctantly.

"What'll happen to Billy?" Bernie wanted to know.

"Well, Ezrah has a policy that he won't approve firing recommendations on the same day," Suzie said. "He says builders are too precious. But, I can tell you what Billy did was really bad. To Ezrah, causing an employee to be fired for no reason is unforgivable. I'm sure Billy won't be working here again."

Candi raised her glass of koamba juice and said, "To sunnier days ahead!"

Everyone joined in that toast.

Good News!

He won! It was official. The Committee told him just hours before. He couldn't wait to tell Alcandor.

As soon as he got home, Bernie rushed to his viewing window, hoping the backdoor would still let him access his universe. He hadn't told the Committee about it, knowing they would never let him keep it.

As Bernie slipped into the familiar universe, he felt something different. There was power here. Enormous power. As he scanned the universe, he detected godly shimmers on Alcandor's planet. From this distance, it had to be the Universe Committee. A single god wouldn't have been visible from so far away. Apparently, they were still looking things over. Bernie quietly withdrew before anyone noticed him.

It wasn't surprising to see them there. He'd left the Committee with a lot of questions. They wanted to know how he'd created his people. He couldn't admit they were the result of a lost jar of universe putty. They might withdraw the award. So he'd politely declined to answer.

Fortunately, the Committee thought Bernie was just being secretive about his techniques, which didn't break any rules. In fact, it was common for award winners to hold back certain information for the books and lectures that inevitably followed. Although they respected his right to silence, it didn't mean they weren't intensely curious.

When Bernie checked, two hours later, they were gone. He rushed to Alcandor's office. He wasn't there. He searched the building and found him in his living quarters, a thoughtful look on his face. For a moment, Bernie held back, enjoying the good feeling he had from seeing Alcandor again.

But his enthusiasm would not be restrained, and Bernie burst into visibility as he called out, "I won! I won!"

Both of them rushed to each other and embraced. Bernie said again, "Everything's okay. It's over!"

"Oh, Bernie. I've never heard more welcome news,"

Alcandor said with a lump in his throat. They held their embrace for a while longer. Alcandor felt limp in Bernie's arms. He could almost feel the tensions and fears as they drained from Alcandor's body. For a moment, it was only Bernie's embrace that kept him standing.

"Every day since we last talked, I was afraid it would be the last. I haven't gone into my lab, or done any research, or even any writing. It just didn't seem important.

"Do you know what I've been doing? I've been visiting old friends. I went to see Gondal, and we talked about how things were when we were young. I even met with Zardok. We used to be friends once. Did I ever tell you that? I told him I was sorry for what happened to Vianna. I told him I loved her too, and I'd do anything to bring her back. I told him I knew she had chosen him, and the best man had won. We talked for the first time in years.

"I was afraid every day would be the last," he continued. "Every night when I went to sleep, I didn't expect to wake up. Bernie, I can't thank you enough for what you've done."

"Actually, I'm not sure I can take credit for it," Bernie said with a twinkle in his eye. "As it turns out, you and your people are the ones who made it happen."

"What do you mean?"

"The Committee decided this world has the most godlike race ever created. They think you're quite an achievement. And apparently, I'm going to get credit for it." Bernie flashed Alcandor a crooked grin.

"What happens next?"

"They took your universe away from me. They discovered a long time ago creators can't resist tinkering, so after they make an award, they take the universe so the creator can't change it anymore. They're going to put you in The Museum."

"But if they took us away, how is it you're here now?"

"Lenny and I installed a secret backdoor that lets me get in whenever I want to. They don't know about it."

"That's great. What about your job? Have they let you keep it?"

"Yes! My probationary period is over. They said they aren't sure what to do with me yet, but they're thinking of using me as a troubleshooter, whatever that is. I'm going to stay with Shemal for now. If someone wants me to troubleshoot something, they ask Shemal, and he sends me to help them."

"But you still have to work alongside Billy? That's not good."

"Billy got fired! Shemal fired him," Bernie exclaimed.

"What happened?"

"The night before the Universe Committee arrived to look at your world, Billy snuck back in the middle of the night. He was going to destroy everything, but Shemal caught him. Shemal was so mad, he fired Billy."

"So there is justice in your world."

"Yes. And there are some perks, too. Suzie says we need to go out to dinner to celebrate."

Alcandor laughed along with Bernie.

Finally, Alcandor said, "Will I see you again?"

"You can count on it."

Awards Ceremony

The Annual Universe Awards Ceremony was a gala event. Everyone who was anyone was there. Even though they'd expanded the banquet room this year, it was still bursting with people. There was one award winner in particular the whole town had been talking about: a young god named Bernie. And everyone wanted to see him.

People had been streaming in for an hour, hoping for good seats. The best seats, of course, were at the front, where the award winners were seated. Each winner had been given four tickets for friends and family to join them at the front tables.

Bernie was flanked on one side by his mother and on the other by Suzie, each of them glowing with pride, confident Bernie would not be there were it not for her. They were both right. Lenny, an easy choice for the third ticket, was basking in Bernie's reflected glory, while occasionally scribbling something in his notebook for whatever charm he was experimenting with that day. Sissy sat proudly on Lenny's shoulder.

For the fourth ticket, several Committee members had suggested inviting his dad. No doubt it would have thrilled the crowd to have the Great Simeon proudly overseeing his son's acceptance of his first Universe Award. It would have been Bernie's chance to show his father what he'd done. Bernie rejected the idea almost before they finished suggesting it. A father was a person who looked after his family, who stood by them through good times and bad. A father was there to protect, to comfort, and to encourage his children. Someone who believed in you and taught you to do the same. Simeon was none of those things. Bernie hadn't seen him in years. He'd certainly done nothing to contribute to this night. So Bernie hadn't acted on the Committee's suggestion. He had a better idea.

It's true he wanted a father, but that role had been filled by another. Next to his mother, beaming with dignified pride, sat Alcandor. His eyes twinkled as he looked around the room, taking everything in. Noticing Bernie's gaze, Alcandor gave him a big thumbs up and a reassuring smile. Bernie could almost hear him saying, "Way to go, Bernie!"

The evening began with officials thanking everyone for helping to make it another great Awards Night. Everyone who had anything to do with anything got to have their name mentioned at least once. Finally, someone took over as the master of ceremonies.

The master of ceremonies, a handsome god named Luke, said, "Welcome, everyone, to the Annual Universe Awards. We're about to introduce you to some of the most amazing and creative talent we've seen in a long time. Remember, all the award-winning universes will be on display beginning tomorrow at The Museum. So, without further ado, let's meet the wonderful new builders who've, once again, set the bar higher than ever before."

~

As the awards went on, Bernie grew more nervous. He hadn't planned a speech. Some winners talked about the source of their inspiration, what motivated them, special techniques they used, and all manner of things. Bernie hadn't planned anything like that.

Lost in thought, he drifted over events that had led to tonight. Too many things could never be explained. The problem, of course, was his world was a gigantic accident. His friends agreed that must remain a secret. Too many things could unravel if people knew his world had been the result of carelessness.

There was more applause as the last award winner took her seat. Bernie was startled from his reverie when he heard Luke say, "It's time now for the award presentation you've all been waiting for. I probably don't need to do much of an introduction since the news has been talking about Bernie's world ever since the Committee first saw it. But I will anyway." Ripples of laughter spread throughout the room.

"This category has been the most fascinating in the long history of our awards. Many great builders have worked to create godlike creatures, and every year we have multiple submissions.

"Why is this category so popular? I believe the answer is simple. We all like seeing and hearing about ourselves. And why not? When a god shows us something of ourselves, it's fun. It's like noticing your reflection in the mirror and liking what you see. Or like receiving a compliment and feeling good." The audience was listening to Luke's every word.

"In spite of all these efforts, there hasn't been a new award winner in this category in over seven thousand years. Let me repeat that. Seven thousand years! And here, some young kid named Bernie comes along and knocks it out of the ballpark." Luke began sounding more and more like a country preacher.

"Bernie has a reputation as a god of few words, so I'm going to tell you about his universe, because I don't want you to miss a thing.

"Let me begin with what the award judges told me. Bernie used a student model configuration—you know the one with a long continent around the equator and two lab continents. The judges found the planet a complete wreck. It had been banged and smashed and ripped in every way you can think of.

"To give you examples so you don't think I'm exaggerating, the judges found earthquakes, asteroid strikes, tsunamis, melted polar caps, extreme weather events, nuclear winters, just to name a few. One judge told me he was so shocked by the wanton planetary carnage he wanted to scratch the entry and leave."

Bernie grimaced with these unflattering revelations, and Suzie, seeming to read his mind, patted his arm.

"But then another judge saw Bernie's higher life forms. They live in small cities scattered throughout the planet. They're a Bronze Era society with a central government. Their cities are full of large buildings made of carved stone hauled from faraway mountains.

"The judges assumed any life forms living through the planetary chaos Bernie threw at them would have been smashed back to the Stone Age. But that didn't happen. They just rebuilt and moved on. One judge said the pluck was impressive, and she considered Bernie for the *Most Resilient Higher Life Form* category because they held up so well under Bernie's relentless oppression. But, ladies and gentlemen, Bernie wasn't done impressing the judges."

Tears began to form in Bernie's eyes, thinking of the people on his world who had become so important to him. Regret filled him for all they had suffered.

Luke continued. "Looking at Bernie's higher life forms, the judges were shocked to find they looked just like us. I mean *exactly* like us. There was only one difference—their skin is a light green color. Maybe we can coax Bernie into explaining that to us sometime.

"Anyway, as the judges examined Bernie's people, they were stunned to find some looked like people they knew! Every person since who has taken a casual stroll through one of Bernie's cities has experienced this phenomenon. You're sure to see a schoolmate, a coworker, a relative, or someone you know from here. There's no doubt that would have made Bernie an award winner. But this remarkable young man still had one more thing to amaze us with."

Bernie glanced at Alcandor, his heart full of gratitude. Alcandor winked as Luke continued.

"Perhaps because the Committee was so astounded by the similarity between these people and ours, it took them several minutes to see the most extraordinary thing of all. Bernie's people have a shimmer! No one in the entire history of the Universe Awards has been able to create another race with a shimmer. The judges were flabbergasted. They called in the full membership of judges to see it. Bernie's universe has caused the biggest stir in recent memory.

"The judges were impressed, and, of course, they all wanted to know how he did it, but Bernie has been tight-lipped. So, unless you can get Bernie to tell his secrets, we may be wondering about this for a long time," Luke said as he gave the crowd a conspiratorial wink.

"Some have suggested Bernie's creation may shed light on the mystery of our own origin. Remember, Bernie forged his godlike race by subjecting them to extraordinary trials and tribulations which appears to have produced amazing strength and resilience. And who do they look like? They look just like us!" Luke had his audience hooked, and they roared their approval.

Luke knew the crowd was ready, and he continued, "And

what do we know about this remarkable new talent? That's where the story gets even more amazing. Bernie just graduated from school this year with his degree in Building Science. After school, he started working for The Business. Nowadays, the first thing they ask new builders to do is to create a universe. Anything they want. The Business wants to make sure new employees have a chance to show what they can do. They don't want someone like Bernie to end up on an assembly line somewhere."

Luke paused for a dramatic effect. "So, ladies and gentlemen, are you beginning to see what I see? Are you ready for this? This was Bernie's *first universe*! And look what he's done! Can you imagine the things he'll do in the future?" The implications of Luke's words were not lost on the audience.

"So let me introduce the young man who brought us this outstanding achievement, the man to whom we are presenting the coveted *Most Godlike Creation Award*. Please, come on up, Bernie. Our audience wants to meet you!"

The audience broke out in cheers and applause.

Bernie's heart pounded as he made his way to the lectern. The long walk to the front was a surreal experience. Thundering applause surrounded him, and his vision blurred as he made his way to Luke, who waited for him with a golden statue in his hand. The applause grew louder with every step. As he arrived, Luke gently guided Bernie to the microphone and turned him to face the audience. Bernie saw a sea of faces. Everyone in the room was standing and applauding. He tried to speak, but the croaking sound that came from him wouldn't have been heard over the applause anyway. Luke let the applause continue before finally raising his hands for silence.

"Bernie, it gives me great pleasure, on behalf of the Universe Awards Committee, to present you with this award."

As Bernie accepted his award, any words he may have planned were forgotten. The applause was back again. When silence finally prevailed, he found his voice and began to speak. "I want to thank the Committee for this award. You'll never know how much this means to me because I... I can never tell you. There are four people I want to thank for sticking with me. Without their help, I wouldn't be here tonight. I would probably be working in a bookstore." The crowd laughed at what they thought was Bernie's little joke.

Bernie looked at the people at his table. Standing taller and with more confidence, his voice grew stronger as he continued. "Mom, thank you for your guidance, and your trust, and for always believing in me. Suzie, thank you for supporting me, standing by me, and for showing me how important it is to trust my feelings. Lenny, thank you for your great ideas, for daring me to try new things, and for your friendship. And Alcandor, thank you for your wisdom, for helping me the world in newer and grander ways, and for giving me a deep respect for all living things. Without all of you, I couldn't have done any of this. Thank you so very much."

Bernie looked out at the crowd and said, "And thank you all. Thank you." And he quickly walked back to his seat. Although it was clear everyone had hoped to hear more, their disappointment did not show in any lack of applause. They stood again and applauded Bernie all the way back to his seat.

The only ones not applauding were the tiny creatures watching from high in the rafters above. They didn't understand what was going on, but they knew their boy was being honored for something he had done. Of course, that didn't come as a surprise to the lookies.

They had known their boy was special for a long time.

Epilogue

Loaded with another stack of old schoolbooks, Bernie materialized in Alcandor's study. *Alcandor's a voracious reader*, he thought as he placed them on the desk. He sensed movement behind him and turned.

"Hi, Bernie," Bowin said, flashing a smile before turning around and calling out, "Hey, everyone! Bernie's here!"

Pouring out of nooks and crannies from all over the library, they came, some of them carrying little ones.

"Can you give your blessing to the little ones, Bernie?" Gower asked the young god. "We have new ones you haven't seen yet."

As they gathered around, Bernie raised his hands above their heads and extolled in his most solemn voice, "I bless you and your children and their children's children. May you live long lives filled with great happiness." Bernie extended his shimmer, sweeping it over the gathered lookies, caressing them with the promise of his words. *They like that*, he thought, as he watched the rapture on their faces.

"Do you like it here with Alcandor?" he asked a moment later.

"Yes," said several of the lookies at once, while others nodded vigorously.

Bernie had been pleased when Alcandor invited the lookies to his world. There were no predators there to hurt them, and Alcandor's people loved them immediately. Bernie made some changes to the lookies when he brought them to their new home. He removed their death directive, so the lookies could enjoy long lives. He'd also adjusted their fertility rate—it would be normal for a few years and then gradually slow until it matched that of Alcandor's people. Bernie didn't want their new world to think they were being overrun and cast them out.

"Where's Alcandor?" Bernie asked Bowin.

Bowin pointed to the laboratory section of the building. "He's working on something really important. He's been in there all week."

As Bernie entered Alcandor's laboratory, he found the man sitting at his desk. Scattered around the room were dozens of Bernie's books. And there, on the desk, propped up on an easel, was a viewing window.

As Bernie looked into the void, he saw a planet as it rotated around a bright yellow sun.

Alcandor, noticing Bernie's arrival, flashed him a big grin.

"Hi, Bernie," Alcandor beamed. "Look at what I made. I think it's pretty good!"

-the end-

(Wait. There's more on the next page...)

FREE Chapters!

I have FREE chapters for you. They tell about the fight between Bernie and Billy that started it all. All the gory details, including what happened afterwards.

It's free, and you can get it here:

www.TheUniverseBuilders.com/TheFight/

Did you like the book?

I hope you enjoyed *Bernie and the Putty*. If you liked my story, I hope you'll do a review for me to help spread the word. Satisfied readers will guarantee more stories from Bernie's world.

These are links where you can post a quick review online.

www.TheUniverseBuilders.com/review-links/

Thank you very much!

Sincerely,

Steve LeBel

Acknowledgements

Writing this book has been a great experience for me. Lots of people helped, especially my wife, Marge, who is my biggest fan. She added her personality to the work, as she has to most of my crazy ideas. And, after 44 years of marriage, we must be doing something right.

I also have an awesome group of reviewers who offered everything from editing assistance to encouragement. Some of them are authors in their own right, like Linda Watkins, Scott Payne, Ella Medler, Julie George, Karen Syed, John Prince, Darlene Blasing, Howard Ruback, and Bob Jackson. I will always be grateful for your advice and support. I also received excellent ideas and suggestions from Ardis Schaaf, Ryan Golombeski, Walt LeBel, Bradley Wargo, Anne Hershey, Larry LeBel, Kathi Prechtel, Bill and Kathryn DeKort, Peggy Brunner, and more.

For the excellent book cover, I am indebted to my daughter, Wendy LeBel Golombeski, Howard Ruback, and Michelle Carter-Hildebrandt. Graphics are not my strong suit; I'm glad it's yours.

Your contributions have been both humbling and much appreciated.

About the Author

Businessmen are serious people, right? Not always. Steve LeBel — hospital president, technology entrepreneur, and stock market trader — is definitely not serious.

Not when he writes.

Whimsy overcomes him at the word processor. And whimsy is at the core of his novel, *The Universe Builders: Bernie and the Putty*, which he tells with a unique balance of seriousness, humor, and imagination.

He lives in Muskegon, Michigan with his wife Marge and their cats, Mindy and Dexter. When not writing, he's busy planning his next trip, cussing out the stock market, or dreaming up new plots for *The Universe Builders*.

Amazon: http://amazon.com/author/stevelebel
Newsletter: http://theuniversebuilders.com/signup2
Facebook: http://facebook.com/stevelebel.author2
Twitter: http://twitter.com/stevelebel
Goodreads: http://goodreads.com/stevelebel
Website: http://theuniversebuilders.com
Email: steve@theuniversebuilders.com

Made in the USA
Las Vegas, NV
16 December 2020